CATHEDRAL

Ben Hopkins

CATHEDRAL

Europa
editions

Europa Editions
8 Blackstock Mews
London N4 2BT
www.europaeditions.co.uk

A catalogue record for this title is available from the British Library
ISBN 978-1-78770-251-6

Hopkins, Ben
Cathedral

Book design by Emanuele Ragnisco
www.mekkanografici.com

Prepress by Grafica Punto Print – Rome

Printed and bound in Great Britain by Clays Ltd, Elcograf S.p.A.

CONTENTS

For Ceylan

Where wast thou when I laid the foundations of the earth?
declare, if thou hast understanding.
Who hath laid the measures thereof, if thou knowest?
or who hath stretched the line upon it?
Whereupon are the foundations thereof fastened?
or who laid the corner stone thereof;
When the morning stars sang together, and all the sons of God
shouted for joy?
—JOB 38: 4-7

PROLOGUE

In the Beginning
(Odile I)

in the beginning was the Light
and the Light was perfect

but there was nothing but the Light
and nothing for the Light to know itself by
and so it created Darkness

and the Light circled the Darkness
and the Darkness circled the Light
and they kissed
and so the Devil was born

and the Devil was lonely
and had no one to play with
so He created His playthings

Matter
Stuff
and the World

know this:

this World is the Devil's World

this world
with all its things

its trees its rivers its stones its lizards its flies its flowers its snakes
its moon and sun and stars
its flesh its bone its blood

is the Devil's world

this world will have no beginning and will have no end
this world
is a decoy
from the real world of the Light

this world
is Nothing

Book One
The Cross
(1229–1235)

BOOK ONE
THE CROSS
(1229–1235)

ANNO
1229

LAMB OF GOD
(ANNO 1229. RETTICH SCHÄFFER I)

It's a story he likes to tell, how he first came to Hagenburg, how he bought his freedom, how he started as a stone-cutter's apprentice, working at the Cathedral. Now he's telling it again, in the *Zum Drecke* in the Fischgass, to Fat Uto and his Boys.

His name is Rettich, like "radish," a name he's had so long that no-one remembers the why and wherefore of it. Maybe it's because his hair is blonde-reddish, and his face is pale and freckled—red top, white beneath . . . so a bit like a radish. But maybe it's something else entirely. Whatever it is, Rettich is his name and he was a shepherd serf in the hills by Lenzenbach, like his father and his fathers' fathers before him.

Anyhow, the story starts when his own father dies suddenly, leaving Rettich master of the family with only nineteen summers on his straw-coloured head. That was the spring when his father was meant to take him to Hagenburg for the first time, to pay their taxes to the Bishop, to buy a new scythe-blade, and to take communion. But the father was dead, and so Rettich, and his young brother Emmle (for Emmerich), walk down from the hills, jump on the back of a cart carrying wood, help unload the wood, then make friends with some boatmen travelling along the Ehle, give them one of their sheepcheeses as a gesture of friendship, and then find themselves like chatelaines, letting the boatmen do all the work as they sit back and let their hands drift in the water whilst the boating boys row and punt them down to the quay at Hagenburg.

Here Uto yawns, and he doesn't even cover his mouth. He drinks and says, "My glass is half empty and you're only just arriving in Hagenburg."

Rettich shrugs, "Well then drink more slowly. Temperance is a virtue."

"A Full Purse is a greater virtue. If you had a big, full purse, you could slap me with it now and again to keep me awake whilst you tell your story."

Rettich joins the laughter. He's not one to take offence at a jest. "Herr Hirschner, let me continue?"

Uto Hirschner, the town crier, waves his hand, granting permission. Buy him a drink, tell your story, then Hirschner has your name and your face. And in the end, so Rettich's been told, everyone who needs something comes to Hirschner.

Rettich spreads his hands, setting a scene. "The quay, the marketplace, the fish . . . "

"The FISH?" says Hirschner, "are you going to tell me about the *fish*? Listen, boy, we're not like you, some shit-drenched hill-peasant a chicken laid out of her muddy village arse, we were born here in Hagenburg. We know what the fish-market looks like."

† † †

In his first nights in the City, lying in the dank storeroom in the Jew's house, he dreams again and again of his coming there, the moments of arrival. Jumping from the boat to the quay. The ground still totters beneath him. The crowd like the Whitsun fair in Schlettstadt, but greater, like both worlds of the Living and the Dead joining to throng the riverside. From the quay, words of thanks to the good boatmen, and then, Emmle's hand grasped firmly, into the shouting market, and seeing, above the frowning gables, a distant dome rising. The Cathedral.

† † †

"Begging your pardon, sir, where can I find the Bishop?"

Laughter from Uto. "You asked, just like that?"

Rettich laughs too, "How was I to know? I had my taxes in my purse, all I know is we pay taxes to the Bishop, so, you see, it follows . . . "

He likes to see Uto laugh, it means maybe he'll sit out the whole story.

In the story, Rettich is outside the Cathedral, asking the milling masons, mortar men and carpenters where he can find the Bishop. These days, now that he's been in the City a few months, he knows how stupid that was. He may as well have had a banner made with the Fool as emblem, and as motto, "Country Dunce."

"Where can I find the Bishop?"

"What do you need, boy, spiritual instruction?" asks one of the Masons. He's trying not to laugh, but his eyes are friendly.

"We all need spiritual instruction," says Rettich.

"And that's true too. The Bishop's not here."

Rettich is sad to hear it. "Where is he?"

The Mason shrugs, "Who knows? Fighting, hunting, riding his lands, checking his incomes. Word to the wise, boy. His Grace the Bishop is *never* here for the likes of us. Now what do you want from him?"

"I want to bargain. About my taxes."

The Mason is surprised. "Hark at that, he wants to bargain with the Bishop." This gets interest from others. They rest their tools, gather round.

"I've heard I can buy my Freedom," says Rettich.

"You can," agrees the Mason, "but I've heard that Freedom is not cheap."

"How much?" asks Rettich. The Mason shows his open palms; he doesn't know. "Why do you want your freedom? Aren't you happy where you are?"

"It's nice, my village. But I don't like the girls."

"Why not?"

"Their beards?"

This raises a big laugh. "So you want your freedom so that you can chase our city girls?"

Rettich laughs too, squinting in the sun, enjoying the attention. "And own my own property. And keep my own fortune."

† † †

Not part of the story, because it would make Uto yawn. Uto knows how the Cathedral is, he's been looking on it since he was born. So he wouldn't know what it was like. To come from Lenzenbach, where the tallest house has two storeys, and see that towering dome. For Uto the doorways are doorways, the arch an arch. But Rettich and Emmerich stood as pilgrims, silent and awed.

Tears came to Rettich's eyes when he saw the portal, and above it, so real it was almost as if it was happening before him, saw the Virgin dying. Her sinking body, received by the mourning, reverent crowd. Her Son, our Saviour, kneeling, holding in his hands a small doll-like copy of her, receiving into his gentle palms her Immortal Soul.

Rettich stood before the Bishop's Church, and cried. He had never seen anything quite so beautiful.

† † †

"Come in, don't hover outside like some damned bat," says the voice from inside, and Rettich (he has left Emmle in the sun with the Mason) walks in, all a-tremble. This is the room of the Bishop's Treasurer, Eugenius von Zabern, in a building a stone's throw from the Cathedral.

Von Zabern looks him up and down. He is tall, dark-haired, dressed in black. "What do you want, boy?"

Rettich is nervous it's true, but he is never shy. "My Lord, I have come to pay our taxes, but also I have two questions. One is whether we can pay our tax this year in coin, not in sheep, and the second is if we can buy our freedom from His Grace, the Bishop."

Silence as the Treasurer takes this in, and looks once again at the straw-haired boy. Maybe something here more than meets the eye.

"Village and name?"

"Lenzenbach, Schäffer."

"In Lenzenbach, everyone is a Schäffer."

"I know, my Lord. We are known as the Straw-Schäffers, because of our hair."

Von Zabern claps his hands and one of the two young Clerks jumps up and goes to the wall of shelving where there are countless scrolls and ledgers. The other Clerk stays seated and counts piles and piles of pennies, flicking the beads of an abacus as he counts. This is the room: wooden panels, endless shelves of ledgers, three oiled muslin windows, two counters, three desks, the Treasurer and his two Clerks, a sleeping dog and Lord Knows How Much Money.

"Why in coin and not in sheep?" asks the Treasurer, sharply.

Rettich takes off his woollen hat, hoping this would make him look more humble. "Last year we gave His Grace ten sheep. In market now, a sheep is selling for eleven pennies. So I am saying I will pay His Grace nine shillings, two pennies, being the price of ten sheep. Is it not fair?"

A smile plays at the edges of the Treasurer's mouth. "Bloody peasant, you want to haggle with His Grace?"

Rettich shrugs, "But it is fair, is it not? The same tax as last year." The Treasurer is silent. So Rettich smiles and nods; "As a sign of good will, we can make it nine shillings, three pennies?"

"One extra penny! His Grace will faint with astonishment. So, lambing was good this year?"

"Why should I lie, it was good."

"So you want to cut His Grace out of the benefits of a good year?"

"Why should we struggle to increase our herd, when the more sheep we have, the more sheep we must give the Bishop? And, when we die, we have nothing, as all of it belongs to His Grace?"

"Insolent egg! Why are you telling me this? You're just a boy. Where is your father?"

"My father passed on this year, My Lord. And my father, God rest his soul, would never have dared to ask this. He talked about it, but he never had the bravery to do anything. But I am not my father, and although, My Lord, my heart is beating with fear, I am not afraid, at least to ask to you this question. Is it *possible* to buy our freedom?"

The young Clerk puts the Lenzenbach ledger in front of the Treasurer, and withdraws. Eugenius von Zabern's long finger expertly runs down the lists of names and numbers, then his dark eyes flick back up to Rettich. "It will cost you twenty-seven marks to buy your family's freedom."

It seems that the Treasurer enjoys the moment of saying this, and the dark, horrible taste of shock that it brings up in Rettich's mouth.

"In answer to your other question," says von Zabern, continuing urbanely, "yes, you can pay in coin this year, but make it ten round shillings. And know that next year, should I wish it, you will pay your tithes in sheep. And don't try hiding any when we come round. Straw-Schäffer, I have been long in this game, boy, and I know *all* the tricks."

† † †

Before any of this worldly talk, tightly holding Emmle's

hand, standing below the altar in the Cathedral's apse. The gilt roof, the patterns, the paintings. And the blocks, so perfectly carved that it almost seems a continuous wall of stone. Waves of different sandstones, their shifting hues made harmonious. And in the window above, Red such as he had never seen, Blue that is bluer than the sky at twilight, a Golden Yellow that captures the rays of the sun and makes Light visible.

In the hall on the way out, statues of the Apostles. Rettich feels a growing shame at his presumption. In his bag, slung over his shoulder, his wooden carvings that he had brought here to sell.

Having seen these works of the true masters, he feels he should empty the sack in the river and forget he ever held a chisel.

Stuttering with shame, he tells this to his brother Emmerich.

"But wood floats, Rettich," is his reply.

† † †

Rettich looks at the heavy silver cross that hangs over the Treasurer's black robes. He can't face looking him in the eye again, not quite yet.

"Twenty-seven marks? How in heaven is any country man ever supposed to be able to find that?"

"Here's a novel idea, Straw Boy, you *borrow* it," says the Treasurer.

"And how do you pay back the borrowing?"

"By robbing folk on the highways, selling slaves to the Saracen, or by good honest work, it's your choice." He smiles. "The Church prefers good honest work."

"So do I. Where do I borrow such money?"

"If anyone lends it to you, come back and tell me immediately. The shock will kill me, and I am weary of this world." The two junior Clerks snigger. Even Rettich is smiling. "Where, my Lord, can I *try* and borrow?" he asks.

"There's a lawyer on Schriwerstublgass, Altmüller's the name. He has little concern for his immortal soul, and lends money sometimes. Or there are the Jews. The Jews offer better rates."

† † †

Some more of the story that won't be told: Rettich comes out of the Treasury House and weeps. Where he's walking he doesn't know. Tears in his eyes break up the sun, blurring rainbows. His sleeve wipes at the saltwater and the snot, his voice keens stupidly, höööö, höööö, like one of his own lost lambs.

People are looking at him, so he turns away. There's a gap in a reed fence and he pulls through that. Solitude. He must be calm before he faces Emmle. He must find something bright and golden to say. Twenty-seven marks is a shadow that blots out the sun. An impossible debt, nearly six hundred sheep.

He is leaning on something; it is a huge block of stone.

Beneath him, surrounded by the reed fence, foundations. Dug deep and wide.

Rettich looks around him and realises these are not foundations of some new building, but of the Cathedral. His keening stops, his tears run dry, he wipes his eyes. Around him, the roofless walls of a Nave. Below him, the newly strengthened foundations. Dotted across the dusty ground, blocks of stone that have yet to find their homes on new, towering walls.

He had thought the Cathedral was Huge, unbelievably high, wide and great. Perfection and wonder and grandeur.

But it is only the Beginning.

† † †

Rettich comes back into the sun, to the building place, to the dusty ground, the blocks of stone, the mortar mixers.

Before he can say anything; "Your little brother tells me that you carve. In wood," says Landolt the Mason. Rettich winks at Emmle, his little accomplice, sits down with them on the large block of purplish stone that is serving them as a bench. Opens his sack and pulls out, at random, a Lamb of God. A little ram, bearing an unfurled pennant on which is written *tollo peccati mundi*, I take away the Sins of the World.

"You have letters?" asks the Mason, surprised.

"No, I copied them—the Priest showed me what to write."

Rettich studies Landolt's face as he holds the Lamb carving in his hands, turns it over again and again. A jab in the ribs comes from Emmerich. It's his elbow saying, "I told you so. He likes it."

"So," says Rettich. "Is there work for me here?"

Landolt laughs a small laugh. "You think you can just jump off a boat, throw a Lamb of God at me and get a position?"

"Yes."

"Here's a boy who wants a position!" Landolt calls out to his friends, who are measuring a stone block with string. They look up, curious. Leave their work, squinting through the dusty sun.

"You don't want to join us, boy. Our work is never done."

Landolt takes two more carvings from the sack, a Virgin, and a St. Catherine with her wheel, entwined in sunflowers. He makes a whistling noise through his teeth. Rettich peers at him, but Landolt's face is saying nothing clear.

The junior masons peer at the carvings, at the Virgin. "This your sweetheart?"

Rettich blushes.

"No? Your sister? Can I meet her?"

The other mason; "Where's she from?"

"From my mind."

Rettich puts his hat back on. There's no more need to look humble. Landolt finishes looking at the carvings and looks at him instead. His eyes are bright. "I'll talk with the Master Stonecutter," he says.

† † †

You cross the Cathedral square, pass the tents where the building workers eat and sleep, turn into the Brüdergass that leads to the monastery, then head for the Mayenzer Tor; you can see it ahead of you, the city's northern Gatehouse, rising above the rooves. Pass the whitewashed Bishop's Palace (where Landolt says the Bishop never stays) and then there's the Schriwerstublgass, a dark narrow street, where the clerks and lawyers are. At the end of that alley, you're there. Everyone knows it, just ask for the Judengasse.

Emmerich is nervous, which is good. It's good because it means that Rettich has to pretend not to be, to be strong, to be the Older Brother, fearless and heroic. Of course they've seen Jews before, who hasn't? But talk to one? Go and stand in Jews' Alley and ask for their help?

"Excuse me, sir, Meir Rosheimer? I'm looking for . . . " The old, white-bearded Jew moves on, shrugging, muttering, hiding his eyes.

For an alley, it's quite wide. Two-storey houses rise on both sides, sometimes three stories. One house has its roof down, covered—they're building a new floor. In the village, he thinks, there's plenty of space; you can build here there and anywhere. In the city, held in by the walls, there's only upwards.

Not many people on the street. There's a woman coming, swaddled in robes despite the sun, her head covered with a scarf and head-dress. "Madam, I'm looking . . . " Her dark eyes dart straight to her feet, her tongue clicks in displeasure. He doesn't exist, not for her.

Rettich stands, looking somewhat lost, and catches Emmerich's anxious glance, watching him floundering. A drowning man reaches for anything, and so Rettich strides to the nearest doorway and knocks loudly.

One, two, three, four . . . Rettich is counting sheep. The herd swarms into the pen, huddling, hiding from the barking dog, seven, eight, nine sheep, no answer at the door, and they keep on coming, the black ones like markers, helping him count, fifteen, sixteen . . . still no answer . . .

After twenty-one sheep, the door opens a crack and a girl stares out wide-eyed at the two straw-haired Gentile fools on her doorstep. "Erm," stutters Rettich, "little girl, we are looking for Meir Rosheimer, . . . "

"In the study house."

"The study house, where is the study house?"

She looks up to the skies as if it's a stupid question. "Three doors down." And she's gone.

Three doors down, and, with a lump in his throat, Rettich is looking through the gap in the heavy oak door at the strange sight inside. Here are rows of desks and tables, piles of scrolls and books, and twenty-two Jews (he counts the herd of them in a glance), some sleeping with their heads on the table-tops, some muttering and swaying as they stand at lecterns and read, some talking with each other, a disagreement here, a joke there.

"Herr Meir Rosheimer! We are looking for . . . Rosheimer," calls out Rettich through the gap in the door, in his bravest voice, which nevertheless cracks with fear.

One of the apparently sleeping men turns round. Handsome, strong-featured, full-bearded, with eyes that somehow seem amused. "I am he," he says. "Let's go to my bureau."

A long, narrow room in the next house. There are five stools, a pitcher of water and five leather cups, an ink pot, a ledger, and a quill. It's dark, the shutters are closed, but Meir's eyes glint in the half-light as he peers at the two boys. "Interesting . . . " he says, "what can I do for you, my Country Eggs?"

Rettich coughs; "Tell me, how do we do this?"

Meir Rosheimer's eyes smile with amusement as he opens the shutters, letting in the afternoon sun. "Well, generally," he says, "you tell me how much you want to borrow. And then, when you can pay me back."

Rettich swallows. "Twenty-seven marks. I will pay you back three marks a year, God willing."

A long pause. Meir Rosheimer sits down. Dust dances in the sunlight, like flakes of gold, rising and falling endlessly.

"Or, in ten years time I can pay it all back. In one go."

"In ten years' time, how much will you pay me?"

Rettich looks at him, only partially understanding the question. "For each year," says Rosheimer, "for every ten marks, you pay me one mark."

Rettich swallows.

"You think I should lend you twenty-seven marks for free?" asks Meir, smiling.

"One in ten, that's two marks and fourteen shillings."

"Well done, Egg, you can reckon . . . "

"Two marks and fourteen, that's your . . . "

"My *interest* in the loan, yes."

"So I pay you twenty-seven plus the two and fourteen. It makes twenty-nine marks and fourteen shillings."

"If you pay me back a *year from today*, yes." Meir looks at Rettich's uncertainty, sighs. "I said '*every year*' I take one for every ten marks."

"So . . . after ten years I owe you fifty-four marks. For every year, two marks fourteen shillings . . . so, fifty-four in total."

"No. It's more than that. You forgot the interest on the interest."

Rettich trembles and a metallic, fearful taste comes to the back of his mouth. He closes his eyes and counts, adding more and more sheep to the pen, and then more and more and more . . . "So after ten years, I owe you something like sixty nine marks, nineteen shillings?"

Silence. Meir closes his eyes, does his own reckoning. Opens his eyes. "How did you do that?" he asks.

"I don't rightly know, sir," says Rettich. "Am I right, sir?"

"You're right."

"Hooray!" Rettich grins and slaps his thigh. Emmerich looks at him like he's lost his mind. Twenty-seven marks has become nearly seventy. Where's the joy in that?

"Tell me, young man" says Meir, still curious. "Where did you learn to reckon?"

"I reckon all the time!" says Rettich. "In the hills at summer, we have all the five herds on the same pastures, and we pitch our tents near each other but then, when it comes to making cheese, it's each herd for itself. So I say, boys, why don't we all come together, put all the milk in the same vat, make cheese together, and so we save time, we share boards, sieves, cloths. And the other boys say; but how do we divide the cheese, we all have different size flocks? So I says it's simple, if we make one hundred cheeses, I take twenty-six, you take eighteen, you take thirty-two and so on, because, you see, I counted all our sheep and there's three hundred and eighty, and I have ninety-nine, so it means I take twenty-six from a hundred cheeses . . . "

"I'm with you," says Meir.

" . . . and it's fair and everyone benefits. So it's what I said to them."

"And what did the other shepherd boys say?"

"They didn't believe me. They thought I was cheating them."

"We Jews have the same problem."

"Do you never cheat anyone?"

"An honest customer? No. Never."

"A dishonest one?"

"Well . . . "

"And is it really one mark for every ten, every year?"

"That's my opening offer. For older, trusted customers,

for long term loans we're more generous . . . " He sighs. "It depends. There are all kinds of deals. In your case, you would be better off paying me three marks a year, like you said first."

"Then I am beholden to you for . . . over twenty years. Twenty-six years or so."

Once again, Meir's eyes widen with acclamation. He leans towards Emmerich. "Are we sure your brother is just a shepherd?"

Emmerich is no fool. "*Just* a shepherd? Our Lord was a shepherd."

"Let's not talk about Him."

"King David was a shepherd," ventures Rettich.

"Let's stick to business, if you don't mind, Country Egg. My other question. What is your security? Where is this money coming from, this three marks a year?"

"I am to be apprenticed as a stone-cutter."

"Congratulations. A good trade."

"My brother will work somewhere. We have a few possessions in the village to sell." Now Rettich lowers his voice, " . . . and twenty sheep the Bishop doesn't know of, that we can trade. Or loan."

"You loan sheep?"

"For sure. The shepherd you loan to, he keeps their wool and cheese. But when the loan is over, he has to give back a bigger herd. Like you, for every ten sheep, one extra must be given back. Or the difference paid in coin, or wool, or . . . Like you said. There are many ways of doing the deal."

Meir smiles, scratches his beard. "Well, I never," he says. "The usury of sheep . . . " He looks up. "Listen. I would never loan twenty-seven marks to a shepherd." He holds up his hands before Rettich can protest. "Nor to an apprentice! But . . . " He stands, goes over to take the ledger. "You will do well, Country Egg. I'm certain of that. And you'll be a companion stone-cutter in five years, I warrant, and then you can pay off the principal quicker, if that's what you want."

He opens the ledger. "I am guessing, but if I loan this to you now, we will close this account before thirteen years are over. Do you think?"

Rettich smiles and nods. Meir turns and looks at Emmerich. "And is little brother as clever as you?"

"More so," says Rettich, proud.

"I need a new Christian servant," says Meir.

Emmerich takes fright, looks to his brother.

"Two weeks trial, and then we'll see?" asks Meir.

Rettich encourages him with a look and Emmerich nods. Meir smiles. "I do need a servant. There are many things we Jews cannot do. One day of the week, it is we who are to blame. The other six, it's you."

He has a quill in his hand, and there is an ink pot on the board beneath the window. He looks at Rettich with sparkling eyes. "Your name?"

† † †

"It's you again," says Eugenius von Zabern, "what do you want?"

Rettich approaches, bows his head to the canon, aristocrat and elder; three times deserving of his reverence. He puts the heavy kid-leather pouch down on the table, and pulls at the strings so that the soft material flops open. Nestling brightly, a cascade of silver coins, minted one shot of an arrow from the Treasury towards the Vogesentor. Brought across town by Meir Rosheimer and now delivered by Rettich Schäffer (" . . . you must give it to him yourself, he won't take silver from a Jew's hands") into the coffers of His Grace the Bishop of Hagenburg.

"I would like to buy our Freedom," says Rettich, simply.

"Did you steal it?" asks von Zabern.

"I borrowed it," says Rettich. "Like you told me, my Lord."

Von Zabern takes a coin in his hand, weighs it in his palm. Shakes his head. "Like I told you? Yes, I told you. *But I didn't expect you to go and bloody do it!*"

† † †

In the *zum Drecke*, the drinkers laugh, cheer and clap Rettich on the back. "There, you showed him! That old bastard!" One more Free Man in Hagenburg. One more apprentice for the Companionship of Stone-cutters. Uto laughs and slaps his fat stomach. "It's a good story, I grant you, Country Boy," he says, and downs his sweet wine. "Maybe one day I'll cry it for you. When you become a Companion, I'll announce you to the world. The name is Rettich, right?"

"Rettich is the name."

"I won't forget. Once a serf of His Grace. Now it's the Jew who owns you."

Rettich nods, smiling. "But every year he will own me less."

† † †

Rettich sleeps with the apprentices now, on pallets in a shed a stone's throw from the Cathedral. And when he can't sleep and all the other boys are snoring . . . then he opens his eyes to the dim thatched ceiling, and imagines that beyond that ceiling are the spheres and the stars, and beyond them all, his father's Soul.

"Look, Father," says Rettich, and in his half-dream holds aloft the sealed parchment from the Bishop's Treasurer. "Who could have thought it. I did it, I bought our freedom."

And his father's Soul smiles. The room is full of breath. It seems that they, the stone-cutter apprentices, are all together, breathing in and out, and it seems that sleep is like a river, like Father Rhine, drifting gently towards some distant, unknown sea.

The Curse of Numbers
(anno 1229. Eugenius von Zabern I)

I am not a bad man, nevertheless no-one likes me. I would have been quite happy, like most of my fellow nobles of Alsace, Aargau and the Rhineland, to live a leisurely life, collect my annual incomes and throw a tantrum when actually asked to do a stroke of work. My family, named for our ancestral township in the Vogesen hills, has had for generations a son placed in the cathedral chapter. And so I inherited this position, I did not acquire it through any quality or talent of my own. But whereas the other cathedral Canons come and go as they please and spend most of their lives hunting, gambling and whoring, I . . . am the Bishop's Treasurer.

This is due to the Curse of Numbers, a curse with which I was born. At times, I come across others of my own kind. Just last month I had in my office a shepherd from Lenzenbach who could reckon. The stone-cutters and masons whose constant chiselling outside in the square is the bane of my life; they can measure, they can subdivide, they can reckon. And the Jews, the Jews . . . God knows they can reckon like Satan himself.

But, sadly, most of the dunces I have to deal with can barely count to twelve.

This is my curse; to know that this is a world made of numbers. Once you know this, whether you are a shepherd, a mason, a Jew or a Canon, you cannot stop playing with them, trying them in different combinations, finding patterns, irregularities and secrets in their series and infinities. The words that sealed my fate were spoken by my elder brother, God damn his idle soul. "This is Eugenius, Your Grace, he is good with numbers."

"A reckoner?" said the Bishop, and as soon as I took orders, he sent me to his Treasury. And now it's been eleven years I have been here, eleven years, two months and thirteen days . . . a total of four thousand and ninety-two days. I myself have been Chief Treasurer two thousand seven hundred and ninety-seven days.

That is a prime number, by the way.

And I have not counted the amount of money that has passed through my hands since that day. I wish I had. It would be a pretty sum.

† † †

Like the farmer and the shepherd in their pastoral paradise, my infernal and cursèd years are seasonal too. I have the joyful spring of the Payment of Tithes, followed by the charming summer of Chasing Defaulters and Debt Collection, the merry festival of the Balancing of the Books, and now . . . my very favourite time of year, the Carnival of Benefices.

This is the season when reeking priests crawl out of the mouldering woodwork of their churches and crawl towards Hagenburg to be paid. It is also the time in which the Great Families of our local lands, who once upon a time used to fight the Bishops of Hagenburg on the field of honour, now instead take from my hands a big purse of silver in exchange for keeping the peace. And finally, bringing with them the blessed stench of incense, come our friends from Rome. Increasingly in the past years, these have been Agents or Legates, hired by our creditors in the curia to come and collect, on their behalf, the golden fruits of our diocese.

So now I have before me a Florentine called Renzo, who is

working for the Frescobaldi family and who has come to take charge of a consignment of twenty-one barrels of our Bishop's vineyards' finest, to be carted to the Saône, and thence down-river to the Mediterranean and all the way to Rome. I ask him for the news from Italy, the health of His Holiness, and for other titbits of news, but he clearly finds my Latin vulgar (how they hate the German accent!), and answers in monosyllables. Very well, the wine I give you will be second grade, you Florentine flounce, and I hope you contract the pox on the way home. "The barrels will be at the Vogesen Tor depot tomorrow," I say politely, and force a smile.

My "smile" scares children. Maybe I should call it some-thing else.

† † †

One by one, or in pairs, our creditors come and collect their silver, their wine, grain and wool. And I don't let one penny go astray. For if I am to have little pleasure in this life (this seems to be my lot), at the very least I can make sure this cursed work is done well.

Around four to six weeks a year, I am so blessed as to be able to leave the Treasury, mount a horse, and travel through the surrounding countryside, accompanied by two clerks and six heavily-armed mercenary brutes. Conversation is limited on such journeys, and so I pass the time in contemplation of the tasks in hand, which are usually to find, humiliate and imprison those who would cheat His Grace out of his dues. Here I am like a bloodhound, searching in every crevice, and, generally speaking I do manage to fish out the malingerers from their boltholes, find the hidden grain, wine and livestock which has been "forgotten" in some forest barn, and protect and amplify His Grace's substantial income.

I wish, sometimes, that there were just one person, just *one*, who could understand what it is I do for His Grace. I have thought about this, and the Jew Rosheimer could maybe understand, he with his hundred debtors and his profits sunk into speculations on a dozen Rhine boats and their cargoes to Mayenz, to Cologne, to Bruges and Antwerp. Or maybe Wolfram, the boat owner himself, who tries to buy cheap Here and sell dear There along the Rhine, the Elbe, the Rhône and Saône. They both must keep complex account ledgers, must make intricate calculations.

But why would I talk to them? A scheming Jew and a tiresome Swiss midget?

And in any case, my Lord Bishop's Enterprise dwarfs theirs like Leviathan a herring. His debtors are legion; the peasants, the shepherds, the goatherds, the hemp-carders, the innkeepers, the estates, the convents and their lands, the vintners, the farmers, the Damned and the Saved, they all must pay taxes to the Bishop.

And on the debit side, the pennies, the shillings and the marks flow outwards to our so-called friends and allies in Rome (some of whom are, apparently, canons of our cathedral, though they have never been North of Florence), to our vassals the once-warring Lords of Alsace (whose loyalty is for sale to the highest bidder), to our canons (more than half live elsewhere), to our churches (more than half need new rooves) and to our priests (more than half are living in sin, or are heretics, or both).

And so the gold flows in, and the gold flows out, and it is my Holy Task to make sure, as sure as the Devil is a Dutchman, that more gold flows In than Out.

† † †

There are many things that I detest in this world, and not many things I love. But I think it is clear that the thing that I detest the most of all is that Bottomless Hole that gapes not fifty paces from my Counting Table: the Cathedral. A constant river of silver and gold flows into that damned hole, providing the wages of the idle, and paying quarrymen, foresters and glaziers for their so-called labour.

How I hate that pile of stones, surrounded by chattering, banging, shouting, clanging workmen who saunter around beneath my windows. On a hot summer's day when the shutters must be opened, I can hardly hear myself think! And the work never ends! Now, for some unknown reason, the foundations are being refitted for a new nave, and of course it is I who must find, from somewhere, five hundred extra marks!

So, this year, on my rounds of Debt Enforcement, I am more assiduous than ever at chasing every penny, every sou. I—let it be known—am the Living Reason why the masons and mortar mixers of Hagenburg can sink a pitcher of wine of a Saturday. It is I alone who keeps the Bishop's revenues in the positive.

One can maybe imagine, therefore, my vexation upon returning to Hagenburg to find two things. One: His Grace the Bishop awaiting me, in person, in my Counting Room. And Two: with him, some zealous-eyed youth from one of the minor Houses of Alsace, his name Achim von Esinbach.

And the two of them telling me that they have New Plans for the Cathedral of Our Lady. And that even one thousand marks will not be enough. Not nearly enough.

† † †

It is doubtlessly true that the penny-pinching nature of my Work has made me jaded and bitter, but I am not insensitive to Beauty. And certainly, my Counting Table has never borne a parchment so Glorious as it does now. There, where habitually there are decked ledgers and accounts and tarnished coins, now lies unfurled a drawing, in full, resplendent colour, of a Cathedral seen from its Western side. A Cathedral in the new style of which I have heard so much: elegant, geometrical and rising to a height that seems to defy the heavens. A Cathedral, let it be clearly stated, of breathtaking Beauty.

And, no doubt, of equally breathtaking Expense.

The Draughtsman of this shamelessly extravagant and exquisite vision is the aforementioned Achim von Esinbach, a young nobleman who has recently returned from the University of Paris, and from the *chantiers* of Reims, Chartres and Troyes bearing in his heart this vision, and in his hands, this parchment. Somehow he has managed to obtain an audience with the Bishop, and, in my Absence, has peddled his lavish dream to my Lord.

"Do not be so shocked, Eugenius," says his Grace, insouciant and amused. "If they can build such wonders in Paris and the Champagne, then surely we can build one here in the Alsace too."

"The Bishop of Metz is starting to build one," adds von Esinbach.

The Bishop of Metz. Our neighbour and our Bishop's greatest rival. And now, all becomes clear. If Metz will have a French Cathedral, then Hagenburg must surely have one too.

"Here, My Lord Canon," says Achim von Esinbach, and turns the vellum on my counting table so that I may see it properly. "Look. And take your time."

And so I look. And I see tiers of statues, arraigned like the Blessèd in Paradise: Kings, apostles, desert prophets, Saints. I see the Virgin, hands clasped in prayer between the two huge portals. I see a Rose Window of intense, beauteous colours, like a sunflower, like a rainbow.

It all swims before me, beautiful, moving and strange, every one of its thousand stones and statues representing for me a bright rill of coinage that must be found from somewhere. I turn my gaze on its Architect, the young von Esinbach, and see a young man trapped in his own fervour. His eyes avoid me, blinking and jumping to every corner of the room, his hands clasping at each other, nervously twitching. He is taut and tense, like the string on a viol.

I sigh, audibly.

And the Bishop laughs. "I know it will be a drain on our resources, Eugenius. But what price the Glory of God? I have made my decision. Now that I have seen Master Achim's designs, my eyes will see nothing else."

But he is not usually so precipitous, my Lord and Master. And so as I sit and calculate, I study his face and see a care-worn, early-ageing man. His eyes are the troubled brown of the Vogesen rivers, his cheeks sag with good sustenance, poorly digested. His nose blooms with the colouration of the local wine. For a warrior, the face is too kindly, too open. And for a Lord, it is too weary.

And so I understand now. He is searching for a Legacy to bequeath to his Diocese and to his City. An Epitaph.

He notices my scrutiny and raises his eyebrows, which rise into questioning points, like wings. "What are you thinking, Eugenius?"

What am I thinking? I am thinking that for eleven years and two months and thirteen days I have protected the fiduciary balance of this Diocese with acuity and cunning. But now I have been outmanoeuvred by this dreamer von Esinbach, and his roll of cursèd vellum.

ANNO
1230

A Devil's Shilling
(ANNO 1230. RETTICH SCHÄFFER II)

His days begin before dawn. Rettich is nearly always the first to wake, and lies in his bunk, surrounded by the breath of his apprentice brothers. From outside their tent he can hear the Cathedral Schoolboys chatting on their way to prayers, he can hear the soft chant of the choir greeting the Lord of the New Day, he can hear the first stall-keepers unlocking the chains and sweeping the grounds, preparing for trade. And then when the first light is seen in the sky, the long, deep bell sounds.

Rettich staggers outside, pulling his coat around him. The Cathedral hulks in the gloom. Towards the sunrise, it is full-grown, complete and towering, with the carved portals that had once made him cry. Then, after the Crossing, the old nave has been taken down, and it is here that they are building. Building a new Nave that will soar the height of three tall trees above the Rhine plain. Slowly they will build towards the sun-set, to where the old frontage and portals still stand. And then they will rebuild these, and thereupon will set proud towers and pinnacles that will touch the clouds.

And no-one knows how long it will take them.

Rettich, beating and crossing his arms on his chest against the cold, walks over to the latrine hut, takes the wooden cover from the bucket, and squats to relieve himself. Latrine duty is the worst of all duties, and it falls to him on the day after Sunday. Then it is he who must carry the full buckets to the cesspits. God forbid he should stumble or knock the buckets against his knees. For then the foul liquid slops out against him, and he must wash his breeches and sit half-naked until they dry. He has but one pair of breeches; all his money is saved to pay his debt to Rosheimer. There is no spare penny for luxuries.

The sun rises, and shadows spread across the Cathedral Square. Lauds and Prime have finished. The schoolboys rush out and play for a few brief minutes before lessons begin. The hawkers start their calls, the stalls are open, the town is awake.

Rettich goes to the Stone-cutters' Lodge, he takes the key from the Clerk, unlocks the tool chest, lays out the Masters' tools on the table. He goes to the back of the Chapterhouse Refectory and waits with the other apprentices; the Masons', the Carpenters', the Blacksmiths', the Ropers', the Mortarers', one of each.

The back door opens and the baskets are given out by the Cellarer's Boy. Rushing across the cobbles to keep the bread still warm, the apprentices run to their masters. In the Lodge, Rettich lays out the loaves by the tools. One small loaf for each Master and Companion, laid on a piece of cloth beside their chisels and hammers. He pours out mugs of ale and water. The masters come and eat, sitting on their stools. It is a silent time, there is not much talking. One of them brings cheese, and shares it out amongst his fellows. A piece of sausage. An apple.

One large loaf is for the boys. Rettich comes out to the Lodge steps, shares it out between them, cutting with his large knife, making the slices as even as possible. The apprentices offer a brief prayer of thanks, and start to eat. In a short time, their breakfast is over.

Then work can begin.

† † †

From Hagenburg one climbs slowly towards the Vogesen

Hills, passing through fields and vineyards, until suddenly the road disappears behind a bluff. This is the first cliff of the Kron Valley, a mighty seam of purplish-brown sandstone. The road runs beside the river, and above its banks, the quarrymen work.

For the first weeks, Rettich was sent here, to see how the raw stone is cut. How the quarrymen search the stone for a fault, and, finding one, chisel out a hole, and then force in their wedges, until the impossible happens, and the stone breaks. How then, with two-men saws, lubricated with water, they carve the stone into blocks. Impossible work, to cut solid stone! It seems that nothing is happening, that the saw is never cutting deeper, but come back at the end of the day, and the saw has cut the span of a hand.

Then, when the block of stone is cut, the ropers come and check the hawsers, and the winch is lifted, a beam poised on a frame made of mighty trunks, and with a team of men pulling on the windlasses, the block is raised and swung out onto the waiting oxen cart.

It will take them two days to carry the stone back to the Cathedral Site in Hagenburg.

The quarrymen work like oxen themselves, like beasts. They come from the nearby villages, and are paid by the block of stone, by the measurement. The stone dust gets into their lungs, and they cough like crones. By thirty summers, they are too ill to continue. The Quarrymaster oversees them, orders them around, hardly lifts a hand to do a thing, and earns thrice what they do. And the Kronthal family, who own the land where the sandstone grows, are rich as Croesus.

In the quarry, there is an atmosphere of brutish, undervalued work. Rettich is ordered around like a Saracen's slave, even kicked like a dog. Fetch water. Heat the soup. Feed the oxen. Light the fire. Carry the rubble. Sharpen the saws and axes. Shut your mouth, you talk too much.

It is a hard apprenticeship. He begins to hate the cold stone. It seems to him it doesn't want to be cut, to be prised from the earth with painful hammer blows. It is not warm like wood, not giving. It is obdurate, it is angry, rebellious.

He sleeps in a barn by the river, and wishes he had never left Lenzenbach. If this is freedom, he thinks, then let me return to my serfdom.

Bruised from beatings, his hair thick with scaly, glistening dust, his five weeks come to an end. He will travel with the oxen back to Hagenburg. On the way, he will lay stones under the wheels when the road is uneven, will water and feed the oxen, will sleep in the cart, and on the morning of the second day, will once again be under the shadow of the Cathedral.

He arrives at noon. The Masons and Stonecutters line up to see his homecoming. They see his sour face, and laugh.

"Rettichle! Rettichle! You survived!"

They run at him, and gather him up, carry him on their shoulders. They canter through the market, singing and laughing.

And from the quay, they throw him in the shallows of the river.

"And now you're clean!"

Gasping, soaked, happy, he has survived his second baptism. He is now, truly, an Apprentice in the Brotherhood of Stone-cutters.

† † †

Rettich's Master is Giselbert, a beak-nosed Burgundian recruited by Achim von Esinbach from the *chantier* of Chartres, white-haired, stooping. He pretends to be severe, but even when berating his shepherd apprentice in his ridiculously accented German, his eyes are smiling.

One day a week, he allows Rettich behind the heavy Lodge curtain. Access to the Mysteries of Stone.

As Rettich enters the sculptors' workspace, Giselbert holds his bony finger to his lips. Silence. He gestures to a stool. Rettich sits. Giselbert closes the curtain, so that the Mysteries should be preserved.

Sunlight floods through the high window and strikes the Blind Woman on the circular wooden plinth. Giselbert pulls at a rope and rotates the woman a quarter turn, so that her lithe body is turned sideways to the light, the sun warming her raised hip, her slender waist. Below the belt that gently pulls her robe around her graceful form, she is not yet realised. Below the waist, she is still a Block Of Stone.

From her height, she looks down upon the seated apprentice. Her eyes are blindfolded, her mouth is drawn in sadness. Her right hand carries a broken spear, from her left hand, a stone tablet is falling. She is the Old Covenant, she is the Synagogue. Blinded, broken, in darkness, unaccepting of the Truth and the Light.

Her sister, the Church, stands nearby, fully completed, Her eyes are open, her richly curled hair carries a Crown. In her right hand, the Cross, in her left, the Grail. Her seeing eyes stare into a bright future.

Giselbert takes his finest chisel, his lightest hammer. He winks at Rettich, and stands at the feet of Synagogue. Poises the chisel at her upper thigh. Starts to cut the falling fold of her dress, making lightest fabric of heaviest stone.

The obdurate sandstone, cracked and sawn from the reluctant cliff, strained over by brutish embruted men, borne by struggling oxen, gives itself sweetly to his Master's hands.

† † †

The unfinished walls of the Cathedral are now covered with dung and straw, protection against the envious ice. Winter wants to creep her fingers in the cracks and wreck the work that summer hands have wrought. Achim, Landolt, the Werkmeister Alenard, take turns surveying the site, checking the coverings, peering at the smooth mortar between the blocks, holding a plumb-line to the verticals, praying that the foundations will not subside, that the Earth will willingly shoulder the new Weight they are asking her to carry.

Most of the workers have been sent home for the worst of the winter. Wrapping spare clothes and tools into a bundle and shouldering their packs, they set off, dun figures on mud-caked roads, heading for their villages in the Vogesen, the Rhine Plain, the Schwarzwald. At home they will lie in hammocks, crack nuts by the fire, tell City stories to the village girls to make them blush. Some have children waiting by those distant hearths, unseen these last eight months, now grown big and strange. In the village doorways, the hatted shadow, the Son and Father returned. A pretty purse of silver jangles in his homesick hands.

In Hagenburg, at the site, the new apprentice Rettich stays on with a handful of stonecutters, masons and carpenters. He will be their factotum and errand boy, eager for even the most menial chore. In exchange, he is accepted into their inner circle, hovering in the corners of the draughty lodge, party to all their jokes and deliberations.

Brother Alenard the Works Master looks up from the designs and sighs. He has been copying, in his precise hand, from Achim von Esinbach's etchings. "When will we get the damned glass?"

The window above the draughtsman is oiled muslin, the light is dim. Alenard's eyes water with squinting. "I will go," says Achim, "and find a glazier."

"The glazier is not the issue," says Alenard. "We have no money to pay him."

"Is the Treasurer not back from his journeys?"

Brother Alenard chuckles. "Not yet. And from that raven you won't get a penny. We are his poison."

Achim flicks his fingers. "In small doses, poison purges," he says. "Let me go and be a purgative. Maybe he will sick up some silver."

"You can try. Just mind that you don't purge him from the other end."

Achim smiles and looks to the floor. Rettich watches him from the corner where he is cleaning and oiling the tools. He looks at his Master's soft face, clean-shaven and boyish, his roving hazel eyes, his fidgeting hands. From the twitching of his body it seems that von Esinbach is always discomforted, ill-at-ease, but whenever he speaks, he is mild and calm, whenever he looks at someone, the gaze is gentle and unguarded. He favours soft clothing of autumnal colours—russet, copper and brown. And he loses himself. His eyes veil over, his gaze wanders, closing off the world and drifting into distance.

And now his eyes land on Rettich, and it seems they do not see him. But when Rettich smiles, Achim returns to the world, and smiles back, in warm embarrassment, realising that he has been staring at the apprentice as if into a Void.

Alenard's voice calls von Esinbach back to the world of work. "For the roof, we need slate. There's no slate here. We need to source it from somewhere. And to underpin the spire, we need tall, strong timbers, with some bend in them, not too much. I've not seen timber like that in the forests near here."

"No, nor I neither," says Achim.

"I have," says Rettich, speaking into the silence. All turn to look at the unbidden voice. "There's a gully below my village. Three trees there are the highest I've ever seen."

"Three won't be enough, Rettich," Alenard smiles benevolently.

"I can find more. And there's some more growing. When will you need them? When will you build it?"

Work pauses. Tension of the Unanswerable Question in the air. Eyes turn to Alenard, who puts down his quill and holds up his innocent palms to the room. "Don't gape my way!" he cries. "Go ask the Treasurer!" Rethinks, rephrases. "Go ask God!"

Still everyone is looking at him. He shrugs. "They are still building the Our Lady in Paris."

"And when did they begin?"

"I don't know. Sixty years ago."

Silence. Rettich dries the tools with a rag. "Then there's time to plant new trees for the steeple. And wait for them to grow."

†††

In the winter months, to save on fuel, Rettich will sleep in the Lodge itself. The nearby apprentices' shack is now cold and empty, the other boys have taken leave and returned to distant hearths and homes. And so, as the short day closes, Rettich fetches his bowl of soup from the Refectory and hurries, clogs clattering over the sodden cobblestones, to the Lodge, the solitary makeshift building at the corner of the Cathedral construction site.

But on this night of sleet and rain he is not alone. Achim is seated at his drawing desk, staring into the darkness. On hearing Rettich's steps, he turns, and his eyes are wide. "I am golden," he says. "Golden, Rettich."

"Master?"

"Tell me, where do ideas come from?"

Rettich is silent. Not because he wishes to be, but simply because he does not know what to say. He has heard the stories whispered amongst the Apprentices, of Achim's madness. They say he has fits of black bile followed by ecstasies that make him rave, drink and spend money as if it were made of water. They say he has a scar on his back from where Satan extracted his soul in exchange for the revelation of the New Cathedral.

"When you make your little wood carvings, what are you thinking?"

"I don't know, Master. I don't know. It's like my mind wanders off on a cloud and my hands do the thinking."

"Yes!"

"The world goes into you through your eyes and ears, Master, and through your nose! The senses! But then it must all mix about like a soup inside you, all those sights and sounds and smells . . . and come out through your hands. That's the way it's always seemed to me."

Rettich blushes. Burbling on about himself like a mountain brook in the presence of his Master. "And you, My Lord, where do your ideas come from?"

"Ah! If I knew that, Rettich . . . If only I knew! From God, I hope. From the angels." And he waves his hands over the draughts and drawings hanging above the working tables. "For could a work like this ever come from the Devil?"

"No, my Lord."

"Rettich, tonight . . . I don't want to be alone. Will you stay with me? Will you drink with me? I have silver in my purse. A handful of pennies! I am made of gold!"

Rettich blushes once more, and looks to the floor.

† † †

The tavern that Achim takes them to is far from golden, merely the first that they passed on their way outside. Smoke-blackened beams and tablecloths whose hems glisten with the pork-fat wiped from hungry mouths. A cauldron of soup bubbling over the smouldering embers, baked clay pitchers of cheap, sweet Rhenish.

But for Achim it is the Earthly Paradise. His eyes shine with wine as he leans back in his chair by the fire. He seems to care nothing that he is the only nobleman present, surrounded by carters, porters and thieves. And yet Rettich is nervous, drinking deep to find Courage at the bottom of his cup.

And suddenly a man is standing in the centre of the room, dressed in a wide broad-brimmed hat and a leather cloak. *In the beginning was the Light*, says this Wanderer, and his accent is strange, an accent Rettich has never heard before, *and there was nothing but the Light and nothing for the Light to know itself by, and so it created Darkness.*

What strange words, and everyone feels it, the tavern becomes silent. The Wanderer, still in his long, patched coat, as if he had just now walked in from the rain and sleet, crouches, raises his arms, sweeps the air, spins.

And the Light circled the Darkness and the Darkness circled the Light, and they fell in Love with each other and created . . . Fire.

He waves his arms, and suddenly there is a small flame in his right hand and the audience gasps! *. . . For Fire, look, my Friends,* and he holds the flame aloft like in the Mass the priest holds aloft the Body of Our Lord, *is a Child of both Darkness and Light.*

Silence in the tavern. Inside, fire- and candlelight. Outside, gentle rain. A sodden coat, steaming by the hearth. Two beautiful young girls, watching the performance, bright-eyed, admiring. The Wanderer's children?

The Wanderer speaks again, hushed. *The Light in the Flame reaches upwards to the Home of Light above, and the Darkness sucks her down . . . down into the wood, the charcoal, into the Stuff of the World, into the Darkness.*

His palm closes and the flame is no more. His pallid face, once lit by the magical light from his palm, now sinks in gloom.

He opens his palm again, and there is nothing. A vulnerable, human hand, shown open to all, held out, the sign of Peace. No trace of soot, no wound, no burning.

Fires burn in the Heaven, he says, holding out his arms,

palms aloft, like a supplicant. *The sun, the moon, the stars. And here on earth . . .* he gestures to the tavern grate *. . . fire gives us warmth, gives us bread, purifies the fruits of the earth to give us Iron, give us Silver, give us Gold.*

My Lord, he says, holding out his palm to Achim, *I and my two girls are fallen on ill times. We are weavers, wandering from place to place, looking for a position, looking for money to start our business anew. So please it God, touch my palm with your charity.*

And the Wanderer's two girls approach and kneel, and Achim looks on them. And Rettich can see how his Master's face begins to glow. For the older girl, of some fourteen summers, is of the kind of beauty that awakens Adoration in men.

Achim bends towards her. "What is your name, maid?"

"Odile, My Lord."

He takes her hand in his. "Odile, will you marry me?"

"No, My Lord."

There are tears in Achim's eyes as he holds his hands up to his face. And pulls off his ring, set with a large amber stone. "But take this ring, Odile. And remember me. Remember me."

And then Master Achim reaches into his coat and withdraws his purse. And into the beautiful girl's outstretched, ivory hand, he places, one by one, thirteen silver pennies, a Devil's shilling.

ANNO
1231

A KNOT OF VIPERS
(ANNO 1231. EUGENIUS VON ZABERN II)

A nd the Lord said unto Satan, Whence comest thou? Then Satan answered the Lord, and said, From going to and fro in the earth and from walking up and down in it. And the Lord said unto Satan, hast thou considered my servant Job?

Hast thou considered my servant Eugenius von Zabern? He too, like Satan, goes to and fro in the mud and walks up and down in it as he marches from one pestilent village to another in January's gloom. And all in the service of our Holy Mother Church and in the search for funds for the New Cathedral.

We are trailing through yet another mud-doused forest on our petulant mules and horses. At the front and back of our train, in case of trouble, ride our armed mercenaries, a motley of delinquents with colourfully painted noses, who, it must be said, are quite willing to fight or take prisoners when called upon. I am in the centre of the train, on my black palfrey, who carries me and our coin. Ahead of me the two asses, carrying our pots, rations and bedding, so that my constant vision, when struggling uphill as now, is of a donkey's anus.

Behind me ride my two junior clerks and our two manservants who make fires, cook, deal with the kitchens and domestics in those places where we pass the night, and who delouse us in the morning sun, if there ever is any (we saw the last sunshine six days ago). We are toiling uphill to one of the castles of the Count of Schonach who has caused us the inconvenience of not being at home in his Black Forest valley residence. For some godforsaken reason, he has chosen to pass this, the darkest month, in his damp pile of stones on the overlooking hill.

Yesterday a rainstorm on the pass forced us to change our itinerary and seek shelter in the village of Blankenau. It is a poor mountain place producing hardy livestock, inedible cheese and a fine-flavoured honey from the pasture flowers. The tithes it pays us are negligible, but I remembered that last year they underpaid us by seven pounds of candle wax. If I am honest, I do somewhat enjoy putting the mortal fear of God into our parish priests by calling by, unannounced. It usually has the result that the missing seven pounds of wax are miraculously found. Usually in the priest's sideboard. And if it's not wax, it's honey, or wine, or good Hagenburg silver.

In Blankenau the priest responded to my unexpected arrival with a panic that was out of all proportion to seven pounds of missing wax. It was as if I were Satan himself, come to claim his immortal soul. His eyes were wide, his Adam's apple bounced. "I will stay with you tonight," I declared. "We will join you and your congregation for Mass in the morning, and then be on our way."

"Mass?" he stuttered, as if he had somehow forgotten that tomorrow was the Sabbath.

I was exhausted, retired early. My host seemed to stay up all night, with the susurrus of whispered voices rising from the lower floor at all hours. Next morning, in the dilapidated church, there was an eerie atmosphere. It was full, but everyone seemed ill-at-ease and strangely silent, and when I looked around, no-one met my eye.

When the priest raised the host and the altar boy rang the bell, I swear I could hear giggling in the congregation, and someone audibly farted.

We left immediately after Mass in hostile silence. The

villagers, dressed mainly in black, scattered away like crows. As we set on our way, an old man spat across our path and covered his cataract-clouded eyes.

Looking back on it now, some hours later on this clammy Sunday, I cannot quite explain to myself the feelings of horror I felt in that cold and ramshackle church. The mass was conducted correctly, the congregants responded in muttered liturgy as they should. Yet somehow in the details it was wrong, as if seen through a mirror. All clear and true, yet reversed, back to front.

And it makes me think of the many rumours I have heard of late, of secret, heretical cults amongst the travelling weavers, of whole villages that have spat upon the cross and apostatised. Of a heretic Abbot in the wealthy convent of Mohrmünster, who claims that he has spoken in person with the Holy Spirit, and who fornicates with the Abbess and with all of her nuns.

One of our horses is sick, we slide in the mud as we struggle uphill. My juniors mutter that the old blind man has cursed us, that the Devil is on our backs. They startle and shiver when a boar grunts in the distance, say it sounds like a screaming purgatorial soul. "It is a boar," I tell them gently, "you idiots."

But the Lord is kind to His Servants, and the muddy ascent is over quicker than I had feared. In the castle courtyard, the servants treat us frostily but with decorum, bring us water, and the horses some hay. The Count von Schonach awaits me upstairs, he does not condescend to leave the warmth of his parlour to greet me. I take no offence. After all, he must receive a never-ending stream of visitors up here in the mists of January. He must be weary of Society.

I keep him waiting and gratefully feed my black palfrey a turnip for having borne me so laboriously. My party is admitted into the servants' quarters for soup, but, at my orders, two armed men climb the castle stairs with me. What I have to discuss with the Count is delicate, and potentially fractious. They wait outside as I am invited into My Lord Schonach's presence.

Fair-haired but balding and ruddy-skinned, he stands before his fireplace, wrapped in a heavy russet-brown cloak. After the greetings and salutations deemed necessary for Courtly Propriety, I am finally handed a chalice (silver-plated!) of warm, spiced wine and offered a seat by the fire. I am so chilled and damp I nearly forget to bless the cup and thank the Lord. But I remember as the chalice is at my lips, and—truly grateful—I silently give thanks to Our Father in Heaven, and drink deep, for the wine is good.

Now, refreshed, to the kernel of the matter. "We hear you prefer to pledge your loyalty to King Heinrich rather than to His Grace the Bishop?"

Schonach dissembles: shock, surprise.

"Is it true? Then you will not be wanting the pension of one hundred marks annual that His Grace pays you?"

Schonach spreads his hands, splutters protest, can't find the words. I find them for him. "There is no truth to the rumours."

"No. That is, yes. King Heinrich needs our support, does he not?"

"He is Our King. Support, what for, exactly?"

"Against the Emperor, who is in the ban of the church."

"Support against his own father?"

"His own father, excommunicate."

"Who has just won Jerusalem back for Christ."

"Without striking a blow."

"If he can win Jerusalem from the Infidel without shedding blood, is this not—?"

The Count interrupts, red in the face, "It's not the ISSUE!"

Silence, as the Count regathers his Courtly Propriety which has momentarily gone astray. To discuss politics with anyone is usually a fruitless experience; everyone states their case ill-temperedly, everyone vociferously disagrees, and, at the end, everyone believes exactly what they believed at the beginning. And then, what's more, to discuss the complexities of the ever-changing relations between the imperial Staufen family and the Popes *with a provincial aristocrat*, this is close to the definition of fruitless. I should know, I come from a family of provincial aristocrats. Praise be to God, I escaped to the bosom of the Church, and the consolation of Numbers.

"And what is the issue, My Lord Schonach?"

"We must be rid of that red-haired heretic."

"You mean Emperor Friedrich?"

"Who else?"

So, the rumours are true. Heinrich is canvassing support in the northern provinces to depose his own father as Emperor. He must have sent letters, messengers, ambassadors to these lonely Lords in their countless castle eyries around the German Lands. To sound them out, implore, cajole. And look at the result: the blotchy, choleric and moaning Graf von Schonach can't wait to start a civil war.

"Tell me, My Lord Treasurer," says Schonach, "if it came to it, which side would His Grace be on? For Heinrich? Or for Friedrich?"

I sigh, look at the Count, and it occurs to me that he is, simply, bored. He is bored out of his tiny, apoplectic mind. In this weather, he can't even hunt. All he can do is sit in his Black Forest hole, throw bones at his dogs, and watch the rain spurt from the grimy gutters. How much more entertaining it would be to spend his Bishop's pension on raising a troupe of mercenaries to go and split skulls and burn down buildings.

Pope Gregory, Emperor Friedrich, King Heinrich fighting like cats in a sack, whilst the Nobles watch on and place bets on who will win. And whilst the Lords of this World fight, unrest, heresy and misrule grow in the fertile darkness like mould on damp, warm rye.

What can I do? Panic? Run back to His Grace with my arms in the air, screaming that the gentry are plotting (again . . .)?

If My Lord Schonach can dissemble surprise, then I can dissemble disinterest. I yawn, take a luxurious gulp from the chalice. "Excellent wine, my Lord."

"The spices are from Acre. I brought them back from the Crusade. From the *proper* Crusade, where we actually *fought* the Saracen, with arms. Didn't just *enact diplomacy* and throw gold at the enemy to buy back Jerusalem. As if money were everything."

He will say the Honour word now.

"Where's the Honour in that?"

It is wearying to be right, on occasion. But the Count Schonachs of this world I have known since I was a boy, and as Treasurer, it is from my hands that their peace and co-operation are bought, twice annually.

"Indeed." I look the Count in the eye. "His Grace the Bishop determines the diplomatic policy of this diocese. His vassals, such as you, My Lord, have signed an undertaking not to take *any* action that may threaten the peace of these lands. You are free to do as you will, but not on the Bishop's pension. If you no longer require the hundred marks a year, you are free. If you wish to receive the next instalment, His Grace awaits you, before the commencement of Lent, in Hagenburg, where you will kiss his hand in the public eye as a demonstration of your continued fealty."

Count Schonach mutters something. It sounds like "bloody extortioner," but it is much of a muchness to me. From his reaction, I gather that, this time at least, we can expect him in Hagenburg before the week is out. Silver chalices do not grow on the Black Forest's branches.

But, despite my success, I am discomforted. There is doubtless something behind Schonach's wavering loyalties; some attempted realignment of the balance of power—a balance which is only very precariously maintained in these fractious Alsatian lands.

"Come in time for the Carnival, why don't you," I suggest civilly to the cantankerous Count. "You will feel better for a dance, a drink, and a change of perspective. These woods are so gloomy in winter, I find."

He looks as if he would like to throttle me, but offers me dinner instead. We have a whole evening of delightful conversation to look forward to.

† † †

What a knot of vipers they seem, the Lords of this Earth, from afar. Heinrich, who would depose his own Father. And Bishop Berthold, from the damp distance of Schonach castle, seems a despot Croesus, a golden spider sitting on a giant web, with all the lands in his dominion spread out beneath his black, unfeeling carapace.

But come closer and see . . . the Bishop is just a man with watering eyes, colic and indigestion. Who looks on a farmer's cart with envy, because there is a simple life in the sacks of corn and swinging children's legs that will never be his.

Nor mine neither. We are up well before dawn like monks, and out on our horses as soon as we can see our own noses in the gloom. Snow is falling, gently. If we are lucky we will make the monastery at St. Trudpert before sundown. The monastery is well provided and its refectory highly praised. If God is willing, let me at least get some good food in my belly before Lent begins.

The snow falls heavier, and my horse is lamed a good distance from the nearest blacksmith. Devil take our luck, we will not make the monastery tonight. We will sleep in some other verminous village and eat stewed cabbage.

It is worse, we must sleep in a barn. *Like Our Lord Jesus Christ's first night on this Earth*, says my junior clerk, sentimentally. Well let us hope that Bethlehem is blessed by more clement climes than a damp hillside in the Black Forest. The manservants strew the straw, prepare the bedding, light a fire, heat the broth. The clerks sit and shiver, keeping a fearful eye on the dark outside, trembling with terror at the bark of a fox. They are Cathedral Schoolboys who only feel safe in cloisters, surrounded by their own Latin-speaking, nib-scratching kind. For them, Nature is full of threat and Evil.

They know that I have learned the Book of Job by heart, and to distract themselves from the terrors of the dark, they question me about it. But I am weary and short-tempered, and have no patience for Latin biblical debates. I would rather listen to the knocks and hisses of the fire, and find in my mind a huge number that I can prove to myself to be divisible by seven.

This is what calms me; the parade and infinity of numbers.

We eat broth and hard bread. Outside the snow falls steadily, and we clerics fall silent. Two of the mercenaries, the Englander and the Danelander, have made friends, and are chatting quietly in some halfway language that they both seem to understand. Maybe it is the mother tongue of some island found in the northern seas between their two countries, inhabited by sea monsters and scaly beasts, who knows, but whatever it is, it sounds like the amorous grunting of toads. Strangely, it is conducive to sleep.

Sinners that they are, they have stolen some plum aquavit from the Count's cellar, and offer me a cup of it. God bless you, sirs. With its stolen sinful warmth in my belly I can lie down like an animal in the straw and hope to find sleep this freezing night.

Then the Lord answered Job out of the whirlwind,
Where wast thou when I laid the foundations of the earth?
Hast thou entered the treasuries of the snow?
Hath the rain a father?
Who hath begotten the drops of dew?
Out of whose womb came the ice?
Where wast thou when I laid the foundations of the earth?
Who laid the corner stone thereof,
when the morning stars sang together?

† † †

Whispering voices, sweet song awake me at dawn. A thrush is singing in the frosted branches, and my clerks are convinced it is a Devil trying to seduce them. They stop their ears against its liquid rush of song, the idiots. I pull out their fingers, and tell them to read the Book of Job and see thereby how proud the Lord is of his Creation. They should not offend God's creatures by calling them Devils.

They have referred to the bird, in their Cathedral School Latin, as a *passer*, which is "sparrow" in the vulgate. I also tell them they should have the respect to call the fowl of the air by their correct name, and this is a thrush, which in our Alsatian tongue is a "Trossle," and in Latin a "*turdus.*" Genesis Two, *and the Lord God formed every fowl of the air and brought them unto the man to see what he would call them, and whatsoever the man called every living creature, that was the name thereof.* This sparks a discussion between the clerks (one is from the Aargau, one is from the Land of Oc) and the manservants (both Alsatian) about the name of the bird that is presently singing. No-one can agree on its name.

Later, after hurried prayers and some more of last night's soup, as we are loading the horses, I hear my clerks discuss Count Schonach's black cats. There were two in the kitchen, apparently. The clerks think these were Schonach's black magic familiars, keeping an eye upon us, and reporting back to their Dark Lord at midnight.

They will be calmer when we reach the monastery. And they will dispense with this demonological nonsense by the time we leave the dark forest behind, and reach the wide Rhine plateau, where the shadows disperse.

† † †

O, Lands of Babel, where one singing bird has a hundred names. Today, on our short, snowbound trudge to St. Trudpert, we pass from Schonach's lands to the Bishop's, whence to the lands of the Dukes of Zähringen, and all are under the same white snow as God made them, without visible border or boundary.

We reach the monastery at noon, and we are grateful for it. The Abbot is an ally of His Grace, pays his tithes promptly and to the penny, and keeps a good Christian establishment of calm and study in these snowy foothills. His cellar is good, his larder well plenished, and we will want for nothing.

† † †

We are back on the Rhine plain, God be praised, and heading for home. In Offenau we stop for food in the parsonage and hear from the priest's maidservant (*cum* concubine, no doubt) that a local landowner of a hundred acres is on her deathbed.

My clerks look at me in silent pleading. They had hoped to be in their own cells in Hagenburg tonight, even if it meant riding the last leagues in darkness. But Duty is Duty, the New Cathedral needs funding, and as soon as we have supped, we are riding off to the lady's manor like vultures flying to the rumour of carrion.

Yet it seems we arrive too late. A smooth Dominican is already there, holding her bony hand and looking pleased with himself. Her heirs, two sons and two daughters, stand at the foot of the bed, looking distraught. In part, because their beloved mother is dying, and in greater part, because she has just bequeathed a good tranche of their inheritance to the Dominican, for the building of his monastery in Hagenburg, and for one hundred years less in Purgatory.

It's twenty marks I could have had for my Bottomless Hole, the New Cathedral. If the Dominican left the room, I could quietly make my counterbid, offer her eternal soul a Mass in one of the apse chapels once a year for the next hundred. But maybe that Preaching Vulture has already offered a Mass at his half-built monastery in Finckweiler? He eyes me charily, kneels to pray for the dying. I and my clerks gather round, we all recite together.

My reverent half-closed eyes flicker over in the Dominican's direction every minute or so. Surely, at some juncture, he will have to leave the room to urinate? Or is it now a contest between his bladder and her mortal frame? Which will hold out the longer?

"My Lady," I say, after a while. Why stand on decorum? "The Cathedral, Our Lady of Hagenburg, is to be rebuilt in the New Style to the Glory of God. It is conceived as the New Temple of New Jerusalem, it will have a roof of Gold, three Towers that pierce the heavens, twelve Portals, one for every disciple and one for every tribe of Israel, nine Altars, and will be one of the great wonders of Christendom. We are offering . . . "

I pause as a bilious secretion oozes out of her mouth, and one of her daughters reaches for the cloth and bowl of water, sending me a recriminatory glance.

" . . . for twenty marks, a mass to be said in a side chapel annually . . . "

The oozing has become a hacking coughing, and suddenly the children are all running to her side. The Preaching Brother, damn him, raises his eyebrow at me, and gently gestures towards the door. We go outside.

Here the snow has not settled, and the plain stretches out in a motley of browns, greens and greys. "Brother Treasurer," says the Dominican, "I have already changed her Will the once, and that took mortal effort. Before she redrafted in our favour, it was promised to the Abbey at Mohrmünster. But have you heard the rumours about that cursed place?"

I lie and tell him that I have heard nothing. And so he whispers to me that he has heard direct witness of how the Abbot fornicates with the nuns (I am meant to be shocked, I think), how the Abbot believes himself some kind of God (this is more surprising, to be sure) and how he propagates heresies, such as that the Holy Ghost had sexual union with Mary (this, surely, if true, is the Abbot's death sentence).

I no longer need to dissemble alarm and outrage with this priggish, preaching fool. If there is truth in these claims, then action will have to be taken.

We thank you for the information, Brother. You can keep your twenty marks from this bilious biddy, I am now hunting bigger game. Mohrmünster Abbey is within the lands of the Bishop of Metz, and is subject directly to the Pope himself. But if it is presently in the hands of heretics, then everything those heretics own, by ecclesiastical law, falls to the hands of the Holy Roman Church.

And I know only too well, the Abbot and Abbess of Mohrmünster alone must be worth several, several hundred marks. And everything they own is now free for the taking.

Mohrmünster Abbey. Dawn. He's shitting himself. He doesn't know it, but this is the day that will change his life. His hand trembles on the hilt of his sword. A dawn raid on a monastery protected by a troop of mercenaries. He's been in the militia three years, but this is different from rolling drunks and chasing thieves. An ambush.

Thick mist from the brook, frost-brittle branches, dim grey light. Snow underfoot, steam from the horses' nostrils. From the nearby village, the dawn bell: once, twice, thrice.

Treasurer von Zabern; aristocrat from a noble house going back countless generations, manager of the Bishop's thousands of marks, and big joyless bastard hated by all, touches his silver cross. It's big, must weigh eight ounces. Manfred calculates; he's learned from his uncle in the Counting House: that's about two hundred and forty silver pennies. Just hanging from that arsehole's neck.

Arsehole mutters something, waves his hands a few times. So he's praying? What will God make of that one? What does God do with all the words lisped at Him? *Lord bless this rapacious attack on one of your monasteries.* Why is it the bastard Treasurer in charge today? And not the Armourer or one of the Bishop's countless vassal knights?

Arsehole waves his hand: signal to get ready. Manfred's bowel loosens, but he gets it under control, pats his horse: a sorrel gelding. Present from his father, God bless him: the horse got Manfred a place in the raid; only mounted men can take part. During the week Manfred hires him out as a pack-horse, and on Sundays he decks him out in fine harnessings and a saddle of Schlettstadt leather, and rides around in search of girls. But they never take him seriously. Girls like the noble boys, in their bright colours. Not some drab Rhine trader's son, smelling of caulking tar.

The Treasurer raises his hand, lets it fall. The signal to advance. Manfred's stomach lurches, his heart pounds. Holy Mary, this is it. Spurs the gelding. Seventeen of them, mounted, armed, hit a canter towards the Mohrmünster gates. Treasure-Arsehole has briefed them: these are heretics and adulterers, unarmed monks and nuns, protected by a handful of lousy mercenaries. A mission for God and the Bishop. He gave them dispensations; blood-spilling here won't count as a sin. And if you believe that, you can believe anything.

But this is Metz's territory, isn't it? Not Hagenburg's?

Friedrich, Captain of the Militia, knocks at the Abbey gate. The troop fans out behind the Gatehouse, out of sight.

Clunking sounds; the gate spyhole opening. The lay-brother idiot gatekeeper looks out, sees the cleric von Zabern, suspects nothing, opens up . . . Screams as he sees a sudden troop of sixteen horsemen bearing towards him. Bertle, Manfred's closest friend and another Rhine Harbour mer-chant's boy, thwacks the gatekeeper with the flat of his sword; "Shut your mouth."

They clatter into the main courtyard and rein in, look around in the surprising silence. Cretin gate-boy is on his knees, clutching his bruised skull. Where are the mercenaries?

They're hired by the Abbot to protect Mohrmünster's lands and treasures from marauding bands. Marauding bands may have been common when Manfred was a boy, when the Bishop and the Staufens were squabbling over every fence and boundary post. But for some years now, Peace has ruined their business.

And so, with no marauders around to test their mettle, the mercenaries have grown paunchy and lazy, and—it seems—they are still a-bed.

Three of them now come stumbling out of the gatehouse, rubbing their eyes, pulling on their armour, waving swords and halberds, wondering what the devilfuck's gone and happened. Seeing them like this, half dressed and half asleep, it's already obvious that the fight's over, but seven of the Hagenburg number are young noblemen, and they've not come all this way just to see three mercenary beer guts and a white flag.

Young Statius von Fegersheim, eager to cover himself in chivalrous glory, charges straight at them, waves his dashing blade and nearly clean cuts off the first mercenary's head. Seeing his bloody success, he utters a scream of horror, which he is quick to convert into a "hurrah" of knightly triumph, as he panic-scrambles his stallion to turn about and retreat . . .

The other mercenaries flinch and look with pale discomfort at their companion's near-severed head, now joined only by the spine and some bloody cordons to his twitching body. Then they fall silent and look at each other. A lake of blood slicks over the cobblestones. They turn to the Treasurer.

"Ten shillings each and we'll leave in peace," says their leader, in an idiotic-sounding Swiss accent; just like the Hayseed Dunce character in the Feast of Fools plays. The Hagenburg troop crumple with laughter. Hayseed Dunce reddens to the colour of cider apples. Von Zabern sheaths his sword, rests his gloved hands on the pommel. "Take three each and consider yourselves fortunate."

† † †

The main part of the troop is sent to the Abbey to round up the monks from their dawn prayers. There might be some fighting, so the knights are needed. Manfred and Bertle get the "soft" detail: shake out the nuns at the nunnery.

That's just royal gold for them; it couldn't be better. Here they are, haring around the herb-garden, kicking up slush from their geldings' hooves, shouting, "To the main courtyard you heretic whores!" and other such niceties. The nuns run, screaming, pulling their black habits over their white gowns. Some men are running with them: monks, lay brothers and other boyfriends: so what Treasure-Fucker said is true; this is more of a brothel than a nunnery.

Bertle has a long spear shaft, has some fun lifting the sisters' skirts with it. They're a fine-looking spread of whores—a better selection here than the worn-out sacks who work the *zum thrunkenen Cahne*.

Beyond the herb garden, a paved pathway runs past the hospital and the leprosarium and into freedom. A group of three nuns and two half-dressed boys are trying their escape into the snowy fields . . . Manfred and Bertle canter up and chase them down.

"Let us get away, what's it to you?" says one of the men. Manfred taps him with the flat of his sword. "Let you get away, and we won't get paid, that's what it is to us." With sword and spear and reeling horse, they sic them like sheep back into the monastery pen. A few blows to their arses send them running to the main Abbey square.

Into the rooms, seeing if any are left in hiding. A long corridor, with the cells in rows on one side. These nuns, unmarriable daughters of fine families, live in luxury: silver plates, dried figs, spiced wine, perfumes, fine linen sheets. In the Abbess' room, a stained glass Holy Virgin illumines an unmade bed of silk and Flemish linen. Golden candlesticks hold three-pound wax candles.

On her bedside chair, a wig of flaxen hair, a box of rouge and kohl. On her writing table, a pouch of silver coin.

Manfred and Bertle share a look.

† † †

In trade, everything connects. This is the lesson he has learned. Nothing is worth nothing. There is no moment that is not an opportunity. In the Counting House at Hagenburg there are Gulden, Sols Tournois, Deniers Parisis, Rappen, Batzen, Bezants, Büssel and Heller, gathered there from the homes of the four winds, carried by foot, boat and horse to their exchange into good, hard Hagenburg coin.

As a child, he used to stare at these coins over the counter. When trade was quiet, his uncle, the Counting House factotum, would hand him a coin to look at, weigh in his hand, bite against his teeth, to dream. From Bohemia, from Visby, from England, from Paris, Basel, Florence, Antwerp, Palermo, Cologne, Constantinople, Alexandria. A web of deals, a network of barterings, promises, investments, gambles and transactions covering our world in threads of living silver and gold.

The night before, at the Inn in Wasselheim, TreasurerBastard gave them all a speech: no looting, no thieving; the Abbey and everything in it is the property of the Church. Now Manfred understands; this isn't just a round-up of heretics and sinners, this is a raid.

And that's why the Treasurer is running things. It's to do with money. Everything always is. At least that's what Manfred's been led to believe.

Money.

Far be it from Manfred and Bertle to disobey the orders of the Holy Mother Church, but somehow the coins find their way into Bertle's underwear, a golden ring into the lining of Manfred's cap, and the wig, God Knows Why, stuffed behind his breastplate.

† † †

"In the name of Jesus Christ, I was chosen. Like the patriarchs of old, it was given me to have many wives. We were wed in the centre of the sun . . . "

Manfred's Latin is not so good, but this is what he thinks the Abbot is shouting as he and Bertle trot back into the Abbey's main square. Screams, wails, weeping. The nuns are being shackled together by the other Hagenburg raiders. The monks are already in chains.

Luckhard the Blacksmith leans against his cart, eating some bread and sausage, in bad humour. He's come all the way from Hagenburg, following behind the raiding party with his cart loaded with chain and shackles. The statutes rule that he owes seven days unpaid work to the Bishop every year, and Treasure-Fucker hit him with this commission: make fifty shackles and lengths of chain and bring them to Mohrmünster. Luckhard hasn't slept in three days, looks ready to beat the Treasurer into sheet metal, cut him into coins.

The morning mists have lifted, a pale sun angles over the Abbey chapel. A servant throws a bucket of water over the mercenary's spilled blood, starts to scrub at it. The corpse has been dragged away somewhere. "The Bishop of Hagenburg is a heretic, not I! What gives him the right to invade my sovereign territory?" shouts the Abbot. No-one pays him much attention.

Friedrich orders the two merchant boys to dismount and join in the shackling. Manfred can think of worse things to do than manhandle nuns, jumps down keenly. Grabs a pretty novice, she struggles, he pulls her close to him, kisses her. She flinches away from his kiss, but weakens. Iron closes around her wrist. Tears fall from her eyes.

Riding into the Abbey now, the Treasurer's Clerks, with rolls of parchment tied to their saddlebags. "Start the inventory of personal goods immediately," says the Treasurer, "begin your work in the Abbot's quarters." The pale, angular young Clerks nod, obedient, dismount. Treasure-Fucker doesn't even want a rusty penny to slip from his fingers; he wants the whole lot inventoried, down on paper, so he can salivate over the lists of goods and chattels.

This place will be worth a fortune.

One of the monks starts shouting in the Treasurer's direction, a mix of Latin and Lothringen dialect. The gist of what he's saying: *yes I always knew the Abbot was a heretic and I always stood against him and I wrote letters to the Bishop and to the Pope and it wasn't my fault if they were intercepted by the Abbots' spies and please don't burn me.*

The Treasurer sighs, speaks quietly; "His Grace has appointed some Dominican Brothers to hear your cases. You will be taken to the castle at Rosenweiler to be tried. Now please shut up."

The mercenary's blood has thickened, blackened. The servant is scrubbing as hard as he can. Pinkish foam gathers round the cobbles' stain. Remembering the sickening moment of the beheading, Manfred's innards turn. He takes the arm of the next nun, an older lady, shaking all over. Her eyes are vacant, demented. She has no idea what's happening. Manfred shackles her wrist.

Von Fegersheim has gone green. He kneels at the Treasurer's feet, begs something quietly, so that the others can't hear. Von Zabern nods wearily, lays his hands on Von Fegersheim's brow—an absolution. So, the young noble has fears for his immortal soul! He's just killed a man, pretty much in cold blood, and it's hit him hard. One of his noble friends says something, Von Fegersheim laughs, overloud. Trying to shrug off the nausea, the shame.

"He'll be alright," nods Bertle, from behind his nun, the last in the line. "He just needs a drink."

"You two!" says Arsehole, imperiously, pointing at Manfred and Bertle. "You'll escort the mercenaries on their way, as far as Pfalzburg. Set them on the Nanzig road. After that you can go home. Collect your pay at the Treasury after Sunday."

Manfred looks at Bertle and shrugs; a nice ride through the snowbound forest with the Hayseeds. If their horses aren't too tired, they can be back to Hagenburg that night. Gibbous moon; last night's was full; they can find their way. And if the Vogesentor is locked, their friends on the Town Guard will let them in if they shout loudly enough.

"Come here first," says the Treasurer ominously.

Manfred and Bertle approach His Lordship, finding expressions of appropriate innocence.

"Empty your pockets, pouches."

Manfred and Bertle exchange a glance, then, like schoolchildren, they obey. Von Zabern arches an eyebrow over their stuff; a couple of keys, some pennies, a small knife, a pair of bone dice.

"Jump up and down."

Incomprehension.

"Do as I say."

Manfred and Bertle jump up and down unenthusiastically. A jingle of coin comes from Bertle's bollocks.

Treasure-Fucker holds out his hand. "Give it to me."

Bertle tries to pull an incredulous face. It doesn't work.

"And anything else you've stolen. Hupprecht!"

The Treasurer summons over one of the young knights to pat the merchant boys down. Before too long, von Zabern is weighing the pouch of silver and the ring in his supple-fingered hands. "What is it about merchants that makes them incapable of honesty?" he asks.

Manfred strokes his pointed, ginger beard, searches for a bright, sharp reply. Can't find one.

"Get going," says von Zabern, turns away.

Manfred and Bertle share a look, then head to their horses. The mercenaries are waiting by the gate, disarmed, ready to try their luck over the border in Burgundy.

"Fucking bastard," mutters Bertle, meaning the Treasurer. Manfred nods. There were a good fifty pennies in that pouch. But he's still got the flaxen wig in his breastplate. And, strangely, it's the wig that's going to make his Fortune.

In trade, everything connects.

SUNLIGHT
(ANNO 1231. RETTICH SCHÄFFER III)

L ie beneath the tree's outspreading arms. Close your eyes. There's a wind, coming from the sun's bedchamber.
The "sun's bedchamber"?

Rettich laughs. Where the sun goes to bed, my Lord.
Ah, from the West.

If you say so, Master. Close your eyes. The wind moves the new young leaves. The sunlight dances.
A dance of shadows, yes.

The wind whispers in your ear. What's it saying?
It's saying that maybe the sun goes to bed over there, but when he gets up in the morning, he rises over there. So what happens with his bedchamber during the night?

Ah, don't you know? Beneath our world there is an ocean.
There is?

And the sun, sleeping, drifts on that ocean, on a boat made of light. His bed is laid on the prow of the boat, and he drifts all night on the seas, and then, when he wakes, he has come to the Other Side of the World. And he rises from there.
I didn't know this, Rettich.

No?
And then what happens to his boat during the day?

It drifts back to where it started. And the whole thing begins again.
There is no-one guiding this boat? It moves of its own accord?

God guides that boat, Master Achim.

Of course.

Quiet a time, if you will, Master. Listen to the wind, watch the dance.

† † †

For the first year Rettich concentrates on simple stone dressing, on measurements and figures, on cutting building blocks to the perfect size, on the making of mortar, on recognising the subtle shades of colour in the hewn stone. Most of his days are therefore spent with the Companions on the site, where they are raising the soaring walls of the new nave along the line of the old.

Rettich has no fear of heights and so he is often sent scrambling like a squirrel up the scaffolds to help with the pulleys and treadwheels. Here, close to Heaven, his companions are the ropers and carpenters in charge of the lifting contraptions, the thick ropes, hooks and weights.

When a heavy block is being lifted, then concentration is deep. Silence is called for in the square below, so that all can hear each other's instructions. The hawkers move elsewhere, the stall-keepers are silent or move into the Apse and Crossing of the Cathedral to advertise their wares to the folk inside. A calm settles on the area, a small hushed crowd gathers to watch.

High up on the top of the wall, the men in the treadwheel start their walk. The ropes tighten, the claws of the lewisson clutch at the stone. The ropemakers watch like falcons for frays, poised with jugs of water to douse chafing cords. Carpenters watch rivets and joins for fractures, watch the wood for any unbearable strain.

Tighter and tighter. Rettich can hardly look.

Then a lurch and the stone is lifted from the cart. The watching crowd gasps. The oxen, sensing the burden's lifting, impatiently paw the ground. The carter keeps them in place, feeds them mangelbeet, calms them down. Masons gather round the block, now at a man's height above the cart, steady its rocking, settle its sway.

Free of the masons' upstretched fingers, the stone now inches its way up the towering wall. In the treadwheel they walk, keeping rhythm, step step step step. If they should stumble, then the block will plummet, the wheel will spin and dash them without mercy. Men have died in this way, too many times.

Rising, a span at a time. The ropes fray and twist. Timbers creak, whimper almost silently like beaten dogs. In Rettich's ears, the whisper of air, here up high, where at dusk the swallows wheel. He listens out for wind, watches the linen rag that hangs from a pole. Should it move, it's his call to cry out "wind!"

The rag hangs limp. Thanks be to God. All is in precarious balance, and any sudden strong gust can break the tensing timbers.

"Wait!" The Carpenter Companion's voice rings out, a marshal command. The load is swaying too much from side to side, and must be steadied.

The treadmill men count together, slowing down in unison, and then . . . stand still. Their weight holds the block in the dizzy void.

All is suspended. In mid-air, the sandstone block sways . . .

"And go!" The Wheelmaster is satisfied. With a forked pole he leans out and steadies the hanging rope as the block inches higher. His apprentice holds him by the belt, his other hand grasped to the scaffold, so that his leaning Master cannot fall.

Higher. Higher.

In the crowd, folk turn away. Look through the gaps in their fingers.

Rettich looks down. His feet touch the edge of the wall. Far below, on one side, the unfinished aisle and the mud and cobbles of the square, on the other side, the unfinished flag-stones of the Cathedral floor.

"Mortar Boys!" It's Landolt giving orders. The mortar is stirred again and trowelled onto its place, not too thick, not too thin, even as possible.

"Ten more spans! Easy! Easy . . . "

The block hovers above the height of the wall. The tread-wheel boys slow to a halt. The stone sways ever so slightly. And then is still.

Weight is balanced, in weightless air.

Now is the most dangerous time. A mistake and all can tumble to the dust below.

"All hands!" Reaching out, vertiginously, pulling the ropes and securing the block to sit exactly over the wall. Judgement of eyes, hands. Rettich offers a prayer, crosses his heart.

"And easy . . . down!"

With a groan of ropes, the block is placed. Final adjust-ments, and then its Weight is given back to it once more. Rock transforms from weightless air to heavy stone. The mortar seeps, the lewisson eases. Pressure sighs its release. Weight runs down the wall, forcing downwards, to the Square, to the Graves, to the Crypts and Foundations, and back into the Earth whence it came.

And then it is gone. There is a new equilibrium. And the stones of the Nave Wall have a new companion.

The builders take a moment, look at each other, pat shoul-ders, wipe brows.

The crowd applauds, disperses.

The hawkers return, call out their wares.

His heart trembling, Rettich scuttles down the scaffolding tower.

The oxen are taken away to be watered. The stall-keepers return.

† † †

Did you use to spend a lot of your time doing this, Rettich?

Watching the leaves and shadows? For hours at a time. Did you never?

No.

Didn't you watch the clouds?

No.

What did you do when you were a boy, Master Achim?

I read books, sat in lessons, stared at the tonsure of the monk in front of me.

You never played outside?

Hardly ever, Rettich.

But, Master, forgive me, once I . . .

What?

I did something I shouldn't.

Tell me. Or a Priest. Whoever is in greater need of knowing.

Once, in the Lodge, alone, I opened the . . . box thing.

I don't understand your German.

Nor do I! The box thing where the parchments are kept.

The escritoire! There is no German word I know for it. Just like there is no Latin we know for "adze."

And I saw your drawings.

This is a sin I will forgive. I am vain.

And on those drawings, Master, there are flowers, leaves . . .

There are indeed.

At the top of your columns. In the windows, surrounding the figures, the people, the saints, the prophets.

Yes.

How can you draw those so well? If you never . . . I mean . . . spent time in the forests, fields.

Those are not real leaves, Rettich, nor real flowers. They are Ideal Flowers, Ideal Leaves. They are from my mind, and from the leaves and flowers of earlier Masters. They are leaves and flowers I have seen in the other churches and monasteries. Transformed.

God has given us real leaves and flowers. Why should we make new ones?

Should we be mere copyists?

Master?

Rettich, have you ever seen a copy that is as good as the original?

No.

So, in praising God and his Greatness, should we merely copy what he has given us, should we hold up a mirror to His World and call it Art? Re-make badly what he has already, perfectly made?

No, Master.

The Cathedral, our Cathedral. It should be a sign. It will be made of mud, lime, rock, earth, sand, wood, it will be made of the mortal Stuff of this World. It will be imperfect. But it will point, in all its stones and mortar, to He who laid the cornerstone, the foundations of the Universe, to He who lives beyond the mud and mess of this world, in Perfection.

So, close your flawed, dimmed, corrupt eyes, Rettich, and see a leaf.

I see it.

But do not see an Oak leaf, do not see a Beech leaf, do not see an Ash leaf. We are not copyists of God's works. We are artists.

See a Leaf. See The Leaf. The first Leaf that was in God's mind, before it was copied into this world of forms. Can you see it?

Can you see it?

That is the difference between you and me, Master. I cannot see it.

† † †

Rettich, this is wonderful.

Pride fills his already-swollen heart. Ridiculous to feel proud, when seated upon a mangy donkey, but so be it. Master Achim has dismounted from his sable mare, and is standing beneath the chestnut tree. He is looking at Rettich's carving of the Virgin, carved from an old trunk, standing by the village spring. Around the Virgin statue, the villagers have left offerings; dried meadow flowers, painted eggs, pinecones tied in ribbon—a bouquet of colour around the Holy Mother.

Achim's fingers gently trace her upraised hands. Are there little tears in the Master's eyes?

"The Priest had her brought here. The villagers always left tokens here anyway because of the spring." Rettich points to the nearby well and trough where the rising water has been captured in stone and mortar. "Now they leave them for the Virgin."

The grove surrounds them; a single chestnut and a cluster of silver-green firs, wind playing lightly in the needles and leaves. Dappled sunlight, a moving tapestry. Young, new grass. Meister Achim nods and turns to look at Rettich, who is perched absurdly on his donkey, his feet nearly touching the ground.

Rettich laughs. "Maybe I should get down before we enter the village."

Our Lord arrived in Jerusalem upon an ass.

"And I in Lenzenbach on my own two feet." He starts to dismount, but Achim protests. *No no no, stay, my friend.* He runs over to the grove of firs, and cuts a frond with his belt knife. *No, you are the prodigal son, and we will fanfare your return as best we can.*

In the village, the children run amongst the houses, calling out in silvery voices, "Rettich! Rettich's come home! Rettich's come home!" Their cries ring out amongst the rough brick threshing yards, the leaning rooves, the dark, open doorways, amongst the spring flowers.

The villagers gather in the muddy thoroughfare that snakes through their houses. Straw-haired Rettich, arriving, laughing, on a donkey. Behind him, a young Lord in a dark-green tunic, waving a fir frond as if the boy were Christ himself. A spectacle, as if from the Feast of Fools. They laugh and taunt, throw clumps of sheep dung at the Returning Son.

When Rettich's sister Amaline comes to her doorway, the boy leaps from his donkey and runs to embrace her with joy. His sister, not seen since last Easter, and now heavy with child. And, beneath her white kerchief, her long flaxen hair all shorn away, like a sheep in May.

† † †

"Was he tall? A ginger beard?" asks Rettich.

Amaline nods. She smiles at Achim as she curtseys to offer him water, but Rettich can read her eyes, and her eyes show shame.

"Rettich?" asks Achim, hoping for enlightenment.

"In the Cathedral Square, on market day, there comes out of the crowds, coming up to me, a young gentleman, tall, ginger beard."

"Yes?"

"He says to me, 'Boy, where did you get hair like that?' and I say, 'On my head and on another place, saving your pardon,' and he says, 'Don't play word games with me my friend, I'm asking where you and your hair are from?' and I say, 'Lenzenbach,' and he says . . . " Rettich pauses.

"What does he say, Rettich?"

"He says 'You'll have sisters, I should reckon,' and I say, proudly, for I love my sisters like my own blood—"

" . . . they *are* your own blood, Rettich . . . "

" . . . and that's why I love them like my own blood, it's true, and I say proudly, 'I have three sisters, sir,' and this gentleman, God damn his soul and God pardon me for saying so, he asks, 'And have they blonde hair like yours?' and I say, 'Two of them has hair finer than the sun, but Grete she is dark for even in a human flock there must be black sheep,' and he says, 'I thank you, my boy', or some such impertinence, for if he is my elder it can only be by one summer and I would say he was a spring lamb compared with me, and that was the conversation we held."

Rettich drinks his water from his leather cup. His eyes sparkle, despite his irritation. The water of Home. He turns to Amaline.

"How much did he pay you, sister?"

Amaline's eyes flicker over, uncertainly, to their Honoured Guest.

"There's no shame before my Master Achim, sister."

Amaline's eyes are suddenly full of tears. "It will grow back!" She runs indoors to cry.

Rettich, regretful, shakes his head. His eyes meet his sister Grete's. "Four shillings sixpence, each," says Grete. "And it *will* grow back." She pushes her own dark hair back behind her ears. "And the ginger beard, his name was Manfred. Thanks to him we won't go hungry this winter."

"You went hungry last winter?"

Mechthild pipes up now: "We ran out of flour well before Lent."

Rettich looks at his eldest sister. Beneath her kerchief, her head is also shaved, and flaxen stubble is growing on her scalp. "Don't your husbands take proper care of my girls?"

"You could send something from the City."

"Only Grete is still my responsibility! I sent Emmle with a purse for her at Christmas!"

"Thank you, brother. It helped. For I am dark, and no-one wants to shear my hair like a sheep." Grete laughs. Amaline appears in the shadow of the doorway, wiping her eyes, smiling through tears. "Ohh, I wish Emmle were here!" she says, and starts to weep again. "Imagine, all us five orphans, together again!"

Mechthild's eyes are bright too, thinking of their absent brother. "How is the little fox?"

Rettich smiles, bringer of good news. "He's in Mayenz! The Rosheimers sent him there to apprentice under their cousins, Rhine river merchants. He's well, he's learning to read and write, and sent me a fine little letter!"

Expiration of breath, happy surprise. Grete kicks at the ground, peevish. "You boys will leave us here to rot. Who here will teach *us* letters?"

Silence a moment. Sunlight, stealing out from under a cloud, makes a halo around Rettich's golden head. Chickens pluck at old chaff amongst the stones, grumbling to themselves. The smell of peat smoke and drying dungheaps. Achim sits in the seat of honour; their only chair, Amaline's husband's oakwood stool.

Curiosity can wait no longer. "Brother," asks Mechthild. "Why are you here?"

† † †

When Rettich arrives in the main room of the Lodge, he can see Master Achim at his tables, studying a series of coloured glass samples. Achim holds up a piece of pale lemon glass to the light, staring at it a long time, turning it slowly between index finger and thumb. He looks disappointed.

"Sir, you summoned me," says Rettich, uncertain if he should speak.

Achim jumps at the sudden voice, and turns. "Rettich."

A moment as the Master seems to come back to this world, and remember why the boy is there before him. "I summoned you."

"Yes. I am here. What can I do for you, Master?"

"Show me your trees."

"Master?"

"You said once that, near your village, there were very tall, straight trees."

"There are a few, my Lord."

"We will leave tomorrow."

Rettich hesitates, caught like a deer in a forest clearing, uncertain of which way to turn.

"I thought you would be happy."

"I am, sir! I'd like to dance on the moon."

"But it is daytime."

"Yes."

"So the moon is not available."

A shadow crosses Rettich's mind. "I have no gifts for my family, sir. I promised I would return with gifts."

"Then tomorrow, before we leave, we can buy some gifts."

"I have no money, my Lord."

"I said *we* can buy some gifts. I will be visiting them too, will I not? So, I can buy them on our behalf."

"You, sir? Visit my family?"

"If you prefer I didn't, you can hide me in a barn whilst you do the visiting."

"No, you will visit them! It will be an honour, my Lord."

"Good. After breakfast we will meet here and then go to the market. Can you ride a horse?"

Rettich wants to say "yes," but in all conscience, cannot.

"A mule? . . . "

Rettich looks sad. Does this mean he can't come?

"A donkey?"

Now he's smiling. And then, once again, he stops, and

frowns. "Sir, I have no permission to leave! I must ask Master Giselbert."

"Rettich, Rettich . . . What makes you think I haven't already asked him?"

Rettich, his heart bounding with joy, bows and takes his leave. The Lodge door swings open to the fresh, spring air. Rettich runs across the Cathedral Square, arms outstretched, like a swallow on the evening breeze.

† † †

Above them the tall trees tower. Straight, lofty in sunlight. Green-gold needled, sifting the wind.

"What do you call them?" asks Achim.

"Trees," says Grete, who has come with them, despite brother Rettich's protest. She giggles.

"Rettich?"

"She's right, we call it a 'tree.'" Rettich laughs.

Achim smiles, "It's a good name for it." His fingers feel the bark. They stand in the hill gully. The splash and gurgle of a brook, steep banks on either side. The sun is about to pass over the crest, leaving them in shadow. "We need to cut one down and season it. If it's good, we need cuttings. Then we will plant a grove of them."

"Here?"

"Nearer the Cathedral, Rettich. In the Bishop's hunting forests." Achim sighs. He looks at the crest of the trees, still bright in sunlight.

"Why sigh, my Lord?"

Achim shrugs, finds a smile. "Everything takes such time, work, effort. And money. If only we could just live in the mind . . ."

Grete looks at Rettich. Her face says, "*What*?"

Achim pats the tree trunk. "But if we do this now, next year we will know if the timber is good. And, if so, we will plant a grove of them. And then they will grow. And then, after we are dead and buried, those who come after us who will build the towers and the steeples will be grateful for what we have done."

Rettich looks at his Master's face, sees that he is glum. "My lord, we will build this cathedral so fast that you will live to see it completed. I swear we will."

Achim looks at Rettich, smiling, but his smile is wan.

† † †

One winter night, Rettich is alone in the Lodge. He sits obediently, waiting for the return of the Clerk, into whose hands he must give the Keys, and to no-one else. The night is cold, a deep frost, and the fire in the stove went out a while ago. He sits, wrapped in a blanket, shivers, and waits.

There is a knock on the door. It is Heinrich, the carpenters' boy, and he is sniggering. "Clerky won't be coming . . . "

"What?"

Heinrich giggles like a child once more. He mimes drinking, drinking, drinking. "Spiced Christmas wine! At the *zum Creutze*. He won't be getting up! Master says you must stay here the night, Rettichlein Rettichlein."

"Then I'll stay. Heinrich?"

"Yes."

"For the Love of God, get me some firewood. Or I'll die of cold."

Later, with wood in the stove, he steals the sheepskins from the Clerk's counting chair and lays them by the fire, folds the blanket, ready for bed . . .

Locks the door from inside.

A candle is burning over in the corner, by the chest where Master Achim keeps his drawings. Rettich goes to blow it out. The chest is not locked.

Temptation is too great. The candle stays lit. Rettich, his heart racing, opens the chest, pulls out a drawing.

Master Achim's hand is so fine, so delicate. Rettich finds, standing before him, a Prophet. Who can it be? John the Baptist? He has long hair, a beard, bright staring eyes, a battered coat and cloak. He is holding his right hand aloft and in his hand a fire is burning, tongues of flame. His left hand is held open in peace, in openness.

Rettich pulls out another drawing, and another, and another, all of them traced in faint, almost invisible lines of the most delicate, greyest ink. And all of them display a young girl of incredible perfection. Her skin is the white of the page, her hair almost floating around her as she leans forward, her right hand outstretched. In her open palm, there is a heart.

A chill runs through Rettich. For he recognises the girl. Odile. The Girl to whom Master Achim had given the Devil's shilling. The Wanderer's daughter.

Another painting. Just one or two more and then he must stop. What if one of the Masters passes by, and seeing candlelight from the windows, comes to investigate?

The next parchment he pulls out is larger. A rose window. Painted in full colour. In the outer windows, petals and leaves and fronds of golden red and green and a sky of deepest, mountain gentian blue. Then a corolla of amber, shot through with rays of deepest gold, fading to the yellow of lemons, bright in sun. And in the centre, a circle of pure, bright, white light.

† † †

"Where are we going?"
"To the pass, Master. It's not far."
"Why are you taking me to the pass?"
"I want to show you something."

Grete, incorrigible, trots along behind them in her clogs, deaf to any commands for her to go home. Late afternoon sunlight chequers the dirt path with shadows. Martins flutter above the swaying treetops. Above and ahead, the wood gives way to open grazing land.

They ride along in silence a while.

"Rettich," says Achim tentatively, "do you have any experience with girls?"

Rettich answers quickly, "No."

Grete laughs, then says, "*I* am a girl."

"It's true, Grete, you are a girl. Let me ask you instead. If someone were courting you, and he brought you a present, what would you like it to be?"

Rettich blushes. "Master, please, Grete is still young and under—"

Grete interrupts her brother, "But I already have an admirer. Hold your tongue, brother."

"You? An admirer?"

"And what if it's true?" says Grete, and turns to Achim. "Something pretty is of no use to me. Ribbons, dried flowers fa la la."

"Something useful, then?" ventures Achim.

"Useful? Will you give a girl a hammer?"

"I see what you mean, Grete. Well then, advise me, poor lost man."

"Something sweet in my mouth, Master. Sugar. Candied fruit. Honey cake."

"Is that the way to your heart, Grete?"

"It may open the door a crack or two. You will need more to have it open wide."

"And are all girls the same?"

"Why do you ask?"

"Because it's not you I'm courting, Grete Schäfferin."

"More's the pity, then I'd have two admirers."

"And so I ask again. Candied fruit, sugar and spice. Will that always find a happy welcome in the female heart?"

"I reckon so. And who is your Belovèd, Master, may I ask?"

Achim blushes, smiles. "I cannot say. She is like an Angel, a Ghost. I have only seen her once. And I am searching for her, to see her again, here, there and everywhere . . . but I cannot find her."

They continue on a while. Rettich looks censoriously at his youngest sister. She makes a face back at him. He wonders who her admirer can be, and prays that it is not Manfred the merchant, who came to their village to haggle prices for her sisters' hair.

And then Rettich turns to watch his Master, who rides by his side, slightly ahead of him. Still thinking of the Wanderer's daughter?

"We're here."

Rettich jumps from his donkey, feels his sore backside. Despite Grete's protests, he puts her astride the poor beast's back. "You wait outside, you witch," he says.

A knoll rises above the pass, with a cross planted in its summit, placed there by the parson when the Bishop passed this way across his lands. Beneath the cross, at the top of the pass, a small chapel. Stumpy, tiny, in drab dun stone. It looks like a chicken squatting to lay an egg.

"You wanted to show me this?"

"Wait, my Lord. Come inside."

Achim shrugs and dismounts as Rettich pushes the chapel door. They pass inside.

Dark, dank. An altar and a rough, naïve and charmless Virgin upon the wall above. Two bunks for passing travellers. A pitcher of water.

"Turn, my Lord," says Rettich.

Achim turns. In the western wall, a window of yellow glass, a bright ochre eye in the dowdy stone.

"Master, I admitted to you earlier that I took a secret look at your drawings."

"Yes?"

"I saw the Rose. The Rose Window."

"You did?"

"Master, it is the most beautiful thing I have ever, ever seen."

"Rettich . . . "

" . . . and I saw the yellows you used, dark golden. But I have never seen a glass that colour on your desk. So I thought of here, my Lord."

"You did well, Rettich."

"At sunset—"

Achim interrupts him, "Yes, Rettich, I can see. In a minute or two, it's coming."

"We are well come on the hour, Master."

"We are indeed. Rettich, you are a marvel."

Achim sits down on the damp pew, holds his head in his hands a second. "Rettich, do you know who made this glass?"

"I do not, my Lord. But I am sure we can find him."

Achim sighs again. "So many pieces to find, to source, to fit together. The work that never ends."

"Master?" asks Rettich, but no answer is forthcoming. Master Achim is silent because the sun is now suddenly shining directly into the chapel.

The window is alive with splendour. The ochre glass captures the setting rays, burnishing them with warm gold, the essence of Sunlight.

The Whores of Rome
(anno 1231. Manfred Gerber II)

He owes his Fortune to Abbess Hedwig and to the Whores of Rome. If the Abbess hadn't been an ugly bald bitch, and if the horny Romans had less cream in their churns, then he'd still be at the docks lugging sacks and making deals for ha'penny profits.

Here's how it happened: a ride on the wild horse of Fate.

Bertle and Manfred leave the Hayseed mercenaries by the outskirts of Pfalzburg on the Nanzig road; there's a good Inn in Pfalzburg, and the Swiss cretins aren't short of money. Unlike their captors, who—as yet unpaid by Holy Mother Church—spur their hungry horses and head back into the gathering dusk.

The road is mainly clear of snow, and they make good use of the remaining daylight, slowing down to a trot as frosty night draws on. As they ride into Ergisheim, the near-full moon is as bright as a winter sun, its pale light gathered and magnified by the snowbound landscape.

On the bridge over the Ehle, they can't believe their luck. Beneath them, old Günther's barge is gliding past on the moonlit river. They call out loudly to the deaf old man so that even he can hear them.

Günther and his boys are glad of the unexpected company. Bertle and Manfred lead their steeds onto the gently rocking barge, then Günther pushes out with his pole and the vessel slides out onto the swirling dark water.

Manfred and Bertle are still excited by the day's events; von

Fegersheim's chivalrous act of murder, the juddering near-headless body, the heady perfume of sex in the holy brothel, the sisters' panic, the whiff of heresy. They tell their story, hardly pausing for breath, embellishing, improvising, exaggerating, lying.

Vague in moonlight, the bone-coloured hills sink gently down towards the Rhine. Manfred and Bertle's story finishes only as the gatehouse of Hagenburg rises above the river, etched against the Milky Way. But they do not stop here; their silent barge slides past the City's river gate, taking the moat that bypasses the walls of Finckweiler, the building site of the Dominican monastery. Bertle and Manfred have no wish to go home to the dullard Merchant Quarter, to their parents and families. In the City, all will be quiet and dark since the ringing of the Angelus bell. One lantern burning in the Cathedral Square, some candles in the windows of disreputable taverns, but everywhere else . . . silence and darkness until dawn.

At the Rhine Harbour it will be a different story. There the *zum thrunkenen Cahne* never closes.

The barge ferries through the lacework of streams, tributaries and marshes formed by the Ehle's widespread fingers as she joins her father, the Rhine. The walls of the City recede, on the banks of small islets fishermen's coracles are gathered by stinking shacks, smoke lazes from their crooked chimneys.

Ahead, a string of swaying lanterns . . . the quay of the Docks. Barges and boats nestle together, tethered to the quay. The faint sound of a woman singing, a flute and drum. Manfred throws his arm round Günther's shoulders. "Let me buy you and your boys a drink."

A wall of warm air hits them as they cross the pub threshold. Fug of sweat, alcohol, smoke from the fire. It's quite full tonight, even here in the Merchants' Snug. In the Boatmen's Ale Room, it must be rammed to the rafters; sounds of music and clumsy, heavy-footed dancing, drunken shouts.

Manfred sinks exhausted into a cushioned chair, orders some stew, wine and aquavit for him, Bertle, Günther. A demi-john of fine *branntwein* has newly come in from Ihringen; the taste of pears, apples and heavenly fire.

Two jugs of wine and three schnapps later and Manfred's in the centre of the room dancing with the Abbess' silky golden wig on his head. Bertle's laughing like a monkey, and Günther's passed out in his chair. As he dances and plays the fool, Manfred catches sight of a small, tanned, fine-coated merchant having a word in Bertle's ear, but doesn't take much notice, as the room is spinning in bright, moronic contentment.

Manfred falls back to the table, exhausted, takes a draft of wine, and sees the sun-wrinkled Southerner peering over at him and asking in Latin, "How much do you want for the wig?"

"Ten marks," says Manfred, without a pause.

The Raisin smiles, shrugs. "Be serious."

"For you, five, because I . . . happy."

Raisin, hearing Manfred's difficulties with Latin, switches to something like *kölsch* German; "Please, I am no fooling, please to say real price." In a fight, it's not clear who would lose; Manfred's dog Latin, or Raisin's mongrel German.

"You say price."

"No, you."

"No less than three marks. The wig was my mother's, it reminds me of her."

Raisin stares, silently. Bertle leans into Manfred's ear, whispers urgently; "*Roman wool merchant, runs Papal commissions. Don't fuck this, arsehole.*"

But Manfred's enjoying himself. "What do you want it for? Your curly brown hair is lovely."

No smile. "It's not for me."

"How many do you want?"

"How many can you get me?"

Pause. The spinning room stops spinning. Manfred sobers.

A sudden, lurching realisation that there could be some real trade here. He erases the schnapps-sodden smirk from his stupid face. "My apologies, sir. We are celebrating a successful day's trading. I can sell you this one now. When would you need the others by?"

"I coming this way still once again in the Immelsfar Fairs."

"By summer I can get you five more."

Bertle looks at Manfred, wide-eyed: *What? Where will you get five blonde wigs?*

But Raisin is delighted. "This is good! Good! Now you say your price."

"For six? Twelve marks."

Pause again. Just for one tiny instant, Raisin's eyes flicker away towards the ceiling, thinking. "It too much."

But Manfred saw it. He *calculated*. It means the price is close! Fuck the Virgin! It's close!

"Say your price."

† † †

They settle on two marks, two shillings upfront for the wig on Manfred's insolent head, and then one and six each for the other five wigs, to be delivered at the Himmelfahrt fair. Manfred keeps a straight, serious face as they shake hands, and then slips outside to the wharf to let out a scream of utter joy.

In the light of the stars and the dim, swaying lanterns he looks down at the silver coins in his palm, clutches them to his breast and screams again. Now he cannot wait until dawn.

Raisin now also leaves the tavern, passing by to his rented chambers in the Cloth Exchange. Manfred hides his childish joy, assays a serious, grown-up face, and tries his best Latin. "May I ask, who for the wigs?"

Raisin shrugs. "Whores." Manfred nods matter-of-factly. "Really?"

"In Rome this days, the blondes can charge double." Raisin pats Manfred on the back and whistles his way down the dock.

As soon as there's a trace of light in the sky, Manfred gathers his grumpy gelding from the stables and walks the raised road through the marshes to the Rheintor city gate, and enters just as it's being winched open.

At home in the Merchant Quarter, he finds his Father already awake at his account books. He puts the two marks' worth of coin down on the table and announces that, with Father's permission, he will sell his horse to cousin Lambert for one mark and sixpence.

His Father stands, and there are tears in his eyes. He embraces his son, holding him tightly. Manfred also bursts into tears of joy. Finally the foolish son has earned his father's respect. "My boy," he says. "My boy." With Manfred's three marks, they can now afford to buy old Gregor's boat. And now the Gerbers will have three trading boats on the Rhine. It's true that that rich bastard Wolfram has twelve, and takes most of the trade. But now they're in contention. In Competition. And they can near double their take.

† † †

"Madam, would you consider shaving your head and selling me your hair?"

"What the Good Lord for, young man?"

"Why, to make a wig from it."

"Who for?"

"For a Roman whore."

The Schlettstadt seamstress gives him a good sharp slap. Ow! No use any further patter about imagining her hair fondled by a Cardinal in a bed of purple silk by the shores of the Roman sea.

Manfred runs away, hides in an alleyway, rubs his stinging

cheek, and rethinks his sales pitch. He comes up with some nonsense about the sickly but saintly Abbess of Bacharach whose hair was burned off in a fire, and a noblewoman of Brabant whose bald pate has lost her the love of her cruel husband and . . . no matter, he'll make it up as he goes along.

He wanders the busy streets of Hagenburg on market day, eagle-eyed for blonde ladies. Where are they when you need them?

His second attempt is an improvement, but still doesn't count as a sale. A farmer's wife, selling beetroot, would be more than happy to help the poor loveless Lady of Brabant and shave her head for five shillings, but then makes the mistake of telling her husband about it. He comes after Manfred with a shovel.

It's not going well. They've put the downpayment on Old Gregor's boat, but he wants three more marks by the Nativity of Our Lady at the latest. In Manfred's plan, these three marks are coming from the wigs, so that all their other profits can go to recaulk their three-boat fleet next winter.

He wanders forlornly into the Cathedral Square, and there, in early spring sunshine, like a Cross of Gold hanging from the scaffolding of the Nave, shines the tousled flaxen head of Apprentice Stone-Cutter Rettich Schäffer.

A Basket of Honey
(anno 1231. Odile II)

He stands in our doorway, the Unexpected Guest. We had heard the warning bell, and thought nothing of it. We had heard the voices in the lane outside, and thought: *a passing beggar who has wandered here in the hope of alms, an unwelcome stranger, who will be shown his way back to the Pilgrims' Road.* For not many come our way, to our hidden hamlet in the banks of reeds and flax.

But the Guest had come for Me. He looks at me and says my name. "Odile. Odile. I have searched for you. Everywhere."

He places a basket in my hands. "Do you remember me?"

"I do, My Lord."

I fold back the cloth that covers the basket. Honey cake and honeycomb, a posy of meadow-flowers. "For me, My Lord?"

"For you, Odile."

Footsteps behind me, and my Father's shadow. I do not dare look in my Father's eyes.

"Young man," he says. "If I send you away now, will you be back one day?"

"Yes I will, Sir. I will be back."

"Then come in now. This must be settled, for good or ill."

† † †

I was born into this earthly form somewhere on the Lower Rhine, and two years later my sister Elise. And then, with the coming of my stillborn brother, the dark years of wandering began.

My Mother died for loss of blood. For us, so the Teachings say, this is no cause for Mourning. My Mother's and my Brother's souls shot like arrows into the wheel of the world, to be reborn again in Another Flesh.

Yet the midwife who pulled the stillborn boy and tried to save my dying mama—she was not one of ours. And she called the priests and the local lords, and we had to flee that place, leaving our dead behind.

We wandered South along the Rhine, and joined a group of travelling players, moving from town to town, sleeping in barns, in corners, in shacks, scavenging scraps of food like mice. In those days, the whisper went along the Rhine, if you are a Friend, make a mark on the door of your house. A white mark on the corner of your lintel, hang a white lantern above the door. It should mean, the Light is Here. In our house, is Light.

We are weavers, and where we could, we wove. But misfortune followed our steps, and we had always to hide from the Whore of Rome. We travelled the Rhine's long river road, up and down, from Friend to Friend, from white lantern to white lintel mark on hovel doors. Until one day, in Hagenburg, this young Lord, who pressed into my hand a ring, heavy with burnished amberstone.

A ring worth a fortune that saved our lives. That bought us this loom, that bought us this shack in this hidden hamlet by Honau on the Rhine's eastern shore. Rising from the river's reeds and from the fields of hemp and flax, twenty wooden shacks, barns, chickens and cows. The apple and plum trees are now losing their leaves as autumn sweeps her cold, golden hand across the world.

And above the twenty silent doors, white lanterns sway in Satan's wind.

††††

"My name is Achim von Esinbach, I am the Dombaumeister of the Cathedral in Hagenburg. And I have come to ask you for your daughter's hand."

In my hand he wants to have and hold, a slice of honey cake. We do not ever eat such food. We eat lentils, dried beans, hard cheese, river fish. No meat. No sweets. No temptation of the flesh.

And yet I bite, and its sweetness melts on my wicked tongue. And I close my eyes.

My Father speaks. "I would ask you why you want her hand. But I think we all know wherefore."

"No," says the young Lord. "I have seen beautiful girls. But none like Odile. And none with a father such as you, Sir. I have seen you, seen you both, in my visions."

"Visions?"

"I have a sickness, Sir, and I suffer visions."

"And what are we in your visions?"

"You wait for me, in light. And you speak, but I cannot understand what you are saying. I have many visions. And from these visions I have designed my Cathedral. And God Willing, we will build the most beautiful church the world has seen."

There is silence for moments; only the sounds of Elise, who is knelt studiously over her bowl, scutching flax.

My father speaks. "Beautiful or otherwise, it is all the same to God. The Lord can just as well be worshipped standing on a dungheap. Your church is vanity."

The young Lord swallows. "It is for the Glory of God."

"*God dwelleth not in temples made with hands. The Godhead is not like unto gold or silver, or stone, graven by art and device of man.*"

"*God made the world and all the things therein.* It is for us to learn to use them, for his glory."

"God makes shit? Pus? Snakes?"

"He does."

"And when your whore-priest waves his hands, bread becomes Christ, and you eat him? And in your gut, Christ turns into shit? And you squeeze Him out into a latrine?"

My father stands. Now Achim stands too, lost. The cramped shack is now crawling with shadow. Achim whispers, pale; "You are not believers . . . ?"

Father grasps Achim's arm. "We are the true believers. There is no salvation from the Church of Rome. Only in Light. Your church is built with Gold sweated by the bastard Bishop from the serfs. Your temple is not for God, *it is the Devil's church!* So leave, now. Our daughter is not for you."

"No. Let her come to me. She will want for nothing."

"Here she has all that she needs."

"You deny her the hand of a Lord?"

"I deny her the hand of a corrupt, lost soul."

Achim gasps, rushes. He stumbles on the raised threshold. For a moment his crushed, tearful silhouette hovers in the doorway, and then is gone.

† † †

The mists drift and the hemp sways, and this world is the Devil's world. The flax shivers and the river flows, and this world is an illusion, a husk, a box of tricks.

I walk outside, and the Guest is gone, the only Guest I have ever had.

I am a sinful vessel, a puppet of vain and mortal flesh.

What right have I to Love?

ANNO
1232

THE BLACK CAT
(ANNO 1232. EUGENIUS VON ZABERN III)

T he world needs clerks and lawyers in the same way as it
needs leprosy, plagues, earthquakes. Without them, life
would be a colourless stroll towards death. But here
they are, proliferating and multiplying over the face of our
earth, and taking ever more prominent positions in the chambers of power. In the olden days, virtuous rulers would surround their thrones with the flower of chivalry, but today the
leaders of our world are ringed by advisers, counsellors, clerks
and Jews.

I should know. I am one of this new cursèd class of quill-
scratching, shadow-skulking *literati*, and I am well aware of the
odium that my "petty penny-pinching" causes in the wider
world. Imagine my horror at finding last year's Cathedral
Accounts containing entries such as "plantation of new forest"
(can one credit the insolence!) and "glass colouration experi-
ments conducted in the Vale of Winzbach, including cost of
travel and accommodation for two" . . . It goes without saying
that I have deducted the cost of these indulgent follies from
next year's construction budget, with a stern warning
addressed to Master Achim that he should, forthwith, start living in the same world in which the rest of humanity is sadly
constrained to live; that is: a world with limits.

But the volume of clerkish paperwork that my Treasury
compiles and creates is as nothing when compared with the
never-ending case of the Dagsburg Inheritance.

In the Vogesen hills lies the County of Dagsburg and it is

the source of all the conflict and contention in our area. The various Counts and Countesses of the small yet nevertheless richly-endowed enclave have, in the sinful panic of their deathbeds, bequeathed the riches of their inheritance to a bewildering panoply of beneficiaries; to the Bishoprics of Hagenburg, Metz and Lüttich, and to Abbeys and Hospitals in the property of the knights of Zähringen and Habsburg. I am told that the various deeds and bequests, collected together, would fill the voluminous shelves of our Chapterhouse scriptorium.

The last of the line of Dagsburg, the childless Countess Gertrud, obdurately and wickedly refuses to die. In bitter, adamant spite of the fact that her death would benefit the gathered realms of Alsace, Lorraine and Aargau, she cleaves to her withered, bilious body and never leaves her castle eyrie to any social gathering where she could conveniently be poisoned. A solitudinous eccentric, she receives no visitors, and refuses to sign any further deeds that might clarify the question of the definitive identity of her County's legal successor.

In view of her incompliance, the paperwork has been sent to no lesser a court than the Curia in Rome. It has been there now for seven years, with all final deliberations suspended until the harridan's much desired demise.

And so, for seven long years, delegations, coin, jewels and gifts have been sent in endless caravans to the Cardinals, from Metz, from Hagenburg, from Lüttich and the castles of the Habsburgs and Zähringen, all to help their Graces in their understanding of the legal niceties of the case. I have personally authorised hundreds of marks to migrate in the direction of their avaricious purses; a haemorrhage of wealth that I shall most bitterly regret if they do not find in Hagenburg's favour.

The raid on the heretical Abbey of Mohrmünster has to be seen in the context of this ongoing legal bickering. It may be seen as an aggressive act against the Bishop of Metz, but this is not how it will be viewed in Rome, if we have gambled well. That Hagenburg should have discovered heresy and fornication on Metz land before Metz himself, and delivered the heretics over to the Dominicans (the Pope's current favourites) for trial, bespeaks well our Christian vigilance. And so we have, to use jousting terminology, delivered a nice, sharp *atteint* to the Metzian cause, and dented the shield of Lorraine.

One can only be certain that the Bishop of Metz will somehow try and turn about and take a tilt at the arms of Hagenburg. Our colours are winning now, but we must be wary of a revenge attack. And if not in the wide marches of Alsace and Lorraine, then in the dusty shelves of ledgers and the murky workings of Rome.

Yet, Metz may not be the most fearful opponent in the tournament. There is, as is traditional in the silly romances beloved of literate youth, an Unknown Knight, carapaced in black, who enters his anonymous pledge at the closing of the lists.

That Pope Gregory hates the Emperor Friedrich is common knowledge. Of necessity, Our Holy Father has rescinded the ginger-haired Emperor's excommunication; after all, he has triumphantly returned Jerusalem to Christian hands. This public, forced rescission must have done nothing but increased the virulence of Our Holy Father's hate.

And it seems it is true that King Heinrich is plotting the overthrow of his own father, the Emperor. Would Heinrich dare such a thing, without the nod and say-so of the Pope? Certainly not.

And if the likes of the Count of Schonach are lining up behind King Heinrich, what exactly has persuaded them to back the son, and abandon the father?

Maybe, over the years, I have become overly obsessed with the Dagsburg case, but I do tend to connect almost everything that occurs within our lands with the files and ledgers gathering dust in Rome. The tentative manoeuvrings of the Count of

Schonach fall into this category. He is related, via his wife, to the Habsburgs of the Aargau; a clan that is energetically expanding its territories through strategic marriages to other local noble families, and who have a strong claim in the Dagsburg inheritance case.

Could it just be possible that one Papal reward for the usurpation of Friedrich is a favourable outcome for the Habsburgs in the Dagsburg case?

Is Albert of Habsburg the Unnamed Knight at the bottom of the lists, the mysterious stranger who will snatch from us the laurels of victory?

But my metaphor is all awry. After all, I am a mathematician, and no Master of Rhetoric. For my jousting metaphor to work the field would have to be open, the Players known, and the Prize named, and clearly in reach.

But in this game, the players are whisperers slinking through the maze of the courts of Rome. They are clerks and lawyers, they are bankers, cardinals, princes and kings. And I, in my small way, sending my promissory notes from Hagenburg to the mouth of the Tiber, my gold, wine and wool, am a player in this shadowy but fatal tournament.

Mohrmünster was a Hagenburg victory. But to win the prize, we still have a long way to go.

† † †

The poison of Heresy, we know not whence, has spread itself through the German Lands and has bred and multiplied so that now there is hardly a town or village that can be found which is free thereof. Therefore we ask our Bishops, in the name of Jesus Christ, to work zealously so that this disgusting weed be annihilated and removed from the field of the Lord, so that it be entirely rooted out, and shall never arise again.

In the Bishop's Palace, mere hours after the arrival of the Pope's letter, His Grace orders me to convene an emergency meeting of the Chapter elders. Such is his alarm, he also invites the Town Mayor to attend. Himself, he thunders through the Vogesentor with the bare minimum of retainers and armoured escort, galloping in from his Haldenheim stronghold.

I am at the Palace gate, awaiting him. I help beat the dust from his cloak. I have warned the domestics, and there is warm food and wine awaiting His Grace as he storms inside with his hounds.

"We must act immediately," he fumes as he tears a piece of bread in two, maybe wishing it was someone's neck. "Lamps! Candles! We need light here! At the reading table!"

Servants rush to fulfil his order as the Bishop limps to his favourite chair, and sinks back into it, stiffly. I note his apparent ill health, but do not comment on it. From his riding satchel, he pulls out the Papal encyclical. "Roll it out on the reading table for all to see."

It is a long, long letter, and needs four paperweights to secure it. As I read by lamplight, outside the Angelus bell sounds, and the overcast, lukewarm spring day fades into night. The sounds of the street recede as the citizens of Hagenburg head for home, firmly closing window and door against a gathering, humid, rain-bearing wind.

The newly-admitted novice is met by a Toad, sometimes in its natural size, sometimes the size of a Duck or Goose, usually the size of an Oven. The novice kisses the Toad, letting its tongue lick around in the inside spittle of his mouth.

If the novice proceeds in the sect, then he is blessed enough to meet the Pale Man with coal-black eyes and desiccated and withered flesh, who kisses the young initiate, chilling him to the bone. Once kissed by the Pale Man, he forgets everything he has learned about the Catholic Faith.

Then the sect sit down to eat in their terrible Meeting Place. At the end of their cursed feast, a Black Cat appears, the size of a Dog, with its tail raised into the air. The Cat makes its rounds of the congregation, who take turns to kiss its foul anus. Then they sing songs of praise to the Black Cat, and chant a terrible catechism in adulation of their ultimate master, Lucifer.

Then the candles are snuffed out, and in the darkness, they all fall upon each other in lust. No care is given as to the sex or the identity of the partners, man ravishes man, sister copulates with brother, and all manner of lewd and disgusting acts are committed.

The Holy Father follows his detailed description of the heretics' rites with a series of threats. Should any of the Bishops fail in their duties, they will be replaced. Any Prince who fails to root out heresy may lawfully be deposed by his subjects. All worldly authorities, mayors, Town Councils or magistrates, are to fall under the same baleful ban. Destroy heresy in your dominions, or yourself be destroyed.

Heavy rain is now battering the streets outside. I look up from the letter to the dining table where His Grace is dolefully eating his soup. The room is now full of light, and I can see more clearly the pallor of his skin, his swollen neck, reddish eyes.

"Your Grace looks unwell," I venture.

He waves his hand dismissively, closing the subject. "The others will be here shortly. Use the time we have to think."

His Grace is, as usual, right. I take my habitual seat by the empty fireplace, and close my eyes. The Pope does not suddenly come up with ideas like this overnight. His Holiness does not wake of a morning and toss fulminating fires at Germany on a whim. A letter like this has been some days in the writing, and many weeks in the preparation. Someone has been whispering in the ears of the Holy Father, lisping tales of heresy, of sin rife as hayseed in the German Lands, of the Black Cat's anus, of the Oven-Sized Toad, the Pale Man cold as Ice.

A knocking at the door. My Chapter colleagues have arrived, dragged at my orders from their Vespers prayers. The Bishop's hounds, maybe disturbed by the storm, start to bay and howl.

† † †

Candles glint in every corner of the room. I, Varenus the Vitztum, His Grace, the Dean, Mayor Müllenheim, the Chapter Chancellor, two Archdeacons, have now all read the letter, and we now sit in silence and brood in candlelight.

Bishop Berthold folds his hands, and turns to his old friend Varenus, his adviser in worldly affairs, and, in my view, an ineffectual fool. "Varenus, what is the political background to this extraordinary encyclical? Illuminate us. What was the last political despatch we received from Rome?"

Varenus clears his throat. "The Holy Father told us, *in confidence and orally via his envoy and not in writing*, that he was looking favourably on Heinrich to depose his father Friedrich."

A slight exhalation of breath in the room, the sound of surprise, the loudest coming from the Mayor, who is not usually party to the internal politics of the Church.

"Meaning?" asks the Bishop.

I clear my throat, loudly, and offer a theory before Varenus can offer his: "If King Heinrich is seen vigorously to deracinate and destroy heresy in our lands, if he is seen as a crusader like once de Montfort in the Land of Oc, then his position is immediately more powerful. He has polished his temporal crown with the radiance of the Faithful Son of the Church. And he can point at his father Friedrich and blame him for allowing heresy to blossom in their ancestral lands whilst he, the Emperor, is more concerned with his temporal problems with the Lombard cities."

The Bishop nods. *I am gratified to see it.* Varenus visibly winces.

His Grace folds his hands. "Eugenius' analysis is probably sound, but it does not change our course of action. We must act, and act immediately. We must do His Holiness' bidding. The positive impression we gave at Mohrmünster must be continued. We must be vigorous against the heretics, and be seen to be so."

He turns to Stettmeister Müllenheim. "Mayor? Are there heretics here in Hagenburg?"

Müllenheim lowers his eyes. "I have heard it said, Your Grace."

"You have heard it said?"

"That there are those who do not attend mass, do not eat meat, that there are those with strange ideas."

"Do we know who they are?"

"There are names."

"And in the villages?"

I, alas, from my annual tours of the Bishop's lands, am the village expert in this company. All turn in my direction. "Yes, Your Grace, I have seen traces of heresy in some villages."

But it is not the Black Cat's anus and the Pale Man that I have seen and heard of in the damp, sad villages of the forests. I do not believe that the peasants meet, worship Satan, and then blow out the candles and fall upon each other in lust. I do not believe that they worship a Toad that comes and kisses them upon the mouth. It is something else. They believe in the things they have always believed in: in wood spirits and fairies, in water sprites and in elves. And there are things they do not believe in. They do not believe in their corrupt and adulterous village priest when he changes the wine into the Blood of Christ. They do not believe that the payment of taxes to the Bishop is for the good of their immortal soul. And some do not believe that ten shillings will buy them one hundred fewer years in Purgatory.

This is the heresy I have seen in the villages. The superstitious and the ignorant, led by poor, verminous priests installed on the cheap by the local lords. The villagers fart at communion and place their trust in kobolds and wood spirits, not in the Mother Church. In truth, it should be our task to save their immortal souls, to cleanse their sins and assuage their suffering. But the only Canon that comes from the Bishop's Church to visit them is I the Treasurer, come to take away their taxes and the hard-won tithes of sheep, grain and wax. This is the sad truth of the situation.

The Dean now stands, dramatically, to command attention. God save us, I was waiting for that old windbag to speak. "I am shocked, Mayor, Treasurer," he says, "that you both state, in cold blood, the existence of heretics in our diocese! As if it were a natural state of affairs. As if it were to be expected."

"If you ever left the Chapter House and cloister, you might see many things that surprise you, Dean."

"Yes, Treasurer? Like what?"

"Well there are these creatures called *women*, for example."

The Dean shudders visibly. Did he emerge like this from his mother's womb? Or did we, the Church, make him like this? Now he blinks at me like a lizard who finds himself in sudden daylight when his rock is rolled away.

"Is it the Bulgarian Heresy? Cathars?"

"I have heard rumours of Cathars amongst the weavers," says the Mayor.

"God forgive us!" The Dean groans, crosses himself, closes his eyes in horror.

The Mayor, a garrulous but capable man, now having been given the word, continues: "In his letter, the Holy Father is clear. It is the Church's responsibility to locate and identify heretics through ecclesiastical hearings. Those who are found guilty will be handed over to us, the secular authorities, for punishment. The accepted punishment is death at the stake. I am ready to set aside an area within our city where the guilty will be immolated without risk to other persons or property. I can also offer certain buildings in our possession as holding cells for the accused and the guilty. All of this will cost money of course. Did Our Holy Father maybe send a promissory note attached to his letter?"

"He did not," says the Bishop, with a grim smile. He is happier now that we are discussing concrete practicalities. The nebulous shadows of politics frustrate him, the refinements of theology confuse him. He is a true Warrior of the Church, believing unquestioningly in her Right and in her destiny to conquer.

"It means we must pay for it ourselves," says the Mayor, and turns pointedly in my direction.

Financial matters. My turn to speak: "We should deduct the costs of the imprisonment and immolation from the distrained goods of those found guilty."

"Ah!" Mayor Müllenheim feigns surprise. "The accused will pay for their own execution?"

"Why should Good Christians pay for the execution of heretics?"

"And if they are well-to-do heretics, and after costs of prison bread-and-water and firewood for the pyre are deducted, there is still a lot left, what should happen to the remainder of their property?"

"It falls to the Church."

"You sit there and say that without even the tiniest blemish of shame on your face?"

"I do."

"The Town wants half. Or I will withdraw my previous offer of help."

"If you fail to help," says the Bishop, who, it seems has enjoyed this exchange, "then, under the Pope's edict, I may replace you with someone who will."

"I am no heretic, Your Grace, I took communion from your very hands last Easter."

"I remember the occasion. The Town will take half and we will deduct prison and execution costs from that half. From our half we will deduct the costs of the Inquisitors. Is it fair?"

"It is fair."

My Lord has spoken and I can say nothing. I would have bargained harder, of course. God forgive me, but there could be good revenue in this heresy hunt.

† † †

So, this was the beginning. Elders and potentates in candlelight, making arrangements, discussing finances and principles.

The next morning we appointed Inquisitors, hired militia, prepared prisons, found suppliers of firewood, chains, shackles, and bargained prices with them. We collected the names whispered from neighbour to neighbour, the names of the Suspects.

The day after, we made the first arrests.

A Profitable Business
(ANNO 1232. MANFRED GERBER III)

They disembark at Honau, seventeen mounted men. Manfred's new horse is a flea-ridden nag hired from the ostlers at the Fish Market; he's brushed her up as best he could, covered her in a fine blanket, but she still looks ready for the knacker's blade. His sorrel gelding is long gone, sold for the down-payment on Gregor's boat, and the nag is all he could afford.

Treasure-Fucker has got together the same company that he used for Mohrmünster Abbey. At Honau, the Inn-Keeper brings them all a cup of cool watered wine and they drink in the saddle whilst von Zabern hammer-haggles the price of two hired carts. Fuck, is the Pope going to go hungry if a Honau carter makes an extra ha'penny on a half-day hire?

They ride inland and downriver, into the reedbeds. They're heading for a weavers' village where it's said every man, woman and child is a heretic.

The wind flays the reeds and grasses, in the sky, clouds race, unravel, reform. As they come closer, they let the carts trundle and fall behind. They canter down the raised, soft earth road. Up ahead, the weavers' hamlet. Getting closer, they slow down again, quietening the horses' hooves. Von Zabern stands in his stirrups, looks around—he wants them to fan out and surround the village, but the ground is riddled with streams and marshes. Little raised pathways run through the swamps, wide enough for one man to run along, but never a horse. They look like escape routes, spreading through the marsh.

The heretics are ready for them. The village bell rings a warning, and before they know it, some younger men and girls are already scattering like rabbits along the raised marsh-pathways, heading for boats and coracles hidden in the rushes. Bertle, on his young stallion, leaps into the reed beds and gives chase, followed by two of the noblemen. Manfred's nag is no use for marsh riding, so he stays with the main corps as they charge into the village proper.

The hairs raise up on the back of his neck. About thirty of the villagers have chosen not to run . . . men, women, old folk, children. They're just waiting, unarmed. Most of them are dressed in white, some in pale blue. A bonfire burns in the village clearing, and they stand around it, holding hands and praying.

In the centre, burning and smoking, a wooden carving of the Virgin.

Von Fegersheim jumps down from his stallion, tries to grab at the statue, save the Holy Mother from the flames. Around the fire, the heretics start shouting: "It's just wood! It's just a piece of wood! It means nothing!"

Von Zabern clutches his brow, shocked into silence, then comes back to himself. "Shackle them!"

The troop dismounts, pulling chains from saddle bags. Von Fegersheim grasps at the burning statue with his mail-gloved hand, but she's too hot to take hold of, her painted, upheld face is bubbling, smoking. The villagers shout, spin, shriek, turn, screech. "Why worship bits of wood? Why offer prayers to stones? Is your God a painted carving?"

One of the noble boys beats a screaming old woman across the face and her cheek splits open. Von Fegersheim yells as he grabs the burning madonna from the fire and sears his hand. The weavers are shouting and screaming at us like lunatics, and then suddenly some of them go silent, serene, and stare upwards into the sun, into the light, almost without blinking.

Von Fegersheim rolls the Virgin in the damp grass, but she's already half burned-away, blackened, deformed. The heretics keep screaming, but don't resist. The troop chain them up, throw the eldest and youngest on the carts, try their best to beat them into silence.

Manfred, after shackling a few of the loons, stumbles off to look in their houses, his sword ready against ambush. But there's no-one left inside—all the homes are empty, and they don't have much to steal. They live like monks, or how monks are supposed to live. At Mohrmünster, the Brothers lived like princes, but these heretics seem to starve like Jesus in the desert. Their houses are bare and cold, like the homes of snakes or lizards.

In one house he finds tools for stripping and scutching flax and four sheets of fine linen. In other houses he finds big looms with linen half-woven. Too big to carry now, but one thing's clear: these weaver folk are headed for the pyre, and nothing will save them. And where they're going, they won't need looms nor shuttles nor sheets.

† † †

The smoke from the burning village palls around them as they ride in slow cortège back towards Honau. Before leaving, they set fire to all the houses. Manfred and Bertle pulled out the looms and laid them on the wet grass, with the hope to come back for them later. They took the sheets and the tools with them.

The devils have stopped screaming, they parade in silence through the outlying barns of Honau. Scraps of ash, spirals of soot carried by the agitated wind curlicue around their sullen faces. The Honauers come and stand in doorways, stare through windows. Some spit, especially when the Treasure-Fucker is looking in their direction. Public display of the One True Faith.

Back at the Inn by the pier, and the barges are slow to be

loaded with their new human cargo. Manfred dismounts for a draught of wine, stands at the doorway, drinking it down, and sees a man running up in panic. He recognises him from the Hagenburg docks: Dagobert the Dyer.

Dagobert sees Manfred, a familiar face. "You're Manfred Gerber's boy," he says. "I am."—"Where are they taking the weavers?"—"To the pyre, no doubt."—"What, all of them?"—"All as we could find." Dagobert blanches like linen, holds his face in his hands. "Then who will weave me my god-damned cloth?"

"Ask the Treasurer there, he's sure to weave you up a few lengths, if you ask him nicely."

"This is no laughing matter, I'm ruined."

"Less ruined than they are."

Dagobert looks at him bitterly. Manfred finishes his wine, nods. "I'm sorry, my friend. How many lengths do you need?"

"Twenty-one. I downpaid for seven. I'll never see that money again."

"It's gone up in smoke."

"Stop making jokes about it."

"Listen, Herr Färber, my father and I will deliver you that cloth."

"From where?"

"We know people. My wife and her sisters are handy with a loom."

"I need twenty one! And well-woven!"

"And you will get them, mark my word—we have all the connections you need." Manfred doesn't mention the eight lengths he and Bertle have already liberated from the flames, baled over the back of Bertle's stallion. "When and where must you deliver?"

"Freiburg. Seven dark blue, seven light blue, seven yellow. Liveries for the Duke. No cheap rubbish. Supple and hard-wearing. By Pentecost."

Something crosses Manfred's mind. Blue. "You'll be needing woad, then?"

"Of course."

On their third boat, coming in soon, God Willing, sacks of woad from Picardy. "Picardian woad?"

"It's the best."

"We'll do this. I'll give you three sacks of Picardy woad for the price of one."

Dagobert's eyebrows raise. He scans the pier, the huddled forms of the weavers crowding the barges, the mounted troop now leading on their horses, the Treasurer at the end of the pier, staring into the grey flow of the waters. "Why?"

"To seal this deal. From now on, the Gerbers will supply you all the linen you need."

† † †

All the holding cells in Hagenburg are full of heretics, there's no more room. At the gates of the city they are redirected to Kronenweiler castle, another two hours' trudge distant. News not joyfully received. They skirt the town walls to the Mayenzer Tor and head out across the newly-sown fields.

This was the third day of the heretic round-up. The first two days, Manfred and his militia brothers had been deployed in the City itself. They were given a list of names before dawn, and sent out to knock on doors. Some of the names caused them no surprise; black sheep, odd eggs, the kind of person people whisper about—she's a witch, he hasn't been to church for years, he has a kobold in his cellar. Many, of course, they'd never heard of—Hagenburg is a big town, after all. Some are folk known to them, good people, shopkeepers, kind old ladies, children. But who are they to question Holy Mother Church, especially when they're being paid tenpence a day?

Some hear what they have to say, nod quietly, collect a bundle of clothes and a hunk of bread, and then hold out their hands for the shackles. Some start shouting and crying. Some jump from windows, twist their ankles, run half-naked through the streets, and they have to give chase. Of course, the Captain of the Militia has posted men at the four town gates to stop any fugitives trying to escape.

But some managed it somehow. Jumped into the Ehle and swam to the marshes. Swung ropes down from the town walls and ran through the fields. Some hid in cellars, in barrels, some hid under sacks on carts and had themselves rode out to the hills. But most of them, willingly or unwillingly, came under their guard and filled up the Mayor's holding cells.

Manfred leads his tired nag by the halter, walking alongside one of the carts carrying the weavers' women. There are two sisters; the younger is pretty and eye-catching enough, but the elder sister is amongst the most beautiful creatures he's ever seen. He keeps looking at her, in spite of himself.

The wind dies down, clouds gather and hide the sun. Kronenweiler Castle hulks above the pointed gables of its village rooves and the knotted vines of the barren brown fields. Spring came and went this year, brought forth the leaves and then retreated, shivering.

The gates of the castle open, their day's work is ending. In the courtyard, dozens of prisoners, huddling under hide tenting. A cattle trough for water, and each of them handed a small loaf of bread from the Kronenweiler baker, standing there in wool coat and apron beside his baskets of loaves. It's a windfall for his tiny village business. Blacksmiths for the shackles, soldiers for guards, bakers for the penitentiary bread, monks and lay brethren as Inquisitors, carters, bargemen, timber merchants, armourers, the ostlers at the Fish Market who hired out Manfred's useless nag. From the Church's pudgy hands, shillings and pence flood down to their legions of helpers and collaborators, and from the ashes of the pyres, the Church pulls the gold of distrained houses, farmsteads, fields.

All in all, a profitable business.

† † †

With Bertle they hire a boat and then a cart and collect the looms from the wind-fired ashes of the weavers' village. At Honau they hail and board a passing barge, straining upriver against the spring-thaw swell to reach the Hagenburg dock by sundown. Bertle and Manfred are set to the oars to help pay their passage.

Manfred Senior is still at the warehouse when Junior stumbles in, half dead from exhaustion. Father ladles out some lukewarm soup, rolls out a turnip from the embers for Son to eat. It's charred and sweetened in the fire, tastes of earth and ash, fills his belly with much-needed warmth.

As he eats, Father pushes over the ledger and a candle so Son can read up the day's transactions. Their third boat, christened the *Grete* after Manfred's new bride, came in today with a mixed load from the Lower Rhine towns; half of it freight borne for other merchants, half of it their own speculations. The woad, from Amiens, was on board. Son tells Father the deal he made in Honau.

Manfred Senior pokes the embers in the hearth, coaxes the ochre flames, nods. "Dagobert has good clients on the eastern bank. You made a good bid. Just make sure you deliver."

"I will."

"I know you will." He sits down, straddling the same bench where his son is sitting. "I only wish this wasn't a business built on the misfortunes of others."

Manfred shrugs. It's the way of the world. Father continues, "The *Grete* boys say they're burning folk all the way down the

Rhine, in every town and city. Either there were heretics every-where and we didn't know it, or the Church has lost its mind."

He takes a sip of wine, rolls its sweetness around his mouth, and swallows. His eyes close. "Nothing good will come of this."

THE LINEN CHEST
(ANNO 1232. GRETE GERBER I)

I only knew my father-in-law a small handful of Sundays. He was taken well before his rightful time.

Our first meeting was not too full of promise neither. Manfred brought me into the house perfumed and garlanded, and said, "Father, this is my bride Grete." I looked pretty as a spring flower and smiled ever so sweetly at my new Dad, but Manfred the Elder shut the door in my face and started on Manfred the Younger with such a shouting as all the street could hear.

It was my first time in the City, and so I stood out on the doorstep of the house with flowers in my hair, and looked at the to and fro of the merchant quarter which was to be my home. By now, Manfred the Younger was shouting back at his Dad, ever so respectfully, but shouting nevertheless, and a small crowd was gathering in the muck outside, making me compliments, to which I curtseyed. I was trying to keep an ear on the shouting inside, but showing an outer face that said "this is the most normal wedding day in the world." This was a challenge, but I rose to it well, and before too long the door was opened and Manfred the Elder was there, red in the face from shouting, but assaying a friendly smile as best he could and saying, "Now let's be looking at you, girl."

So, I did my prettiest curtsey and smiled, and for some reason I winked at him. Whatever I did, my Father-in-Law was suddenly embracing me and saying, "Well, my boy, I give you, she's a jewel."

The heart of the matter was: my Manfred had been meant to marry a merchant's widow but—as he told me—he'd rather go to bed with a sow. And so, as I was for the taking, he took me, and I was right happy to be took.

But his father wasn't pleased at all, not until my Manfred shouted at him that Father Manfred as a young man had done exactly the same thing, and married for Love against his own father's wishes. And didn't he always say that he never regretted it one minute? Well, Manfred the Elder didn't take so kindly to have his own song sung back at him, but in the end he couldn't tell the Kid not to act the Billy Goat. And so he gave me a hug and passed me over to Manfred the Younger, who carried me over the threshold.

Then they sent out for my boys to join the party, and Emmle came first from the Judengasse. How he'd changed! A bit of fur on his lip, pale and with a deep voice! And talking clever, like a priest!

Rettich, well, he'll never change. He ran up with the messenger boy, looking the same as ever, and on hearing that I was now Frau Gerber of the Rhineboat Gerbers, stood a while tongueless, and unable to decide between looking like a cloud about to spit lightning, or the happiest elder brother on earth. In the end it came down to Money like it normally does, and his troubles were two: one, that my husband had shaved our sisters' heads for four and sixpence each, and two, that I had no dowry to speak of and that he had planned to marry me off in four years, by which time Rettich would be a Companion and able to fill a linen chest with fine sheets and silver, to make me a proper bride.

My husband, who had a clever mind for such things, took me and Rettich to the bridal chamber and showed Rettich the empty linen chest there. I had come from Lenzenbach with nothing but a small bundle of clothes and a box of pins, carding combs and other bits and bobs. Now Manfred put my bundle in the linen chest and held a pretty speech. He said, "Apprentice Rettich, your sister's smile is, for me, worth all the rubies of India, and I am in want of nothing. But look, sir, if you want to honour your sister with a dowry, this linen chest will be yours to fill any time you wish, and we will accept your future gifts with the gratitude of a loving sister and brother."

And like this, he saved my Brother Rettich's shame that he had no money to put on me on my wedding day. And now even Rettich could smile, and Emmle could dance. Manfred the Elder sent to the tavern for a barrel of fine wine, and so, in the end, my wedding day continued in drunken happiness, as well it should.

But it wasn't long after that they started burning the heretics. My Manfred was signed to the city militia, which usually meant he spent one day in every seven pretending to patrol the streets at night, whilst really sitting on his behind in the guardhouse, drinking and gambling with the other night watchmen. But now it meant he was called on to put the heretics in irons and take them to the holding places for them to be tried. It wasn't joyful work to be sure, but it was well paid, and Manfred reckoned they were Enemies of the Church, and so someone had to deal with them, and it might as well be him.

I hadn't been long in the city, and hadn't had time to get used to it at peace before it broke out into war. They dug a ditch out by the Mayenzer Tor, and made a big pyre there, and that's where they threw the heretics to burn. Many folk went to watch but I didn't have the stomach for it, to begin with. Like a good young wife I waited at home for my husband to come back from his work, and made him as comfortable as I could, for his labour those days was a dark one.

I knew he didn't relish the work of putting souls in chains, but even so, after a while I could see he and his father were worried about something. The fools thought that I was some country dunce and couldn't understand, so they didn't tell me nothing about it. I wish they had. My Manfred learned later that I have a good head on my shoulders for solving riddles and straightening out bends, but he didn't know and trust me then, more's the pity.

So one morning, it's dawning outside and we just heard the Cathedral bell when there's a knock at the street door. And then a pounding and a shouting. My Manfred obviously knew what was coming, for he grabbed me straightaway and lifted me up in his arms. "For the Love of God," he said, "you promise me to be silent and not say a word." I nodded though my heart was leaping like a hare in a snare. Manfred nods back at me, kisses me gently and . . . puts me in the linen chest! He puts a wool stocking by the lock so it doesn't close properly, so that there's a gap so I can breathe and can get out later. Then he pulls on a shirt and goes down to the soldiers outside.

I hear the voice reading out, "Manfred Gerber the Elder and Manfred Gerber the Younger, you have been charged with the grievous sin of heresy." They quickly search the house but I can hear my Manfred say, "She went back to her village to see her sisters, I swear," and no-one found me.

The house went silent and then the street outside. And then I crawled out of the linen chest like a mouse out of its hole and sat on our bed and didn't know what I should do. I first thought of my two brothers and maybe they could help me, but I was now a grown and married lady, and I shouldn't go crying like a little girl to the men of the family, now should I?

I don't know why, but my only thought was to go out and see for myself. Who these heretics were, and who the people were that were burning them.

And so I dressed and walked out into the near-empty streets, and headed for the smoke, the ditch and the fire.

†††

At the Burning Ground, to get people in the mood, Uto the Town Crier was standing on a cart and shouting out a story.

There was a man, and he was a heretic, and he was took by the Inquisitors and they seared his arm with the hot iron until he repented of his evil beliefs. As soon as he repented, through the Love of Christ, his terrible burns stopped hurting, and he was as new and reborn. He went home to his heretic wife, who listened to his tale and then made him a nice, warm dinner and took him to bed. In bed the wife started to whisper in his ear, saying that they had fooled the Church, that now they could secretly return to their sinful ways. The man, for love of his wife, reluctantly agreed, and immediately his burns opened up again, red weals all over his arms. He started to scream. His whole body was on fire, as if Devils were pressing him down into white, searing coals. He grabbed his wife, screaming, and as he grabbed her, his hands burned her flesh like his hands were made of red-hot iron. And her flesh began to burn as well, and she began to scream too. The pain was unbearable and so they ran to the river and threw themselves in the waters, hoping that they would hiss like glowing horseshoes thrown to the blacksmith's brine. But they did not hiss and extinguish like iron, there was no relief for them in the waters, and they thrashed and screamed and howled and drowned, and their souls were torn from them by Devils and were pulled down straight to Hell, where their torment continues to this day and to the End of Time, without relent, without rest or respite. Amen.

That was the story that Uto was telling when I came to the Burning Ground. The fire in the ditch was already hot, and behind the ditch a pyre had been set a-flaming. As I arrived, the vintners of Engiskirch were there, delivering their old barrels and timbers as their contribution to the fire. Their serving boys were out in the crowd, selling leather tumblers of their last year's wine.

From the streets by the Rheintor tower where the poorer folk live, from the Brüdergass that leads to the Cathedral Square, and from across the fields beyond the walls the people were coming, beckoned by the rising grey smoke. Most were peasants dressed in black, and the fire had charred and wizened the grass and so it made me think of a murder of crows on a wheatfield after the harvest, all black, brown and burned yellow.

Priests from the town churches arrived, and some of the Lord Canons of the Cathedral. Noblemen trotted up on their horses, watching from the back of the common crowd. Children gathered on the ramparts of the town walls. Mothers shouted at them to leave, but they were not heeded.

The Rhine Gate opened and the first cartload of heretics came in. They were weavers from a village on the far bank of the river. Manfred had been in the troop that brought them to irons. And now he himself had been taken.

I looked round for someone to ask how to find him, but I was still just a girl from Lenzenbach. How did I know who was a magistrate, who was on the Council, which of the Fathers was an Inquisitor? I chose a Dominican who had a kind-seeming face, and was trying to summon the courage to approach him, when Uto started up again, shouting out the names of those who were to die.

He said they were Cathars or Satan-lovers or something, I don't rightly know, but whatever they were, they weren't Christian. They had confessed their hatred of Rome, derided Communion, denied the power of the Pope and his Bishops. They never attended church, did not eat meat, and swore that this world belonged to the Devil and not to God.

Some of them tried to say something, to shout to the crowd, to give us some final words, but you could hardly hear them, as the crowd was shouting back. Some people threw things at the heretics, dung, pottery shards, pebbles.

Then one by one they were taken by the soldiers and thrown to the pit or the pyre.

How they would scream when they went on the fire. Just think how you snatch your hand away from the flame when you mistakenly reach over a candle, think of the throbbing, piercing pain that comes from a burn when you're clumsy with the fire and burn your wrist, and then think of that pain, all over your body, and lasting for a good long long time. And all that time they are screaming as if they're already in Hell.

And you can see. You can see what the flames are doing to their flesh. See it charring, smoking, cracking, peeling, you can see the fat, juice and blood running . . .

Sometimes the heretic would manage to scrabble from the pit or leap from the pyre, his or her body a smoking red-black weal from head to foot, and run like a flaming demon from Hell. Then the guards would prod her, him, with their halberds and push them back to the flames. And the crowd would laugh.

I looked around at the faces. Some were like me, pale and sick, but most were mirthful, laughing, like this was a parade, some kind of Saint's Day spectacle, the End of Carnival.

It's when they brought the girl out that I couldn't take it anymore. She was about my age, and had the looks of an angel. She was dressed in white, in a white shift. To humiliate her, the soldier cut the shift with his dagger, so that she stood there naked before us all. The men in the crowd went quieter when they saw her like that. Probably they all wanted her then. They were thinking they'd rather take her a-bed than watch her burn.

Some older women shouted some insults at her, and the soldiers remembered what they were there to do, and started to prod her towards the fire.

In the crowd someone started screaming, and I recognised Dombaumeister Achim, my brother's Master, him with the nice brown eyes and the soft, sweet voice. But now there was something wrong with him. There was froth at his mouth, like a dog with the rage, and his face was all twisted and he was screaming and screaming, "Odile! Odile!" He seemed to be attacking the others in the crowd, trying to run at the pyre himself, but the men at the front jumped upon him and held him down, shouting out, saying, "there's a lunatic here," and "the young Lord needs help."

Now my eyes flicked back from Master Achim to the fire, and I saw what had driven him mad.

And I swear I saw that girl burn like a candle. Silent she was. Her face looking up at heaven, with her eyes now all burned away and sightless. But no scream came from her. And around her, somehow, a rosy purple flame, like the colour of the setting summer sun. And its shape, the shape of the flame, like an iris. Like a tall, slender flower, holding her silently.

Into Thy Hands
(ANNO 1232. ODILE III)

1 am sorry for many things
i am sorry i have not tasted mulled wine and meat
i am sorry i have not tasted the spiced Christmas candied
fruit that
they make into round cakes in the winter markets

i am sorry i did not take the invitation of the girls at Speyer
when they asked me to come and play
i am sorry, at Bacharach in the burning summer, i did not
jump into the cool
water, and swim

i am sorry i have not tasted love

it was offered me by gentle Master Achim
but i could not take it

i am sorry that i will not know
if just for one night
how man and woman become lovers

i am sorry that i will never bear a child

children are brought forth in sorrow into this world of lies
but—who can deny it?—they smile at a gentle touch
and gurgle with life at the shine of their mother's eyes

*

i am sorry
that i will never bring my own human child to smile

i am sorry for many things, but sorry to whom?
not to God, whom i have well served
not to my Father, whom i have well obeyed

i am sorry to that Judge who resides in Me
and weighs the balance of my life
and finds it short
and lacking

i will be, they tell me, a blaze of light
i will be, they tell me, a star in the firmament
glinting at night
sign of the Light
guide to the Truth
in the Darkness

. . .

our sister has been lost to us
she repented

she turned to the Whore and will keep her life in the world
of lies
her hair will be shorn
she will be paraded like a Saracen's slave through the markets
she will be used by the Roman abomination as an example
and she too will be sorry

and yet alive

do i envy her?

no
i shall be a blaze of light, a star of the heavens

Achim, i did love you, forgive me
i thank you for my only taste of honey cake

they are taking me now

father has already gone before me
by now his earthly frame
this shirt of flesh our souls must wear
will be made of ash and smoke

the soldier tells me
the fire is now so hot it needs no more wood
the human fat from heretic flesh has become its own fuel

we are the fuel that feeds the fire
we are as firewood, as coal, as charcoal,
the stuff of the world

shouting, braying
the crowd's faces are twisted in hatred

but some soften upon seeing me

i try a smile

he is cutting my linen shift to show me naked
could this not have been spared me?

i can feel the fire on my back, on my buttocks, on my calves already from here it is too hot

o, i am sick

i will be a point of light, i will be a star, i will be in heaven

o i am sick
o i am scared

i cannot tell Thee why, my Lord,
but i do not want to lose these clothes of flesh

not in agony like this

they are pushing me towards the fire

it is written

can i run?
it is too late

into Thy hands my Lord, receive me

† Odile 1216–1232

D ays and nights in Kronenweiler, prisoners. Former
Merchants of the City, payers of tithes and taxes,
donors to the Cathedral Fabric. Citizens. Now treated
like the Bishop's dogs, curled on the floor of the Bishop's castle kitchen, trying to keep warm under stinking sheepskins.

Father's seniority has earned them a place near the fire, but
even there, in relative warmth, Manfred can't sleep. He wanders the restless castle courtyard, full of prisoners huddled by
braziers, terse, anxious groupings, discussing their fate, asking
the same question that Manfred asks himself: Who has
branded them as heretics? *Who* has named their names?

Is it Wolfram, owner of twelve boats on the Rhine, killing
his next-in-line competition? Michael of Müllhausen, whom
they refused to pay for his third-rate leather? The once-merry
Widow Rosamunda of Mayenzer Gass, now jilted for Grete?
Rettich Schäffer, in revenge for shaving his sisters' heads? A
childhood enemy? Grünlein, whom he used to bully with
Bertle for his clubfoot, his stumbling walk?

Manfred tosses and turns, thinking, thinking again. Who?
The heretics of Honau? Revenge for their capture? They were
being taken to the Burning Ground just as Manfred and his
father arrived, passing each other on the road. The girl was
amongst them. She looked straight through him. She was pale,
absent, clothed in white.

Who?

† † †

On the morning of the third day, they take his Father to be questioned. All four rooms in the castle keep are being used as courtrooms. Two Inquisitors for each court, all on the Bishop's shilling. A profitable business.

Manfred waits for his Father at the castle door. When he comes out from the interrogation, he's trembling. Son puts a blanket around his shoulders, but he throws it off. It's not from cold he's trembling, but from anger.

"What, Father?"

"I denied the charges, I said I was a good Christian and had no heresy on my conscience."

"This is dangerous."

"Why?"

"If you confess and repent, you go free. Your hair is shorn, a yellow cross is sewn onto your coat. It is bad, I grant you, but you go free and live. But if you deny, you are still under suspicion."

"Should I lie?"

"And? What did they say?"

"They asked me why they should believe me and not the witnesses who have accused me."

"There. You see."

"I said, 'Tell me who these witnesses are, or bring them here before me, and let them testify to my face, and then you shall judge the truth of it.' They said that this was not necessary, that the witnesses had already proved their commitment to the truth."

"Which means that they confessed to heresy themselves. By confessing, they showed their *commitment to the truth.*'"

"I know it. And if they were heretics it is well that they confessed. But now I am undone. Undone by the tongues of folk who either denied our Church, or who were Christians but who have lied on oath, and damned their souls. Manfred, the world is upside-down."

"Let us live and set it right."

"How should we live?"

"By lying like Pardoners, and saying we are heretics. Then we will live."

"Then, as confessed heretics, how should we set anything right?"

"As corpses, what can we achieve? Father, confess to heresy."

"And lie? On oath? And damn my immortal soul?"

"Absolution for lying can be bought later. You know how it works."

"You do not bargain with God, Manfred. And this is a fool's dance I cannot join. If you confess, then you must name names. Names of those who were with you in heresy. And so it goes on and on and on, and all are damned. Doubtless some poor soul, terrified of death, has named our names and brought us to this perdition."

Then he turns, and his eyes are burning, but calm. His face is pale, but decided. He says, "I have made a demand to the Inquisitors."

"What do you mean?"

"I am a merchant of this city, and all my life I have worked and paid my dues, I have left money on the Cathedral altar every Christmas, and when I die, five marks will go to the Fabric, paying for one statue of a saint. My demand was this; that if I am tried by the Church, I be tried as a citizen of the City of Hagenburg, by Canons of the Cathedral where I worship. Not by these hired Dominican vultures."

His voice is calm, but underneath, Manfred can hear his anger. Father says "I have sent a message to the Bishop, requesting an answer to this demand."

"You sent a message to the Bishop? How?"

"I had nearly a shilling in my purse. It was considered enough money."

"And in your letter, you made this demand to the Bishop?"

"I did. I requested an answer by noon tomorrow."

Manfred holds back tears, he has not wept before his father since he was a small child. "They will kill you!" He looks away, rubs his moist eyes. "You will die unshriven."

"For the salvation of my soul, I put my trust in the love of Our Saviour. Not in this pack of cassocked jackals."

† † †

Some fools were trying to make light of fate, their skulls grinning in firelight, spitting out jokes which failed to spark. But most sat grimly in the gloaming of the flames, searching for the words to say to tease out clemency from their Judges' hearts. Conversations were clandestine, whispered, quieter than the spitting of the damp firewood. But urgent; the whisper of confession, the hiss of conspiracy.

Manfred, sleepless again, wanders around, joining familiar faces, faces he knows from the streets, from the river trade. Everyone is asking questions; whose names should I name, what should I say when the Judge asks my confession?

"Say you met in a barn at dusk, and it was dark, and there were many people there, and they closed the doors and then their priest said some things you didn't understand, and then candles were lit, and the big Black Cat came, the size of a dog, and danced with everyone. And say that you danced with the Cat and kissed his arsehole with your lips, and kissed the other Brethren there, and danced in the darkness."

"Won't they ask for more?"

"Yes, for some details."

"And?"

"You make those up. Then they will ask who else was there."

"And what shall I say?"

"Say it was dark and difficult to see, and then name names of a few people who have already died or been shorn."

Others rocked back and forwards, clutching their knees, thinking and thinking again . . . trying to work out why they were there. "I think I know who did it. I think I know." It was their neighbour who always hated them, the neighbour who wanted their land, it was their half-brother who wanted their inheritance, it was a business rival, it was the priest who was in love with their wife . . .

And he sat too, by the embers of a fire, leaning on the stone of the castle wall, wrapped in his oily sheepskin. And in the white and orange flames, he saw two faces, one of Love and one of Hate. His young, pretty wife Grete, with whom he had had such short but joyful times. And the wooden carving of the Virgin he'd seen in Honau, blackening and blistering in the heretics' bonfire.

† † †

Father wakes him around dawn. No message has come from Bishop or Chapter.

"Listen my boy," he says, sitting down next to him. "When these great Lords in the Cathedral Chapter, these von Zaberns and von Diezes and von Moders, when they let good Christian citizens of Hagenburg burn to death, then our city is at War, do you understand? Someone, somehow, some way, has to show the Lords of the Church that they cannot do just as they please with us. It is we who pay the taxes that keep them in wine and ermine. It is our money that builds their Cathedral. Do you hear me?"

Manfred nods, "Father I hear you." Then Manfred's name is called from the keep doorway—it is time for his interrogation. He kisses his Father's hand and stands. His

Father looks up at him. "Good luck, my boy. I'll be waiting for you."

His Inquisitors are called Konrad Dorso and Johannes Jahn, lay brothers of the Dominican order. They are sitting at a high table, breakfasting on ale, porridge and cheese, and looking down on Manfred as he walks in. Both of them are ugly as pigs. A young clerk sits beside them on a stool, scribbling notes.

Manfred just wants to get out of that damned place as quick as he can. He tells them dirty tales about barns and sheds and black cats and candles and everyone fucking everyone in every which way. The Brothers love it, and ask salacious questions like *and did the toad kiss you full upon the lips?* and *was there incest there, between brother and sister?* and Manfred always says, "Yes, yes, Brother, yes," with a mournful and penitent look on his face. At one point, Dorso, a half-blind cripple, limps up close to him, sniffs his face, waves his hands over his head, and says, "Yes, truly I smell heresy in his soul." This is how he finds heretics: by smell, by second sight. Manfred resists the desire to spit in his face. Who are these grotesque dwarves, lording it over the fates of men? They're like jesters, jongleurs, acting a play. And yet, with their Dominican scapulars, they have the power of life and death.

Dorso limps back to his perch and they then start to ask him who had been *with him* in the barn when the Black Cat had come. And he says that the barn had been dark, and many of the initiates' faces were painted. They repeat the question and say *And your Father was with you, we know* and Manfred swears he never saw his father there. *Your Father was with you!* "He was not!" *He took you there with him!* "He did not! I never saw him there!" *Liar!* "I am not lying, I swear!" *He was there!* "He was not!"

This goes on endlessly, but Manfred doesn't relent—his father was never there, never there, never there. They press him again and again and again, becoming more and more frustrated, more angry. *He was there with you, he took you there.* "No!" *Where was your father?* "I don't know! At home! Not there!"

Jahn bangs his hand down on the desk and shouts: *Who else was there with you?*

"It was dark."

WHO WAS THERE WITH YOU?

"I saw some of the weavers of Honau," murmurs Manfred.

"How did you recognise them," sneers Dorso, "in the darkness?"

"Some of their girls are beautiful," says Manfred, "I would recognise them anywhere."

"Did you fornicate with the girls?"

"I don't know, it was dark."

Jahn cackles, "You fornicated with something, but you know not *what*?"

Manfred thinks; *yes, with you, you bastard,* but says instead; "I was forced to, Brother. I am truly sorry."

"What else did you see? Whom else did you see?"

Manfred wants to say he saw His Grace the Bishop riding on a Satanic crab that rose from the Rhine, that he saw the Canons of the Cathedral bent over a bench, being fucked up the arse by a bunch of Jews, that he saw the Pope sucking Lucifer's huge horny cock. He wants to shout and scream, he wants to name all his merchant competitors; Wolfram of Basel, Michael of Müllhausen. He wants to say he saw Dorso and Jahn there with their fingers up each other's bumholes.

Instead he says, "It was dark."

You saw your father there.

"I did not. Who is supplying you with your yellow cloth?"

This question takes them by surprise.

"For the penitential crosses sewn on people's backs? Who is supplying it? I can do you a better deal."

Silence in the chamber, for the first time. The clerk's quill hovers in mid-air. This part of the conversation will not be a matter of record.

Dorso clears his phlegm-blocked throat, a disgusting sound. He speaks with quiet threat. "We hold your immortal soul in our hands, and you want to haggle with us?"

But Jahn is interested. "It's true," he says, getting up from his chair and approaching, "we have the ear of the Bishop's Treasurer. Maybe we *can* make you the supplier. We'll take a commission, of course."

Manfred shrugs, "Of course."

"And we want something in return."

"Yes?"

Silence. A teardrop of ink falls from the clerk's poised quill . . . .

"Tell us you saw your father at the barn."

Manfred sighs. "No."

"Other people saw him there. Admit it. He was there. If he admits too, and repents, he will be saved."

"He was not there."

Jahn's voice rises. "Your father refuses to repent. He will be burned. You can save him. Confess that he was a heretic like you."

Dorso has also approached. "The Church is *generous* to the penitent."

Manfred stares at the ground between his feet.

"He was not there."

† † †

Outside, hours later, people look away from him, they won't meet his eye. He rushes to where his Father had been sitting, but now there are two old women there, their heads shaven, weeping.

A voice whispers in Manfred's ear, the voice of Hildebrand, a miller's boy. "They took him to the Burning Ground. Whilst you were inside."

Manfred wheels round. "It's too early!"

Hildebrand hisses. "He was making trouble. Telling us to rise up, to attack the guards, to escape."

Manfred cannot bear it. A howl builds up in his throat and then releases itself. He falls to the ground, screaming. One of the old women clasps him, and he collapses into her ageing, wrinkled bosom, abandoning all shame and honour.

† † †

Evening. Rumours come back to Kronenweiler of his father's end.

They say he paid sixpence to the executioner, and was rewarded with a moment to speak. It was a Sunday, and the crowd gathered there had come from Mass. From the Cathedral Mass, the Bishop himself had come, the Dean, the Treasurer, some others of the Chapter. They were gathered there at the Burning Ground.

They said he began to shout that that the City belonged to its people, not to the nobles or the church. That the people deserve justice, and to have a role in writing the laws of the land. They say he had only just started speaking, when, at a sign from the Bishop, he was pushed into the pit and spoke no more.

† † †

Five days later, they shaved Manfred's head and set him free.

Grete is waiting for him on the Hagenburg road. She gives thanks to God and wipes the cross off his forehead with ditch-water.

A storm is coming. They hurry home, not talking. After the town gate, they take the back streets, looking at no-one.

At home, she cooks him meat and pearl barley stew, pours him wine. She heats a bath and washes him and then, in bed, holding each other, they cry like children.

In his young wife's arms, Manfred finally can sleep. He feels an emptiness around him, filled with silent rest and peace. He wants to sink into that darkness and forget everything, start again from blackness, from nothing.

But his Father's words keep on coming back to him, as if out of a huge, empty grave.

We are at War.

ANNO
1233

THE MORNING ALTAR
(ANNO 1233. RETTICH SCHÄFFER IV)

I n the forests, after the birds' bright aubade, silence drifts through the leaves and needles. Slowly, a humming rises from the fertile ground; the buzz of insects, the cicada, the thrum of life. And the Cathedral is like a forest, sounds flooding and ebbing through its stones, the rising columns are like trunks reaching up towards the forest canopy, the light that angles through the stained windows is filtered into patterns just like the sunlight that falls through shifting leaves. And like the forest, just before dawn, the Cathedral resounds with song.

Rettich has been here all night. He has sat alone in the darkness, watching the uncertain light of the votive candle until the Choir starts to fill for Lauds. The flagstones now resound with footsteps; quiet, reverent ones heading for worship. The clatter of the portal's chains echoes through the Crossing, coughs and throat-clearings rise and fall from the domed ceiling, and then the Precentor's first, sung *te deum laudamus* reverberates, calling all to the music of prayer. The sounds filter themselves, concentrate, and unite in chant, into one voice, praising the Lord of the Universe.

Rettich listens and looks to the East window, where grey Day will soon be dawning. He has been sent here by his Masters for one week of meditation and prayer before he begins the fifth and last year of his Apprenticeship. It is his fourth day and already he feels he is sinking into the stones, becoming part of the building, one with its rhythms and rituals. His back aches from fitful sleep on flagstones and benches, he half-wakes, half-sleeps through the five psalms and antiphons, he drifts in and out of the words, half-learned, half-forgotten . . .

Pleni sunt caeli et terra maiestatis gloriae tuae . . .

Heaven and earth are full of the Majesty of Thy glory . . .

Omnis spiritus laudet Dominum . . .

Let all who have breath praise the Lord . . .

Then a clattering of feet, the Precentor files out, followed by the Canons who have attended, by the residentiaries and chaplains, the Cathedral Schoolboys heading for lessons. Sandalled and hooded, the Warden snuffs the candles of the Choir; the wicks spit and exhale their final smoke, spiralling upwards, joining with the traces of incense. The last words of prayer seem to diffuse gently into the silence, falling slowly to the Cathedral floor. There they eddy, drift and subside, lying amongst the dust.

And all is still.

† † †

Boom . . . the South Portal door is pushed wide open . . . and the Cathedral is ready for business. Now, one by one, the weekday regulars file in and take their positions. Three beggars, a seller of embroidered prayers, hawkers with almonds, dried currants and fresh bread rolls . . . and the apprentice boy bringing Rettich some bread and a slice of Lenzenbach sheepcheese.

Rettich sits in a corner and devours the breakfast. This week he is on a fasting diet of a bowl of soup, a hunk of bread and a slice of cheese a day. Already his dreams are being invaded by visions of roasted meats, a stew of beans and pork belly, a thick slice of bread smeared with cream and mountain honey.

The first tradespeople are arriving, stamping the mud and

dust from their shoes at the doorway, and then slipping inside. They genuflect, cross themselves, make for their favourite chapel to offer a prayer to their chosen saint, and then sit on the benches that run along the South Transept wall, waiting for their colleagues, customers, waiting for their meetings.

Passing the St. Martin chapel, through the spider-work of holes in the carved wooden screen, Rettich can see the criminals stirring from their sleep, gathering up their straw bedding to store beside the altar. The hilt of a dagger glints in the candlelight as the Murderer stoops to snuff the wick. The guttering flame hisses in his spittle-licked fingers.

There are three men sleeping in the chapel this week, seeking sanctuary. It is more than usual, but since the fires of the Burning of Heretics, disorder has convulsed the land. When the prisons were emptied and the repentant returned to their homes and villages, many were the acts of revenge on the Namers of Names. Farms were burned, fields razed, priests hanged by their parishioners, men and women slain in their beds by vengeful hands.

The murderer in the St. Martin chapel has been here for one week. They say he is from Saxony, a mercenary and a hired assassin. He murdered Konrad Dorso the Inquisitor in a tavern as the Dominican ate his supper.

They say he cut open Dorso's stomach and pulled his guts out onto the table so that the last thing that he would see in this world would be his own liver.

They say that many in the tavern, eating and drinking near Dorso, were the murderer's paymasters, who had paid a Mark each so that they could watch the public spectacle of the Inquisitor's death.

They say that the murderer then raced through the streets to safety in the Cathedral, and no militia tried to stop him, as they too were in the pay of those who arranged Dorso's murder.

They say that the assassin's paymasters are many merchants and tradesmen of the city. And they say that Dorso's murderer is waiting for safe passage out of the Cathedral to be arranged by those who hired him.

"Boy, here!" calls out the assassin. A freckle-faced lad jumps up from the bench where he was sleeping and rushes to the murderer's side. "Take this chamberpot to the pits. Bring me some sausage and poppyseed bread."

The glint of coins as money exchanges hands. The boy slips out of the chapel, tenderly holding the chamberpot at arm's length, heading for the northern portal and the public latrines.

"Attention!"

Now is the time for morning masses. The chaplains of the apsidal chapels and their helpers are sweeping the floors, lighting the candles and preparing for work. "I will now say mass for the immortal soul of the Knight Rudolf of Kalben!" calls out Chaplain Malo from the St. John Chapel doorway.

The Chaplain retreats into his chapel, followed by three older women from the merchant quarter, wrapped in the black shawls marking a recent bereavement. Following them, a feverish-looking young man seemingly in need of religious consolation.

The chaplain's soft chanting begins, absorbed into the rustles of morning movement, into the sudden beating of a pigeon's wings as, disturbed from its rest, it flutters upwards towards the light of the Eastern window.

Gathering by the Morning Altar now, the daily meeting of a group of City Merchants. They come here to share news, make deals, discuss issues. The Dean has requested that they meet elsewhere, in a tavern, in a shop, in the tollhouse, but they defiantly demand their right to congregate here, in the City's church that is theirs as much as anyone else's.

Rettich has seen how they talk and laugh loudly, purposively disrupting the prayer and quietude around them. At other times, they huddle together like a herd of cows under the rain and whisper conspiratorially, making all who watch them wonder what secrets they can be so fervently discussing.

Amongst them, always, is Rettich's brother-in-law, Manfred Gerber.

Rettich slinks into the shadows of the half-built northern Aisle. Like anyone else, he has heard the rumours. Last Christmas, most of the City's merchants and traders left no money on the Cathedral altar. When old man Gerber died, the five marks he bequeathed to the fabric were not given, but sent instead to the monastery of St. Odile. Other bequests from townsfolk have not materialised, wills have been altered in favour of other institutions. The Cathedral is losing money.

And the Merchants' Guilds have bought a plot of land near the former Burning Ground, near the Rhine Gate. The shape of the plot of land is large, and cruciform. They want to build a church.

The foundations have already started to be dug.

From the shadows, Rettich watches as Manfred leaves the group of whispering merchants, and wanders towards the North Transept. On the way, he genuflects and crosses himself beneath the painted wooden statue of Our Lady.

And then he enters the St. Martin chapel.

Rettich knows that, at this hour, the chapel is empty. The only person there is the Saxon assassin, eating his bread and sausage.

From the altar steps, a loud voice calls out. "Dietzheimer wine! A special offer for all our citizens and pilgrims!"

Rettich sighs. The last three days, this wine has been cried to the eaves of the Cathedral between every Holy Service. He knows every word by heart. "The new wine now broached and tasted, and found to be of the sweetness of honey, with the scent of lilacs and diverse flowers! Only one penny ha'penny a measure! Or a shilling a cask!"

"And the Bishop personally pissed in each one!" calls out one of the merchants at the Morning Altar.

"The harvest of the Dietzeheimer vines is personally blessed by His Grace the Bishop!" continues the crier, raising his voice. "It is a wine that enlivens the tongue and thickens the blood. It is a wine that takes away sorrow and care! Available in the Cathedral arcade. Please come, taste and buy!"

Rettich has tasted the wine. He and his Apprentice colleagues pooled their ha'pennies and bought two pitchers for the Johannisfest bonfire. It was fine indeed, golden and half-sweet, half-lemony, gentle and cheerful.

"Sell it in a wineshop like anyone else, you lackey!" shouts out another merchant to the crier's retreating back.

Applause from the other merchants. "Silence!" calls the Chaplain of St. John's chapel. "Shame on you!" cries one of the widow women, emerging from mass, shaking her head. The merchants shrug, and turn back to their gossip and conspiracy.

Emmle has explained it all to Rettich. The Dietzeheimer vineyards belong to the Bishop. And, by selling the wines in the Cathedral arcade, they are exempt from the taxes that all the other merchants of the city must pay. All the stalls in the arcade by the Cathedral's western walls are exempt from taxes, can charge a lower price, and turn a pretty profit. This is the way of trade in Hagenburg; as in all things, the Bishop is Lord.

Manfred crosses back towards his colleagues from the St. Martin chapel, a slight smile on his face, hand running through his reddish hair. There are nods, words exchanged, hands shaken, and then the merchant dozen begin to disperse, heading for the southern portal and their businesses in the harbour and the market quarter.

Near-silence returns. Rettich counts the people moving through the building, as he once used to count his flock. One two three four five six seven . . .

A round sixty. Rettich's eyelids droop.

Velvety silence. And now the soft sound of mass being chanted in the side chapel. The sibilance of shuffled footsteps, the mutter of private prayer. The distant crepitation of a cart passing in the square. The metallic song of chisel on stone behind the temporary nave wall of mud and straw. The rustle of the pigeon's wings. The Chaplain's voice.

Lamb of God, who taketh away the sins of the world, have mercy on us.

†††

"Brother, wake up. Pssst! Wake up!"

Emmle's voice.

Rettich rises from the corner where he has been lying, looks round with grey-filmed eyes in the gloom.

"I could hardly find you," says Emmerich, "lying in this dark corner like a barn cat."

"I was tired. I was awake all night," mutters Rettich.

"Doing what? Playing dice with the murderers?"

"Thinking, Emmle."

"Oh, that's not good."

"Watching the votive candle. Praying. Reflecting."

"It's getting worse. What are you, a monk? Sleep at night like a man with a good conscience. Or do you not have one?"

"I have my worries."

Emmerich smiles, takes his elder brother's hand. "Come, let's move away from the merchant benches." He means the townsmen and traders in the South Transept, sitting at their discussions and meetings. One of them is looking over at Emmerich with an even, hostile stare.

"He owes my master money," whispers Emmerich, "and it's me who reminds him every godgiven day."

When he started working for Rosheimer, Emmle did the

cleaning and on the Jewish sabbath he lit candles, made fires, carried water, did those things forbidden the Jews on their holy day. Then there was a new boy who carried out these tasks, and Emmerich was apprenticed in Mayenz, in the family's trading business. Now he's back in Hagenburg, runs errands in the city, collects debts, talks to the merchants in the marketplace and in the harbour. He is Rosheimer's eyes and ears.

Seated in the far corner, they smile at each other. Always in the same city, yet in different worlds, never meeting.

"Tell me, big brother," says Emmerich, "what troubles you?"

"I must get married, Emmle."

"Is that troubling you?"

"It is a law that all Companions must be married men. I have one year to find a wife."

Emmerich's hands sweep around, indicating the busy city around them, the thousands of people. "Well, choose one."

"How?"

"There were some village girls as liked you."

Rettich shakes his head.

"But there is a fairer choice here in the city. Who has taken your fancy?"

Rettich shakes his head once more.

"Is there *no-one* you like?"

"No-one. Master Landolt has shown me his cousin, a baker's daughter."

"And?"

"If I want her, it can be arranged."

"And how is she?"

"I know nothing about girls, Emmle."

"Nothing?"

Silence in the vast Cathedral. *Terce* prayers must have passed whilst Rettich slept. The time for the midday meal is approaching, and the benches and chapels are nearly empty.

An ancient, crooked man is bending, slowly and painfully, to kneel before the Virgin. Somewhere in the dome, a pigeon coos softly.

"I know a place. I can take you there," whispers Emmerich.

"A place?"

"Where there are girls. Women. They can teach you."

Rettich looks at his younger brother, his eyes widening. "This place, have you been there?"

Emmerich looks at the flagstones, saying nothing. Silence stretches out between the brothers. Rettich looks at Emmle, remembers the little boy, playing with the newborn lambs. Throwing pebbles at the geese, laughing at nothing.

Emmerich breaks the silence. "Is it Holo the Baker's daughter, by the way?"

"It is."

"You could do much worse than her."

Over by the portal, the hawker has sat down to eat his last, unsold bread roll himself. As he chews, his eyes are closed, as if trying to sleep whilst he eats. Rettich tries to picture Ällin the Baker's daughter, her cheerful, round face. Tries to picture her naked body, pressed against his . . .

"What did the Canon say?" asks Emmle, after a while.

Rettich looks up from his fruitless reverie, clears his throat. "He says that the Church Synod was clear on the matter. All who work for the Jews are in the ban of the Church. Your soul is in danger, Emmle."

"Herr Rosheimer and I have a solution."

"Which is?"

"We will set up a subsidiary trading and investing company, in my name. To start this company I will borrow money from Rosheimer, and follow his instructions, at least to begin with. And I will pay myself wages from this company's profits. When profit comes in, whose money is that? Money has no owner, it's always changing hands. It means I no longer work *for* the Jews."

Rettich looks at his brother with troubled eyes. "Do you think God is a lawyer? When he judges your soul, do you think he looks at contracts?"

"Show me where in the Gospels it says that it is a sin to work for the Jews."

"You know better than the Holy Fathers?"

Emmerich shrugs. "What I know is that for two marks a year I can buy a dispensation from the Church that will allow me to work with Jews, without sinning."

"Then buy it."

"Why pay good money to that pack of fraudsters?"

"You mean the Church?"

Emmerich shrugs.

"When was the last time you went to Mass, Emmerich?"

For a while, Emmerich says nothing. Then he turns to his elder brother. "Have you really never, with a girl . . . just kissed, maybe?" he asks, mischievously.

Rettich cannot help himself, and smiles. "Friede, in the village, one Johannisfest."

"And?"

Rettich winces, laughs. "I ran away!"

"Oh, my brother . . . " sighs Emmerich. "The baker's daughter is used to carrying heavy baskets of loaves. She'll hold you and won't let go."

† † †

Rettich presses his ear against the temporary wall of the Nave. It is made of wood, mud and straw, and is there to separate the quiet of the Cathedral from the noise of the Site. With his ear pressed against it, Rettich can hear, muffled and distant, the sound of his brothers chiselling stone. Looking up, he can see the temporary Nave roof above him, the height of a tall poplar tree . . .

In the four years Rettich has been working there, they have built two arches of the Nave. Now they are completing the arcades. Once they are ready, and strong, they will help support the weight of the Nave's soaring walls . . . and once more they will build upwards and onwards towards the Western façade.

Achim, his friend and master, is sick. It is a year now since he was taken from the Burning Grounds, restrained by three men, frothing at the mouth like a dog with the rage. For some days, locked in a room in the Chapter House, he raved, screamed and attempted the sin of suicide, and then, exhausted, he sank into a dull Lethargy. And in this state of sullen darkness he was taken away to the monastery of Avenheim in the foothills of the Vogesen, where the Mad of good families are held in silence.

Rettich remembers. The last good times he and Master Achim spent together, crossing into Winzbach in Lothringen in search of the maker of the yellow glass. Forest paths, dappled sunlight, a night of rain in a parish church, wrapped in woollen blankets on straw. A hamlet of foundries and charcoal-burners by a churning, sand-bedded river, and an old man with rheum-ringed eyes, the maker of the glass.

The glass-maker remembered the yellow batch—he had been trying to make red, but had used the sand from higher up the river bed, and it had come out ochre. He laughs that now his mistake has brought him good fortune. Master Achim leaves silver in his palm, makes him promise to teach his grandsons the secret of the yellow glass so that, when the Western Rose is built, the colour of sunlight can flood the Bishop's Church.

After his collapse, Achim lies in his bare cell in Avenheim Monastery, hardly moving, hardly eating, drinking, speaking. Rettich visits him on Sundays, chatters away into the dismal silence. His friend's back is turned to him, lying on his pallet, facing the speechless, blank wall, immobile.

One Sunday Rettich brings with him the contents of Achim's "escritoire," his drawings, sketches and designs. Images of the statues of the Western Wall, paintings of stained glass windows for the Clerestory, the beauteous Rose.

"Master, I have brought your Work. I hoped . . . maybe . . . if you saw it. You would remember. Remember your calling. Remember your Voice."

But when Achim speaks, he says that all of Creation is a decoy, a distraction from the Real World, which is hidden behind a curtain. He says that, because of him and his sins, the world has become a copy. Because of him, the whole world is a shadow.

If someone will kill him, he says, the world will be restored.

These are the kind of things that Achim has been saying in the cold cells and corridors of Avenheim. And there is now talk of abandoning his plans and designs for something more simple. For the Lord knows, these are maybe the designs of a madman . . . even a heretic.

Rettich looks at the windows of the Apse, the colours and figures that had moved him so much when first he came. Now that he has seen Achim's work, he can see how lacking they are. To Bishops, Kings and Emperors, Achim prefers Prophets, Saints, Martyrs, the Ancestors of Christ. He prefers profiles, rapt figures, arms outstretched, bodies twisted, hips swaying, fabrics falling from coiling limbs, fluid shapes, a feeling of uplifting, spreading, rising . . . He favours floral patterns, leaves and petals, animals rampant, the world in rapturous essence. *The first Leaf that was in God's mind before it was copied into this world of forms* . . . His vision, beautiful, strange, evocative, worshipful, must be retained. He must be saved from his own mind.

As the last notes of the Compline prayers subside into silence, Rettich prays. "Good Lord, protect your servant and my friend and Master, Achim von Esinbach, bring him serenity, heal his mind, Amen."

These last days, he cannot think straight, he is tired, his mind is so full it is like a swollen stream in the thaw, running over its banks, spreading everywhere and running nowhere . . . his thoughts loop back into each other in exhaustion, finding no solutions.

And yet he feels a strange kind of elation, a closeness to God such as he has rarely felt before.

Rettich wishes Achim were here, so that he could touch him, hold his hand. A thought rises in his mind, unbidden. "If only I could marry Master Achim, I could take good care of him."

Rettich blushes, shudders, drowns the thought back into the eddying waters whence it came. Then he smiles. What nonsense we think sometimes. What nonsense.

Compline has passed like a vision, a mirage, and the congregation is filing out into the autumnal darkness. The Warden snuffs the last candle in the choir, and, carrying a flickering lantern, walks quietly to the door.

The Cathedral falls silent.

In the vast darkness, only the one votive candle trembles. Rettich is alone in his part of the nave.

In the chapel, the murderer and criminals are sleeping. Over by the Southern wall, some travellers and beggars. It is almost as if he can hear their breathing.

The candle's tiny flame flickers, the Eternal Light, dwarfed by the silence and darkness.

ANNO
1234

NINE CIRCLES
(ANNO 1234. EUGENIUS VON ZABERN IV)

I am not quite sure what, really, I was expecting. But not this. This bordello.

In my imagination I had seen Our Church's splendour magnified, wide streets, grand basilicae, processions of the devout. Instead, I am presented with the stench of an open sewer, and crowds of lousy, stinking thieves.

Rome. The sun is like a hot iron on my back and shoulders. My black Flemish robes are too heavy for the climate—I will have to buy a new set of clothes; I may be here a while.

Magnus, our guide, turns and shows his apologetic face. Again. "It is not far," he says, for the third time. Maybe I am to blame. To save a couple of shillings, I said we could walk from the Tiber to our lodgings near the Basilica of St. Peter. We make a pretty sight; a gaggle of pasty-faced Germans, sweating and trudging through the filth of the streets with a train of laden donkeys.

There are hordes of cutpurse children swarming around us. Tan faces, loud voices, starving eyes. They chatter and scream in their vulgar Italian, their hands make gestures, doubtless obscene. Our mercenary escort can hardly keep them from the pack animals and their precious cargo. I see one boy skirt past, cut one of the leather straps holding a sack with his little dagger. He runs off into the crowd, disappearing instantly. Then another boy, doing the same.

"Armund!" I shout at our brawny Englander who is meant to be guarding the animals, "the straps!"

"Huh?" he grunts back. I try in Latin, but it's no use. I try and push through the crowd to get to him. Thanks to God, I had the foresight to hang my own purse round my neck, deep in my robes—no-one can get to it there.

Bang! The devils! Between them they have cut enough straps for the donkey's burden to come crashing to the ground. Like ants over crumbs, the boys swarm onto our unravelled cargo.

Armund strikes out with the flat of his sword. His colleagues come running to back him up. One boy takes the edge of a blade on his wrist and screams. Spurts of blood.

"Quickly!" I shout. "Out of here! Now!"

† † †

The wintry weeks of Lent, in the episcopal castle in Haldenheim. The Bishop, wrapped in furs, rubs his watery eyes. And looking at him, diagonally propped on his bed and countless cushions, swollen and immobile, he seems like a prize boar laid low by the hunters' spears; a once great and noble beast, brought down.

His two dogs lie beside him, shifting in their sleep. "I summoned you here, Eugenius, because I have a dropsy that the doctors cannot seem to cure."

"My Lord, I am saddened to hear it."

"Walking is becoming difficult. My legs are beginning to swell like gourds, barrels."

"We can find new doctors."

"I fear new doctors will only find new ways of torturing me."

"We can send to Cologne, to Salerno, to Paris—"

"Who would leave Paris in midwinter to cure an ageing man?"

"I have an emergency fund, Your Grace. It is worth many

hundred marks, it is quite sufficient to pay for a fancy doctor. And you are not old."

"I feel old." The Bishop's ringed fingers reach out and caress his dog's ears. "Keep the investment. Let us not throw the diocese's money into my grave." His Grace's eyes flicker up at me, commanding and serious. I am instructed. "There is an Italian Prince who, I am told, lived with this form of dropsy for several years, and died the size of a cow."

"That is encouraging."

"Isn't it? But I just wanted to make clear that my death seems not imminent. Nevertheless I would be remiss if I did not now turn my attention to my legacy. Eugenius, there are four major candidates to be my successor. Varenus. The Archdeacon has expressed an interest. As has the Dean."

"The Dean is dreaming."

"He is a Man of God. Let him dream."

"The fourth?"

"Is you, Eugenius."

"I have not declared myself a contender."

"Nevertheless I will put forward your name as a candidate. If you have no objection."

I say nothing and look to the floor. His Grace continues; "The Dean has no chance, all the Chapter know that he has no worldly understanding. Varenus; he always seeks consensus, which makes him popular, but weak. Archdeacon von Stahlem is well-liked, however, and may well be the Chapter's favourite. Eugenius, your defect, if I may say it, is that you have never courted popularity with your peers."

"An understatement, Your Grace."

"Begin now. You are not as antipathetic as you think you are. At times you even have charm."

"What should I do? Bake cakes?"

"Use your emergency funds. Increase the refectory budget, have more meat pies served and sweets, and better wine."

"Are my fellow Canons so simple-minded?"

"Most of them."

"And for those Canons who are never in Hagenburg?"

"Send them gifts. They will know why."

"Can not His Holiness appoint His own candidate?"

"Yes, but I don't believe He will."

The Bishop's rheumy eyes cloud over, troubled. "Varenus . . . ." he says and sighs. "As young Canons, we made a deal to help each other. He would help me become Bishop, and I would help him become Dean. But, in the end, Vitztum was the highest office I could get for him. He never fulfilled his youthful promise. He will be very bitter if I give my support to your candidacy."

"I can live with the Vitztum's bitterness."

"They said I appointed you too young. But you have been my greatest helper, Eugenius."

He looks at me, and the whites of his eyes are veined with blood. "I need you to go to Rome."

† † †

Our entry into our august lodgings is hardly decorous. We run red-faced and panicked through the heavy oak doors, pelted with filth by the baying Roman crowd. The doormen seem unsurprised by our precipitous entrance, however, and close the gates on the *plebs romana* as if it were a daily occurrence to rescue German ecclesiastics from a mob howling for blood.

"Welcome to Rome my Lords," says the director of the establishment, bowing respectfully, as if nothing untoward had happened.

"We were robbed!" I exclaim, "by thieving children! And when we tried to recover our stolen property the crowd turned on us! Not on the thieves!"

"Very regrettable," says the director, bowing again. His

white hand slips out of his Benedictine robes like a snake from a stone. "Let me show you to your chambers, My Lord Treasurer."

The Director leads me up a scuffed marble staircase to the second floor. Flaking, whitewashed walls surround an inner courtyard where the scent of flowers competes with the stench of the streets and achieves a temporary victory.

He opens the door to my room; wide, white, and decorated with roses in silver-plated vases. White sheets, white walls, white shutters, white roses. Peace and purity, unblemished.

He opens the shutters, and I am moved to see that my room looks out on the Basilica itself; seemingly only an arrow's flight away, the Church founded by Peter, beloved of Christ! Its bell tower, separate from the church itself, rises over the rooves of the city, over the domes and spires, over the sea of terracotta tiles, smoking chimneys, circling doves, over the thousands of Romans, pilgrims, clerics and thieves. The sun is setting, and an auburn light deepens the lengthening shadows of the stones. From a hundred churches, the soft toll of vespers bells. And beneath my window, an old lady squatting to defecate in the street.

† † †

"Why me?"

His Grace passes me a short letter, in poor handwriting and in poorer Lothringen German, addressed from Dagsburg Castle. *Lady close to deathe.*

"From my spy at Dagsburg," says the Bishop with a wink.

"We have heard this before, many times."

"As soon as the thaw comes, you'll go. By sea from Provence, not over the Alps—it will take too long for the passes to open. I need you in Rome as soon as you can get there."

I fold the letter and stare into the leaping flames in the

grate. "I am to persuade the Curia to judge in our favour? The Dagsburg Inheritance?"

"You are."

"And how much will that cost?"

Berthold shrugs. "I don't know. But somehow I judge that you will get a better price than Varenus. You are a fine haggler."

I look up at His Grace. "I had better succeed. We have sore need of new revenue."

"We do?"

"Our bequests are down, Your Grace. A long way down."

He nods gravely. "Our people are punishing us. We struck a strong blow against heresy, and it was well received in Rome. But here, it feels that we struck too hard." He looks up at me. "When you are Bishop, Eugenius, these are the books that you will have to balance. Not everything is counted in marks, shillings and pence."

"In my world, Your Grace, it is. I will have to reduce our outgoings this year."

"Do as you need to do. I trust you. Just," and here he raises an admonishing finger, "do not touch the Cathedral."

An unhappy silence.

"I am afraid I will have to. The work will have to be slowed. Workers dismissed. One in four."

The Bishop shakes his head. A pause. He clears his throat. "One in six."

"One in four. Or would you have me borrow from the Jews?"

"Everyone else does."

"I will have to borrow, already. To pay the Curia. But I prefer to raise that from the banks in Rome."

"If we win the Dagsburg case, then we will pay back the loan immediately."

"If."

His Grace folds his hands. "That Cathedral is my legacy to Hagenburg."

"One in five, effective immediately. Even that will leave us exposed."

A grunt. A nod. "One in five."

††† †

I had never expected to see this. I thought I would spend my days pushing pennies and abacus beads in the Counting House. I thought I would die at my desk, or, failing that, be stabbed to death in a forest by some embittered landowner on my way back from collecting his taxes.

I never thought I would come to Rome.

It is Sunday morning, the day after we arrived. We flow through the huge gateways into the basilica courtyard, surrounded by columned arcades and crowds of people; I am adrift in a sea of pilgrims and supplicants from all four corners of Christendom, from Ireland, the Baltic, from Portugal, from Dalmatia. From Alsace.

Magnus pulls at my sleeve, and my junior clerk stumbles behind as we push our way into the shadow of the bell-tower, now tolling for mass, and rush towards the Basilica's sun-dazzled portals. I am surprised to find myself excited like a child at the idea of taking communion in St. Peter's. It is as if I have shed two decades of weariness, disappointment and cynicism. I feel elated, blinded by the bright sunlight, hopeful of holiness.

At the doorway, liveried wardens usher the congregants to their places. As we stumble inside one of them looks us up and down, as if a slave-trader estimating our value, pauses, and then, as we say nothing, gestures us to his right at the back of the Nave. We obediently follow, taking our place in the crush of the crowd. The basilica is already full to bursting . . . and we were just in time; they are now closing the doors behind us to still the flood of pilgrims.

There is no room to kneel, to bow, to genuflect. We are like sheep herded together to be shorn, pushed into a pen. I look around (thanks to God, I am a head higher than most of the congregation) and cannot help but notice we have been ushered amongst the poor and indigent at the back of the Basilica. Some twenty paces ahead there is space, light, and room to move. There are even benches where one may sit, and these pews are dotted with priests and nobles, colourfully dressed Ladies, and velvet robed Lords.

I look over to our Usher, who shrugs at me with an insolent face, and looks away. Curse him and the bitch that bore him. Why have we been accorded this insult to our station?

There is a tug at my sleeve. I look down and see a Roman boy with a dirt-smudged yet bright-eyed face. "*Luca summa*," he says in his dog Latin. These Romans add at least three syllables to every word they speak. They call me "*Eugenio Vonnalazzabberna*"—just as an egregious example.

"Yes, Luca?" I say.

"This issa no place-a for a gran signore like-a you, sir," he says and tugs at my sleeve again. "I take-a you?" His grinning face nods in the direction of the front benches. "Yes, take me," I say, gesturing to my retinue to stay where they are.

Luca pulls me out into the slightly-less-crowded aisle. "One half *augustale* for middle-a, and one full-a *augustale* for front-a," he says.

"You take me for a fool?"

"No, signore is gran signore. Today papa issa in massa, and price is alto."

A gasp ripples through the congregation. I look towards the marble columns of the Choir, but can see almost nothing; here I am in the thick of the crowd. Luca explains: "Papa issa entrato."

The Holy Father is here, and I cannot see him. I dig in my purse and pull out—God forgive me—a golden *augustale*. Luca grins triumphantly, takes the coin and runs over to give it to the usher.

The usher, God damn his soul, nods superciliously and comes to escort me to my place near the Transept. He enjoys his smirking triumph at having milked me for my gold, and, with practised dexterity, pushes the crowds aside as he leads me forward through the envious horde. Ahead, the choir has begun its chanting and the Basilica's marble resounds with song. Here the crowd is denser, and it's only with difficulty that I arrive at the wooden fencing that corrals the people in their pen.

With a pretence at ceremony, the usher swings open the gate, and bows deeply as he takes his leave. I am now in freedom, and can choose my place from the few remaining empty seats, amongst nobles, Bishops, canons, and—by the look of it—courtesans.

I slide into a vacant seat between a tiny Spaniard nobleman attired in black velvet and an over-painted, dark-skinned strumpet with flaxen gold hair gleaming through the loose folds of her wimple. I nod a greeting to the nobleman, shun the whore, and look up to the splendour of the Choir and its gleaming windows, lit by the rising sun.

We kneel. The sound of thousands of people falling to their knees as one before God; a holy sound. As I close my eyes to meditate, I see a man looking at me intently. Bright green eyes, trimmed dark beard, clothes of a beautiful, dark blue silk . . . When I open my eyes again, he nods at me; welcoming, respectful.

I look away, to the Crossing and the Choir. In the distance, by the altar, Our Holy Father Gregory the Ninth. A little, bent old man, heir of St. Peter, swaddled in gold thread and jewels.

† † †

Outside, the sun dazzles me, and an elegant, manicured hand takes mine. It belongs to the man in blue silk. "I am Guido Terzani. You are the Treasurer of Hagenburg?"

"I am."

"I am a banker. Please come with me, I have some information for you."

His soft hand tugs gently at mine, guiding me away from the flowing throng, towards a door in the marble arcade, guarded by two Papal Soldiers. The Soldiers recognise Terzani and step aside, and we are admitted into a quiet courtyard where flowers and herbs grow in profusion.

"The sun is too hot for you?" asks Terzani, gesturing questioningly towards the seats in the bright herb garden.

"My clothes are too heavy for the climate. I must have new ones made."

"Tomorrow I will bring you to my tailor." His hand springs once more into life, turning and gesturing towards one of the arcade benches in the cool of the shade. "We will make some fine new clothes for you, signore. Please sit."

"I thank you."

We sit. Other notables are filing in from the courtyard door, coming from mass, taking places in the arcade and garden, talking in the Italian style: all at the same time as each other, and moving their hands around in intricate gesticulations.

Terzani's green eyes look at me as I gaze at the new world that surrounds me. "This is the first circle. The Basilica Courtyards—a place for conversation, discussion, for gossip, for news. The Second Circle . . . the front steps and hallway of the Papal Palace—a place to make appointments, to manufacture chance meetings, to accost the Cardinals' messengers and servants to request an audience. The Third Circle, the office corridors where one can meet face to face with the clerks of the Curia, the Fourth Circle, the rooms of their personal secretaries, the Fifth, audience with a Cardinal himself, the Sixth, to be heard *in camera* by a sitting of a quorum, the Seventh . . . "

"The Holy Father?"

"Oh no! The Seventh, the Holy Father's personal secretaries, the Eighth, the Holy Father himself. And the Ninth . . . "

"There is a Ninth?"

"The Ninth is to be heard by God. Or the Devil. Whichever is of more value to you."

I concede him one of my warped smiles. It's nice patter, and I am intrigued, but not yet impressed.

"Tomorrow," says Terzani, "you will be charged with murder, but do not worry."

This gets my full attention. Terzani's eyes are sparkling; he seems amused at my doubtless ashen expression. "It seems you or one of your entourage cut a child's arm, and later he died."

I am shocked. "The child died?"

Terzani shrugs. "Maybe he died, maybe he didn't, it is not relevant."

"It seems so to me."

"The point is, the child is probably running around happily, with his arm bandaged, and another child has been registered as dead, in any case, tomorrow a bailiff will come to you and charge your party with murder, and you will have to pay bail and a security, and they will set a watch over you to make sure you do not flee the city and so on and so on. Do not worry, this is just intimidation."

I try and maintain a level expression, as if this were all perfectly normal. Terzani continues volubly, his elegant hands dancing, emphasising, punctuating the flow of his beautiful Latin.

"I know officials in the Tribunal, in the courts, in the

authorities. With the right donations, the charges will be dropped."

"I understand."

"But this is just the beginning. You have walked into a trap, Treasurer, a labyrinth. And you will need a guide to help you to escape and win a victory in the case of the Dagsburg inheritance."

"And that guide would be you, I take it?"

Guido shrugs, lifts his arms to the sky in a gesture of modesty. "You are a genius, Treasurer! You see everything!"

Even though this man is doubtless a fraud, I cannot help but like him. There is charm in the way he does not attempt to hide his machinations.

"You are being . . . " and his two hands make a truly obscene gesture, "*fottuto.* Is it Metz? Or Lüttich? They both have a claim in this inheritance case. Or even the Zähringen and Habsburg families? They have a claim. Are they *furbi,* foxy enough to seek local help in Rome to *fottere* the competition?" And his hands gleefully fornicate each other once again.

"I very much doubt it."

"You underestimate your opponents?"

"They are German nobles. So am I. I know them well. This is not their *modus operandi.* Nor is it mine."

"Then it must be Metz or Lüttich. But listen, Treasurer, to the winds of politics. The whispers in the Second and Third circles . . . His Holy Father. Whom does he hate more than anyone else?"

That is an easy question. "Emperor Friedrich."

"*Bravo.* From what family is the Emperor?"

"The Staufen."

"*Bravo.* They are saying . . . the Pope, he wants to give support to a new noble family in Germany, to a new clan that can take away the strength of the Staufen. And the new clan is the Habsburg. And . . . they have a good claim in this Inheritance."

"That is interesting. But Hagenburg's case is stronger. And we too have been resistant to the Staufen. A strong Hagenburg is the greatest rock His Holy Father can rely on in the German Lands."

"A nice speech, Treasurer. But now your words fall on deaf ears. You are paying the wrong Cardinal, and not nearly enough. You need new advice, new champions. And a new bank."

The sparkle dims from his eyes, and they harden. Here it comes. "I can help you. With everything. And it won't be as expensive as you think."

† † †

The Ides of March. The Vogesen snows are melting, the Sâone will be a-swell with the thaw and will speed me to Lyon, whence via the Rhône to Arles and the sea. I am packing my things for the journey to Rome. Countess Gertrud is dead. This time it is incontestable; His Grace had his Dagsburg spy stick pins into her corpse, just to make sure.

My personal possessions are few, and are packed in a few brief moments. The Dean has given me a St. Christopher statuette for the journey. I would be touched if it were well-intended, but it is probably smeared with poison. On balance, I feel I will "forget" to take it with me.

There is one more thing I want to do before I go.

At last, a knock on the door. My Clerk Hieronymus.

"You are late. Come in."

He bows, and kisses my ring.

"Hieronymus, last year we raided a village of Cathar heretics near Honau. Some escaped, but most were captured and were burned at the stake. Very few repented their sins and returned to the Church."

"Yes, My Lord."

"I must go now. Whilst I am gone, look into the records, and see if you can find the whereabouts of the surviving converts. And go quietly to where they can be found, and ask them . . . if they know Achim von Esinbach."

Hieronymus looks up at me, surprised. And then comprehension creeps into his eyes.

"If you value your life, you will tell no-one of this."

Hieronmyus nods.

"Although the Dombaumeister is manifestly mad, the Mason's Lodge and the Bishop remain loyal to him. And so von Esinbach's extravagant, costly vision remains uncontested. But if he were a heretic . . . ?"

"I see."

"Report to me your findings by letter. Now, I am for the road."

"A safe journey, sir."

I shoulder my bag.

"Sir, you've forgotten your Saint Christopher?"

"God damn you, Hieronymus."

Mists are rising from the Ehle as we embark on the barges that will take us upriver towards Burgundy. Despite the cold, I sit on the prow and stare ahead as we creep slowly against the swell. The thick fog repaints the world as a variation in grey and shadow, a world without forms or definition.

In my mind, a day of high wind, in the reedbeds by Honau. The village of the Heretics, and amongst them, the two sisters, remarkable in their beauty. And then, some days later, at the Burning Ground, as the elder girl began to burn, Master Achim von Esinbach, raving, and calling out her name. "Odile!"

The ravings of a Madman? Or of a Lover?

The Lover of a Heretic? Or a Heretic himself?

The world of mists gives no answer. The brown waters churn and swirl, making patterns and shapes. A heron, surprised by our sudden emergence from the fog, launches upwards, disappearing in the direction of the invisible sky.

This is how journeys begin.

ANNO
1235

This is an "A"
(ANNO 1235. MANFRED GERBER V)

The Merchants' Church. Difficult to believe, but it was originally Bertle's idea. One evening a short time after Manfred Senior's murder, they were drinking in *zum thrunkenen Cahne* and Bertle slammed down his mug and said, "And if their big bastard church is too good for the likes of us then we'll build our own bloody church and go and kneel there!" And there was a short silence at the table; one of those silences in which an Angel seems to flutter past and perch on your shoulders, and Manfred looked at Günther and Günther looked at Rolo and Rolo looked at Manfred and they thought . . . *Our own bloody church?*

And that was the Idea. But an Idea is nothing without hard facts, and the hardest of all facts is Money. They spread the word over town, in the markets, in the shops, in the Ehle and Rhine harbours. A Merchants' Church, St. Niklaus, to be built with their donations, and fuck the Bishop and his Cathedral.

We are at War, his father had said. And here was Manfred's opening battle. But what fool is just going to hand over his silver to some ginger-haired idiot boat-freighter to make a church? Manfred curses himself for not listening to his father more often when he was around. He realises that building a church is not so simple. His church needs a Committee, and a Treasurer, and someone to check the Treasurer's accounts and report to the Trustees, and a Werkmeister and a Lawyer and some friends in the Council to approve the land sale and builders and workmen and donors . . . And, in the end, let's not forget. A Priest. To run the fucking place. And, in this diocese, whether Manfred and his friends like it or not, the Priest will be appointed by . . . the Bishop.

So. Best not go around shouting too loudly about this being the Fuck the Bishop Church. Manfred calls a meeting of his co-conspirators and says, *Let's just tone it down, boys. Keep that kind of thing to ourselves. We can't do anything without the right friends.* Friends in the Cathedral Chapter, in the Rathaus, in the lawyers' offices in the Schriwerstublgass, in the Counting House, the Treasury and the Guilds.

Manfred learns quickly. Every day after Prime prayers he's at the Morning Altar in the Cathedral with the other Merchants of the City. When he can he does the rounds of the shops and markets and warehouses, talks to people, gets his face seen. Everywhere he goes, Manfred makes Friends.

He's never been so busy. He wishes there were double hours in the day, that he could go somewhere, anywhere, and buy an extra Month or two, to give him the time he needs. And he spends the Hours that he does have running from one place to another. Over here to the Rathaus to draw out a parcel of land for the church, over there to the fields of flax to make a downpayment on the harvest (a favourable rate by paying half in advance! God willing, it will be a plentiful crop . . .), over here to one of his looms, over there to lick some aristocratic arse to help oil the wheels of permits and permissions, over here to bow and scrape to the Bishop's household in search of diocesan work commissions, over there to make the deal with the Saxon murderer to take revenge and kill an Inquisitor to hike his popularity amongst his peers, over here to inventorise his boat just docked in from Flanders and Cologne and over there . . . when there's blessed time . . . to see Grete and his newborn son, Manfredle.

The boy's little feet make him laugh, kicking at nothing. His tiny hand pushes and pulls at Manfred's finger. His mouth gurgles, dribbles, twists. "He smiled this morning," says Grete. "If only you'd seen it!" She throws up her hands, pulls a pretty face of pique. "I wanted to come running to find you! But I'd no idea where you were, as usual."

"At the Cathedral. How's the weaving?"

Grete snorts. "Is that all you've got to ask me?"

Grete had looked a bit put out when he brought home one of the Honau looms and told her to get to work. Maybe she'd thought that a wife's life in the Merchant Quarter would be all leisure and luxury, grapes and honey cake from silver platters. Thought she'd let her hands grow soft and ladylike, not pluck at flax, pick at carding combs and shuttle shuttles.

She felt better when two more looms made their way to her sisters' houses in Lenzenbach, and when he put her in charge of the workers, the schedules, the deliveries. Grete Gerber of the Rhine-boat Gerbers, Manageress of Delivery of Cloths and Textiles.

The Gerbers now have some twenty-one looms working for them in the city and in the villages, and out back where once the neighbours grazed their pigs, a water trough to soften the flax. Twenty-one women. When their babies are sleeping, when their husbands are sated, when the household can be left a while to its own sweet life, then they sit down to the loom and start to shuttle and weave. Tuppence ha'penny a cubit.

"Looks like you haven't done much today," says Manfred, nodding at the loom in the corner.

Grete puts Manfredle down, her face flushes apple-red. "Look you," she says. "I can't run the business, take care of you two Lordships and weave like a heretic all at the same time!" She slams her fist down on the table. She has a temper on her, his wife does. And the Devil knows she never showed it until his ring was on her lilywhite finger. "I need a bloody servant! Now! So get me one!"

Manfred picks up the nearest thing; his drinking flagon,

and throws it at the wall. Bang! It breaks. Grete flinches, even though it goes nowhere near her. Takes Manfredle in her protective arms, as if Manfred was about to hit him too. Like an accusation. Manfred loses any control he had left. "You're a LADY now, are you, you fucking bitch?"

It takes him three big cups of wine at the tavern before he can calm down. And when he's finally calm, and looks up from the dregs of the third tumbler, he's looking straight in the unforgiving eyes of Wolfram of Basel.

"You're back," Manfred says, faintly.

Wolfram says nothing. Rather than be taken by the Inquisitors, he disappeared, leaving his brother to run his boats from Basel.

Absence hasn't helped his business. Manfred's taken over five of his accounts.

Wolfram. Glaring at him. "Was it you, you bastard?" he growls.

Manfred checks. Wolfram is armed. A long dagger at his belt. Weak words crowd the back of his throat: *What me? What are you talking about? Ha ha ha the very thought of it . . .*

He throws them away. Stands. "And was it *you* who named *our* names?"

Wolfram stands too. But he's hardly three cubits high, the midget. "So it was you?"

"No. Was it you?"

"No."

Two Freightsmen, between them they hold the Hagenburg Rhineboat trade. Wolfram has twelve boats, Manfred is just building a fourth. Staring at each other, looking for a lie in the corner of the eyes.

Wolfram blinks first. But his hand is still on the pommel of his dagger. "So who was it, Gerber?"

Manfred swallows. "I don't know." He finishes the dregs of his cheap tavern wine; a mouthful of sediment. "You lost some trade, Wolfram. I'm sorry. But I lost my father. Someone told lies about us. And when I find them . . . " Manfred falters. "Someone told lies about us. But it was the Church that gave us false trial. And the City that lit the fire. Think about it that way. It helps."

† † †

In times of war, moments of peace are precious. Before the Angelus bell softly tolls, bidding all to hearth and supper, Manfred leaves the tavern, checks his purse for pennies, and knocks on the Stationer's door in the Schriwerstublgass.

Coming home, their anger still rings in the air, a buzzing of flies trapped in by the window shutters. The shattered tankard is still on the floor, left as a sign. Grete sits in twilight, far from the lantern that hangs by Manfredle's crib.

Silence as Manfred opens his satchel, places parchment, ink and a quill on the table. The dim light catches in Grete's eyes, the trace of a smile.

"Come, bring that lantern over here," he says softly, and is relieved to see that she obeys. Without a word she places the light on the table, and pulls up her stool, ready. He sits beside her.

"This is an A," he says, and dips the quill in ink, and draws the letter, simple and bold. "A is for Apple, for Aaaaaaachen, for . . . ."

"Aaarsehole?" says Grete, with an arched eyebrow.

"Don't start," says Manfred, raising a warning finger, but unable to hold back a smile. "And this . . . " his pen strokes upwards, downwards, in two generous curves, "is a B. B is for Bishop. B is for Bertle. B is for—?"

"Bastard."

"Bitch."

Grete laughs. This is more enjoyable than he'd feared. For

weeks she's been nagging him, and he always finding excuses. Ink and parchment are expensive. He was a bad student, so he'll be a bad teacher. Where can he find the time?

"Now you try. Hold the quill like this." He shows her.

He hated study. He envied the porters' boys who'd spend their summer evenings by the banks of the Ehle whilst he, Bertle and Rolo, a fraternity of resentment, sat at lecterns in the cold presbytery with Father Bernard. Reading, Writing, Arithmetic and Latin as the hours of play drained away into dusk. A torture paid for by their families' shillings, and their poor progress rewarded in beatings by the teacher's switch and their fathers' belts.

Those evening-golden hours of play are long lost and will never come again. Now, in this time of war, in soft lanternlight, Grete's hand wobbles over the page, the nib splutters speckles of ink, turns, curves and comes to rest.

An A. Her first A.

Manfred gives her a look of congratulation, trying not to be patronising. It doesn't work.

A further gesture of peace. A generous olive branch.

"I'll ask about a servant in the morning."

Grete smiles.

"Now clear up that mess there and we'll move on to B and C."

Grete's smile fades. But she's still happy.

† † †

The woodshed is at the back of the house, beyond the trough that they now use for softening flax. In summer, it is concealed from prying eyes by the old apple tree's spreading arms. A secret place.

The maidservant Elise seems to know what's expected of her, and doesn't put up any resistance. Turns her back to him and leans on the woodpile, lets him lift her skirts. A few summers younger than Grete, a perfect peach. Manfred knows she's been "broken in" before, but this is his first try-out. He'd taken her off Gaufried's hands when Frau Gaufried had walked in on her husband giving it to her in the storeroom up against a five-gallon barrel of Molsheimer. "Real honeysuckle, this one," lisped Gaufried in Manfred's ear, "you won't find better . . . "

Manfred's waited what seemed an eternity for Grete to leave Hagenburg to check on the village weavers. But now she's gone, and Elise's beautiful buttocks are in his hands as he takes his time with her, sliding it in and out, hard and fast a while, then soft and slow. She doesn't seem to mind.

A strange fish, Elise. Quiet, diligent, obedient. Pretty, auburn hair, petite body, chirpy bright face. But haunted, accusing eyes. They follow you wherever you go, those dark brown, even reddish eyes. If you look up from the dining table, she's in her corner like a barn cat, watching you. Come in from the outhouse, she's sweeping the floor, her hands flick the broom sightlessly, her eyes are on you. As if she's recording everything for some later reckoning.

But then speak to her, and her voice is meek, obedient, calm. "Yes, Master, straight away, Master." Every morning at dawn, she's first into St. Stefan's church. Two years of shaven-headed contrition in a Vogesen nunnery has put the fear of God into her, and she prays four times a day. After mass, she slips quietly back and sweeps the house, then sits to the loom and shuttles like there's no tomorrow. There's no faster weaver than Elise. And she knows flax, hemp and wool like a Flemish Draper. Her father taught her well.

When Grete summons her, she comes quietly and immediately. Elise is tender with the boy, her mournful face breaking out into smiles as he gurgles and sings. And when he's moody, she will rock him in her arms, whispering lullabies in the dialect of the Northern Rhine, lays she learned as an itinerant child on the River Road. And she has Letters. In the afternoon, as Manfredle sleeps, she and the Mistress sit to the dining table with pen and ink, and Elise helps the Mistress to write and do arithmetic. And now Manfred has bought them a ragged, faint, seventh-hand copy of the first parts of *Tristan*, and they read that together and giggle, and wipe girlish tears from their eyes.

Manfred feels it coming, can't hold it back any longer, pulls himself out of her, groans and shoots his seed onto her thighs. There'll be no bastards in the Gerber house, as long as he can help it. Panting, he sinks back down onto the chopping block. Elise's breaths subside. Her skirts slide down around her ankles. Saying nothing, she returns to the house. From the shed, he can hear her pouring out water to wash.

He tries to think of the first time he saw her.

A day of high wind, the raid on the hamlet near Honau. Cantering into the village and seeing the flames, and the Virgin burning, charred and black. And all around, the heretics screaming defiance, scorn. Her father and her beautiful sister, now both burned to ash. And she somewhere in that baying crowd, intent on damnation.

† † †

Manfred is checking cloth samples in the sunlight when there's a loud knocking from the street outside. A fist pounding his door like on the dawn of his arrest. Not a neighbour. Not a tradesman—they know to stand by the doorway and call out the Gerbers' names. The knock of a stranger. Manfred rushes inside.

Coming in from the bright light of the backyard, the hallway is plunged in thick greenish shadow. "There's someone at the door, Master," comes Elise's soft, faintly accented voice.

"Well answer it," says Manfred, rubbing his eyes, still dazzled by the sun.

The door opens, sending a jagged diagonal burst of light into the hallway. A tall, black silhouette stands in the threshold.

Manfred's eyes adjust, see commanding eyes, sun-browned skin, a large silver cross.

Treasurer-Bastard.

"My Lord, I thought you were in Rome?" says Manfred, confused by conjecture. *What can this visit be about?* Fear pumps at the valves of his heart. The murder of Dorso? The pilfering of Cathedral bequests for their new church of St. Niklaus?

"I am, as you can see, returned from Rome, Gerber."

Manfred swallows, ready to run. From the woodpile he can jump to the cesspits and through the drain to the Ehle. He wouldn't be the first fugitive to fetch up at the Rhine Harbour soaked in shit and river water. "What can I do for you, my Lord?" he asks, and his voice trembles.

"It is not you I have come to see, Gerber," says von Zabern, and fixes his sharp eyes upon him. "Though I hear that we would have plenty to talk about. Your name seems to crop up with a dispiriting frequency these days."

Manfred feels something unfamiliar rise in him, dispelling his fear. It is pride. "If it is not me you've come to see . . . .? My wife is at market . . . " His confidence ebbs as uncertainty once more comes over him. Von Zabern's eyes probe the shadows of the hallway, find the flexuous petite figure silhouetted in the back room threshold. The Treasurer speaks softly, as if to an infant, or a fool. "I have come to see little Elise." And his finger points out to her. "Is that she?"

† † †

Grete comes home to find her husband with his ear pressed to the back room door. He gestures frantically to her to be quiet.

She, perplexed, obeys. Why does a man eavesdrop in his own house? And to whom? To the maidservant talking with his baby son? She slips off her clogs, tiptoes to join him at the door. A cheeky, quizzical look to her husband, and then she crouches to listen too.

Manfred blushes at the thought. That he invited a von Zabern into his own home, allowed him to sit at his table, interview his servant, drink his wine, sit in his chair, whilst They, the Master and the Mistress of the House, crouch eavesdropping in the hallway like a valet and maid.

And he came there many times?

Not many, no, My Lord, just twice or thrice

And why did he come?

My Lord, to see my sister

Your sister? Why?

He wanted to marry her, My Lord

Grete looks at Manfred: *What? Who?*

Manfred makes her a face: keep quiet, or else . . .

Where did they plan to get married?

I don't know.

In a church?

I don't know.

But they had different religions, did they not? von Esinbach was a Christian. And your family . . . Cathars.

But now I am a Christian, My Lord.

I know, my dear. And as a Good Christian, I want you to tell me. Was Achim von Esinbach a believer in your religion?

No, my Lord.

Are you sure? But he was going to marry your sister Odile . . . ?

A bitter silence. Sound of von Zabern's expiration, the shuffling of his feet. And then he is still again. The silence spreads, black and cold like ditchwater.

In his mind's eye, Manfred sees the Treasurer's eyes burning across the silence. He sees Elise look down in fear and then look up again to face that probing gaze. A gaze that says, *tell me what I need to hear.*

Elise' voice is soft. Tears catch at the edges of her words.

But he said he would consider . . . to convert. He wanted to marry Odile so much. He said he might leave the Church.

† † †

Arses in moonlight. Pale globes emerging from the Rhine's dark surface. Three of them swimming, showing off. Manfred treads water, the cold river flowing around his naked body.

The musicians play. Flute and drum. Lindalisa yelps and sings, slaps her big thighs. *Mir han nen Bischofen, nen Narrenbischofen nen Dreckbischofen, habemus Arschepissco-popum! . . . a foolbishop a filthbishop, we have a new Arsebishop!* Song from the Feast of Fools, when they crown the town idiot in the Bishop's mitre, make a beggar the Mayor, make a cripple Emperor. The joys of an upside down world celebrated for that one dark, midwinter day.

But now it's the first warm night of spring, and the party has staggered out of the *zum thrunkenen Cahne* and onto the quay. "Be quiet, you damn idiots!" shouts a desperate trader from his sleepless room. But tonight the night belongs to the young merchants of the Morning Altar, and there won't be sleep till dawn.

The source of their unexpected joy has already left them to his quarters above the Cloth Exchange, where all the wealthier Latins stay. His name is Renzo, a collecting agent for the Pope and Curia, who spends his life drifting through the German lands and escorting consignments of wool, wine and silver to his Roman masters.

And tonight he brought them the news from Rome. Not news that will be shared with the citizens of Hagenburg, for

Uto will not cry the Bishop's ruin. And in one breath, the news is: Treasurer-Bastard got his arse fucked in Rome.

And how they fucked him! "*He bend over so nice for us!*" exclaims Renzo, pinching his thumb and forefinger together in a Florentine expression of delectability. "*A little plum . . . .*"

Renzo switches between faulty, accented Rhenish German and racy Tuscanised Latin. Difficult to follow at times, but always flavoursome, spicy. *The Terzani family they reeeeeel him in like a fishy, they give him a slicey, they gutting him good, sprinkle some timo here some rosmarino, they eat him all up and cacca him out into the sewer. Nearly two thousand marche they gutting him! And for what? For zero, zilcha, nihil, nix. Salute!*

Renzo downs a glass of Dietzheimer. He's bought a whole keg for the table, and has his own beautiful Venetian wineglass, with a delicate, rose-coloured stem.

I see him today to collect my annual tribute. Normally he try some chitty-chatty, some how is Holy Father and this and thatty, but today he look how you say . . . constipato. Like he wait for ten days to shit. He say nothing. Just: "Herr Renzo." Renzo's face contorts into the grave, constipated face of Treasurer von Zabern. His voice drops to an Alsatian bass, sober and sombre. The assembled Morning Altar merchants dissolve into hysterics. Their noses are flowering, rose and maroon. "Herr Renzo. This year I give you only sicteen barrel."

Only sicteen, Signore Treasurato? But what will I say to Big Pappa?

The booming, von Zabern voice again: Say what you like. It is sicteen barrels this year.

He is a bit angry, isn't it true? Like little boy he is shaking his little fist at Big Pappa. We'll see, we'll see.

The Terzani, they are clever. They do everything right for Treasurer, for Haggenburgo. They take his money, they bribe the right officials, they give Vonnalazzabberna the right contacts, they bring him two new Cardinali to be friends of Haggenburgo,

*they do everything so nicely, and Vonnalazzabberna is paying
and paying and paying.*

Just one thing they do not tell him.

"And what's that?"

*That the Dagsburgo decision has already been made. Three
years before.*

Laughter falls like confetti, spring blossom. The Germans
slam their tankards down, turn the spigot, fill with wine.

*And everyone knows it, apart from Lazzabberna! Pappa is no
fool, he is a Conti from Agnani, they are all banditi. For years he
pretend he make no decision, and so all you German sheephead
cretini, you throwing money at him, at the Cardinali, from
Aaggenburgo, from Metzi, from Liodium, from the Absburgi, the
Zerringhi, o you German names are too hard, I am drinking
again, salute!*

Cheers as another glass is downed. Renzo's fine little glass
wouldn't drown a mouse, and even after five toasts, he's still
sober enough. The Alsatians, however, who each time down a
sizable tumbler . . . their world is sliding into fug, fog and nonsense.

*All you tedeschi-germanichi-cretini keep on throwing your
money at the banditi from Agnani, gold and silver, for years and
years, and all the time the Pappa knows what he will do anyway
with Daggasburga inheritance, with all those lands and those
castles, all that mud and forest and pigs.*

"And so what was it? The decision?"

*He divide it equally between the parties! Why should he do
different? He wants to make no enemy! Just a bit extra he give
the Habbasburghi, because he want them to go and fukka the
Staufani.*

Renzo shrugs, raises his glass again. *Congratulations,
Aggenburgo! You now have new lands in the Vosgesi, new cold
freezing castles, new fields of mud, new piggies! But it has cost
you so much, more than it is worth. And your Bishop, so rich, is*

now so poor. And the Terzani fuck Treasurato so nicely. Like a nice ripe fruit! Salute!

Cheers! The Dietzenheimer flows.

It all fits together.

Manfred stumbles outside to the warm spring evening. Lanterns hang from ropes along the quay, pools of light glow from barges where boatmen are hanging their hammocks for the night. The lights are broken in the water's surface. Damp, fragrant air, the resurgence of spring.

It all fits together. Treasurer-Fucker's visit to his house, the questioning of Elise. To brand Dombaumeister Achim a heretic and halt the work, cut the workforce, save money. Von Zabern, badly bruised from his arsefucking in Rome, comes back to take revenge on the thing he hates the most, the biggest drain on his funds. The Cathedral.

It all fits together. Manfred must meet with the other merchants tomorrow. They will need cash. Silver you can bite on and break your teeth. Soon. As soon as the Cathedral masons are laid off, and in shock. Then offer them a helping hand, employment building the new Merchants' Church. At half the price.

Manfred turns his head to the heavens. Stars are faint behind a warm veil of cloud and riverine mist. But they are there, dim, half-seen, promising the granting of wishes. Did I really deserve this Good Fortune? he asks the stars, his father's ghost, that distant, unseen God. Did I?

Shouting. The door bursts open and the drunken rabble of his friends flops onto the wooden boards of the quay. Friedel the Draper's already ripping his trousers off, and Hagar's leading out the band and Lisalinda the whore to sing.

Shirts, socks and hose thrown to the quay. Screeches, abandon. Hands pull at Manfred's laces. "Come on you ginger bastard, you can swim."

Is there any point in resistance?

THE MINOTAUR
(ANNO 1235. RETTICH SCHÄFFER V)

A day of high wind, coursing downriver from the Aargau, carries with it the scent of new life. On the washing lines the shapes of human bodies sketched in hose and blouse, smock and tunic, quiver, flutter. It is a day of hurry, of action. No-one can sleep or tarry whilst the air itself is agitation, invigoration and dance.

On the steps of the Tollhouse, Uto rings his bell. The scattered townsfolk, hurrying through the whirling winds, race to form an audience. Uto himself is crying today, not one of his boys. It means that something important may have happened.

Uto's apprentices and helpers stand behind him on the stairs. They will learn his cry, and then take it to the parishes; to St. Stefan's and St. Lorenz, to the shacks of the poor by the Rhine Gate, to the merchants' huts and the warehouses of the harbour, to the tall, fine gabled houses by the Bishop's Palace. And from these places, the passing carters, beggars and wandering monks will take the news into the fields, to the villages, to the distant cities beyond the horizon.

Uto's bell comes to rest, he cups its ringing bowl in his sausage fingers.

"Honoured people, hear me!" he bellows from the top of the stairs, "Citizens, gather and hear me!"

Passing the three-pound bell to his Boy, his hands now free, he strikes a pose. One hand on his ample stomach, one raised aloft. The news will be tragic, dramatic, of portent.

"The word comes from Wimpfen, beyond the Black Forest,

that King Heinrich has accepted defeat from his father's hands. He has knelt before Emperor Friedrich, his father, he has bowed his head, he has been stripped of his crown. Citizens of Hagenburg, behold the price of rebellion against one's own father! King Heinrich is King no longer, he is a prisoner. He will be conveyed from his German Lands to a fortress in the far south beyond the mountains. He will face shame and ignominy. The traitor's treachery has been punished. Amen.

"Citizens, Emperor Friedrich's second son, by Yolande of Jerusalem, has been named as the new King of the Germans. He is already King of Jerusalem, his name is Konrad, a good German name! And hear this, he is six summers old!"

The townsfolk laugh at the idea of their new minuscule King. Their new sovereign, with his wooden sword, his play-things, his big crown falling from his golden head.

Rettich sees a picture in his mind of the King of Jerusalem, now King of the Germans. A flax-haired boy, riding upon a Lamb. In his upraised arm, a banner, carrying a flag announcing the coming of Christ. Rettich closes his eyes, smiles, feels the sun on his hair, feels the buffeting winds on his cheeks.

"Hagenburgers! Bid welcome to a citizen of promise, of integrity, of honour! I give to you Reichart, known as Rettich! Rettich Schäffer, formerly of Lenzenbach, Honourable Companion of the Guild of Stone-cutters! Present yourself, Companion Rettich!"

Rettich, laughing with embarrassment, mounts the last few steps, with his wife Ällin's arm crooked in his, to the applause of the crowd.

"Five years ago, my ladies, my gentlemen, Rettich came from the hills to pay his tithes. Arriving at the Cathedral, he walked up to the Masons and asked them 'Pray tell, where is the Bishop? I need to give him my taxes!'"

The crowd dissolves in laughter.

† † †

Happy day. Companion Rettich, Ällin, already with child, Grete, Manfred and their baby son Manfredle, Emmerich, now fully grown, tall, bearded and wrapped in a cloak trimmed with fine red squirrel fur, Mechthild and Amaline, their husbands and children. All ranged round the Gerber hearth, with roast lamb, lentils and red Burgundy wine.

The last time they had gathered together had been his wedding day, last summer. A modest gathering, bakers and stonecutters, masons and millers. Wine and dancing, a flute and drum. A wedding jester, with new, feeble jokes for the occasion. *If the Schäffers fall on hard times, they can always sell their children's hair to their in-laws! Will Ällin soon have a loaf in her oven? Can she keep it warm nine moons long?*

That eve, in their bedchamber in the boarding house on the Steinmetzgass, they come together in coy twilight. By the light of seven candles, Ällin disrobes for him. Slowly. One garment at a time. Her milky body blooms pale in the dark room. The air is fragrant with plum blossom scattered by the bridesmaids.

Rettich's freckled cheeks are blushing with shame. She takes his hands, lifts his bridegroom's smock.

Shy and trembling, they are in each other's arms, they are lying together.

Rettich never went with Emmle to the Women's House beyond the city walls. He knows little of what to do. But Ällin has taken whispered lessons from her friends, her aunts and confidantes. She reaches between Rettich's legs, and he gasps. She rubs and pulls, like milking a cow, her hands damp with sweat and ardour. Rettich closes his eyes, lets his body respond. Eyes still unseeing, he is pulled on top of his young, panting wife, and she guides him inside her.

"Push," she whispers. "Push, my love."

He has seen the rams, the bulls, the billy goats, he knows

what he should do. He pushes, her maidenhead tears, gives way. She gasps. He falls inside. Groans with sudden joy.

He lays his shameful head against her neck, and they writhe and rock together, sweat and moan.

They are husband and wife.

† † †

Eugenius von Zabern, the Bishop's Treasurer, his face still bronzed from his year in Rome, stands upon a block of sandstone and tells them the news they already feared. Last year, the workforce was cut by one in five. Now there is a further cut: one in four. The plans of Dombaumeister Achim von Esinbach will be frozen. Evidence has arisen that he was a heretic, that he was in the cult of the Cathars of Honau. His plans must be investigated by the Chapter to see if they contain secret heretical influence.

Meanwhile a more modest building plan will be drafted. A new Dombaumeister will be found. Thank you for listening. Get back to work.

Sullen faces and scowls. The porters and apprentices kick at loose stones. "Lose one in four of your pension's gold marks!" shouts a Mason at von Zabern's back as he strides away towards his counting house. "Lose one in four of your banquets. One in four of your palfreys. One in four of your silver plates!"

The Treasurer doesn't turn. A Judas in black and silver, with his heavy cross, his boots of Cordoban leather, he rounds the corner of the Apse wall without a word.

Waiting nearby, Rettich's brother in law, Manfred, wearing a grim smile.

"Don't be downhearted, my friends!" he shouts to the milling, grumbling labourers. "Our new church of St. Niklaus needs working hands! I will take two dozen after the

Annunciation Fair! We pay nearly as well as the Bishop. And our soup is better."

Nearly as well? They pay only just over half. The porters, carters, mortarers rush to Manfred, calling out their names.

In the Lodge, Rettich looks to his Master Giselbert, who nods reassuringly. Rettich's position is safe. It would be cruelty indeed to lay him off now, only one Sunday before his Companionship, with his first child on the way.

Shadows in the Lodge doorway. The Treasurer's soldiers, the Treasurer's Clerks. "We're taking von Esinbach's drawings for examination."

Brother Alenard stands, holds up his hand, demanding pause. "Tell me this. If this is a matter of suspected heresy, why is it the *Treasury* that is running things?"

Clerk Hieronymus arches an eyebrow. "It is we who uncovered von Esinbach's connections with the weavers of Honau. We will pass materials to the correct authorities once we have collected them all. Until then they shall be in our safekeeping. Proceed."

He waves his hand, a gesture of power, borrowed from his overlord von Zabern. The soldiers clatter into the lodge, steel-capped boots on the worn wooden floor, and start to tear all the technical drawings down. And Rettich gives thanks to the Lord that he had taken all the other designs, the ones secreted in the "escritoire," and brought them to safety in Monastery Avenheim.

† † †

The roads are full of peasants and tradesmen, making their way to Hagenburg for the Annunciation Fair. Girls in bright kerchiefs ride on the back of oxcarts, farmers bent double under wicker baskets carry cured hams and sausages from the winter's slaughtered swine. Laughter, chatter and expectation throng the well-trodden roads to the Vogesen passes, newly opened by the thaw. Rettich is one of the few riding westwards, rising away from the greening valley.

The monastery buildings squat on empty, muddy fields, snakes of mist curl around the silent belltower. Rettich dismounts and knocks on the door. He waits.

The gateway arch is made from Kronthaler sandstone—he recognises it immediately; the quarry of his first apprenticeship, five years before. His hand reaches out, smoothes the damp stone, stained by fine films of rain now drifting from the hills. In the corner of the stone, the Steinmetz has made his mark: ⩒. Soon, Rettich must choose his own signature to carve in the stones he works. His fingers feel the grooves cut by the chisel in practised, familiar blows . . .

"Who's there?" comes the voice from the silence beyond the door.

"I've come to visit Master Achim."

The gatekeeper opens the spyhole, looks at him darkly. "I've been told to record the names of those who visit him."

"You know who I am. I've been here often enough."

Achim is in his cell. A board for a bed, a basin, a lectern, a stool. His eyes are dim today, it seems that maybe he has been weeping. He embraces Rettich, gives him the kiss of peace, says nothing.

Rettich sits beside him on the board, holds his hand. Sometimes they have sat like this whilst the Hours pass by, from Sext to Nones, without saying a word. Outside, silence creeps the corridors, the window frame judders softly, buffeted by the uncertain wind.

Rettich breaks the silence. "By Sunday I will be a Companion! If God is willing . . . "

Achim turns to look at Rettich. His eyes are sad, but he tries a smile. Rettich grasps his hand more firmly.

"Master, I promise I will do what I can to protect you. To protect your work."

Achim's shoulders form the shadow of a shrug.

"Your humours are imbalanced, an evil planet is working on you. You will recover and we will prove that what you saw came from God. I know it."

Achim faintly shakes his head.

"Master, I need to take the drawings, all the drawings that I brought here to you. They will be safer with me. If those vultures find them here, they will impound them and see what they choose to see, I need to keep them safe until we can find a Champion for you, someone to stand up for you, someone on the Chapter, I don't know, the Dean, the Pope, God himself, the Stettmeister, the Count of Habsburg . . . "

Achim holds up his hand, smiling at Rettich's gabbling.

"So, Master, where are they? Your drawings? The ones I brought. From the escri, the escrit, from the box thing?"

Master Achim's smile fades. "Rettich." His voice croaks, rasps, like a leper's.

"Master?"

"I burned them."

"Burned them! God in Heaven, what a sin! All of them?"

"Except the Rose. The Rose I kept . . . And I hid it well."

† † †

He can still see them in his mind's eye.

So many times, alone in the Lodge, he has gazed on them. Sometimes, together with the Master, when his mind was whole, he has studied them. The statues of the Prophets, rising from the deserts, wild-haired, right hand uplifted to God, eyes upraised, receiving visions. The Girl, Adoration, her ivory hand held in offering. He has seen them all, and remembers them, penstroke for penstroke.

Tears film his eyes as he leads his weary donkey home. Burned them?

He can re-draw them. His hand is not like his Master's, but it will be a start. And then he can show them to him, and as sure as God is Good, Achim will smile censoriously, pick up his pen once more, and correct Rettich's uncertain work. His Cathedral will be born again.

The donkey stalls, kicks the ground, reaching for the grass by the wayside. Dusk is gathering early on this damp and sombre day. Not for the first time, Rettich wants to run. He wants to run back to the hills of Lenzenbach, and back into the past. He wants, one more time, to be a Shepherd Boy, lazy in sunlight, little Lord of his gentle flock, knowing nothing but sheep and the childish woodcarving of his dreams . . .

But the road he is on leads to Hagenburg, and the Vogesen Gate. It leads through the narrow streets behind the Judengasse, across the stinking Fish Market, then through the warren of lanes in the Cathedral's shadow, to the Treasury.

Rettich stands before the Treasury in the last glimmer of dusk. No light comes from its three windows. No guards stand by. All coin has been taken to the Pfennigplatz counting house for the holidays.

Distant, the sound of music, dancing. The fair continues in the Cathedral Square. Screams of laughter, last year's wine, newly breached. The coming of Spring.

From his belt, Rettich takes his chisel. "Hello?" he calls out.

In the courtyard, nothing moves. The Kronthaler sandstone of the Treasury stares blankly at the lone Apprentice. The oiled muslin windows like dull eyes, seeing nothing.

Rettich slides the blade of the chisel in the gap. Near the lock.

"God forgive me," he says, hoping that God will hear him.

A wrench of the chisel, a splintering. Rettich looks. It will take some work. But this door will open.

† † †

His Master's eyes are moist with joy. "Rettich! You are a miracle." The sketches slide through his delicate fingers; prophets, angels, gargoyles, Christ.

"My hand is nothing like yours, Master." Rettich kneels beside him in the cell in Avenheim. April raindrops gather on the windowpanes. "And I have only just begun to replace the drawings that are lost."

"Sssh, Rettichlein. The miracle is that you have remembered well what I have preferred to forget. And that is what touches me."

"I'm glad, Master. And you seem so well."

"I do feel better."

"Soon you can start work again."

"I do not think so. I am accused. They are pressuring me to confess to heresy."

"But they have no case."

Achim looks up from Rettich's drawings of the Western Façade, sketched from memory; the statues for the portals, the sweep and symmetry of its rising forms. "Thank you, my friend." He looks at the young Companion, and hands back to him the drawings. "And you had better keep these too, lest I burn them again!"

"Master? Would you . . . would you burn them again?"

Achim's face darkens. "I do not know what I will do."

Rettich takes his Master's hands, "You will escape, My Lord. You will rise from the darkness.

Achim looks to the floor. "I am not so sure.

"But Rettichlein," Achim says, shyly, and looks up, smiling. "There is something you could do for me."

"Yes, Master?"

Achim is embarrassed. "Would you delouse me?" His eyebrow arches, recognising the oddness of the request. "It's been weeks, and no-one here will touch me."

But Rettich is delighted. He stands, gestures. "To the window, Master. I'll see better there."

Achim pulls a stool to the window, where a grey light filters through the droplets of rain. Rettich, at the edge of the bed, takes his Master's head in his hands, a trophy. "I am a champion delouser," he says, and runs his fingers through Achim's fine long chestnut hair. "At home in Lenzenbach, I would do the whole village. And after them, I'd start on delousing the dogs. Do you know what the Lenzenbachers used to say?"

Achim shakes his head.

"*That Rettich, he could delouse a louse* . . . Funny thing to say of course. Do you think lice have lice? Really tiny ones? I hope they do. 'Twould be a kind of justice wouldn't it?"

"It would."

Rettich shakes his head, decides to be quiet. He is gabbling again. And he realises, with a pinch of sadness somewhere within, that he doesn't really talk like that anymore. At the Site, at home with Ällin, he is serious, a man of few, well-chosen words. A Companion of the Guild of Stone-cutters. The Man of the House.

Only with Achim can he be how he used to be, a boy with a chattering tongue in his head.

But for now, meditative quiet. The rain falls, Rettich's hands do their work, Achim stays still, watching the muddy horizon vanish under veils of grey. Lice crushed by Rettich's nail drop on the windowsill, on the dappled stone. Gently, methodically, Rettich moves on, from tress to tress.

"I am happy, Master."

"Then so am I."

And that's how he'll remember him, his Master Achim. His face turned to the window streaked with rain. A faint smile on his lips, and his hair in Rettich's supple, chisel-calloused hands.

† † †

"Daedalus was his name. He was the greatest builder of his time. He lived in Crete, an island in the hot seas beyond the mountains. The Queen of Crete was known as Pasiphae, and she mated with a white bull, and gave birth to a monster which was half man, half animal."

God preserve us.

"That monster was known as the Minotaur."

The night of Rettich's initiation. The seven Masters have led him here, to the Cathedral Crypt, in darkness.

Each of them carried a lantern before them, and now the seven lanterns burn on the slab of white marble. Rettich is kneeling on the cold flagstones. Around him the tombs of Bishops and Lords, their names carved in stone. One of the graves is open, awaiting the day of Bishop Berthold's death, when God will gather him.

The Seven Masters stand above him, behind the altar-like slab. Alenard is speaking, quietly, so as not to disturb the dead.

"The Minotaur was a terrible creature, but of royal birth. Queen Pasiphae did not allow him to be killed. But he needed to be contained.

"So Daedalus, great master builder, constructed a Labyrinth to hide the monster in. A building of corridors, stairs, chambers, a maze of such intricacy that the monster, the Minotaur, could never escape."

Alenard falls silent. For long moments, no-one speaks. The Cathedral hulks above them, unseen but felt. Its grandeur, its centuries.

"We are the children of the Master Builder Daedalus, Apprentice Rettich. God be praised, we live in Christian times. We seek salvation. Through virtue, through good works.

"We have no monsters, no Half Men. No Minotaur.

"But we are constructors of Labyrinths. We work together,

Masons, Stone-cutters, Carpenters, Ropemakers, Mortarers, Blacksmiths, Painters, to create something where all pieces interconnect, hold each other, raise each other. All our work unites to form a whole, a Unity, for the Glory of God.

"And in our Labyrinths, we have a monster to contain. To defeat.

"So we have brought you here, Apprentice Rettich, to ask you this question. Here, in the foundations, beneath our building, beneath our work, the labour of our hands. The question. What is the monster that we must contain, imprison, defeat?

"What is the Minotaur?"

Seven pairs of eyes look down upon the kneeling Apprentice. He knows the answer. Nevertheless he trembles as he speaks.

"It is Weight."

The Masters nod.

Alenard speaks again. "We are a brotherhood, and we work for each other." He smiles, wry, cunning. "If for instance, an *Apprentice* were to break into the Treasury and steal some documents, some technical drawings and plans, he would have to be reported and reprimanded."

Rettich swallows. But his Master Giselbert is smiling.

Alenard continues. "Yet if a *Companion* were to do such a thing, then we would keep our silence. We would assume that the Honourable Companion would have had his reasons, and that would be sufficient for us. But be warned, Schäffer. Never bring our Lodge into disrepute."

Rettich looks up, contrite, accepting. Alenard nods gently. One by one, the Masters take their lanterns in their hands. Only Master Giselbert's remains upon the cold white stone.

"We will leave you now, Apprentice Rettich. You have one lantern. Long before morning comes, the oil will run out, the flame will extinguish, and you will be alone in darkness.

"Face all your Devils now, Rettich. In the morning, when

you hear Lauds, you will rise from the Crypt, like once our Lord Jesus Christ.

"And we will welcome you in our brotherhood.

"Until then, we wish you peace."

They file out, almost soundlessly. Their boots scuff and hiss on the stairs.

The sound of the Crypt door, creaking on its hinges, closing. The Key in the lock, turning.

Rettich, kneeling, offers a prayer to God, *Preserve me, my Lord, preserve me.*

He is alone.

He prostrates himself before the Light. *Let me serve you well, my Lord. Save my Master Achim from the demons that torture him, save him from doubt, show yourself to him, so that he can know you again. Let him return to this holy work, let us build a church in your praise, in image of your greatness. The work of my hands is offered to you, My Lord. Amen.*

Dreams and nightmares crowd the backs of his eyes, waiting to be born. He thinks of what Achim told him. That God was a corpse. That there was no God, that this world was a dream, this world was a labyrinth from which the only escape was death.

He kneels again, holds his hands together, bows his head. Devotion. Silence. The trackless time passes, counted only in the dwindling flickers of the flame. He prays, repeating all the good, godly words he knows, again and again, crowding away the thoughts that come from the Devil and from Darkness.

And then the light gutters. Hisses. Extinguishes.

Black.

Rettich raises his head, he twists it from side to side, but all Looking is futile. This is a darkness complete, without flaw or blemish. A void.

And Rettich thinks to himself. This is the Absence. This is

the Absence, this is the Nothing from which God created the World. This is the starting point. The blank page.

But, he thinks to himself, it is not empty.

I am Here.

There will be light. The door will open, and Companion Rettich will climb the stairs to the dawn.

It won't be long.

I, Rettich, am here. And so is God.

Even though it is meaningless to do so, Rettich looks up. His gaze, eyeless, bleak and born of Nothing, reaches upwards through the void. It rises through the arches of the crypt, through the stone, into the Crossing, into the dome above, into the starless sky.

All around him he senses the Cathedral. He sees nothing, but he can sense it is there. Its hundredweights, its thousandweights, its millionweights. Stone, interwoven, layer upon layer by the labour of hands. Reaching upwards to an unseen but yearned-for God.

And trapping the terrible force that pulls it ever downwards.

END OF BOOK ONE

BOOK TWO
THE SWORD
(1241–1255)

BOOK TWO
THE SWORD
(1241–1255)

I: THE WAXEN HEART
(ANNO 1241. EINOLF I)
*

II: INNOCENCE
(ANNO 1241. RETTICH SCHÄFFER VI)
*

III: THE PAVILION
(ANNO 1241. GRETE GERBER II)
*

IV: SCHWANENSTEIN
(ANNO 1242. BARON VOLMAR VON KRONTHAL I)
*

V: LAMPBLACK
(ANNO 5002. YUDL BEN YITZHAK ROSHEIMER I)
*

VI: THE RISE OF MAMMON
(ANNO 1242. EUGENIUS VON ZABERN V)
*

VII: FEAST OF FOOLS
(ANNO 1243. MANFRED GERBER VI)
*

VIII: THE CROWNED SHADOW
(ANNO 1243. EUGENIUS VON ZABERN VI)
*

IX: FOUR SACKS OF TURNIPS, TWO POUNDS OF RICE
(ANNO 1243. MANFRED GERBER VII)
*

X: ABOMINATION
(ANNO 5003. YUDL BEN YITZHAK ROSHEIMER II)

*

ANNO
1241

The Waxen Heart
(anno 1241. Einolf I)

A nd then what happened?"
Between his feet, crushed lilacs and river rushes.
"Look up, Boy. Tell us."

Tears haze his eyes and blur the flames of torches held in pages' hands.

"Be gentle with him, My Lord," the Countess' voice whispers, hardly heard above the hiss and creak of the hearth. Outside, hounds howl at a dirty moon, servants' clogs clatter across the broad courtyard flagstones. Inside, smoke stings the young Boy's eyes. He looks up. Teardrops snail-silver his cheeks, snot clots his nostrils. The Count of Schwanenstein, tall, bald, face of a hunting Black Kite, looks at him. Attempts a milder tone. "Boy. What's your name?"

"Einolf." His trembling voice, babyish and broken. The young Countess, all in white and gold like an Angel, smiles. Her hair coils like little rams' horns. "Come, my little squirrel, tell us. You had set sail on the Rhine for Cologne . . . "

A sob breaks forth like a turn of a lock, and then an unchained cascade of words . . . "Father Bodo wanted to stop the night at the Pilgrims' Inn, but the Boat Owner said it's a full moon and they can make good sailing at night on a full moon and Father Bodo said to him you just want to get out of paying the tolls . . . "

" . . . yes we know that trick . . . " a shadow of a smile on the Count's bleak face.

" . . . and the Boat Owner said what's that to you, you and

your pilgrims'll get to Cologne and the Three Magi one day earlier so don't complain. And so we sailed at night."

"Where are you and the other pilgrims from, boy?" The Count von Schwanenstein stands from his throne-like chair. His boots clatter on the wooden dais, his dogs swarm around his feet, a brown tumult.

"From the Breisgau."

"A Country Egg. Is it your first journey?"

"Yes, My Lord."

"So you are sailing at night down the Rhine, to avoid the river tolls." A valet pours wine into the Count's glass, straight from the skin, and curlicued flames outline the silhouettes of Lord and Servant. The hearth is huge, the size of a mountain barn.

"Yes."

"And then what happens?" The Count turns to face the Boy. His voice is soft, encouraging. Einolf can't see his eyes, only the bright, leaping flames behind.

"We're sailing, and it's cold, and the moon is shining. Some of us tries to sleep, but it's cold, so Father Bodo starts us singing a hymn but the Boat Owner says shush you never know who's listening. And then we sail on and then there's this terrible rattling under the boat, like it's run on ground, like it's running over stones and then we're stuck and not moving."

"And you're not run aground on the shore?"

"No My Lord, we are in plain river."

"How strange."

"It's because they put chains."

"Who? Chains? What?"

"You see we're stuck there and then we see some lights and it's a lantern held by a man and his woman and they've just come out of bed from a house on the banks and they're saying, 'Do you need help?' and we say yes we do. And they say they'll get help, and soon there's coracles coming from the village and twenty people and they rope up our boat and tug it ashore. And they help us all get out and say, 'You can stay here with us in the village.'"

"What village was it?"

"When we get ashore, there's no village, just one little hut. And the Boat Owner starts shouting *I knew it I knew it,* and grabs in the water and pulls out this chain that's run across the river, and that's what made our boat stop. And then then then . . . "

"Oh little squirrel . . . " The Countess holds out her arms. "Metta, comfort him!"

A serving matron's arms wrap around the Boy's dirty shoulders. Metta's voice whispers in his ear, her cockerel jowls wobble against his cheek. "Come, boy, don't cry. The Count and Countess have saved you. Show them some Grace. Tell. Tell."

"They cut off his head. With a sword."

"Who, Boy? Whom?"

"The Boat Owner. They cut off his head. And Father Bodo starts crying to God and they drag him to the ground and kick him."

"A Priest? They kick a Priest?"

"And they all have knives and they take all our bundles. A few of us fight and they get knocked down with knives and axes, and there's all this blood and screaming. And my Mamma takes hold of me and says Einolf run, but I can't run nowhere, my legs won't go and my Mamma how can I leave my Mamma. Two horrid men are dragging her and our women away and she puts something in my hand and says run Einolf run, she screams run boy run and so I run. I run into the dark wood!"

He can't continue, his face is one mess of snot and tears, buried into Metta's smoke-reeking shoulder. She cradles him.

"Poor boy, poor boy!" the Countess cries. "Sebald, we must do something for this poor boy, Sebald, we must do something."

The Count of Schwanenstein stands to the side of the fire, the huge hearth of the Great Hall of Castle Schwanenstein. Below him, around him, his two score hunting dogs, one score servants, a dozen liegemen. "Boy. Is there anyone waiting for you back home in Breisgau?"

"No, Sire."

"Then I will pledge a covenant for you. An annual sum that will keep you at the Hagenburg Cathedral Orphanage until you come of age. Or, until your Mother is found. In a satisfactory state."

The Boy snivels and whines. He doesn't understand. Metta takes his wet cheeks in her withered hands. "It means the Count will look after you, Boy! Say thank you! On your knee, Boy! On bended Knee!"

The boy of eleven summers, a marionette, flops to his knee and raises his palms in thanks. Sobs break from his chest in shuddering waves. The Countess glides from the dais towards him, eyes shining amber and gold.

"Don't come too close to him, my Lady," says Metta, "he's stinking filthy, poor lad. Been in the woods three days."

The Countess stoops to him, keeping one pace distant, and smiles until his sobs subside. "What's that in your hand, Boy?" she asks.

"What my Mamma gave me."

"Show me."

The Boy opens his palm. A pine-cone-shaped Heart, fashioned in red candlewax.

"What is it, Boy?"

"A heart for the Holy Virgin in Cologne. That's why we were travelling there."

"A heart? What for, Boy?"

"Our Dadda died last year of the Ague. My Mamma wanted the Virgin to cure her broken heart."

INNOCENCE
(ANNO 1241. RETTICH SCHÄFFER VI)

Master Stone-Cutter Rettich sits alone in the Lodge as dusk gathers in the Cathedral square. He sits in silence, waiting. A click of the latch and the Lodge's apprentice boy arrives, bringing water from the Cathedral Well to clean the floor. He bows and smiles at Rettich, almost a girlish curtsey, starts to work on soaking the washing rags.

Rettich watches him a long while, his fresh, youthful, open face. As he himself must once have looked, twelve summers ago. The boy, Friedl, feels the Master's gaze upon him, glances up from the floor. Rettich clears his throat. "You may finish early tonight, boy. I have work here and will lock the door when I leave."

Friedl pauses a while, kneeling. Looks up at Rettich, bright-eyed in lantern light. "Is there anything else my Master needs?"

Rettich looks down at the drawing table, hiding his eyes. "No, my boy. That will be all. Until tomorrow."

Friedl nods, a bit sadly. Hangs the rags in the corner to dry. Heads to the door and steps outside where swallows shimmer against the sky. The door closes behind him.

Silence. Outside, curfew's quiet hours stretch through the streets. Rettich should go home, but he has no wish to be there. He lights the lamps and swears to himself that this is the last time.

Spread out on the draughting table, Rettich's copies of Achim's drawings, those that were burned.

Master, forgive me.

The day of his friend's death, he had been working on them, drawing out the last copies from memory; the Western Façade, the Virgin and the Prophets, the Vices and the Virtues, the statuary, tier after tier.

Rettich had wanted it to be a surprise.

Master, forgive me, that I did not come to you.

Instead, two days later, he had made his solemn way to Avenheim and an open grave outside the cemetery walls in the space reserved for sinners and suicides. The Abbot, hurrying his muttered valediction under the drizzle, throws a perfunctory sprinkling of Holy Water, a half-hearted petition that the young Lord might escape Hell. The monks rush back inside to warmth and prayer. The lay brothers scoop up the purplish earth.

Thud.

Thud. Clods fall on the faceless coffin until Master Achim is cut off forever from the light of the world.

Rettich stands in twilight in Achim's empty Avenheim cell. By the bed, a prayer book, opened at the first chapter of John, Achim's russet cap of Anglian wool, and the hunting knife he had used to stab his own heart.

Rettich takes them as tokens. He searches everywhere; on the shelf, in the cracks in the walls, in the straw of the mattress. He asks the passing brother monks if they know where it can be. Shaken heads, nervous eyes, hurried steps.

Achim's drawing of the Cathedral's Western Window.

The Rose.

† † †

Before him on the Lodge's draughting table, all that remains: his inexpert copies. The Virtues, holding lanterns aloft, one at hip height, one at waist, one at breast, one at shoulder, one on high, representing the rise of the Sun, the growth of Light. The Vices, with their snakes, basilisks and devils, sinking from crown to waist to feet, the temporary, nocturnal victory of Darkness. The triumphant Virgin, flanked by two massive portals, beckoning the pilgrim to enter the temple.

And now his poor copy, newly drawn from fading memory, of Achim's glorious Rose.

Rettich stacks the drawings away. He rolls them tightly, binds them in ribbon, and places them at the bottom of Achim's old escritoire with all the other discarded parchments.

What is in the Past must stay in the Past.

† † †

The next day at dawn, Friedl awakes him. His fresh face hovers above his, peering at him, wondering what brought the Master to sleep on the apprentices' bench.

Rettich takes the boy's hand. "Friedl, would you do something for me?"

"Anything, Master."

"Then come with me."

Together, they scale the scaffold above the Southern Portal. To the plinth where Rettich's sundial statue stands. Below in the square, the City is yawning awake. Rettich holds out his hand, pulls Friedl to the working platform.

"Is he ready, do you think, boy?"

Friedl, surprised by the question, catches his breath and stares. His eyes sweep gently over the youth's carven form, his graceful body, his outstretched hand, his upturned face, his expression of enduring hope, the proffered sundial, held towards the light.

In the statue's upraised eyes, salvation and love. In the posture of his body, yearning, and at the same time, melancholy. He holds out the sundial like a gift, but who will receive it?

At this height above the southern portal, there is nothing but the Void. And so, Master Achim bequeaths his gift of illumination to Emptiness.

"He is beautiful, Master."

"I know. But he is only a copy." Rettich turns away, looks out over the rooves of the town. "Tell the boys to take down the scaffold. We are finished here. From now on, only the pigeons will see him properly."

† † †

Dombaumeister Durand raises his eyebrows in surprise. "I accept your apology, Master Rettich, though I am not sure it was necessary."

Rettich still looks at his calloused hands. "No. I have been difficult for you. I have obstinately stuck to my own projects. I was very attached to the old master, and was slow to accept change. But now I accept it. The sundial is completed, and now I am at your disposal."

The Speaker of the site translates Rettich's Alsatian into Latin for Durand's benefit. The new Dombaumeister, like Alenard, has come from France, bringing with him a small team of cutters and masons from Troyes. Durand speaks. "I am glad to hear it. The world has changed. And we must change with it."

Rettich nods. His Latin is sufficient to understand this.

Durand continues. "You will join the Nave work detail, as we discussed. When there is no work, you will teach the apprentices."

The Speaker translates. Rettich stands. It is as he expected. Statues will be carved by Giselbert and the other foreigners. "So I am a Master, but only in name."

Durand's German is sufficient. He nods at the Speaker to indicate he has understood. "If you wish, you are welcome to seek employment elsewhere. Your skills will find you work if you should seek it."

Outside, Rettich sits in pale sunlight and smiles a pale smile. The fight is over, and even if it brings little satisfaction, it does bring some peace. These last years of struggle have wearied him, chiselled lines into his forehead. It was a struggle born out of remorse. But now he has laid down his arms.

† † †

Six summers ago, after Achim's death, everything fell apart.

Treasurer von Zabern cut the expenditure until a new Dombaumeister could be found. A small, bitter-faced workforce arrived each morning and struggled to find the energy to carry on. Poor funds meant constant delays: masons idle because no stone had been sent from the quarries, roofers waiting on the masons, glaziers waiting on the blacksmiths for their frames, the blacksmiths refusing to take on more work until they were paid.

In the Lodge, tension and uncertainty reigned. Werkmeister Alenard continued for some months, trying to stay true to the dreams which had brought him there from France. He had come because of the grandeur of Achim's designs and the promise of a regular flow of gold from a wealthy diocese. But now all had turned sour.

One Saturday, Master Alenard collected his pay and packed his things. After hurried kissing of his colleagues and their reluctant blessings, he set his horse's hooves on the long road to Bohemia. He had received an offer to build a convent in the distant city of Prague.

When asked on Monday, the Lodge knew nothing. They protected their own in silence. *We came to work today and he was gone. We know not where.* The Bishop sent out armed bailiffs on the four land roads to bring him back, to punish him for his breach of contract. But Alenard was never found.

They had no leader, no plans. They agreed between them to complete the walls and arcades they had started, to finish the windows and statuary already commissioned. And then wait. Wait for His Grace to appoint new masters.

And then, one year later, Durand came. A practical man, an appeaser, a manufacturer of compromise. By agreement of the assembled Masters, Rettich was asked to show Alenard and Achim's technical drawings, those he had saved from the Treasury's purge. Then, one by one, Achim's goals were scaled down and moderated. Expenses were cut, trouble-makers were dismissed. Landolt and Rettich argued for Achim's vision as long as they could. But their battle was a losing one, and they knew it.

And now they have lost.

Rettich sighs, closes his eyes and thanks God for his blessings. He has work, a fine living wage, property in the Steinmetzgasse, a family.

A family. That is his next task. Peace must be made at home, with his neglected wife, with his sisters and brother. And once he has peace all around him, maybe he will find his inner peace too.

† † †

"Get up off your knees, you're worrying me."

Grete, his little sister, ordering him about. From the back of a mule, no less. Not only has she learned how to wear silks and silver girdles, how to boss servants and shout at tradesmen, she has also learned how to ride.

Rettich gets up from where he has been kneeling, in front of his own shrine. The Virgin, one hand on her breast, one opened out before her in a gesture of beckoning welcome, carved from oak by his own young hands.

"What've you got to pray about, anyway?" gabbles Grete. "You're virtue itself. If all the stories about you are true. Are they?"

Rettich doesn't reply.

"Stop pulling that miserable face. This is a happy day. Be happy."

"Is that an order?"

"Yes."

"I should put you over my knee and give you a spanking. Like I used to when you were a cheeky little mouse."

"That's more like it. Let's get going."

Rettich looks over to his young family, who are spread out on the grass: his wife Ällin, his daughters Mechthildlein and Lysa. The girls' uncle Manfred, feeding them raisins. A happy day, by order.

Rettich gets up from the ground before the shrine. "Come on, girls, hoopla!" He lifts Mechthildlein onto the donkey, helps little Lysa into the linen sling around Ällin's shoulders. "Not long to go now."

Mechthildlein: "Is it far?"

"What did I just say, monkey? I said 'not long now.'"

Mechthild's face scrunches. She scratches her ear. "Is it faaaaar?"

Ällin laughs, Rettich shrugs. What can you say? "No, it's not far."

"Is it faaaaaaar?"

†††

Triumphant return to Lenzenbach, a story the children will remember in rheumy old age, the story of how Father and Auntie Grete paid for the new church roof. All the village turning out to greet them, the Priest kissing their hands and blessing their munificence, a gift to Mother Church that will be remembered by the Angels at the gates of Purgatory, flicking their abacus beads to total up sins and remissions. Aunties Mechthild and Amaline, Uncle Hannes, the four cousins dancing with them on the village threshing ground.

Only Uncle Emmle is missing. "Whhhhhyyyyyyy?"

"He cannot come, his business keeps him in the City."

A little lie for the little ones. To Grete's proposal that he should contribute to the village church roof, Emmle had laughed and replied: "Let it fall down."

Rettich talks with the villagers who will do the building work, gives instructions, takes measurements to reckon how much timber, how much lead guttering, how many roof tiles, gives warnings about what will happen if the work is not completed by the autumn. They grumble and smile at him. And nod, bowing, as if he were the local Bailiff.

The midday Feast is laid out on planks before the church. The whole village has gathered, contributed; loaves of bread from the village oven, stacks of cheeses, honey, sauerkraut, slices of sausage. Grete takes pride of place at the Priest's right hand.

Manfred turns to peer at his brother-in-law. He chuckles. "What's your secret, Radish?" Rettich doesn't follow, rubs his eyes, blinking in sudden brightness as sunlight bursts out from behind a cloud.

"I mean, once you could never stop talking. And now you hardly say a word. Tell me why, so I can use the same medicine on my wife."

Despite himself, Rettich's face breaks into a faint smile.

"Just a little clue. It could be worth a lot of money, Master Schäffer. I'd pay a whole shillingsworth for every hour of silence. Just look at her."

They look over to the "high table" where Grete is chattering loudly to Father Konrad and the Lenzenbach Bailiff. Seeing them watching her, she gestures that they should come to her at once, as if summoning dogs or errant children.

Rettich obeys, yielding to his little Sister just as he yielded to Durand, for the sake of Peace. As he takes his seat, he looks over at Ällin, laughing in sunlight, chasing their daughter around the threshing ground. She stops to catch her breath, sees him watching her. Smiles.

Harmony.

† † †

Outside the church, the second wine barrel has been breached and the dancing has begun. Rettich whispers in Ällin's ear that he will go for a walk "to the old pastures," and slips away.

The wind has softened and now makes only gentle spirals and somersaults as Rettich stands above the village, looking down. A scattering of thatched rooves, dusty threshing floors and dungheaps, surrounded by gently swaying beech and fir. A tiny place, but once, for him, it had been the whole world.

He walks further uphill, pausing to catch his breath on the paths he had once tirelessly cantered up as a child. It is years since he has held an innocent Lamb in his hands, felt its gentle trembling, the almost frighteningly racing tempo of its tiny heart. Years since he slept under the stars or wrapped in wool blankets in a shepherd's tent.

They call his old pasture Hasenlenz after the hares that dance there in spring; it was allocated to the Straw-Schäffer flock for generations, but now that the Straw-Schäffers are Free Men, the Jackdaw-Schäffers' herd grazes there; sheep and goats, two cows.

Evening sunlight gilds the meadow flowers, sends the vast Rhine valley into yawning shadow. Up here, at the top of the world, there is air and brightness, a capricious wind. Rettich breathes in deep, sits down to rest on the grass and clover.

A shape racing towards him . . . black and white, a dog. It

starts barking. Rettich stands, puts his hands round his mouth, makes the Lenzenbach cry. The dog falters at the familiar sound, falls silent as the call is echoed back from across the pasture.

Rettich can see, faint in the dusk, a shepherd boy waving at him from further uphill. A tent of sheepskin and wooden struts. A fire, a skinned rabbit waiting to be cooked. His flock, dotted around him in the upper meadows.

The boy is sixteen summers, called Ludo, not a Jackdaw-Schäffer, but an orphan from another village, taken into the Jackdaw clan as part of a marriage deal. "I've heard of you," he says, shyly, to Rettich, as he turns the spitted rabbit above the hot embers, "everyone talks about you here. All the boys want to be like you."

A warm feeling suffuses Rettich's heart: an ambush of unexpected pride. "Like me? Old and worn out?"

"You're not old, master."

"I feel it. Especially today. Coming home."

The last sunlight is brushing the ridge of the Black Forest above Offenau, the first stars are silver points in ultramarine. Venus, pale blue, gazes from her crystal sphere, offering solace to those who yearn. Rettich drinks from the shepherd's cup, cool springwater.

"How was lambing this year?"

"Good, master. Just two stillborn. And only one ewe died."

"Foxes, wolves?"

"No, master. Blackie keeps them guarded well." His young hands ruffle the dog's head, and the yellow, canine eyes close with pleasure.

"Forget 'master.' Call me Rettich. I used to be a shepherd boy, just like you."

The boy smiles and turns the rabbit once again. "Won't you be heading down, before the dark?" he asks coyly, and nods to where, far below, a bonfire burns in the village square. Faint, almost inaudible, the sound of music, dancing; an echo from a busy, more crowded, troubled world.

Rettich shrugs, and then laughs, unbridled. He, the stone-cutter, has been carrying a block of stone these last twelve years, and now, finally, he lays it down. Settles it, rests it in the summer meadows of his childhood home.

† † †

The fire has sunk to its embers, the dog stands guard. The flock's thirteen bells sing an evening roundelay. In the tent, Rettich and Ludo lie together.

When Rettich was a boy, sometimes the elder shepherds came to his tent, and put their cocks between his legs. When he himself grew of age, they showed him how to do it too.

And he's tried to keep it from his mind ever since, but it's always been there, an indelible, shadowy sin. As he walked up the hill to visit his childhood pastures, he told himself he was only coming for the innocent memories of his shepherd's life.

But inside he knew why he was here, again, after so many unsatisfying and melancholy years.

THE PAVILION
(ANNO 1241. GRETE GERBER II)

It's six years now since we got our first Big Diocesan Commission; to make the cloth pavilion and the liveries for the Imperial Visit. Since then I've known no rest, but I can't complain: money's flowed through my hands like mill-race water.

But what's ill got is ill fated they say, and it may be just old wives' tales, but when I think about it, a shiver runs up my back, and the hairs on my arms stand on end.

That summer, once we'd pinched ourselves to make sure the Imperial Visit Commission was real, we got straight down to work. We had our old team of weavers in the city and villages, plus the heretic whore Elise, who was still in our employ back then. I went racing round the whole wide open world, from Lenzenbach to Honau, from Rheinau to Egersheim, to supervise the girls and prepare for the fulling and the dyeing. I spent all the last pennies we had. I swear, on the last day, my flour barrel was empty and the cupboard was bare, and we'd've gone hungry if it hadn't worked right.

When you think of one thing and one thing only and dream of it too and live and breathe and drink it, and then, finally, when it comes true in front of your eyes, it's the strangest thing. We stood with the throng in the fields down by Finckweiler and watched as the Emperor, with trumpets a'droning and drums a'pounding, rode up on his white stallion. The little balding ginger dwarf! He needed a box to get down from his horse! And then the Bishop, swollen like a beer barrel, had to be carried by two men-at-arms so that he could kneel before the Emperor.

What a pair, a midget and a wallow-hog! But all Manfred and I were thinking was *God forbid the pavilion will fall down God forbid the livery is wrong God forbid the fabric will tear.* It was windy that day and with every gust our hearts lurched into our mouths.

Bishop and Emperor spent all day in the pavilion in discussion. They discussed the division of the Dagsburg lands, the Emperor cancelled some tariffs on goods crossing the Alps to Lombardy, and He made the Hagenburg Jews his subjects. Inheritances, Jews and Taxes. That's what they were talking about all day in our bright and sturdy pavilion, the Bishop and the Emperor. And then they retired to their Castles—the Bishop to Haldenheim, and the Emperor to the old Staufen fort at Kronenburg.

And Manfred and me, we stood there in the field as everyone wandered off, as the servants took down the trestles and scattered the fires, as the minstrels and musicians wrapped up their lutes and flutes and as the Bishop's kitchen boys handed out the uneaten pies to the poor.

At ringing of the Vespers bell it was just me and Manfred and the Pavilion left standing there. "Maybe the Bishop's men will come by and take it down in the morning?" said my Manfred, and shrugged.

I laughed and kissed him, and said, "Whatever will be, let's go home and celebrate." On the way home we passed the Fleischmarkt and bought a suckling piglet and a barrel of Doroltzheimer from *zum Creutze*. We invited our neighbours and our weaving girls, and had such a revelry that the Town Watch came past to close us down. But Manfred handed each of them a tumbler of wine and a wedge of pork, and they made merry with us too until the ringing of the Matins bell.

The next day, feeling a bit tender, we wandered back out to

the Finckweiler field just outside the City walls. The Pavilion was still standing there, empty, with no one around. Today, Bishop and Emperor were meeting for Mass in the Cathedral. Yesterday the Bishop bowed before the Emperor. Today the Emperor will kneel to receive the Bishop's blessing. And then he will ride over the Alps to Italy to his endless battles with the Pope.

And the Pavilion is standing there, alone in the field, empty. Three hundred ells of best-woven cloth. "We better just . . . take it down? And store it? In case it rains?" I ventured. My husband and I looked at each other. And then we ran to get some helping hands.

Months and months passed and not a word. The first days I would jump at a knock on the door, thinking that it was the Bishop's provost come to claim the pavilion. But soon I forgot to worry and life went on.

We hired some laid-off workers from the Cathedral site to come and re-build the backyard stables, adding shuttered windows, a proper roof, and a hearth for winter heating. We bought trestle tables and benches, kitted it out as a proper workhouse. And that was our first proper cloth atelier, with its seven busy looms.

Manfred said one day soon after the Emperor's visit, "I'm giving the whole textile trade to you, Gretl sweet. I've more than enough to deal with on the river boats and the new church." And that's how we divided things from now on. Two trades, two concerns, and two money chests, his at the Pfennigplatz Counting House, and mine in the home in the Müllergass.

One year passed, and more. At dinner I turned to Manfred and said "Männle, you know that pavilion cloth?" And he cut me short and said "I don't want to know." So I took that as a "yes" to do what I wanted to do and I started to cut sections from it and sell them at ninepence a length. It was beautiful cloth—sturdy and supple and with a shine to it, perfect for an overcoat. In fact Elise made me one as a present, trimmed with red piping, I still wear it today. My Empress Coat I call it. That was the last thing Elise made me. The day she gave it to me I found out she was opening her legs to my Manfred and had her thrown out on the street.

I'd already sold half the pavilion cloth when that knock on the door actually came. I was at home resting, I'd just lost the baby; my second stillborn. Little Manfredle was playing with the puppy, the boy's screaming and the puppy's yapping, and then there's a pounding at the door. The new maid, Maria, who's ugly as a pugdog with the scabies (I choose the domestics now), goes to answer and comes back with a tall, stooping Benedictine. "Brother Hieronymus from the Treasury to see you, ma'am."

My heart's in my throat and I nearly bite it in half. "Sit down, Brother. Maria, let's have some calm around here." Maria packs off Manfredle and the puppy and the Brother looks at me, peering, like he's short-sighted. "Eighteen months ago, we ordered a pavilion from you, madam, and took delivery of said pavilion." He's trying to speak like the Treasurer, but he's got an upper Aargau accent, and it doesn't work. "We paid the agreed sum, thereby fulfilling the contract. But a recent inventory of the Bishop's household possessions revealed . . . no pavilion. Madam, do you know where it is?"

"I have no idea where it is, Brother," I say, as calm as a cow on the cud. "We made it, delivered it and after that it is no concern of ours. How could it have gone missing?"

"It seems the Bishop's Master of Ceremonies celebrated rather too enthusiastically on the occasion of the Emperor's visit. He forgot to order the pavilion to be dismantled, and . . . well, we do not know what happened to it subsequently."

That was five years ago. I had quite forgotten about the

whole thing. When, now, I am suddenly summoned to a meeting with the Bishop's Treasurer.

† † †

"Frau Gerber! Follow me."

He is standing waiting for me on the Cathedral's south steps, beneath the statue of King Solomon. His long, elegant hands, heavy with silver, gesture towards the church's interior. "Let us find a place to sit."

We walk inside. His long strides leave me tip-tapping in his wake like a Saracen wife behind her Pasha. What possessed me to wear my Empress Coat cut from the pavilion cloth I will never know, but indeed I look very fine, with my cream-and-red trimmed overcoat, my gown of night-blue Ghent, my silverthread girdle hanging low, and a soft black hood trimmed in foxfur.

The Treasurer even seems to notice my finery. As he gestures to a bench in a quiet corner, I note his eyes flick up and down my figure. Let him look at what he can't have. I don't mind.

I am not often in the Cathedral, and I am surprised by the crowds. It seems more a marketplace than a Church, with all its hawkers and salesmen and beggars and the business meetings going on all around.

The Nave has extended by another arch towards the West. My brother and his colleagues are working slowly, but they are working. The new Nave soars as high as three tall trees, flooded with coloured light . . . until the screen that cuts it in half, blocking out the building site.

"You will be wondering why I summoned you to this discussion?"

"I will."

It doesn't look like he's about to have me hauled in front of the town executioner. He's even attempting a friendly smile. He speaks softly. "The new church roof at Lenzenbach. Your husband's church of St. Niklaus in the Brandplatz. Not to mention the many donations I have heard about. To the new Dominican church and nunnery in Finckweiler."

He pauses, and I raise my eyebrows. I have no idea where this is leading. And why me, here, with him, now?

"My question, dear lady, is this. You, *the merchant estate*," (he says these words as if talking of the clap or the secret name of a demon), "seem most open-handed. Most generous. Most desirous of securing your salvation by Good Works."

I nod tentatively.

"But you do not give to . . . this splendid Cathedral. And, for a few years now, I have been wondering why."

As well he should.

"And so, I thought, I would simply ask you."

"My Lord, you should speak with my Husband. I am just a Woman."

"Please do not assay false modesty with me, Frau Gerber. You are a person of achievement . . . " I swear I even blush at that point. Compliments from a Canon! And me born with clogs on my feet.

" . . . if only of the commercial ilk."

I should have waited for that.

He leans towards me. "Tell me why, if you would be so kind."

And so I tell him. And once I open that door, there's no easy way of closing it.

"Well, why should we pay and get nothing in return? We have no say in the Cathedral, how it looks, who it is for, how it is built."

The Treasurer raises his eyebrows. Smiles his acidic smile. I just keep going. "And look who is a Canon! Two Cardinals in Rome and three other Italians who have never been here. Or

Count von Schwanenstein. A gambler, a fighter, a drunk
. . . Why does he deserve an annual golden prebend from the
diocese money?"

Von Zabern waves his hand. As if he's saying *Keep going,
dear Lady. Hang yourself with your own rope.*

"It's our trade that keeps this City going, it's us merchants
who bring in the meat and the milk and the cheese and the
wine and the thread and the fabrics, it's we who feed and
clothe and water everyone, and every second pace we take,
there's a toll to pay, a tax, a tithe. We can hardly walk from one
City Gate to another without paying away all our profit in tolls
and taxes. And so why should we give one farthing more than
we already do? We're not noblemen, so we can't be canons nor
town councillors. We give the money for you to play with, but
we're not allowed to throw the dice!"

Canon von Zabern looks at me and shakes his head in disbelief. "I had heard you had an insolent mouth." He chuckles quietly. "You think, if you commoners could be Canons
and Councillors, then Hagenburg would be the earthly paradise?"

"I think we could run things better."

"Power looks so easy from the outside, dear lady. To exercise it is a burden. A complicated and challenging one."

"Oh, is it so?"

"Tell me this," he says, stroking his clean-shaven chin. "If
you could *buy* a place on the Council, or a Ministerial Office,
or any position of influence, how much would you pay?"

"Quite a lot."

"I thought so."

He straightens his back, stretches his limbs. It seems our
interview has finished. "I thank you, Frau Gerber. This has
been instructive."

I am angry with myself. I had an opportunity, and all I did
was grouse like a brat.

"Is there anything I can do for you, my lady? You have been helpful to me."

I have? How? Before I know what I'm doing, my mouth is flapping away. "The Council is drawing up the charter of a Drapers' Guild. They are talking about Master-membership of the guilds being only available to men."

"Are they?" He frowns, looking bored. An impatient Crow in a long black robe.

"They are trying to . . . cut me out, my Lord. It is not just. If anyone in this City is a Master Draper, it is me."

"Indeed. I will have a word with my cousin the Burgrave. Frau Gerber . . . " He stands and bows the slightest of bows. "It has been instructive. My thanks to you."

And he walks off, striding like the sun won't rise tomorrow, to a small, hidden door at the side of the Choir. And he's gone.

And I'm left alone in my corner of the Cathedral, and wondering what's happened.

I walk outside where the autumn sun is setting. Time for home. From inside, the sounds of the Vespers chants. People stream out of the southern portal, on their way home before the Angelus bell. I look up. High above the doors, my brother's statue, holding the sundial.

"Admiring my work?"

Rettich is at my shoulder. I turn and embrace him, happy for the surprise. Beside him, carrying his tools, a young apprentice boy, fresh-faced and jolly. He bows low, lower than is really needed. "Madam."

Rettich presents him; "My little apprentice, Friedl. My little sister, Gretl. What brings you here, sister?"

† † †

A week later, I've been paying the fishmonger for the month's fish and the butcher for the month's meat, and I'm walking back home along the Market Quay. As usual, boats are unloading and Thelonarius Thieme is there, calculating how much money the City needs to steal from the merchants and call it "toll," and he sees me walking past and frowning and he says, "I thought you'd be smiling, Frau Gerber, today of all days."

And I say, "What's there to smile about? My purse is five shillings lighter than it was an hour ago."

He says, "Oh, haven't you heard?" and I say, "What?" and he says, "The new Guild of Drapers has published its statutes and they're allowing women as Guild Masters!"

I walk away and my heart is leaping like a lamb at springtime. I will be Mistress Gerber of the Honourable Guild of Drapers! And all thanks to that Crow, Eugenius von Zabern!

I bustle my way back to the Müllergass, give ha'pennies to all the beggars waiting outside our shop, go out back to the atelier and sit in the cold sun, just dreaming of my happy future and how I'll thank Canon Eugenius and how I'll tell Manfred and how envious he's going to be . . . when Manfred's messenger boy comes tearing up from the Rhine Harbour. He's run all the way, he's out of breath, and his face is pale.

I pour him water from the jug, watch him drink long and deep. "Well, out with it, boy."

"Master bids me tell you they've lost a whole ship."

My heart starts thudding. Like I've seen a ghost. Like the Devil touched my shoulder. "A whole ship, lad? It went down?"

"No ma'am, it was attacked by river pirates. Like with the pilgrims' boat this spring, they ran chains across the Rhine, brought the boat to ground. They took the lot, ma'am. The lot."

That Devil's hand, it just keeps on running up and down my back. My skin goes cold and clammy. And in my mind's eye, what do I see? I see the damned pavilion, the pavilion I stole from the Bishop. Its white cloth and scarlet-trimmed pennants fluttering in the wind. The trumpets sounding, the drums pounding.

God has a way of Justice, and he gives with one hand. And with the other hand he takes it all away.

ANNO
1242

SCHWANENSTEIN
(ANNO 1242. BARON VOLMAR VON KRONTHAL I)

A re you Elise?"
It's a simple enough question. I get no bloody answer. But I suppose I must look quite daunting saddled up on my charger Jerusalem. He's a good sixteen hands and I'm no midget neither. So I dismount to look at her more closely.

She's standing exactly where Emmerich Schäffer said she would be, outside the Jewish tailor Mannekint's shop, all dressed in spotless white. Strange, staring eyes, auburn hair, gap-toothed, tiny, but sweet and pert as a rosehip bud. And as I look her up and down like a slavegirl for sale, she doesn't seem to mind. Clasps her hands behind her back and does a little dance, swaying from side to side.

"Aye, My Lord. I'm Elise," she whispers in the end, like a mouse.

"Can you ride behind me, or do I need to sling you over the horse's neck?"

"I have ridden before, My Lord, when I was a Girl."

"And you're not a Girl now?"

"No, sir. A Woman."

"You look like a Girl. Family name?"

"The nuns gave me 'Gottlieb' so that I should love God."

"And do you?"

"I do love God, sir. Very much."

"Why? What's He done for you?"

"He has brought You to me, My Lord."

"That's a bloody fine answer." She's got spirit too, just like Schäffer said. "Shall I lift you on? Or can you . . . ?"

"Let me assay it, My Lord." And she tries to get her little foot in Jerusalem's stirrup, but it's just too high for her. It's like watching a mongrel trying to mount a mastiff. I could let the stirrup down for her, I suppose, but it's an opportunity I don't want to miss. So I grab her by the waist and lift her up and over Jerusalem's back. She's as light as a lamb.

"Are you comfortable like that, you tiny girl? With your legs spread as wide as . . . as . . . "

"My legs have been spread wide before."

"No talk like that once you're in the Lady's presence."

"What Lady?"

"Your new mistress."

"And who is She?"

"I'll tell you on the road." And I swing myself up into the saddle. "Take hold of me here and here, and grip with your knees. Ready? Hold tight!" And Jerusalem leaps off at a canter through the streets, scattering all before him. "Road! Give me Road!" I cry at the hightailing Hagenburgers, and behind me Elise screams with excitement like a giddy bridesmaid at a wedding dance.

† † †

He'd made it sound intriguing enough, God damn him. He has this way of wheedling his way into my thoughts, making me do things I would never otherwise do.

If your Lordship were to go to Mannekint's, the Jewish tailor's, on the Schneidergass, he says, *she'll be waiting for you outside, all decked out in the new maid's costume I've had Mannekint make for her. She's sweet as honeysuckle, and she'll make a perfect maidservant for your cousin Countess Adelheid.*

"Why do you say that?"

Because she knows some Courtly Poetry.

"Courtly Poetry?" I stutter. "What's a maidservant doing reading that nonsense?"

We're standing outside my drinking den, the *zum Sterne*, in the sunlight. Me and him, Emmerich Schäffer, my adviser, my fiduciary counsel.

"I don't know for sure," he says. "She's an intriguing little fox. Grew up with an educated, itinerant family. Performers, travelling players, heretics, that kind of thing. Then when they died, she was taken to a convent, and then worked as a maid. Got into trouble with one of her Mistresses—to tell the truth, it was my own sister Grete. Who caught her with her skirts hiked up in the woodshed."

"I follow you, Schäffer."

"After that she fell on hard times. Her name's Elise. And it just occurred to me that I could help her. And help your Cousin. And help you too . . . "

"Help me? How on earth is this going to help me?"

"Didn't you tell me that your Cousin Adelheid's husband, the Count von Schwanenstein, sold you a parcel of land last year? For a song?"

"I did."

"Well, it wouldn't hurt you, would it, if we had a friendly pair of eyes and ears at Castle Schwanenstein? Just in case the Count needs to raise more capital one day?"

I see. So she's not just a Handmaiden, she's a Spy, a new pair of eyes and ears in Schäffer's network of snitches and informers.

"And there's another reason," he says, raising a finger. "Seven Rhine boats attacked and plundered in the last year, all between the Albe river and Illingen. All within a day's ride of Castle Schwanenstein. Maybe somewhere on the Count's extensive lands, there are some bandits hiding. We've written this letter," he takes off his glove and presents a sealed roll of parchment, "asking for the Count's assistance in the matter."

Always scheming, this Schäffer. He makes me dizzy, just

thinking about him. But it's been a long time since I've seen my Cousin Adelheid, and Castle Schwanenstein is always worth a visit. Adelheid loves poetry, music, song and dance, and keeps an extravagant kitchen. It's all revelry and dissolution from dusk till dawn. Quite a change from my virtuous life with the Baroness at dull old Castle Kronthal.

† † †

We gallop down to the Rhine, and then trot along the banks until we come to the Erlbach stream and a pretty little grove of willow trees. Elise holds me tight all the way, as if she's scared of falling. "Oh? Must we stop?" she says, in disappointment.

"Horses need to eat and drink sometimes, you idiot. And so do I. There's food in the saddle bag. Serve it."

And I lift her from the saddle. She stands there, dazed, for a few moments, and then remembers her Duty, and fetches the saddle bag. Lays out the horsehair rug, unwraps the provisions. Cuts me a big hunk of bread, a lump of Lenzenbach cheese, four slices of sausage.

I start to eat. Hagenburg bread, a bloody disgrace.

Elise kneels beside me, cutting out more bread, cheese and sausage, her staring eyes never breaking their gaze.

"What are you looking at, girl?"

"At you, My Lord."

"And is it pleasing to you?"

"Very."

"Are you hungry?"

"No, My Lord."

"Liar." I tear her some bread, take the knife from her hands to cut her some cheese.

"No, My Lord, do not serve me."

"Why not, girl?"

"It wouldn't be right."

"I decide what's Right. Eat."

And she eats, covering her mouth with her hand.

"Eat properly. Not like a damned mouse."

She laughs and drops her bashful hand. "Where are we going my Lord?"

"Schwanenstein. You'll serve my cousin, the Countess. If she likes you."

"A Countess!"

"Schäffer told me you can recite Poetry. That's good. My cousin, it's all she cares about."

She finishes eating and I take her hand. "But I regret it now, this idea. To bring you there. I'd like to keep you all to myself. Who knows what will happen to you there?"

"Is it such a terrible place, My Lord?"

"It has a reputation."

"A rep . . . ?" Before she can speak, I kiss her on the mouth. She shrinks, surprised. And then kisses me back.

"If I don't take you now then someone there surely will."

"Then take me, My Lord," she says.

† † †

It's a fine sight, Castle Schwanenstein. Rising on a hillock and an outcrop of rock overlooking a bend in the silver Rhine, a lofty Keep with a slate roof, fine outhouses and stables for the countless guests that swarm in for the Countess' banquets and tournaments, and all circled by high, proud walls. A hearty Alsatian stronghold, unconquered for centuries.

In the keep's Great Hall, Cousin Adelheid circles Elise, looks her up and down with arched eyebrows. A real inspection. "This is she? She doesn't look like much."

"There is more to her than meets the eye, Cousin."

The train of Adelheid's overcoat hisses in the dried rushes of the flagstoned floor. "How do you know, Volmar?"

"We have been having a conversation."

"Oh? A conversation?" Now she looks *me* up and down.

I chuckle. "Schäffer says she knows poetry."

"Who is Schäffer?"

"The young man who works for . . . He is my fiduciary counsel."

"Whatever that is. Something to do with money."

"A capable young man. Sharp as a blade."

The Countess comes face to face with Elise. Her eyes blink, coquettish, and then fix on the young maid. A test. "Recite for us, my girl."

Elise shifts, one hand slowly unfolds, reaching out from her breast. Her mouth opens. Her voice sings out:

ein wunderlichez wunder,
Blantscheflur sine swester da:

On talking of Blanchefleur, Elise's upraised arm gestures, sweeping through the air, at Countess Adelheid.

ein maget, daz da noch anderswa
schoener wip nie wart gesehen.

Adelheid's eyes shine. Flattery and amazement. "The girl knows *Tristan*!" She laughs. "She's wonderful. I'll take her."

Now the Count approaches, stalking. From his height, he looks down on Elise. His cat-grey eyes stroke her calves, thighs, hips. "We thank you, My Lord Volmar. Very kind of you."

A scraping, a singing. A high ringing note hovers, trills, echoes against the stone. The Count, surprised, turns and looks:

It's my sword, drawn from its scabbard in one swoop. I hold it aloft.

Seeing my naked blade, the Count starts. Liveried servants stand. Schwanenstein's liegemen's hands clutch their pommels, move to block the doors.

"Listen all of you," I call out into the great hall. The point of my sword swishes round to point at Elise. I look around the room, looking everyone in the eyes in turn. "Be good to this woman. Or answer to me."

All turn to look at the new servant; petite, gap-toothed and trembling.

"She is under my personal protection."

LAMPBLACK
(ANNO 5002. YUDL BEN YITZHAK ROSHEIMER I)

nd it did not come. We waited and it did not come. And in my heart I knew it would not come and yet I waited. In our hands were letters from the great Rabbis of Spain and Italy, saying that it would come, that the year 5000 would be the year of our Salvation. Even the Rokeach, he of blessed memory, had sent letters from Worms. And in my library I have a computation, rigorous and strange, that claims that the year 5000 will mark the end of the dominion of the Hanged One, may his name be blotted out.

*Yet all these speculators are Liars and Frauds. We have proved ourselves unworthy of redemption, and truly Judah the Pious of blessed memory says that it is a sin to divine the time of the Coming. I say with the Rambam, he of blessed memory, **I believe with full faith in the coming of the Messiah, and even though he tarries, I await his arrival with every day.** Amen.*

Silence is a slippery thing, it is hard to define exactly what it is. Yudl stands in the empty house, eavesdrops on this so-called Silence, and finds that it is full of creaks and crepitations, of cats' whispers and spiders' weavings.

Yudl's hand trembles on the Forbidden Book's red leather binding. The Slippery Things bother Yudl, they slide and slip round his head like snakes. The Slippery Things. Like Silence. Like Eternity. Like Nothing, Everything, What came Before and What will come After. The forbidden questions. They crowd in the corners of the dark, between the letters of the Law.

Floorboards in the upstairs room knock and crack, the echo of the morning's footsteps, or a ghost?

His Father, suddenly home from the beth midrash?

The whole house creaks, stealthy, like a thief. Shelves lean down towards his shoulder, dust fingers his neck.

Yudl's palpitating heart races in his mouth. He slips his Father's red leather book back into the secret shelf. Takes the key and locks the Library. Runs upstairs, kisses the key so that it will not betray him and eases it back into its hiding place in the straw of his parents' mattress.

Then the boy of ten summers stands on the creaking stairs, his blood pounds at the door of his heart. *Then your eyes shall be opened, and ye shall be as gods, knowing Good and Evil.* His trembling hands flatten the unruly fair hair beneath his cap, shake out the Library dust, all trace and sign of his Transgression.

His eyes have been opened, he has read his Father's Secrets. Two years ago Father was awaiting the coming of the Messiah. And yet he said nothing? And yet they did not prepare for His Coming? Why did they not clothe themselves in sackcloth and ashes? Put their feet in icy buckets and repent their sins? Wait on the roof of the house for a golden cloud to carry them to Jerusalem?

He runs down the stairs and out of the creeping, leaning, secretive house. Out into the courtyard, and through the alley to the bright, busy Judengasse street.

✡ ✡ ✡

Yudl had first seen the secret red book two weeks ago. He was in the courtyard shelling peas with his Aunt when he heard his Father calling his name. Which can mean only one thing: he's done something wrong.

Yudl stands in the tiny Library; little more than a large cupboard. His Father is at his reading chair, surrounded by the tottering shelves. A lamp twists on a chain, hanging above his Father's inclined head. He doesn't turn round to face the boy. "Where is the Alphabet book I lent you, Yudl?"—"The Alphabet book, Father?"—"*The Alphabet of Rabbi Akiba*, Yudl."

A pause fills the room. "I lent it to Barukh."

A longer pause. "Yudl. Did you ask my permission to lend it to Barukh?"

A third pause, even longer. "No."—"Come here." Yudl takes three steps forward and his Father's hand grabs his collar. "Kneel." Yudl kneels. His Father's face is dark with anger, he holds out a crumpled scroll. "Do you know what this is?"—"The catalogue, Father."—"And did you write in here, that you have lent our book to Barukh?"—"No."—"And what did I tell you to do, if any books leave this house?"—"To write it in the catalogue."—"And what will you do now?"—"I will go and fetch the book from him. Straight away, Father. Straight away."

Yudl races down the narrow stairs and into the yard where his Aunt is still at work with the peas. "Where are you going, Yudl? Your work isn't done." No time to explain. Yudl hurries across the yard to Cousin Barukh's, knocks on the back door, kisses his right hand, touches the mezuzah and enters.

There is the beautiful Leah, plaiting her black hair. "Is Barukh at home?" asks Yudl. "No," says Leah. "Where is he?"—"How should I know?"—"At the beth midrash?"— "*Am I my brother's keeper?*"—"Don't be frivolous."—"Don't be cheeky."—"Can I go out by your front door?"—"Don't we always tell you, our house is not an alleyway. Go round the side."—"Why?"—"You'll make the floor dirty and I've just cleaned it."—"My shoes are clean, let me in."—"Said the cat to the mouse. Get out."

Yudl runs back out to the courtyard. The chickens cluck

and flutter out of his path. His Aunt shouts at him. "Yudl, come here and finish your chores."—"Not now, Auntie." He turns to his left down the alley, past the office room rented by the Strawhead Goy. And there he is, Strawhead, walking in from the Judengasse. "Hello, Yudl."—"Hello, sir."—"Where are you running to?"—"Nowhere."—"You're running nowhere fast. Where's your cap?"—"Inside."—"Don't you need it?"—"No."

Yudl slips past Emmerich Schäffer in the narrow alley, through the wooden gate and into the Gasse. Late afternoon sunlight, rattling carts, the smell of dung. Yudl's uncovered head glints gold; he too has fair hair like the Goy; rare, strange.

Yudl runs the fifty paces to the beth midrash. Praise be to the Eternal One, Barukh is there, trimming candlewicks. "Barukh!"—"What?"—"I need back that book I lent you."—"Ask Aberle."—" Why?"—"I lent it to him."—"DID I SAY YOU COULD LEND IT TO HIM?"—"Did you say I couldn't?"—"No, but . . . "—"So don't shout at me."—"I'm sorry."

Rabbi Menahem, at his lectern, looks up sternly at Yudl. "Why are you shouting? Is this a tavern?"—"No, Rabbi."—"Behave. Or get out of here now."

Adonai Adonai, protect me. May Aberle be home and have my book in his hands . . . Five doors down the Judengasse, through the rickety ashwood gate, down the muddy, smelly alley where chickens peck in the day and rats run at night. At the wall of the Jewish Cemetery, turn left, say a blessing for the dead, spit to ward off ghosts, skirt the Nachmann stables and the shokhet's slaughterhouse where dogs and cats wail for scraps. Into dark, dank Sheol Street, which the goyyim call the Sumpfgass. Two-storey shacks totter in stinking shade. On the other side, in the sun of the Rhinegate Street they sell shining soup pots and strawberry tarts, and here, in the rented shadow of the shops, ten families crowd and swarm.

"Aberle! Aberle!"—"Who's calling?"—"Yudl!"—"Which Yudl?"—"Yudl ben Yitzhak!" An attic shutter opens and Aberle's downy chin pokes out, followed by his beaky nose and his blinking eyes. *If I were like Aberle my father would be proud of me*, thinks Yudl, *all he does is read.* "You have my father's Alphabet of Rabbi Akiba!"—"Yes." *Praise be to the Eternal One! He has the book!* "What about it?" asks Aberle, irritated. Yudl must have interrupted him reading the Song of Songs, dreaming of the dusky skin of the Queen of Sheba. "My father wants it back, that's what."—"Come and get it tomorrow."— "No, now."—"Why now?"—"Why ask 'why now'? Whose book is it anyway?"—"Books belong to no one, knowledge is a commonwealth."—"Tell that to my father."—"I will tomorrow at schul."—"But give me the book first."—"No, you midget, go away." He closes the shutter.

Yudl runs to the doorway, kisses his right hand, touches the mouldy mezuzah and rushes inside. A sooty hallway. Aberle's mother sits in silence and spins wool with distaff and spindle, her cote torn above her breast in sign of mourning. She has recently buried two boys, lost to the Ague.

She looks pale and exhausted, herself a ghost. "I must talk with Aberle."—"So I heard. Talk with him, don't shout. The girls are sleeping. For once."—"I can go upstairs?"—"Go, Yudl, go, and don't let him bully you. He's a terror."

Yudl walks up the creaking steps, spotting spiderwebs in the ceiling corners. The house used to be noisy with children, but now is silent. Dustballs float on the stairs, a whole house in mourning, gone to seed and ruin. Wind whispers through a crack in the wooden boards; magic spells, incantations. A finger of ice strokes the flaxen down behind Yudl's ears. The hairs on his arms rise in dread.

The attic doorway, Yudl swallows. He knocks imperiously. "It's Yudl."—"Go away."

Yudl opens the door regardless. Two planks propped on

crates, scattered with straw: Aberle's bed, once shared with his brothers. A lectern of sorts; three boards held loosely together by three nails. A lantern, a sheet of parchment full of scrawls, letters and diagrams, and Aberle. "GET OUT!"—"NO! I WANT MY FATHER'S BOOK! NOW!"

Aberle's lanky limbs block the way. He has to crouch; the ceiling is too low for him to stand. "Why do you want it, midget?"—"My father wants it." Aberle leans forward, his ugly face leers. His finger touches Yudl's sweaty forehead. "Then tell me which letter is the most exalted."

Yudl doesn't know.

"You haven't read it? You moron?"—"I didn't have time to. I lent it to Barukh, and then he lent it to you. When should I find time to read it if you lot are throwing it around town as if it belonged to you? It's my father's, now give it back to me."

Aberle's face, unrelenting.

Yudl feels in the hem of his cote. It is still there, his gift from Uncle Meir. Hard, round, the size of a fingernail. Tarnished silver, opener of rusty doors. "I will give you a Ha'penny." His quivering hand proffers the coin.

Aberle stares at him a while. "The book is wasted on you." He reaches into his stuffy room, under the bed, and pulls out the *Alphabet of Akiba*, bound in green vellum. "How did your Father—a great scholar!—ever produce a dunce like you?"

✡ ✡ ✡

And he bows before his Father, the Great Scholar, and proffers the book in its green jacket. Father takes *The Alphabet*, studies its condition briefly, turns a few pages, sniffs its inner leaves. "Damp," he says, and glowers at Yudl. "Aberle is never to take a book from here into that filthy damp hovel again, do you hear?"—"I hear you, Father." And then Father slides the green-jacketed book into one of the higher shelves, and . . . it happens. A small, fat, red leather bound book falls from its hiding place onto the lectern.

"What is, that book, Father?"—"Never you mind what this book is Yudl, get going."—"No, really, what book is that, Father?" Father's cheeks flood red. The curls of his hair twist and writhe. "Do not ask me about that book again." His hand flinches, spasms, strikes Yudl across the cheek. He turns and places the book up high, in the crooked corner of the shelf.

Yudl's cheek stings, his eyes flutter, resisting tears. His tongue tastes the sour taste of hatred. *I will find what is Hidden from me. I will do what is Forbidden.* As he leaves the Library, his mind teems with the words of Solomon. *If thou seekest knowledge as silver, then thou shalt understand the fear of the Lord.*

✡ ✡ ✡

Once a week it is his job to collect the lampblack from the beth midrash lamps. He has two horsehair brushes, one larger and one tiny one for the difficult crannies in the lamp's mantles. He brushes the lamps over a white-painted plate . . . and the soot gathers, falling like black snow . . . drifts of dark powder, the precious, wonderful magic of lampblack.

And then he goes around the houses of the Jews, knocking on the shutters and calling, "Lampblack! Lampblack!" And he cleans the dirty lamps and takes away the soot in his wrap of blackened cloth.

At rich Uncle Meir's he can usually collect two good pinches of soot from the office lamps. "I've been working late at night," says Meir, ruffling Yudl's hair. "What have you been working on, Uncle?"—"Business."—"Of course. But what business?"—"Business that is good for your business. The more I work, the later I stay up, the more oil I burn, the more lampblack for you."—"You're not answering my question."— "You're too young for business, that's why. And your Father wants you to be a Scholar."—"Then he should have a different son."—"Why so? You're good at Torah study. Better than I ever was."—"That's not a compliment, Uncle."—"Insolent boy." Uncle smiles, and Yudl sits down to work. It's true. Father can recite Deuteronomy backwards. Uncle Rosheimer, for all his gold, reads the Torah in a high-pitched voice that sounds like a peacock and he needs the Gabbai's help with the vowels. For shame.

The door opens, Emmerich enters, pulling down his fur-trimmed hood. Following him, a young Jew, red-haired and blinking. Yudl has seen this stranger before; a commercial traveller from one of the communities downriver. Emmerich holds up a bunch of papers. "Letters from the *Grete*, just docked."

The stranger, Mordechai, bows to Uncle Meir. "Greetings from my Father. I have a promissory note."

Rosheimer takes the scrap of parchment, examines it carefully, checks the seal against a sample in one of his ledgers. "Six marks, sixpence?" Mordechai nods.

Rosheimer counts out the coins, passes them to Emmerich to check the balance. As the Goy counts, flicking the coins expertly from one hand to another, Yudl bends back over his lamp, brushes at the soot. He does it slowly on purpose, not wanting to leave.

"Welcome once again, Mordechai," says Uncle Meir. "Go to the beth midrash for your meal tickets, and the Gabbai will allocate you a bed. I've forgotten whose turn it is to take in travellers. It might even be ours!"

"That would be an honour, Reb Meir."

"What business do you have here?"

"We're awaiting a shipment coming over from the Danube. I have to pay and find a boat for it, take it back to Mayenz."

"Tell your Father that his credit balance here is getting precarious. We need to draw coin back from him next time one of our associates is in Mayenz."

"I will tell him. He will be glad to reimburse you."

Emmerich finishes counting. "The sum is true. Here, Mordechai, please count."

Mordechai shakes his head. "There is no need. Here." And he holds out his wallet to receive the coin. Emmerich slides the silver across the tabletop. It rains into the open pouch, chiming bright. Uncle Meir becomes thoughtful, shuffles his feet.

"Mordechai, tomorrow is shabbat and of course, as an honoured visitor, you'll be offered to read the Torah portion. If you wish to, please do. But I know it's my brother's turn to read it and.... well ... it's so *important* to him, and he does it so well and ... "

Mordechai holds up his hands. "Say no more, Reb Meir! I will be glad to refuse the honour. My reading voice is poor, in any case." Uncle Meir claps his hands together high in the air, a gesture of relief and gratitude.

After Mordechai has left, Emmerich takes out two letters from the pile. One is a mere scrap of parchment, torn from a book, bearing a brief scribble of ink. Uncle Meir raises his eyebrows. "And what is that?"

"A note from the serving girl I had placed in Schwanenstein. She says she has asked around amongst the servants and they say that they think some bandits might be holed up on the marshes at the end of the River Albe. But she can't leave the castle to look for herself ... " And then Emmerich holds up the second missive—this time a full scroll, bound with a ribbon and a seal. "From Our Lord Count von Schwanenstein. In response to *our* letter. About the Bandits."

Uncle Meir's eyes flick over to Yudl, who, despite being as slow as possible, has now nearly finished his work. Emmerich follows Rosheimer's eyes. "It's alright, let the boy hear." He unfolds the letter. "There's nothing to tell anyway. In short His Lordship says that he takes no orders from a bunch of

Merchants and Jews. He's sorry we lost some merchandise, but the bandits could have come from anywhere. If he finds any on his lands of course he will put them to the sword as he has done in the past. But now he has more important things to worry about than our commercial misfortunes. The matter is closed, goodbye, good riddance to you."

A pause. Uncle Meir folds his hands. "Well, it was nice of him to find the time to write."

Emmerich chuckles bitterly.

"And the Albe River? If the maidservant is right? Is that on his land?"

"The River marks the border of his land. So the jurisdiction is unclear."

A contemplative silence fills the room. After a short while, Emmerich breaks it. "In the meantime we can put armed men on the boats."

"They will need to be paid. It will drive up the price of all goods. Yudl?"

Yudl looks up from his work, brushing the soot into his folded oily cloth. "Yes, Uncle?"

"Are you ever going to finish?"

✡ ✡ ✡

The day after shabbat, home early from the beth midrash to mix the ink, he stands in the doorway and listens. Footsteps above, a snatch of song. Auntie Esther is home, as usual.

Not that he can see her. He thinks; *is she only there because I think she is there?* How do I *know* she is there?

The Slippery Things, once again.

Yudl goes to the kitchen and collects the ink pot and a jug of warm water from the cauldron hanging above the hearth.

He thinks: probably someone is in the schul latrine now, but if no one is there to see them, are they really there? And what of the desert, the waste places, whose only witnesses are jackals and screech-owls? Are they really there, those lands of sand, blasted thorns and darkness?

Yudl shivers. They are there. The Eternal One has set them there. And he sees them. And so they are there.

But does The Eternal One have Eyes? No. That would be to limit Him. To give him organs, fingers, hair, hands. Ridiculous! Like the Goyyim do with their idolatrous sculptures! (Spit twice! To left and right!) Their horrible, twisted, bleeding Hanged One. And the "Mother of God"! As if God was once born! Once a Baby!

Back to the topic. Job asks God: *Hast thou eyes of flesh and dost thou see as a man sees?* and Zophar the Naamathite answers *Canst thou by searching find out God?*

Rabbi Menahem explains it thus: How can you search for God when God is already Everything? What can it mean to search for something that is even the Searcher himself?

And so God has no eyes. God IS all eyes. God has no flesh. God IS all flesh. And so it goes on, and so it goes on, and so . . .

Yudl slaps his forehead.

Stop thinking the Slippery Things, Yudl.

Turn to The Chore.

Yudl mixes the magic mix: lampblack, water and fishbone glue, just like his Father has shown him. He stirs the ink pot with the quill. Still too viscous. He adds a spot of warm water, just a spot. Perfect. Tests the ink on a scrap of parchment, writing his name. Yudah, ben Yitzhak. Son of Yitzhak. Rosheimer, the new surname Uncle has chosen for them from the nearby town of Rosheim. Rosheimer.

Yudah. Ben Yitzhak. Rosheimer.

He blows gently. The ink dries to a glossy, deep black, with slight grey ghosting where the nib stroke was too light. A good ink. Maybe his father will be pleased. Maybe he will even smile.

"Yudl, I'm going next door." It's Auntie, standing at the foot of the stairs, pulling her cloak over her shoulders. "How long, Auntie?"—"How long what?"—"How long will you stay next door?"—"How long is a rope?"—"Just tell me how long."—"Why, what mischief are you planning?"—"Mischief? How easy you think evil, Auntie."—"Evil thoughts are first to the table."—"How long?"—"Until I need to come back."

Auntie Esther harrumphs and clatters out the yard door, heading across the courtyard to Cousin Barukh's, sending the chickens scattering.

Yudl's heart starts to beat faster. It is a Sin. But he cannot help himself.

He stops to listen to the house's guilty silence. His blood judders in his heart, sickening him to his stomach.

✡ ✡ ✡

. . . she said, "Why not make love to me not as duty, but just for pleasure?", and I of course said that would be frivolity and she frowned, so next shabbat I came to her in our chamber and desired her and spoke soft words to her and complimented her hair and her lips, but she turned her back and said, "You have not understood at all," which truly was not untrue, for who, since the beginning of our world and Eve in the garden, has understood women's whims?

We must study the Law and not be distracted by shameful thoughts, and for this Adonai has given us marriage so that we should be fulfilled and not succumb to the temptations of demons. But what should a man do if his wife will not have him? What if, when she does so, she does it only as duty, and takes no pleasure in it?

Yudl's blood races. He feels he will faint. He can hardly

hold the book still, his hands tremble, his arms shake. He knows he should not read more. But he cannot stop.

I cannot stop thinking of her. Not just me with her. But her in the arms of others.

Thud. Thud. The door opening, closing.
Downstairs.
Yudl nearly retches with fear. His legs shake uncontrollably. He wants to scream.

Quick. He stands on the chair. Slides the book back in its top shelf. Tries to come down quietly. Bang! His wooden sole sounds like thunder on the boards.

Quick. Out of the Library, the key is still in the lock. His breath comes fast and deep, like a foundry bellows. Turns the key and slips off his shoes, tiptoes upstairs, kisses the key and slides it beneath the mattress on Father's side . . . .

"Who's that up there?"
A voice from below.
"It's me, Auntie, just going to schul!" His voice quavers. His feet clatter on the stairs, racing for the door.

The study house is full. As Yudl enters, shaking, the usual bored glances greet the new arrival. *Only the bored look up. The truly pious are too engrossed to care who has just walked in,* as the Gabbai always says. Caught by his own snare, it is the Gabbai who looks over at Yudl from where he is instructing the boys in the weekly Torah portion. This week is Numbers. *Take the Levites from among the children of Israel, and cleanse them.*

The Gabbai points a finger at him: *come here now.* His crooked, white finger resembles the *yad* used to point at the Torah scroll. Yudl shakes his head, his eyes scour the room . . .

When he sees his Father, nausea rises from his stomach. A flush of shame. Yudl takes hold of the nearest lectern, as if he is about to plummet to the ground. His Guilt must be written across his forehead, like the mark set upon Cain. He looks down at his feet, awaiting the thunderbolt. The blow.

But nothing comes. Yudl looks up. Praise the Almighty, his Father has hardly noticed he is there. Father reads aloud, closes his eyes, memorises, reads again . . . and only sends one brief, dismissive glance in Yudl's direction.

Yudl looks at the lectern he is holding for balance. Unfurled on it, the book of Ruth, lazily left there by the last reader. Yudl starts to read aloud, swaying gently backwards and forwards— *wash thyself therefore and anoint thee and put thy raiment upon thee . . .*

But he is not really reading.

Of course he knows something of it. Mitzvat onah. Lying together in bed. On the eve of the Sabbath. Making babies. But what is it like? And why does Mother not like it? *They made me, didn't they?* And two more sons who died as babes, taken by the envious demoness Lilith.

He thinks of his Mother and Father lying together.

And then one line he read comes back to him and sickens Yudl like the Ague. He closes his eyes and it crowds in the darkness behind his eyelids like Nightmare.

. . . her in the arms of others.

Yudl's mind writhes and twists, a nest of snakes. And around him as he sways he can hear mutterings and susurrations, dozens of pious mouths whispering and reciting, lisping and singing the eternal Word of the Lord.

L ike the brattish child that tugs at the sleeves of its parents, exploding in tantrum until its whims are heard, thusly has the Merchant Estate, in its incessant whining from its wharves and warehouses, sought to inveigle its way into my attention. Previously they had merely wheedled at the foot of the High Table in the hope of a few crumbs of privilege or the lowering of a Noble or Episcopal ring to kiss. But of late their entreaties have taken on a strident and even rebellious tone, and have become truly difficult to ignore.

Furthermore, they are beginning to set up their own institutions and companies, founding Guilds, Corporations, Travelling Societies to spread their risk and increase their mutual profit. They are building their own churches, making their own investments in both this world and the next. They seem to believe, because they have money in their purse and the freedom to spend it, that they have the God-Given Right to Everything and Exactly How They Wish It, as if Blood and Breeding and Culture had played no role in determining society's Hierarchies! On the altar of Mammon they sacrifice their humility and saunter knavishly into our Cathedral as if into a market tavern. Such a din and clamour do they make that the Cantor can hardly hear himself singing the Psalms and Antiphons.

God Damn them, but one cannot ignore them. They are, as they know only too well themselves, our Diocese's breath and blood. Their wealth is increasing, one must concede, by dint of cunning and hard graft, by the building of networks that now spread to England, Flanders, Italy, even to Constantinople and the Holy Land itself. Hagenburg is a passing port in this spidery web of waterways, and our Merchants are the ambassadors who know the by-laws of its pathways of silk.

I have been holding meetings with a small selection of them. The unctuously friendly Tollmaster Thieme Isenheim, whose work brings him into contact with all who dock at our city port. Wikerus the Grain Merchant, the senior trader of the town, slowly losing his wealth and status to the younger generation. And Grete Gerber, an attractive but insolent and ambitious woman who maybe should be pitied for being the wife of Manfred, epitome of all that is low and loathsome in the mercantile class.

In my interviews with them, conducted out of the necessity to learn our rivals' strategies and *modus operandi*, they have made it clear. They have thousands that they could contribute to the Diocese. But for this, they would want something in return. Power. To share Power with the Bishop and his *ministeriales*. To wield Influence over the workings of the Diocese.

Distasteful and unacceptable as this request might be, it is most clear, and easy to understand. I cannot claim to like these Merchants, but I do comprehend them.

Perplexing and alien to me, however, are the Jews. This peculiar people, scattered to the Four Winds, their Temple destroyed not merely once, but twice, persecuted and reviled wherever they go, believe stubbornly, and in the teeth of all the evidence, that they are the Chosen People of God.

This might be easier to understand if one could familiarise oneself with their impenetrable customs, but they keep apart and to themselves. It seems they only have their occasional dealings with us Christians out of necessity, and even these exchanges appear somehow dirtying or shameful for them.

One cannot escape the sense that they, from their lousy gutter, *look down on us.*

Opinion of the Jews has not been much helped by recent revelations, posted from the Holy See to all the Bishops of Christendom by a certain Nicolas Donin, a convert from Judaism. One presumes that this former Jew knows whereof he speaks when he claims that the Jews' *Talmud* contains terrible blasphemies, not least of which the assertion that Our Lord Jesus Christ is punished in the afterlife by being boiled in a vat of faeces.

In the Kingdom of France, the horror of these revelations has led to trials of the Jews and their works, with Donin himself as the Chief Prosecutor. I am glad that here in Alsace this controversy has mainly gone unnoticed. For after all, do we not need our Jews?

When I was a boy, most trade was carried out by barter and by the exchange of services, by mutual arrangements. Most of the tithes and taxes were paid in goods; in sheep, wool, wax, honey, wine, grain, in indenture of servants: *my son will work in your Household three years, and you will charge me no tithe for five.* These were the deals that were struck. Goods and labour, agreement and exchange.

But now it is all Money. Tarnished pennies, clipped hellers, golden *augustales* stamped with Emperor Friedrich's head, promissory notes, payments on account, reckoning coins and *lettres de foire.* And I must confess it is to my detriment that I have spent the first forty years of my life ignoring these two classes of people whose expertise is Money.

Jews and Merchants. Merchants and Jews.

† † †

"I am the Bishop's Treasurer, I have come to inspect your community's tax payments."

I stand stooped under the lintel. It is the biggest, finest house in the Judengasse, but still its doorway is much too low for me. In the hallway, a beautiful dark-eyed Girl is looking askance at me. Hovering at her shoulder, a Boy with bright blond hair sticking sideways out of his cap like a scarecrow overstuffed with straw. "I'll get him," says the Boy. "No, I'll get him," says the Girl. They scuffle and struggle to be first up the stairs. "Yudl!" curses the Girl, "Leah!" curses the Boy, amongst words that I confess I do not understand.

I turn to Hieronymus, who is, as usual, standing behind me like my shadow. "You will wait outside," I say. He stutters his disagreement, "My Lord, are-are-are you certain? There there there could be . . . trickery." I look levelly at my loyal, long-serving Clerk. "Hieronymus. I will be fine."

The boy, Yudl, has won the struggle. Leah returns to sulk in the shadows of the stairwell, emphatically flicking her broom at pointless dust. Yudl bows and gestures that he will lead me upstairs.

I am admitted into the room on the first storey that serves as Rosheimer's bureau. Everyone stands as I enter: the Rabbi, Rosheimer, and his Gentile assistant, Emmerich Schäffer, of whom much is said, but little known.

I dislike Society, and always have. Awkwardness, Uncertainty, Humiliation. Wondering whether to bow, shake hands, give the Kiss of Peace? Who should sit first, to whom may one turn one's back without giving offence? These questions are a plague. In my view, a universal series of Rules and Regulations should be written out by a Papal Clerk and the Proclamation hung in every public space so that forthwith no social uncertainty should ever arise.

Emmerich bows and kisses my ring. This is "correct," but in a Jew's House it feels somehow inappropriate, and he does so with a nonchalance that verges on the insolent. Then he grins and waves his hand towards his two Jewish colleagues, announcing in a clarion voice "Herr Meir Rosheimer and Rabbi Menahem HaKohen Hirsch . . . the honourable Lord Canon Treasurer von Zabern!"

The two Jews' right hands twitch at their sides like suffocating fish, as if uncertain whether to raise them for a handshake. Of course, a Kiss is out of the question. I resolve the uncertainty by aiming a slight bow in the Rabbi's direction. This is maybe more than I should have conceded to him, but Let It Be. The sooner this farce is over the better.

The two Jews, seemingly grateful to me for taking the initiative, now bow, quite deeply and gravely, in my direction. "Please sit, My Lord," says Rosheimer, gesturing to the chair behind me. It is hardly a throne or chair of honour. But it has four legs, and even a cushion. I sit in it, and the others follow, with the boy Yudl perching in an alcove by the doorway.

The Rabbi's hand now waves in the air in some kind of dismissive gesture. "Herr Rosheimer will answer all your questions," he says, "I understand nothing of money."

It is as I have heard. The Rabbi of Hagenburg is a religious scholar of some renown, but of little worldly understanding. The community has its *de facto* leader in Rosheimer.

The Rabbi speaks in a thick mid-Rhenish dialect, from Mayenz or Worms, but when Rosheimer speaks, it is in good Alsatian: "Welcome, My Lord Treasurer, would you like some wine or other refreshment?"

"I thank you, no," I reply, and go straight to the matter in hand. "How is Business, Herr Rosheimer?"

"Thank you, My Lord, business is good, but has been better."

"In what wise has it been better?"

"You will have heard of the piracy on the Rhine near Illingen?"

"I have heard of it."

"Now seven cargoes and two ships have been lost there,

and we have had goods on all of them. I'm glad you have opened up this subject."

"I wasn't aware that I did. But please continue."

"We have information that these pirates may be holed up near the mouth of the Albe, on the edge of the land of the Count von Schwanenstein."

I raise an eyebrow.

"We have written to the Count, asking him to deal with this problem, but he seems preoccupied with other matters, such as tournaments."

"That is regrettable, but it is his land, and he is master on it."

"The Count is also a Canon of your Cathedral."

The Rabbi, hearing this, snorts. Just about audibly. Rosheimer, undistracted, keeps his eyes on me and continues; "Have you no influence over him?"

Silence for a long moment. "No."

† † †

His Grace Bishop Berthold is still dying, but his body, bruised and bloated, seems in no haste to give up the ghost. And so the question of his Succession, which, a few years past, seemed to be a smooth transition either to me or to the Archdeacon Heinrich von Stahlem, has gradually become a tiresome political struggle. Factions emerge, make their requests, join with other factions. Silent pacts are made between individuals and parties, plots are whispered in the chapterhouse corridors, and the two candidates are forced to woo the support of men like the Count von Schwanenstein, who by quirk of tradition is indeed a Canon of the Cathedral, despite living a life of sin and dissolution.

In short, it is an unholy mess, and I am caught up in its centre. Bishop Berthold's political Genius consisted in his insistence on never choosing sides, never clearly favouring the policies of the Pope or of the Emperor. Staying inscrutably Neutral. But now he is dying, the Diocese is beginning to splinter, crack and divide.

My "faction," which I did not choose, but who instead came to me, mainly comprises members of the older families of Alsace with property in the City and the surrounding estates. The opposing "faction" has centred around those families that the present Bishop, in his thirty years of rule, ennobled, promoted and patronised in the farther marches of Alsace. My faction, broadly speaking, holds its loyalty to the Staufen Emperor Friedrich, and the opposing faction, broadly speaking, to the Pope.

When it comes to a vote, von Schwanenstein's old Alsatian hand will swear its pledge to me. And so I do not want to trouble him with tales of pirates. He cares for only two things: his Wife, who tortures him, and his Hunting Dogs, who worship him. Until I am chosen Bishop, I am in the unenviable position of being at his, and my other supporters', disposal. To retain their cooperation I must tread carefully around them, must flatter and delight them, and bring them gifts and perfumed tributes.

It is all highly tedious.

† † †

Emmerich Schäffer leans forward, his unnerving grey eyes fix shamelessly on mine. "Surely the Bishop, as Lord of the City, should act to protect the City's trade?"

"His Grace is too ill to deal with such matters as pirates now."

Emmerich sighs. Rosheimer looks at his hands.

"However, if I am elected Bishop, I will deal with the matter," I say.

They rally. "We hear that you are the Favourite to succeed!" says Rosheimer. "They say it is inevitable."

"And we hear you have been holding meeting with merchants, that you look favourably upon the world of Trade," says Schäffer. "Is it true?"

I look studyingly at this youngish man. Grey-blue eyes, stonier than his brother's. The same straw-coloured hair, but elegantly brushed and ruled, not like Master Rettich's tousled mop. A cocky cap, tilted at an insolent angle. A hood of Carelian sable that many a nobleman would envy. A cote such as lower grade merchants and salesmen wear, but trimmed with coloured silk. A mixed picture, piebald, hard to define.

But knowingly so. Emmerich Schäffer is someone who is trying to be different from Everyone Else.

"There is maybe some truth in what you say. I am . . . exploring possibilities . . . " My words trail off. From the street outside I seem to hear the distracting sound of Hieronymus roaring like a wounded boar. My chair is by the window, and the shutters are half-open, so I stand to look.

I find that the tonsured and black-robed Hieronymus has become a kind of Ogre figure for the Judengasse's children. They gather around him, hiding behind hand carts and the trunk of a solitary linden tree, creeping closer and closer until . . . Hieronymus makes a terrifying face and utters a monstrous roar. Whereupon they scatter in childish terror and hide.

I cannot help smiling. It is probably the most entertaining afternoon that Hieronymus has had for some time. Schäffer and Rosheimer, now also looking down into the street from their end of the room, smile too. For a brief moment we look at each other, united in mirth.

Emmerich folds his long, lady-like hands. "Is Our Lord Treasurer maybe interested in other proposals that He might consider, should He have the good fortune to become Bishop?"

My face indicates that I am listening.

Emmerich speaks. "A sewerage system for Hagenburg. We will start by clearing the Rheintorgässel and digging drainage for that pestilent part of town, and then continue until all main streets within the city walls are provided for with running channels of water."

"The Diocese has no funds for such huge projects."

"Impose an excise tax such as they have in Cologne. Even a small one will raise substantial funds. We will match the Diocese's expense on the sewer project one penny to the Diocese's two."

"And who will carry out the building work?"

"I will found a company to provide this service. With the Diocese, of course, as equal partner. The citizens will understand why they are being taxed. Clean streets, fresh air! Taxes are only burdensome if one cannot see the benefits of paying them. But here they will understand."

"Will they also understand that your clients the von Kronthal family, who own the Rheintorgässel, will make thousands out of this?"

"How?"

"By building new genteel properties where the shacks are now, and renting them?"

Rosheimer and Emmerich exchange a brief look. Rosheimer smiles, shrugs his shoulders, raises his palms to heaven. It says: *he's seen through our plans, but who cares.* "My Lord is very sharp-sighted. Herr Schäffer's plan is beneficial both for the City in general, and for our Client Baron Volmar von Kronthal in particular. If the Diocese were also our Client, we would offer the same service to you."

"The Diocese cannot go into partnership with Jews."

"I am not a Jew," says Emmerich, "and the Diocese's dealings would be with me."

"Look over your young shoulders, Herr Schäffer, and one sees Meir Rosheimer. Do you have any other proposals?"

Emmerich looks to Rosheimer, who briefly closes his eyes and his mouth, giving Schäffer the reins.

"Invest the Diocese's money with us. For Baron von Kronthal last year, we delivered a profit of nine *per centum*. An excellent return on investment. You may see the books if you like." Emmerich's delicate hands flutter towards a pile of ledgers at the corner of their Counting Table.

He leans forward. There is zeal in his falcon-grey eyes.

"We were so glad, My Lord, when we heard that you intended to visit us! We thought '*at last*.' An opportunity. An opportunity to wed the capital of the Diocese to our success as lenders and investors. A truly auspicious match. Profitable for both of us, My Lord."

In truth, I must admit, I am interested. Terrible is the temptation to make money, to make money grow like grapes on a vine, to make Profits swell like rivers after rain. Why earn one's bread in the sweat of one's brow? Just pay for one loaf now and lie down in the shade and sleep and wait. Then wake up, rise up and go to the Baker. And there, waiting for you on the shelf: not just one loaf, but two.

Who would not choose this easier path?

And yet Usury is a Sin.

Emmerich's grey eyes are glittering gold in the autumn's afternoon sun. Dust specks turn somersaults in the rising warmth. It looks like the Rabbi has fallen asleep. But I look again: his lips are moving, muttering some kind of soundless prayer.

I look back at Emmerich. He nods slowly, taking my silence as a confession. He smiles warmly, seeing that I am interested, understanding that I cannot say so. Yet.

His hand rises and he chews his little finger, deep in thought. Then an idea comes to him. "Half of business is information, My Lord Treasurer."

I nod. I know what he means. Foreknowledge is Golden.

"Here is some help I can provide for free. As a gesture of Goodwill."

He fixes his gaze on me. Pauses. Draws out the silence until, with anticipation, I can hardly breathe.

"Have you heard what is happening in Rome?"

ANNO
1243

Feast of Fools
(anno 1243. Manfred Gerber VI)

I t was the Jews who came to him. All smiles and talk of shared interests and mutual benefits. "We have information," they said, "about the whereabouts of the river bandits."

"And where do you have this information from?" asks Manfred, who's heating some soup on the little hearth in his Harbour warehouse. Just after Christmas. Cold, dark, the freezing arse-end of the year. The Harbour like a graveyard, empty boats bobbing on their tethers, even the Whorehouse silent.

"That we cannot tell you, Herr Gerber," says Rosheimer and holds up his shrugging hands.

"A source we trust," says Emmerich, as if that's helpful.

Manfred nods vaguely, grunts. "Well that's reassuring." They always have their secrets, the Jews. Their clever ways of knowing things. "And what do you want from me?"

Rosheimer dusts his stool with his sleeve, sits down. "They're on the Count von Schwanenstein's land."

"Just," qualifies Emmerich. "Right on the border."

"But he won't do anything."

"And the Bishop can't do anything," continues Emmerich. "He's on his deathbed."

"He's always on his deathbed."

Schäffer moves closer to the fire, lifting his coattaile, warming his behind. "Exactly. We can't wait. If Eugenius von Zabern becomes Bishop, then he would help us. But that could well take a while."

"That old crow? Help us? What makes you think that?"

"Well, we have Information about that." Once again, Rosheimer holds up his open palms. *But don't ask how.*

All this secrecy is beginning to crawl up Manfred's craw. "So? I ask again. What do you want from me?"

"Manfred. If no-one else will do anything, why don't *we*? We'll put up half the cost of an armed raid. We're looking for partners. Are you in?"

"I'd like to see you two waving a weapon." Manfred laughs.

"We'll be silent partners in the raid," says Emmerich, somehow managing to say it with a straight face, and without blushing.

"You mean you'll stay at home and warm your feet by the fire whilst some real men go and risk their lives?"

Emmerich's eyes grow cold. "We've found the bandits. We're putting up half the money. We're doing something about this problem. I grew up in the Vogesen, watching sheep. No one ever taught me how to kill a man. Now, are you in or are you out?"

"Do you want some hot soup?"

Emmerich looks at Manfred a moment, assessing the offer. Then nods. "I'll have some, thank you."

Manfred looks over to Rosheimer. Rosheimer bows, holds his hand to his heart, declining.

"Come on, eat with me."

"No thank you, Herr Gerber."

"It's good soup."

"Thank you, but no."

Manfred holds Rosheimer's gaze a moment, two moments, three moments. "All right, suit yourself." He ladles out two bowls. Split beans, pearl barley, ox bones. And plenty of *polvere forte*, the hot spice mix from the Levant. Burns your mouth, makes your nose run, gives your arsehole a stinging goodbye-kiss the next morning.

He watches as Emmerich takes his first spoonful. Tastes it.

Gasps a bit, then nods. "Hmm, spicy," he says, and eats some more.

Damn. Most people who eat his soup run screaming to the nearest pitcher of water. Disappointed, Manfred shrugs, takes a big gulp, drinking straight from his bowl. He looks around the warehouse, shelves laden with rolls of fabric, with sacks of grain ready to sell in the weeks before Lent when they fetch the highest price. Now, in the Dark Weeks, commerce is quiet. But as Lent wears on, the roads open again, the River Trade starts to flow.

The pirates, those Parasites, will be waiting.

† † †

The fifth barrel of wine is being breached in the Cathedral Crossing. Sleeves wipe mouths as the cups are handed around. The New Year's Wine, a gift from the Bishop to his congregation. The Masons have brought a barrow, and they're piling the drunks on it, pushing them to the South Portal and throwing them outside.

Laughter. The crowds push and pulse. No one's ever seen the Cathedral so full before. It's always crowded for the Feast of Fools; the World and his Wife, but not like this, not so's you can hardly move.

A wide, moon-like child's face. A Mitre atop his head, a Crosier held upside down in his shaking hands. Riding on a donkey, round and round, round and round the Crossing, circling the wine barrel. The Cathedral Orphan Einolf has been enthroned as Bishop for the day. The drunken crowd slap the donkey's flanks and kiss the Orphan Bishop's spit-shiny, trembling cheeks.

The Lord of Misrule, the subdeacon, is dressed as the Pope. He stands in the pulpit, ringing Uto's bell, and shouts. "*Good News! The Virgin got knocked up! By an Angel! Be happy!*

Gaudete! Three Kings have come from the East! And they're all three of them fools! Rejoice!"

The musicians squeeze their way through the crowd. The Big Drum sounds. You feel it in your stomach. Boom boom. Like the heart of a Giant beating in your guts. Boom boom. Boom boom. The band surround the pulpit, and the Lord of Misrule sings: *Mir han nen Bischofen, nen Narrenbischofen nen Dreckbischofen, habemus Arschepissco-popum! . . . a foolbishop a filthbishop, we have a new Arse and piss bishop!*

It's the same song as every year, but this year it feels different. This year there's no Order at all. Over in the Choir they're trying to carry out a proper service and Liturgy, but Lord knows if they'll ever get to the end and bless the bread and wine. The real Bishop, Berthold von Dietz, hasn't been seen for a year. And there's no Pope. Gregorius died, and Pope Celestine was only on the Roman throne a few months before he croaked too. Now the Cardinals scrap and screech like fishwives and can't agree on a new Holy Father. Rome is the capital of a Disorder hooking its arms with the reeling, drunken, Upside-Down World. The Pope is a Satyr, the Bishop an Orphan, the Cathedral is a whorehouse tavern, swarming with drunks and bawds.

Manfred climbs a pile of stones near the Nave scaffold, takes a swig from his wineskin, looks around. A hundred candles burn in the crown-shaped iron chandelier. The cornices and turrets that hold the candles are shaped as buildings, an image of the Holy City, Jerusalem. And beneath its holy lights, Pandemonium. Surges of people, swirls of movement. Dances break out and fall apart.

Manfred feels a power here, something raw, unformed. The People's Power, lost in drunken chaos and unbridled abandon. How to harness it? How to target it, like a crossbow quarrel, at the Diadem, the Crown, the Mitre, so that they can all Take What's Theirs? So that Manfred can rise to be like them, the Lords of the Sword and Cross and Pen?

Manfred looks over to where Grete is drinking with her Draper friends, all in their finery, surrounded by their seamstresses and apprentices. Over there the Drapers, over here the Cobblers, in the corner, the Silversmiths. The newly formed Guilds of Hagenburg, new colleges of strength, new unions, but each to his own. How to yoke them all together, to haul the drunken, dragging world to a new horizon?

Grete sees him perched on his throne of stones. She raises her bowl of wine to him. The Lord of Misrule shrieks. *Habemus Arschepissco-popum!*

Manfred sinks down, rests his legs a while, sits. Why not go into business with the Jews this time? The City's Merchants, striking a blow at banditry. Solving our own problems, our own way. Let the Count go and fuck his dogs, if that's all he cares about.

But one thing's clear, Manfred must lead the Expedition. And as the main risk-taker, his capital downpayment should be lower. One fifth. Let the Jews raise the missing three tenths themselves.

It's a risk worth taking. If he routs the bandits, who's going to remember who paid for it all? They'll remember the Hero who wielded the sword, not the Fools who paid the gold. And in business, Reputation is everything.

He'll do it.

Manfred raises his wine skin and drinks to himself. Suddenly the Cathedral bell tolls, loud and low, bringing him to his feet. What's this?

Uto has taken his bell from the Deacon. Standing in the pulpit, he begins to swing it, slow and loud. His face is a picture: sombre respect. His left hand rises slowly into the air, commanding silence. High above them all, the Cathedral bell tolls once more.

Something has happened.

Shouts and whispers snake through the crowds. *Quiet!*

Stop! Listen! Uto lets his bell ring into the rising, hushing swell. It fades out, silver to the last. A pause.

"Our Lord and Master, Bishop Berthold von Dietz . . . " Uto's voice breaks with tears. Real emotion? An Act? " . . . this morning, in his Castle in Haldenheim . . . " The crowds are now silent. Uto's voice resounds, a cracked bell. " . . . has passed into Glory. God rest his soul."

Gasps and some titters. A Fools' Day joke?

"The Canons of the Great Chapter have been summoned. Many, such as Our Lord Treasurer von Zabern, are abroad, in Rome. The convocation may take some time."

Manfred, shocked, excited, turns, his eyes raking the congregation . . . and finds Emmerich. Schäffer's grey eyes had sought him out too. Their gaze locks, confirms. They understand. Everything has changed.

Uto continues. "The funeral will take place the day after tomorrow, here in the Cathedral. And now, in mourning and respect, we declare today's celebrations over."

A wave of sound breaks into the silence. Wails and laments, a crash of chatter. Gossipers, stoked by wine, turn to their neighbours and gasp, exclaim.

Manfred jumps down from the stones, struggles towards Emmerich in the throng. "Let's wait this out, Gerber," says Schäffer. "Why pay for a small expedition, when Bishop Eugenius can mount a proper raid?"

Manfred peers at Emmerich, doubtful.

"Gerber. The man told us himself. Everything is set to change."

Manfred pulls away from Schäffer. He looks for Grete amongst the gossiping crowds, and smiles. On the Feast of Fools, the World is turned upside down. And as the world is topsy turvy already, it means, on the Feast of Fools, everything is turned the Right Way Up.

For once. Just for one day.

THE CROWNED SHADOW
(Eugenius von Zabern VI. anno 1243)

From my balcony near the Basilica of St. Peter, I can watch the gangs roaming the streets, searching each other out. A confrontation: the two gangs face each other, shout imprecations and insults, throw stones and horse dung and rubbish at each other. Then the bravest will run forward, flashing a blade. The briefest of skirmishes, a feint at an arm or leg, a flood of insults, howls like a pack of starving, stray dogs, and then they retreat their separate ways.

Over a year and no Pope. And amongst the Cardinals, the different factions struggling for Supremacy. Those who would excommunicate Friedrich, cry "heretic," plunder the Papal coffers, pay to send an army to Imperial Lombardy and claim it for the Pope. And Those who believe in some form of balance between Emperor and Church, who owe something to Friedrich and the Staufen clan, whose home territories have Imperial loyalties. These two main camps, and every shade of colour in between, and not even one shadow of Compromise.

Over a year and no Pope. The disunity has spread from the Curia to the streets, each faction hiring agitators and protectors, men with clubs and blades. Rome is like a wedding dance, with the squabbling conclave of Cardinals as the unmoving centre, and all around it the drunken guests wheel, turn, crash and collide, spinning in violent and vertiginous circles.

It is two weeks after Epiphany and I have only just heard of His Grace's death. A letter has arrived from Hieronymus in Arles, where I left him on route for just this purpose; a messenger-boy halfway between Hagenburg and the Holy City. I am needed urgently in Hagenburg. It is now time for our own Conclave, our own election.

But there is one last thing in Rome that I need to do.

The rain is falling again and the roaming of the gangs has momentarily ceased. The Sext bell has not yet struck, but it will be timely to use this lull and set out. I pull on my cloak. Outside in the courtyard, my men-at-arms are waiting for me, sheltering in an alcove, warming themselves with branntwein in the absence of a fire.

† † †

Sometimes it is better to act in darkness. Even when one cannot well see what one is doing, it is better that there are no witnesses. When the sun rises and light returns to the world, then will your deeds be judged.

In these days of Chaos, the sun's sphere is hidden and the world has turned on its dark side. Mother Church has no Holy Father, the Infidel Hordes surround the walls of Jerusalem, and the fierce armies of the Mongols are at the gates of Christendom. All is in turmoil and flux.

Of the chaos in the conclave I had of course heard from our Curia contacts, and something of the disorder of the Roman streets had been related in their letters, in outraged tones. But it was the Merchants' news that resolved me to come. The Jews and Merchants may know nothing of the Cardinals' deliberations, but they know everything about their own idol, Gold.

They told me in urgent whispers: *the Gold is moving*. The Banks are quietly, secretly fleeing the insecurity of Rome and the Status Pontificius. They are moving their capital North-West, up the Via Cassia. To Florence. New families are emerging, new financial potentates, new opportunities. Rome, the

City where I lost thousands, is in chaos. Rome, the City that undid me, is undone.

Time to return, to rewrite the books under the cover of chaos and darkness.

† † †

I kiss the Bishop's warm and swollen hand, keep hold of it, a dead weight in mine. I kneel beside his dying body and whisper to him of my Roman plan.

A constant stream of tears wells from his rheumy eyes. He blinks without ceasing, struggles for breath. His body is nearing ruin, but his mind is clear, and his ears are listening.

"I want this chance, My Lord, to make amends for my earlier errors. I was led astray by Terzani, who promised so much and delivered so little. We should move our accounts from the House of Terzani to the Bardi of Florence. Our money will be safer there. And, whilst making this move, we will be able to restructure our financial relations in Rome."

His Grace's eyes narrow, move. He is indicating the small pile of kerchiefs that lie beside his pillow. I take one, and wipe his eyes for him. He breathes in deeply. "Restructure?"

I must confess, I am nervous. In times of Peace and Sunlight, I would never even think of what I am about to suggest. But in times of chaos and darkness . . . "Let us cut the prebends of Carducci and the Vittorini. Cut them for good."

My Lord's face is a picture; a perfect marriage of shock and grudging admiration. His swollen lips contort into a smile. If he could breathe better, I am sure he would laugh. "*You fox!*" he rasps.

"Their influence in Rome has been waning for some years now. A river of gold flows their way from Hagenburg, and coming back to Hagenburg from them? Nothing at all. Let us cut them free."

His hand, two pounds of dropsied, swollen meat, squeezes mine. "And their benefices, Eugenius, their Canonries?"

"They are in your gift, Your Grace."

"You must have someone in mind . . . ."

"I would not presume . . . "

"*Who?*"

"Liebenheim, the Dean's protégé. Our Chapter needs some young blood."

"And you will get the Dean's vote for this? And all of his faction in the Chapter?"

Why hide it? I nod. His Grace's face forms into a strangled approximation of a smile. "Then let's give the second benefice to von Kolzeck."

"That old sycophant?"

"Not him. His younger son."

"He's not yet eight years old."

"Maybe so. But then your election is certain, Eugenius. The waverers will come to you. Your complexion was too Staufisch, too Imperial, too *Old Alsace*. With a gift to Kolzeck and a young, rising noble family, you look open to compromise."

The words come slowly, and at great effort. The Bishop's breath falls harder, rasps. A coughing fit comes upon him. Immediately the two valets are at hand, running from their stools by the fire, rolling his bulk forward onto his stomach where the coughs come easier, saving him from suffocation. His hunting dogs, sensing his discomfort, rise and scatter round the room, moving in agitated circles.

It is a good, long time before His Grace can breathe again. The dogs settle at his feet, the valets return, silently, to their chairs. His watery eyes fix on mine. "Do it, Eugenius. Do it, and you will win. Go to Rome."

His hand lets go of mine, moves slowly back to rest on the bed. "I fear I will not see you again, Eugenius." He sinks onto his back. His eyes stare at the ceiling, where the fire's flames send a dance of shadows. "I had a dream last Sunday. I saw you enthroned. With mitre and crosier. All shining gold."

His eyes are bright with water, rivulets run down his cheeks. "The new Cathedral, Eugenius. Promise me you will keep the work going. Promise me."

"I promise you, Your Grace."

His eyes close.

† † †

We are not the only ones venturing out under the cover of the rain. Old Roman women with baskets waddle to the market, priests and monks hold tight to the shelter of the walls, their hoods pulled down low, hurrying from Church to Monastery.

Gathered in a group under the archway of a grand house, one of the gangs, eating bread and soup, watching the passing traffic of the street. Their leader is the only one standing, tossing a knife into the air and catching it. Each time it spirals three times before landing safely in his palm. He doesn't need to look whilst doing it; instead he eyes my troop as we pass, nods me a sarcastic greeting. *Groosgott, bastardi.*

It is a short walk to the place we have chosen for the meeting. A small hall built adjacent to the German Church, paid for by German merchants as a meeting place and storeroom. I am early, but already they are both there. Ludovico, agent of the House of Bardi. And Guido Terzani.

Terzani's eyes are cold, but he puts on a show of a smile. Like a peacock opening its beautiful tail and screaming its eerie cry, the combination is unnerving. "*Signor Tesoriere!* I swear you are even taller than when last we met. Have you grown?"

"I doubt it, Signor Terzani."

"In boldness, certainly. I am taken aback by your brazen

courage. You are moving all your accounts to this gentleman's bank?" His hand springs towards Ludovico, a gesture both elegant and rudely dismissive at the same time.

Ludovico bows to me. "Welcome, Signore von Zabern."

But Terzani is in full flow, "And closing your, shall we say, *alliances* with Carducci and Vittorini? A bold move."

"Their fortunes are declining."

"And so are mine, I see. Why? We Terzani also have a bureau in Florence, if that is your concern. I understand. Rome is no longer safe."

I have seen Terzani in my dreams for nine long years. And in my dreams I have strangled him, stabbed him, broken him upon the wheel, had him flogged in public on the steps of St. Peter's, and enjoyed every minute of the spectacle. Now I hold out my hand. "The deal is done. Your signature is required, that is all."

He shakes my hand with sarcastic warmth. "It has been a pleasure, *Signor Tesoriere*. Fortune's wheel is turning, and I am falling with Carducci and Vittorini, and you are rising. You will be Bishop, I hear?"

"There will be an election."

"Fortune's wheel is always turning, is it not? Don't you ecclesiastics always lecture us on this point? Today a King, tomorrow a Beggar, today a Bishop, tomorrow a Leper . . . Why strive and struggle for the vainglory of this transitory world? The true Life comes after Death."

"You should have been a priest."

Terzani smiles, a bright, sudden smile like the slash of a knife. "But I actually believe in what I am saying."

An uncomfortable silence settles on the room. From outside, the gentle chatter of the rain. Inside, the hall's caretaker, a bent old man, takes his broom and starts to sweep the dusty corners. Two German Merchants are asleep at one table, their elbows touching, their peaceful snores synchronised.

Ludovico breaks the silence with a gentle cough, and pours out three glasses of red wine. His hand gestures to the table, where the account ledgers are lying open, waiting to be signed.

† † †

The news from the harbour is good; the sea wind is from the South. A propitious time to set sail along the coast for Arles and the mouth of the Rhône. With Good Fortune, we can be in Hagenburg before Lent.

Good Fortune. Terzani's strange words have stayed with me. They echo in my mind, unwelcome visitors. *Why struggle and strive for the vainglory of this transitory world?* It is a question I have often posed myself, and answered thusly: all is Vanity.

All is Vanity. His Grace put the idea in my mind that I might be Bishop. Since then this idea has grown, taking on gigantesque proportions, eclipsing all my other thoughts. And why? Why am I now so concerned to become Bishop? Why will it make such a difference if I am enthroned, and not Archdeacon Heinrich von Stahlem? And will it not transform my Life into a continuous stress and torment, agonising over the exercise of power, deciding the fates of the Diocese and Upper Rhine?

Why do I therefore run towards this dream and embrace it with such passion?

And His Grace's final request, to preserve the Cathedral as his "gift to posterity." What is this new Cathedral if not the product of two vanities, the Bishop's and Achim von Esinbach's? Their desire to see their Will glorified in living stone?

My saddle bags are ready. I sit, prepared, wrapped in furs on my freezing balcony. The moon lights the bell-tower of St. Peter's. It is an hour or more until dawn.

The journey will be a wearying one. An unruly sea, and then a land frozen in snow and ice. On our way here, it was my first crossing of the Vogesen in winter. Our horses' legs sinking to their hocks in the drifts, in the lonely mountain villages, peasants staring at me and Hieronymus, taking us for apparitions, harbingers of disaster.

A raven followed us for three days, always flying above us, alighting always on the snow-deep road ahead, a Guide. As we descended from the frozen mountains towards the safety of Bisanz and the Burgundian plain, the Raven began to cry. And as we approached the City walls, it circled thrice above us, cawing with such insistence that we paused.

There was a Calvary by the roadside, dedicated to St. Arbogast, Hagenburg's founding Saint. The Raven, hoarse with crying, swooped down and landed there, high up on the Calvary Cross. It uttered one last cry and then launched itself into the freezing air, heading back to the heights whence it had come.

Hieronymus turned to look at me. "This is a good omen, My Lord."

"Don't talk like an old woman," I said. But, God forgive me, I had had the same thought.

And in Arles, five days later, on Sunday. After weeks of cloud, darkness, sleet and rain, there rose the most perfect Sun in a pure sapphire sky. We took Mass at the Cathedral. The sun shone through the eastern windows of the Apse, blessing the congregation with weak but long-awaited warmth.

I gave passionate thanks to God and prayed for safe journey on the seas to Genoa and Rome. My prayers took quite some time. As I left the Cathedral, it was nearly empty. The low sun shone through the stained glass, throwing my shadow, unnaturally stretched and tall, all the way up the length of the Nave. I stopped. God forgive me, but I took it as another Sign:

Around my shadowed head, a crown of golden brightness, a corona of haloed light.

† † †

Finally the Lauds bell sounds from the tower. I gather my bags, swing them over my shoulder. Call out to my men, sleeping nearby.

Inside my room, I blow out the lamp.

So much of our human striving is but Vanity. To leave a mark. A sign that we were here. A trace of our passing on this passing world.

† † †

The wind is fair, all is ready. The last merchandise is being loaded onto our barque. They will take us as far as Genoa, from where we can most certainly find a ship for Marseille. The harbour is noisy, crowded with working men and men looking for work. I retreat into the St. Christopher's chapel to pray for a safe journey. As I kneel down before the altar, I note with wry amusement how devout I have become of late, preparing for my coming role as pastor of fifty thousand souls.

Exiting the chapel, I hear raised voices. My armed guard, three Germans, a Dane and an Englander, are exchanging words with a local gang. As I approach, I can hear the words "Emperor" "heretic" "Pope." I sigh. Politics.

I do not know what my men-at-arms understand of politics, but I do know they profess loyalty to Emperor Friedrich but also have sworn lifelong allegiance to Mother Church (at seven shillings a week). They are probably somewhat confused.

"Come, let's embark, forget this!" I order. But their Roman interlocutors have no wish to end the discussion. In a doggerel mix of Latin, Roman dialect, and the occasional German word (mainly, "Scheisse"), they passionately explain that the Emperor is a heretic, a homosexual and a German.

It is hardly a new discussion. "Let's GO!" I shout, pointing imperiously at the ship.

One of the Romans approaches me. His face is scarred, his body squat but powerful. A street fighter. "What do you say, German Scheisse?"

"We have heard this discussion before, and we must leave. Good day."

"You don't like speak with us, Master?"

He pulls out a knife. A ridiculous blade! Shorter than my little finger, its point a cross, two tiny blades welded together. It appears more a cobbler's awl, not a weapon. I laugh. I am almost twice as tall as him. "I am leaving now."

Suddenly a fluttering. Something passes over my eyes, a brief shadow. I cannot move my arms.

It was a rope. It is now holding me tight. I try and cry out but the air has been taken from me by a sudden kick to the small of my back.

A leg. A leg hooks into mine, throws me. I plunge to the ground.

In a brief moment I see that the Romans have surrounded my men-at-arms, shouting. Blocking sight of me. My men have not seen me fall.

The small scarred man leaps onto my chest. Squats on me like a spider, holds aloft his hand. "This is a message to you, *Tesoriere*. From your Roman friends."

I now understand the little blade. But it is too late.

His hand strikes down, the strike of a serpent, into my eye. He pushes, tears from side to side. I scream, but his left hand is over my mouth. The pain makes my body convulse in waves, but I am trussed like a Christmas Eve pig, and his unseen accomplice's hands hold me fast.

"You understand?" he says.

"Please . . . " I beg. Pointlessly.

His hand strikes down again. A shudder of pain, a thud. A spasm of light flashes in my mind.

A final image. His scarred face, grinning.

Immediately he jumps from my chest. I can feel his weight going into some unseen void. The rope is released. The two hands that were holding my head slip away. I can hear voices, the argument. The argument is suddenly over. The sound of running feet, shouts, screams. Milling chaos. Footfalls around my supine body. The gang is escaping.

"My Lord! My Lord! My Lord!"

I want to cry, but there is nothing to cry with. Blood is washing over my face in the place of tears. My throat convulses into sobs.

And in my mind. That beautiful sight, in Arles Cathedral, after Communion. The sun behind me, and my shadowy head crowned in mocking gold.

Four sacks of Turnips, Two Pounds of Rice
(Manfred Gerber VII. anno 1243)

It doesn't get any easier. Each time he straps on his sword, fastens his chainmail, dons his helmet, the fear of death loosens his bowels, paints his face pasty white. He tries to control it, plays with his moustache, smoothes his beard, gives orders, makes jokes to the men, but it's always there, a pressure, seeking release. His stomach juices sluice through his guts, his hands twitch and sweat.

And so here he is, Captain Manfred, squatting on the latrine at the barge's stern, letting it all out into the Rhine's grey waters.

Setting a fine example, for sure.

None of the men seems to care. A cheap, desperate lot, lured from the Rheintorgässel with the promise of silver. Labourers, pimps, thieves. Using vermin to chase out vermin. God willing, he, Bertle, Rolo and the other Town Watch soldiers can keep them bridled.

This weather doesn't know what it wants to be. Dawn came up bright and sharp, frosting the grass of the riverbank. As they struck camp and slipped their moorings, they slid into a bank of white, drifting mists. And now, gliding into the eddying water, soft flakes of late winter snow.

Manfred splashes some water on his arse and ties his braies. Hitches his armour back into position. Walks the length of the boat, patting shoulders, punching arms. Primping his own Courage into bloom. "Get ready, men, we'll be there soon. From now on, silence. Not a bloody word."

He reaches the prow. Günther is ship captain. Old, deaf, but no one knows the waters better. He points his bony finger at the reeds and banks of silt half-seen in the mist. "The Albe," he whispers, "prepare to row." Günther signals to his punt-men. They raise their poles as Günther steers into the upriver swell.

The men slide out the oars, dip and pull. The puntpoles slide into the silt, push, and come up slick with freezing slime. The barge turns, lists, heavy with its cargo of men.

Those not rowing steady themselves against the rocking with their spears, clubs, swords. The barge lurches as it finds its new course, sends two men tumbling. Stifled laughter. Manfred turns, shows a stern face: *Silence!*

Günther has turned it well, ruddering through the banks of silt into the only clear channel in the labyrinth of weeds and sand. A canal not much wider than the boat, lined with mud and rushes, leading into drifting mist.

No turning back.

† † †

In the meagre first days of Lent, Manfred meets with his fellow Merchants at the Morning Altar, they thresh out the plans for the coming, fatter months. All is in tension. The City awaits the return of Eugenius von Zabern from Rome, the Convocation of the Great Chapter, the Election of the new Bishop.

Manfred walks with Wikerus the grain merchant up and down the length of the Nave. Wikerus needs a boatload of grain transported from the granaries of the Meuse to arrive in Hagenburg in time for Easter Week.

"Prices are going up, Wikerus. Name me one thing that costs the same as last year. Listen, old man, even the priests are charging more for funerals. When it's getting more expensive to Die, then you really know . . . "

Wikerus holds up his hand. "Wait, Gerber, something's happening." A ripple of rumour is snaking its way through the Cathedral crowds.

Outside, the Lent market-stalls are mean, bare. Between the melancholy trestle tables of cabbages, turnips and kale, a ragged procession is making its way. From all directions, the Curious come, a noisy tide of gossipers that then ebbs into silence.

Manfred and Wikerus join the hushed crowd. At the centre they can see two clerics, both tall and stooping. A voice says, "It is this way, Sire, we are nearly there." Hieronymus, the Treasury Clerk. He is guiding someone over the cobblestones.

It is von Zabern. His proud head bowed, shadowed by his cowl. An invalid, a beggar, led by Hieronymus' underling hand. A staff, like a pilgrim's, he holds before him, feeling the air. And then his head sweeps upwards and the crowd exhales. Two black, encrusted Wounds where should be his Eyes.

† † †

Screams. Hoarse, full-throated. Inhuman.

Sweeping down through the mist, fluttering shapes, then twisted arms.

A willow, leaning over the river. And fighting in its branches, two jackdaws and a crow. The loud retort of wings like the sound of a pennant whipped by a high wind. Some of the men cross themselves. The willow's bony fingers scrape the deck.

The reeds and rushes are thinning out now, the banks becoming more solid, formed. On one side, the mist is clearing, revealing flooded, churned fields of muddied ice.

Manfred stands on the prow, looking for a sign of human life.

Two coracles pulled up on the shore. Logs laid across marshy puddles; a jetty. A path dug by struggling feet zig-zagging up the bank.

This is it.

Fingers to his lips, Manfred gives the signal to land. Already five torches are burning in the hands of the Rheintorgässel men. This is a raid of destruction, retribution. No mercy, no house left standing, no prisoners.

Manfred crosses himself, faces the men.

A whisper. "Let's go."

† † †

A darting flash of iron. A spark flies from the nose-piece of his helmet, burns his eye. The blade glances, slicing his cheek. His left arm sweeps out, grabbing the shaft.

The bandit tugs hard, tries to pull his spear back. But Manfred holds fast. With his right he flails with his sword. A panicked strike, but a good one. The bandit's arm cut to the bone. The spear comes loose into Manfred's grasp. A Rheintorgässel pimp grabs the spear, flips it round, plunges it into the bandit's fleeing neck.

One more down. Smoke gutters from the sodden straw rooves. The pirates are running. Some are already in coracles, paddling like drowning puppies. Others plunge and flail in the mud, grabbing at the boats' tottering sides. Three or four tear along the embankment, heading for the highway, pursued by Rolo and his men.

Five, who stayed to fight, lie dead or dying in the mud.

Blood stings Manfred's eye. Its salty, metallic taste in his mouth. He holds his sleeve to the wound. Just a small cut, but deep. He'll have a scar! Girls will trace their soft fingers along it and he'll tell the story, pulling them onto his lap. He laughs with manic excitement, feels like vomiting, holds it back.

He turns the dying man over with his feet. The bandit's eyes flutter, roll. His limbs twitch, reach spastically for his neck, where it hurts. His mouth spits, looking for purchase on the

Word he so much wants to say. "Mmmmur, mmur." Murder? Mummy? Mercy?

"Who's your leader? Where is he?" shouts Manfred, kicking the man's ribs.

The pirate grins, a bitter rictus. "You'll . . . never . . . find him. Bast . . . ard. He'll . . . kill . . . you. Bast . . . "

His mouth stops moving. Yawns, lips curling back from his teeth. Face contorts into a scowling skull. The last slack tremors and then rigidity.

So that's what Dying looks like. It doesn't look like much fun.

Manfred strides into one of the huts. Hammocks, sacks of straw gathered round a central fireplace. Smoke-blackened wicker-work of branches, wattle. A threadbare haunch of meat, sacks of turnips. A pot of uncooked rice.

His cheek throbs, stings. He should wash the wound. His mind is racing, high with excitement. He needs time to think.

"Is this a joke?" It's the Rheintorgässel pimp who speared the bandit, grabbing Manfred's shoulder. The Pimp looks at him, eyes dark and hostile. He kicks at the turnips. "Is this our booty?"

"You'll get your money. Calm down."

The Pimp's hand flashes out, grabs Manfred's jerkin at the neck. "I saved your life."

"No you didn't."

"They said there would be booty. Not fucking turnips."

Time to leave. Set fire to the place and get out before Mutiny can whisper and spread. "You'll get your money. I need to wash my wound."

Manfred strides back outside, where the smoke is thickening. Bertle is coming out of the third hut, shares a look with Manfred, shakes his head. Nothing.

Manfred thinks of the stolen cargoes. Coin, silks, tapestries, rolls of Flemish cloth, raw wool from England, wine. Copper from the Harz, swords from Magdeburg. Amber, soap, perfume. Grain.

"Bertle," he whispers. "Where is it? Did they *spend it all*?"

"Be happy, Fredle. These bastards won't trouble us no more."

A butt, full of rainwater. Manfred kneels beside it, scoops up icy handfuls and cleans his wound. The first hut's roof falls in, consumed by fire. Sparks somersault upwards, meeting the sparse snow as it spirals down.

All gone. Sold? Hidden? And these men, squatting in misery through the bitter winter in makeshift huts, waiting for the spring trade to return. What profit did they have from it? Just hired mercenaries?

If so, then hired by Whom?

Father Arnold gets down from the boat. On a normal day he sweeps the Cathedral steps and says mass at a side altar in St. Peter's by the Vogesen Gate. They hired him for a shilling; the cheapest they could get. But he's ordained, and God listens to what he says.

He starts his work, waving his cross and chanting over the dead. Nine bandits, two of ours; Rheintorgässel thieves who got themselves in the way of a blade. The Priest gets an extra sixpence for every Last Rite he gives. He was probably praying for a massacre.

"Start digging a pit for their nine. We'll take our two back with us," says Manfred to the gaggle of cold, disenchanted men standing by the pillaged sacks of turnips and the pot of rice. "There are shovels on board."

They turn to look at him. Their hungry eyes are sharp and cold.

Manfred remembers the Feast of Fools. After a skin of wine and in festival candlelight, the power of the People looked so fine, like gold, a blessed force that would tear the Sceptre from the undeserving hands of Kings. Here it seems different. Black gaping mouths, snow settling on their sackcloth hoods like shrouds, hearts full of cold disappointment, a short step away from Mutiny.

Manfred's armour alone would keep them in food and wine for a fortnight.

"Come, I'll help you dig," says Manfred. No time for Lording it now. Time to get his hands dirty, like he used to before Fortune raised him on her Wheel. "Bertle, let's warm up some wine. And spice it fine. These men deserve a good warm drink."

When in Doubt, pour out the Wine.

ABOMINATION
(ANNO 5003. YUDL BEN YITZHAK II)

Keep not thy silence, O God: hold not thy peace, and be not still,
O God.
For, lo, thine enemies make a tumult . . .
Do unto them as unto the Midianites; as to Sisera, as to Jabin:
make them as the stubble before the wind . . .
persecute them with thy tempest, and terrify them with thy
storm . . .
Let them be put to shame, and perish:
That men may know that thou, whose name alone is YHVH,
art the most high over all the earth.

His Father told him: make fish glue. Go forth amongst the
Gentiles and buy fish bones and bring them unto me. He told
him, "Think of the Psalm *keep not thy silence, O God,* as you
wander amongst them. I always do."

Yudl must concentrate as he walks to the Fischmarkt.
Normally, he never leaves the Judengasse. He only knows the
one route that his father showed him; left here, straight on,
here left again. The route is a red thread unravelled through
the network of Hagenburg streets; a path of safety. On either
side of it, lies the Labyrinth, lies the Unknown.

Yudl keeps his eyes fixed on his wooden-soled shoes as
they march through the mud and cobbles. His eyes flick
upwards when they have to, register the landmarks, keeping
an eye out for possible trouble. And he realises the obvious
truth. His Father has taught Yudl this route so that he can go

in his stead. So that, from now on, Father never has to leave his Books.

But doesn't Father go on journeys every day? When he opens a book, he spreads his wings, he floats into Eternity and resides there. His travelling companions are the Letters of the Alphabet, burning with fire, racing through the spheres like comets. His Father's Soul sits in the curve of Beth as in a chariot, a chariot pulled by the horses of Vav and Zayin and Nun. Ahead, beckoning him to follow them, silent Ayin and Aleph, burning on the distant horizon, the imagined world of perfection. Isn't reading itself a pilgrimage into the Eternal Mysteries, into the . . . ?

"Where am I?" asks Yudl to himself. "Oh Lord, where am I?"

He stops and looks around. He doesn't recognise this street. The horrid Cross stands high above him over the gate to a building. Two monks pass through the gate; it must be a monastery. A monastery he has never seen before.

Looking back down the way he came, he sees a large wooden sign, carved: a feather quill and a pot of ink. The Schriwerstublgass! He has walked right past it!

Yudl retraces his steps. "Don't get distracted and lose your way again," he says to himself. "Concentrate."

Yudl reads the Red Book whenever he can. It is his obsession. To wait for silence in the houses, in the courtyard. To steal upstairs . . .

. . . the angels must have cried to see it, ophanim and galgalim, the hosts, the spirits of Israel. The Talmud, burning, and the goyyim rejoicing at the fire . . .

His Father's words. In the red leather book. The Book of Secrets. The Book of All Things That We Hide From Yudl.

In a square in Paris, they made a huge bonfire, and there

they burned one thousand of our books. And think of this! The goyyim had first set the Talmud on trial, with judges and priests as prosecutors and Rabbis as defenders and they had found the Talmud guilty, and thrown it to the fire! And no one told Yudl about it. Not even a word. Not even in passing. "Yudl, collect our bread from the oven and by the way, did you hear? The Goyyim burned a thousand Talmuds in Paris." Not even that.

But Frankfurt he had heard about. They couldn't keep that quiet. Much as they tried, much as they whispered it to each other once the children were asleep. News like that finds its way to all ears, eventually. The Rabbi of Frankfurt and his pupils shot with bows and arrows. The Jews of the city hiding in a tower, and slaughtered to a man.

The Rabbi says, "Fear not . . . if they are planning such things here, the Strawhead Goy will warn us. He is our eyes and ears in the City, he has spies in the Rathaus and the Bishop's Palace. He will warn us."

Lord forbid, our lives are in the hands of He Who Has No Name.

In Frankfurt a Christian and a Jewess had a child. They found out the child had not been Baptised. And that's when the trouble started.

Yudl stops. At the corner of Seilergass and Fleischmarkt. Something has come to his mind. The Gentiles' Abomination.

Its dome can always be seen, towering above the sloping rooves, above the gable shutters, the chimneys. When he left the Judengasse, it was in front of him. But now it is behind his back. How can that be?

How can something that was in front of you end up behind you? Without walking past it?

Yudl shakes his head. This is confusing. Like everything else in his life. With the point of his shoes he tries to draw in the mud at the side of the road; geometric patterns like the Rabbi has shown him. The triangle in the circle, with all its sides the same. The Abomination in the centre of the circle, and Yudl's trajectory . . . going . . . round . . .

"Move, boy, you're in the way."

A porter wants to push past with his handcart. Yudl steps aside, and the wheels of the cart dissect his circle, straight through the middle.

It's true. He has walked in a semi-circle. The way his Father has shown him is not the quickest way. It is a route that avoids the Abomination. The Abomination that Yudl has never seen.

Yudl moves on. Everyone is looking at him. Strange little boy, drawing signs in the mud. At the corner of Metzgergass, he looks back to where he had been standing. A man and a woman are there, hands on hips, looking down at his diagram, shaking their heads.

Yudl moves on towards the nearby Fischmarkt. He thinks about the Jews of Frankfurt, the boys hiding with their Rabbi in the Beth Midrash, reciting the *Shema Yisrael* and praying that they will not be found. Then the pounding on the door, the breaking of the locks. The soldiers rush in . . .

And Yudl can think no more.

In his Father's fantasies, all the Goyyim's evils are avenged, the Jews' exile is over, their sorrows are at an end. *The day when we shall wear golden garments and the Edomites will serve us as kings, when their murderers shall be dashed against the wall, when the blood of martyrdom shall be revenged.*

The Fischmarkt. His nose tells him he has arrived. He looks up from his mud-spattered shoes to the trestle tables laden with their silvery, slippery cargo, the water in the barrels wriggling and writhing.

First to the back of *zum Creutze*, the tavern nearby. His

Father made a deal with the serving girl there. She keeps fish-bones in a sack that hangs from the outhouse ceiling, where the cats can't get at it; the customers' leftovers.

He knocks at the tavern's back door. An angry-looking cook opens. Red-rimmed piggy eyes glare at Yudl from above his three chins. "What do you want, boy?"—"Is Guda there?"—"I'll get her."

Guda comes, looking flustered. Her eyes look blank an instant, and then recognise Yudl. She pinches his cheek. "How are you, my treasure?"—"Thank you, I am well, Fräulein."—"Such a polite boy. Come with me."

In the outhouse, Guda reaches up with a hook on a pole to detach the hanging bag. Her gown pulls tight around her but-tocks. *Look away. Sinful thoughts begone.* "A big bag this time, Yudl. What do you use the glue for anyway?"—"To make ink."—"Ink? For books and that?"—"That's right, Fräulein."—"Well aren't you a clever boy."—"That's for oth-ers to say, Fräulein."—"Well I'm saying it. Give me tuppence ha'penny."

At the fish market, Yudl selects a carp. "Not too big, not too small," said his Mother that morning, "a middle-sized carp, Yudl."—"But how should I know a middle-sized carp when I see one?"—"Yudl, find the biggest carp in the market, and then find the smallest. And then buy one that is right in between."

The fishmonger pulls out the carp by the gills and gives him a sharp mallet-blow to the head.

Walking away from the fish market, he hears their voices before they are upon him. "It's the Jew-Fish-Boy."—"Didn't we tell you never to come back again?"

Yudl looks up from his shoes to the three boys he met before, on his last Fish Glue adventure. "You did say that, sir, but nevertheless I must come."—"He called you 'sir.'"—"He's making fun."—"No, sir, I am being polite."—"Who asked you to speak?"—"I don't need to be asked to speak, sir, now let me past, please."—"You're not going anywhere, Jew boy, give us your money."—"I would but I've just spent it all, sir."—"Let's *baptise him!* Grab his arms."—"No. NO. NO!"

The bag of fishbones and the basket with the heavy carp fall to the ground. And Yudl is lifted into the air. He screams. The boys, laughing and shouting, drag him towards the jetty by the Ehle. "We're going to make you a Christian, boy!"

Yudl screams and writhes like the carp in the barrel. He howls. The boys' pace falters. Conscience seems to slow their steps. "He's screaming, Fritzo."—"Let him scream." Yudl contorts, twists, bites at their grasping hands.

"He bit me! The bastard!"—"Let's beat him!"—"Can he swim?"

"PUT HIM DOWN!"

A voice thunders from nearby. The boys' hands fumble, falter, let go. Yudl slips heavily to the ground. Thud.

The voice comes again; "What are you doing?"—"Just having fun, sir."—"Is that any way to have fun?"

Yudl's face in the mud at the side of the road. The wind knocked out of him. He can't move. More voices come. "They're right to get him. He was drawing magic signs at the side of the road."—"Magic signs? What nonsense is that?"— "Curses probably. They can do magic."—"Magic? He's just a boy. I know his family."

Yudl has already recognised the voice.

✡ ✡ ✡

Yudl looks up at his rescuer. A rosy-cheeked peasant face, long, slightly curly straw-blond hair, framed by a sable fur-trimmed hood. Emmerich Schäffer looks down at him, smiles. "What happened back there with those boys?"—"They were going to baptise me."—"They can't baptise you, Yudl."—

"They can't?"—"For that they need a priest."—"Oh."—"Can you swim?"—"No."—"They can drown you, which would be worse. Mind you, I can't count the times I was thrown into the millrace back in my village."

Emmerich leads Yudl through the market. Around them, butchers cry their wares, flies buzz, customers haggle. "You're better than them, Yudl. Don't forget it."—"How do you know?"—"I know your uncle, I know your mother. They talk about you."—"You know my mother?"—"Of course. We talk sometimes. I do investments for her. Zipporah is a fine lady. And she says you're a clever boy."—"She does? What does my father say?"

Emmerich smiles. Rueful. "I don't speak with your father much. I don't think he likes me. Come on."

Strawhead Goy takes Yudl's hand. Yudl likes this; the comforting touch of an adult palm, guiding, protecting. If only his Father ever held his hand.

"Not this way, sir." Emmerich is turning down the Seilergass. "Not this way?"—"This is not the way my father taught me."—"But it's the quickest way home."—"It's not the way he taught me."—"It's all right, Yudl. I'll show you a new way."

Yudl smiles. The secrets of the Labyrinth will be opened to him, the streets of the Unknown City beyond the safety of his Father's red thread. And he no longer has to keep his eyes on his shoes. He has protection now, from one of the magical Goyyim, to Whom the World belongs. He looks up at the three-storey buildings that lean into the narrow lane. Shutters, chimneys, pigeons flapping past through the narrow gap of sky. Coils of rope in workshop doorways. Ropemakers sitting on stools, rubbing their rough and calloused hands.

And then the lane opens up, and light pours in, and a huge Square folds out in front of him. A Square full of stalls and people. And there, squatting like Behemoth in the centre of the Square, the Abomination.

Yudl trembles to see it, its hugeness. It sits there, solid as the World, and asserts its power. Purplish sandstone rises higher than the tallest trees, topped by a half-seen dome. Statues adorn its high galleries, depictions of the Hanged One, the Hanged One's Mother.

It is being built. Re-built. The new section, gleaming with fresh-cut stone, dwarfs the older construction and seems to swallow it up, like the Serpent devouring the Mouse in Yudl's Bestiary. Enormous, grotesque, like a demon squatting on the idolatrous earth.

Yudl covers his eyes so as not to have to see the monstrosity. Emmerich looks down at him, and smiles. "Is it really that horrible?" Yudl says nothing. Emmerich chuckles. "I remember, when I was your age, I went with my brother to your schul."—"You went to our schul?"—"We were looking for your uncle, to borrow money from him. I was scared, just like you. We saw inside . . . all the Jews swaying and chanting and reading out these strange words. It seemed like . . . devilry. But it's not of course."

They walk on, passing an oxen cart loaded with stone. Yudl likes the way they are talking, the openness of it, the guiding touch of Emmerich's hand, his gentleness. Why is his Father so stern? So angry? "Are you going to Uncle Meir's office, sir?"—"I am."—"Can I come with you?"—"Why?"—"I like it there. I want to learn commerce."—"Aren't you meant to be a scholar?"—"Yes, but who needs another scholar? All we do is read."—"It sounds like a good life to me."—"Then why don't you do it?"—"I have to earn a living."—"And why doesn't my father have to earn a living?"—"Your uncle and mother support him. He doesn't need to earn a living. They work so that he can study. Everyone says what a great mind he has."—"But no one likes him."—"Yudl!"—"Even my mother doesn't like him."

Emmerich stops, lets go of Yudl's hand. His eyes look

worried, perplexed. He bends down to Yudl's height. "What makes you say that, Yudl?"

Yudl shrugs. He cannot say.

"This is a bad thing to say. You know that, don't you?"

Silence. They are back in the Schriwerstublgass, beneath the sign with the feathered quill and the pot of ink.

"Don't listen to the gossipers, Yudl."—"Which gossipers?"—"Any gossipers."—"Which ones?"—"Any ones."—"What do they say?"—"Forget it. Forget I mentioned it."

Emmerich takes his hand again and they walk on.

His Father's strange words come back to him.

The whisperers, the slanderers at the back of the beth midrash, who whet their tongues like swords.

They turn into the Judengasse. Uncle Meir is sitting out on the street outside his house. He's brought a stool, leaned it against the wall and is catnapping contentedly in the spring sunshine. The River Bandits have been defeated, and Uncle Meir's investments are growing like never before.

"What's that smell?" he asks, without opening his eyes. "It's the Fishbone Boy," says Emmerich. "I saved him from some bullies in the marketplace." Uncle Meir's eyes ease open a crack, blink in the sunlight. "Thank you, Emmerich."—"Don't send him out tomorrow. Best you all stay at home tomorrow. Keep Quiet." Uncle Meir sighs. "Ah yes, the enthronement."—"What's an 'enthronement'?" asks Yudl.

Emmerich's hands reach out and reset the cap on Yudl's rebellious head of flaxen hair. "The new Bishop. He sits down in the Cathedral and they give him . . . a crown and a sceptre. That kind of thing."—"Who's the new Bishop?"—"Heinrich von Stahlem."—"And why should we not go out?"

Uncle Meir stretches, yawns, grudgingly waking from his sleep, "The Christians will be celebrating. They won't want to see us walking around looking miserable."—"And why should we be miserable?"—"What use to us is this new Bishop?"—

"You wanted the other one to be chosen, didn't you, the One Who Was Blinded?"—"We did."—"Why?" Emmerich shrugs. "He understood . . . the world. How things are changing. Come on, I'll take you to your mother. You can give her your carp."—"No, I want to stay."—"Run along, Yudl."

They walk on. Yudl looks up at Emmerich. His kind face, his flaxen hair.

The whisperers, the slanderers at the back of the beth midrash, who whet their tongues like swords.

They stop outside his mother's haberdashers. They can see her through the shutters, as she sits and waits for custom.

And then it comes, her face dawns alive from its reverie. Her coal eyes glow, and sunrise comes to her dusky cheeks. She smiles at Emmerich, a warm, beauteous smile. Her face tilts, looking at him from the corner of her eyes.

And then she notices Yudl, and her smile falters, fades.

She blushes.

Yudl begins to feel sick in his stomach.

The slanderers.

My loveless wife.

In the arms of others . . .

He Who Has No Name.

My son, with the golden hair.

Yudl runs.

ANNO
1245

The Rood Screen
(Rettich Schäffer VII. anno 1245)

Take your wax tablets in your hands. Draw one vertical line in the centre of the tablet. And one horizontal line near the top of the tablet. What do you have?

A Cross.

The Cross.

The drawing in your hands is just made of two straight lines, but yet it is full of meaning. It means the Passion of Our Lord Jesus Christ, his Death for our sins, the promise of the Resurrection in the Life to Come.

Look at your drawing. Is there anything like your drawing in the Real World that surrounds you? Is there anything in the seas, in the forests, in the fields, that looks like those two lines?

No.

What you have in your hands is man-made, two scratches of the stylus on wax.

Just two scratches, but full of meaning.

Take something real. A Squirrel. Let's make a statue of a Squirrel. Let's spend weeks carving and cutting, sanding and etching . . . and then—why not?—painting. The perfect shade of red. With those little whitish tufts on his belly and tail. Let's put jewels in for his eyes, our little squirrel. Dark garnets. Let's put a pine-nut in his hand!

Look at him! He's perfect! Our Squirrel looks just like a Real Squirrel! How clever we are. Aren't we?

This is what my Master taught me, and what I am now teaching You. *Leave that kind of work to God.* Let God make the Squirrel.

But let us draw those two lines into a Cross. A symbol, a sign that make us *think* of God. Think of God and Wonder. Wonder at how he created all things. Including the Squirrel.

† † †

It is two years since the new Bishop, Heinrich von Stahlem, was enthroned. Two years of a New Regime.

The New Regime has spread out roots and fingers, it reaches into every cubbyhole and cranny, every hidden, dusty corner of Hagenburg life. At the Feast of Fools this year, no donkeys, no masonry carts full of drunks. The Lord Bishop himself is there, and Uto calls for silence. "In previous years, this ceremony has become a disgrace to our City. Our Lord Bishop bids us celebrate with Joy, but with Restraint. Those drinking to excess or behaving indecorously will be removed."

The Bishop's militia carry staves and mingle amongst the crowds, enforcing the new Order. Many of the congregants leave to the taverns in disgust.

The same men with staves patrol the church in the days of the week, calling for silence when the services begin in the Choir. Bitter unease gathers in the arcades where the townspeople meet, breaking out into defiance and shouts. "I'll talk here if I want to! Whose Cathedral is this? It's the City's!" Staves are raised, beatings given, protestors are taken to the stocks, to the Gatehouse Prison for a day's bread and water.

And the new Lord Bishop has given the Cathedral a new Dombaumeister; Werlinus von Nordhausen. A tall Cistercian mason originally from Quedlinburg in the Harz, thin as three sticks tied together, hands long like a scarecrow's. A kind, drooping face. Like Achim von Esinbach, he had travelled to Chartres, Reims and the lodges of the Champagne. Unlike Master Achim, he has a worldly intelligence, an understanding of his political role.

And his role is to do the Bishop's bidding. The Cathedral had become a place of Disorder and Misrule. It must be calmed and made serene. And so a Rood Screen will be built to separate the Canons from the People. A screen of stone across the eastern end of the Crossing, blocking the Apse and High Altar from view. In the screen, facing the Nave, seven altars are to be built, including the Morning Altar of the city's merchants. "It will be of mutual advantage to both Church and City. Our Lord Canons will be able to conduct their services in peace, behind the screen. And the daily life of the Cathedral will continue on the other side."

Master Rettich looks at Werlinus' design, spread out on the drawing table of the Lodge. A seven-arched wall, each arch topped by the crown of an equilateral triangle, supporting six statues and an intricate gallery of corniced stone. Pretty, in the style of the Cathedrals of France and the Champagne.

But it cuts a line through the church. It blocks the Apse, the Choir, the High Altar. It breaks the sweep of space that the Cathedral will have once the Nave is complete. Squatting at the end of the Crossing, it seems to pull the arches lower, making them dwarfish and stout.

It destroys Master Achim's design.

Rettich glances over at Landolt, who meets his gaze a brief moment and then looks away. The same thought crosses through their minds: ten summers ago, they would have cried out, protested. But times have changed.

The New Regime. Know your Master. Submit. Obey.

Landolt clears his throat. "That's a lot of work, Herr Dombaumeister. Who will do it?"

"You all will. Work starts tomorrow, measuring and ordering the stone."

"And once we start building the Screen, what will happen with the Nave?"

"The priority now is the Rood Screen. The Bishop wants it

completed as soon as possible. The work on the Nave will stop."

Rettich nods mournfully, looks at the floor.

The New Regime.

† † †

There is a space behind the little arches of the triforium, a cubby hole, decked out with straw, linen sacking and a blanket of Anglian wool. And now Bishop von Stahlem's regime has reached its probing, spidery fingers here.

For three quiet years, Rettich has worked on the triforium and the upper galleries, diligently carving Master Achim's designs; rhyming patterns of *acanthi*, mythical monsters, gargoyles. And when work was quiet and he had no novices to teach, he would sit there a moment, lay down his chisel, let his legs dangle high above the Nave. He would look to the Cathedral floor, make sure that there were no prying eyes, and then would nod to his apprentice Friedl, send him a wink.

They pulled up the ladder silently, rung by rung. A final look around, and then they crawled inside into the warmth of sacking and straw. Quietly they made love and laid back to rest in each other's arms.

Across the Nave, the opposite clerestory stood empty, an open frame, awaiting its glass. As they lay together, the swallows wheeled in the evening sky, pigeons perched in the paneless windows, grumbling, cooing witnesses of Rettich and Friedl's Love.

But now the work on the Nave has been stopped. For the last time, Rettich and Friedl sit and pack their tools, legs swinging over the unfinished void. They check no one is looking. Kiss a final, memorial kiss. Then they take the bedding from the cubby hole and tie it into a bundle, make it fast with rope, toss it to the Cathedral floor. Then they lower the ladder, the now-broken thread between their secret Heaven and the lower, purgatorial world below.

† † †

Look now, boys, at this Gargoyle that I have made. Wings of a dragon, face of a devil, legs of a goat, a human trunk. Do you like it?

Some say that it is wrong to make Gargoyles. That it is not for us to make creatures from our fantasy, to make inventions. That in doing so, we blaspheme, and indulge ourselves sinfully. They say we should leave Invention to God, and reflect the World as He has made it.

But some, like my Master before me, say that to copy God's creation is nonsense, for how can we do any better than God? Why be God's copyist? My Master said we should let our minds seek out new forms, put our dreams into our hands and let them guide the chisel. Let God flow through us as we create.

God made this world for us, for Adam and for Eve. And as he made this world for us, let us make our works for Him.

These last two, three years I have been up that scaffold, forty ells above the ground, making dragons and monsters. My sister asks me why I bother, as no one can see the work I do, as it's so high above the Cathedral floor.

But God sees it, boys. It is my Work, for Him. And that's all I can ask for in this World. To work and work well. To work as best as I can, for God.

For all there is in this world, is Work. Every blade of grass, every cloud, every drop of water is a sign of God's Work. And all I will leave behind me when I am gone is what *I have made*.

All there is, is Work.

† † †

"Master Rettich. A word."

Dombaumeister Werlinus' quiet Saxon voice halts him at the Lodge doorway. Rettich turns. His Master is seated, as usual, at the Draughting Table. Seven candles in the candelabra above him, a crown of quavering light. It is late in the day, the Apprentices are clearing away the tools, the dust.

"Yes, Master?"

"Take a seat."

Rettich sits, awaits the Topic. Werlinus intertwines his long fingers, like wicker-work. "The theoretical line you take in your lessons, Master Rettich, I am not sure it is appropriate."

Rettich smiles; his best defence. *Your smile would charm the devil*, Friedl tells him. "I am just teaching what my Master taught before me."

Werlinus smiles back. "Master Achim was a brilliant man."

"He was."

"But he was . . . confused about many things."

"He was?"

Werlinus leans forward, speaks more quietly. "He was a theologian, a scholar, a Master of the Paris University! His experience of . . . practicalities . . . was limited. And, as you know, he was . . . " Werlinus closes his eyes, hoping to find the right words in darkness. "Afflicted. See his creations! Prophets with wide, upcast eyes! Majestic, aloof, staring Kings. Sometimes I look at his ideas, and . . . I am lost."

"They are beautiful."

"No doubt, no doubt. But this phrase. *God's Copyist!* 'We should not be God's Copyists.' It is absurd. Those who pray wish to see familiar figures. The delight of the eye in recognising a true human form, one of God's animals, or fowl, perfectly rendered in stone!"

"Master Achim said the delight should be felt looking on God's original works, not on our copies."

"Why? We honour Him in replication of the wonder of His creation."

"No. We honour only ourselves, by showing off how clever we are at copying."

"God gave us hands and minds so that we can worship Him, by displaying His grandeur."

"God gave us minds so that we could search for Him, where He is Hidden."

"What do you mean, Master Rettich?"

Rettich's mouth purses, closes. His eyes wander to the seven candles, their silvery reflectors, the flickering light. *Be careful now.* He tries another smile, but it comes out twisted, defiant. "The glory of God's creation is clear to anyone. Just look around you and you will see it." Rettich turns to his Master's narrowing eyes, looks deeply into them. "Copying what is already there is not a Search, it is not a Pilgrimage. Close your eyes, Herr Dombaumeister, don't look for God in the world. Anyone can find him there. Seek Him in the hidden places of your soul, seek His Light in the shadows of your imagination, and then express your search with your hands. That is Art, Herr Dombaumeister."

Silence.

"That is, at least, what my Master Achim taught me."

Werlinus nods silently, sadly. His kindly face is in shadow as he looks down at his hands. "Master Schäffer, maybe it will be best to relieve you of your teaching duties."

Cold fingers trace the length of Rettich's spine. The Dombaumeister continues. "In *my* Lodge, a statue of a dog must resemble a real dog. In the real world." He looks up, and there is fear and maybe anger in his eyes. "If we copy God's creations, we cannot err. If we follow . . . an Inner Voice . . . Then, Master Schäffer, how do we know it is not the voice of the Devil?"

Rettich says nothing. The Dombaumeister finally untwines his fingers, lays his palms flat on the Draughting Table. A sign that the interview is coming to a close. "And maybe it will be good to keep you away from the younger boys."

Oak Apples
(ANNO 5005. YUDL BEN YITZHAK III)

W*omen. None but the honourable honoureth them, none but the despicable despiseth them. Have I fallen so far from the ways of the Righteous that I should despise my own wife? Have I lent my ears to the whispers of the Wicked?*

Who can divine the truth? I look into her eyes and see nothing. All love for me is gone. But am I not author of this contempt? For I have called her contemptuous?

Unto thee O Lord do I lift up my soul. Show me thy ways O Lord, guide me in thy truth and teach me, for thou art the God of my salvation.

Redeem Israel, O God, out of all his troubles.

✡ ✡ ✡

There is a Conspiracy. A Conspiracy against Yudl, to tell him Nothing. To keep him in the dark.

The Conspiracy has another name, it is called Sex. And everyone is involved in it, and no one will tell him anything about what it is.

Sex is driving his Father mad. He wants his wife to Love him, but he doesn't know how to make it happen. So he thinks his wife hates him. He thinks everyone hates him. He even thinks the Rabbi hates him. And his Secret Red Book is full of terrible things. The Whispers that Yudl had never heard, about his fair hair and the Strawhead Goy. That the Goy may be his real Father.

The Conspiracy. The plot of silence. And if Yudl had not sinned by eating of the forbidden fruit, by reading the Secret Red Book in the locked and mysterious library, he would have known Nothing. Which is what everyone wants him to know.

Nothing.

But if the Jews won't tell him, maybe the Gentiles will. And so Yudl begins to follow Emmerich Schäffer when he leaves the Jews' Quarter in the evenings. Yudl slips on a dark cloak, pulls down the hood, and follows the Strawhead Goy into the narrow streets. Sees how goes into an Inn to eat a bowl of pottage, all alone. How he sits a while longer, leaning back against the wall, thinking private and melancholy thoughts, drinking a pitcher of wine. And then how he wanders down a few more alleyways to his lonely lodgings on the Langer Weg, a stone's throw from the market gates.

On some evenings, Emmerich has company, meetings. He strolls over the Square and enters the Abomination. Or walks further on to the Merchant's Quarter, to the fine, narrow, four-storey houses of Müllergass or Spitzengass, and sits with the merchants in their shops, drinking wine as a servant lights the lamps in the corners and closes the shutters against the passing traffic of the street.

Twice Yudl sees him go to the notorious tavern *zum Sterne*, where an armed guard, liveried in black and argent, stands at the door. Schäffer is not allowed entrance to this Old Family meeting place, merely announces himself, and waits outside. Presently, the tall, commanding Baron von Kronthal steps out. Emmerich presents the Baron with a sheaf of papers and then they walk up and down the street, their hands behind their backs like Rabbis, as Schäffer explains, and von Kronthal listens . . .

One late spring evening, after his pitcher of wine, Emmerich's eyes seem clouded, melancholy. Instead of heading home, he walks back past the Judengasse. Yudl has never seen him take this route before. Curious, he follows, holding to the shadows.

A balmy, tentative breeze steals through the streets, and for the first time since winter, the houses' shutters are open. The sounds of family suppers, arguments, laughter echo from the open windows to the lonely road below.

Emmerich goes deeper into the alleyways of the Mayenz Gate district. Left here, right there, right again. Yudl fears that he will never find his way home. The evening's purple gloaming is hardly to be seen between the gable rooves. Crows search amongst the scraps and broken pots behind the houses. Mice scuttle.

A long, crooked, narrow street. Suddenly a rainbow of colour, an echo of the celestial spheres. Lanterns burn above the doorways; a purple moon, a golden star, a red globe, swaying.

Standing in the coloured pools of light, women. Women without caps or scarves, with open, flowing hair. Women with blouses open to their breasts. Women with skirts hitched to show their knees and calves, and (God forbid!) their secret, soft thighs.

Yudl slinks into a shadowed doorway, hiding, burning. His stomach twitches, cavorts, his loins dance. He covers his eyes, but through his wicked fingers, shamelessly stares at That Which Should Not Be Seen. At calves, necks, breasts.

Emmerich dances the length of the lane, spinning round, turning, taking in the women like wares on market stalls. They call out to him "Come on, Master," "Try me," "I'm yours." He waves his hand, passing. An old, cracked jade jeers, "You've got no chance! He likes them dark!"

At her doorway, his girl waits for him. A girl from the South, dusky, plump, the Queen of Sheba. Emmerich dances up to her. There are silver pennies in his hand.

Suddenly behind Yudl, the door opens. A man hurries out, hastily pulling his hood around his face. A momentary impression, his cold eyes, startled by the boy. Yudl jumps out of his way, and then the man's gone, half-running into the rainbow-coloured lane.

Behind him, a woman, ripe, red-haired, full-lipped, fastening her blouse. She takes hold of Yudl's flailing, running arm, holds him tight. "Slow down, love," she says, "Waiting for me were you?"—"No, madam."—"Oh, '*madam*' is it?" She giggles, reaches out to pull down his hood.

"Oh my!" she coos. "Just a boy."

Hot blood rushes to Yudl's face. "Sorry, madam, I must go."—"No, wait a while, my boy, you must've come here for a reason."—"No reason, I should go."—"Now be polite, my lad, and tell me your name."—"H- H- Heinrich's my name."—"Can I call you Heinl?"

Her hand slips inside his cloak, reaches downwards. Yudl gasps like a carp. "Yes, I thought you liked me." Her hand moves up and down, touching him through the fabric of his hose. She pulls him close, into her breast. Yudl feels something inside him, rising up like sap, bursting. He groans, gasps, in torture.

Explodes.

The woman laughs, a cascade of cracked bells. "*Oh Jesus, he's gone off already!*"

Yudl, pale, ambushed, sinks against the lintel, breathing hoarse and fast. "I . . . I . . . I . . . Sorry! Sorry sorry sorry . . . "

And he runs.

The woman's voice calls out after him. "Don't worry, Liebling. No charge!"

✡✡✡

The Magical World of the Goyyim. Sodom without cataclysm, without the rain of brimstone of a Vengeful God. In this Wonderful World there are women who show their ankles and whose love can be bought for sixpence. In this Wonderful World one may drink wine until one can drink no more, without even pausing once to bless the cup, to praise the Almighty. In this Wonderful World, the Gentile awakes and opens his eyes without obligation to thank God, he burps and farts his way to the commode without ritual ablution. He goes to his abominable Church when he wills, he offers idolatrous prayers when he wishes, he goes hither and thither as he pleases, eats as he wishes, devouring every kind of filth and uncleanliness, and yet He is the Lord of this World, and we Jews are his shadows.

We, even before opening our eyes in the morning, must offer the correct Benediction. And then get up, wash, urinate and defecate according to the Law. Determine when it is dawn according to the Law. And then scuttle through the half-light to the beth midrash to join our fellow Jews for the recitation of the Amidah, Israel raising its voices to the Lord. And only when we have finished may we the Elect of God begin our day, a day spent as far away as can be from the wide, busy avenues of the Gentiles. For we prefer to cleave to our own, private Mourning. For we have no Homeland. Our Temple is but rubble, and the woes of our thousand year Exile have no end in sight.

Mannekint the Tailor, who had a shop in the Schneidergass and sold silks and made robes and tunics for the Hagenburg Lords, who sewed beautiful gilt patterns on kerchiefs and wimples for the finer city ladies, has lost his shop, lost his livelihood. And alongside Mannekint, many other Jews have been banned from their trades.

It is a new ruse, such as the Gentiles often invent to humiliate and break the Jews. And the new ruse is called "the Guilds." The Guilds are societies to which, of course, only Gentiles may belong. And laws have been passed saying that the only tailors allowed to work in Hagenburg are those who are members of the Drapers' Guild of Hagenburg, the only goldsmiths who can trade in Hagenburg must be members of the Guild of Goldsmiths, the only cobblers members of the Hagenburg Guild of Cordwainers, and so on, and so forth, and the end result of this Christian scam is to remove all Jewish craftsmen and artisans from the marketplaces of the city.

But Trade is still allowed the Jews, at least for now. Moneylending, peddling, buying, selling.

Trade.

Emmerich Schäffer enters the office, frowning. Yudl, a refugee from Torah study at the beth midrash, looks up from his corner, where he is reading the account ledgers, the mysterious records of every purchase, every sale, every loan. "What's wrong, Master Schäffer?" he asks.

Emmerich sits down in his silk-cushioned chair by the shutters, closes them against the breeze. The room darkens. He now also has Uncle Meir's attention.

"Gerber is talking about a River Trade Union."

An Angel of Silence passes through the room. The unruly breeze nudges the shutters open again, ruffling the pages of Emmerich's ledgers. He bangs the books shut.

Uncle Meir chuckles sarcastically. "Right, I see. A Union that, of course, we won't be allowed to join."

"Gerber wouldn't dare. We're his biggest customer."— "And his biggest competitor."—"We've made him rich."— "He's a merchant, Emmerich, he'd sell his own mother."—"All right then, then let's do what we've talked about doing."— "We've talked about doing a lot of things."

Emmerich stands, fastens the shutter wide open. White midday light, the hawkers' cries. *Sharpen any kniiiiiiives?*

"Make this company Christian. Call it Schäffer and Associates. Move our office out of the bloody Judengasse and into the Merchant Quarter. Hire fat, blond, sausage-eating apprentices. I marry some merchant's daughter with big jugs. Make it all in my name on paper. And then let them try and call it a Jewish company. Let them try."

Yudl senses something. A tension. But Uncle Meir's voice is calm, even warm. "And I come in by the back door?"

"YUDL!" An angry voice from the street. Uncle Meir's eyes flinch, reflex of guilt, and then flash in Yudl's direction. "*You told me your lessons had finished!*" he hisses, going to the window. "Yes, he's in here, Yitzhak."—"Send him down now!"

Uncle Meir turns, shaking his head. His finger rises in the air, points harshly at his nephew, a lightning bolt. "*Don't do this again, Yudl,*" he hisses, emphatic. "Decide. Trade or Torah. You can't do both. Get out."

Outside in the milling street, his Father grabs his arm. His black eyes are serrated, sharp. "The Rabbi is expounding on the Book of Job, and you're not there? YOU'RE NOT THERE?"

Yudl looks down. "I know the Book of Job, Father."

His Father's hands grab his lapels, nearly knocking him from his feet. "You KNOW the Book of Job? It contains multitudes, layers and layers and layers. Even if you studied it seven years you would not KNOW it."

"But Father . . . The River Trade Union . . . I just wanted to . . . "

Yitzhak looks at his son, incomprehending. Anger and disappointment struggle in his eyes. "Yudl, don't be foolish. Gold comes and goes. But there is Nothing. Nothing. Greater than the Word of the Lord. Come."

Fifty paces and they are there, back in the world of the beth midrash. The lecterns, sides worn from the grip of a thousand

hands. Parchment, vellum, curled and yellowed, blotched and fil-
igreed with black, traces of a thousand scribes, men and boys like
Yudl, bent over books with quill and ink. The smell of male sweat,
dried on linen shirts in the summer heat. The buzz and hum of
prayer, the sway and dance of recitation. The gaze of Gabbai
and Rabbi, the unpeeling onion layers of text, commentary,
interpretation, all circling the eternal mystery: the Lord Adonai.

Yudl bends to the book before him. Job's words buzz in his
head like wasps.

And the words fade away into silence. And he thinks. He
thinks of Uncle Meir's business ledgers. Written there, like
some strange, mysterious Alphabet, rows upon rows of numbers, sums and reckonings, subtractions and additions, a complex and ever-spreading network of figures, every bit as
absorbing and mysterious as the Words of the Lord.

✡ ✡ ✡

*I have eaten ashes like bread, and mingled my bread with
weeping. For Thou has taken me up and cast me away.*

*Three weeks! My turn to read the Torah portion delayed!
Three weeks. They are running out of excuses. A bridegroom, an
honoured visitor from Mayenz, Michen whose wife gave birth to
a son. What new excuse will they find next week? Let us see.*

*They are conspiring against me, the Whisperers, the Impious.
Rabbi Menahem cannot look me in the eye. He now prefers the
company of that fool Aberle and his absurd pilpul, his pedantic
glosses on the Torah. I am losing everything, my wife, my standing, my son.*

My son?

✡ ✡ ✡

In the village of Rosheim, there are just enough Jews to form a minyan, hold prayers in their tiny schul, maintain a teacher and a mikve, pay the ritual butcher. Yudl's father's family came from here. They're leather traders, tanners, cattle sellers, but as soon as a boy is born here who has a gift for the Torah, he gets carted away to Hagenburg to study under a proper Rabbi. And that happened to his side of the family three generations ago, and so all that's left in Rosheim are cousins and cousins of cousins.

Yudl has no wish to be here, but it is the month of Tammuz and the time has come to harvest oak apples from the forests that grow around Rosheim, the little gourds that swell from the old oaks in high summer, ripe and bitter with black gall. Oak apple gall, copperas and gum; the ingredients for the perfect ink, the only Ink used for the Holy Script, for the Word of God.

They are sitting on stools in the courtyard between the leather workshop, the tanning shed and the shokhet's slaughtering house. A smell of cowdung, fatliquor and blood. Father's critical eyes fix on the mezuzah on the door post. "The mezuzah looks rotten."—"It's the winter rain, it comes straight in from the hills, blows right in under the roof."—"Do you want me to check it?"—"If you like, Yitzhak."—"If the writing is damaged, it's a sin."—"God forbid."

Father stands to open the little mezuzah box on the doorpost, pulls out the tiny scroll from inside. Goes into the sunlight to examine the writing. "Some of it's faded. I'll touch it up for you."—"God bless you, Yitzhak."

Later, at dinner, he takes over all the blessings, studies the kitchen knives for nicks in the blade, checks the division of the bowls for milk and meat. He looks like has hasn't slept for days. His eyes shine with edgy fervour as he fingers cousin Aaron's tabard. "Where did you get this?"—"This? From a peddler."—"From a peddler?"—"It was good and cheap. Why?"—"It's shatnez."—"What?"—"It's a mix of linen and wool . . . Take it off."—"What?"—"You can't wear it, Aaron, it's forbidden. You should buy nothing from the Gentile."—"That's easy for you to say."—"Come to Hagenburg for your cloth and buy from Mannekint; it will be a mitzvah, he has lost all his Gentile clients. Take the Law seriously, Aaron. Don't wear shatnez."

Aaron takes off his shirt, stands stupid and bare-chested in the courtyard, ashamed.

They walk through the Forest, carrying the ladder, his Father in front. The sun is high and bright, filtering through the trees, a shifting tapestry of gold and green. Despite the lustre and brightness, his Father is nervous, always looking about him as if expecting the trees to bend down and strike him.

His wild eyes narrow, focus. "Here are some," he says, pointing to the high branch of an oak. "Up you go."

They lean the ladder against the twisted trunk, and Yudl climbs up into the canopy, slides along the branch. "Don't worry, it will hold your weight."—"That's easy for you to say."—"If you fall, I'll catch you."

Yudl looks down at his Father, standing small and anxious below him, holding out his hands, absurdly ready to try and catch his fall. Yudl takes his little knife and cuts the gourds from the tree. Swellings from the oak twigs and branches, the size of acorns, rough and gnarled to the touch. He tosses them down to his Father, who puts them in the basket. "Good. Now come down."

Yudl swings onto the branch, clutches on for a moment and then lets go, plummeting heavily to the forest floor. The jolt takes the wind out of him.

His Father shakes his head. "I said 'come down,' not *jump down*.'"—"Jumping down is easier than climbing down."—

"All right, but be careful. I nearly died of shock."—"How many more do we have to collect?"—"A lot more."

Yudl walks on in glum silence. Today they are opening the new office of "Schäffer and Associates" in the Ehlestrasse, and he wants to be there, to see the new sausage-eating apprentices, the crucifix hanging over the lintel, the idol of Saint Christopher above the desk, the new, Christian face of Uncle Meir's Money. The biggest business in Christian Hagenburg.

Instead he's here in a forest, carrying a ladder, looking for stupid gourds and swellings.

"Yudl!"—"What?"—"You just walked straight past an oak full of them."—"I didn't see anything."—"Look up there!"—"All right, Father . . . "—"Keep your eyes open, boy!"—"But it's boring!"—"Boring?" Yudl throws the ladder down on the ground. "You're just teaching me this so you don't have to do it yourself!"—"And so? Why do you think my father taught *me* how to do this? And his father before him? It's the way of the world, Yudl, from father to son. And you'll teach your own son the same."—"No I won't. I'll teach him to *make money* and send a servant to *buy ink from a shop*. Why make our own ink when you can buy it?"—"Because this is the Way, Yudl. The Way We Do Things."—"For what? For *what*? So we can sit in the beth midrash our whole lives, sit in the Judengasse and read and read and read and do nothing until the words come out of our bloody ears?"

Silence between Father and Son. Five heartbeats, seven, nine.

Suddenly his Father's hands are grabbing at Yudl, beating at him, slapping his face, pushing him to the ground. Yudl curls into a ball in the mulch of leaves. His Father's eyes are bulging with blood, veined with rage. "GET UP THAT TREE! DO AS I SAY!"

"NO."

His Father's hand curls, writhes. Then it rises in the air and comes down hard.

✡ ✡ ✡

Sundown in Rosheim, the Cousins have been tenderising hides, the courtyard is awash with stinking, yellowish fluid. "What happened to the Boy?"—"Oh, what a bruise!"— "What happened, Yudl?"—"I fell off the tree and hit my head."—"You should be more careful."—"I know, my Father says the same thing, don't you, Father?"

Yudl and his Father have to share a narrow bed in the reeking house, pushed up against each other. Neither of them can sleep. Yudl thinks *the eye that mocks a father will be plucked out by ravens*, but what if your Father is not your Father? What if your Father is an impersonator, a monster?

What if your real Father cannot claim you as his own?

Yudl closes his eyes, feeling his soul swell with hatred. Gall and bitterness swill in his guts, and he sees the Temple of Jerusalem, and King Solomon before it, calling for a sword. And tugging at Yudl's hands, pulling him apart, his so-called father Yitzhak and the man his Mother truly loves, the Strawhead Goy.

Yudl turns in the bed for the thirteenth time. He cannot hold it back. "Where does my fair hair come from, Father?"

A bitter silence fills the darkness. The smell of tanning fluid, horsehair and polish seems to rot, ripen, grow. Yudl opens his eyes, but the air is like pitch. His Father has frozen. He doesn't move.

"From your Mother, Yudl." His voice seems to come from the distance. It trembles. "But her hair is dark."—"She has fair cousins."—"Where?"—"They live far away. In Prague."— "Have you seen them?"

"No."

Father and Son's breaths shudder in the perfect blackness. It is so dark that all things are as one, confused and fumbled together, indistinct. Truth, Lies, Half-Truths, Fears, Speculations, Desires . . . all lie together in the same stinking, narrow darkness, crowding the invisible spaces between Father and Son.

THE NEW REGIME
(RETTICH SCHÄFFER VIII. ANNO 1245)

T he New Regime spreads out its cold hands, reaches into every cubbyhole and cranny, every hidden corner of Hagenburg life. It crawls along the rillets of sewerage that seep through the stinking alleys, spreads like a shadow from the Rheintorgässel shacks to the whitewashed walls of the central streets.

After a dull day's work carving the cornices of the Rood Screen, Rettich wanders, dawdles, drinks. He dreads the idea of going home to Ällin's cold, turned shoulder, his children's questioning stares. On Holidays he makes melancholy pilgrimage to Avenheim Monastery in the Vogesen foothills, to Achim's lonely grave beyond the convent walls.

Hagenburg is fat, overstuffed, bursting. Every Spring brings new hopeful faces, stumbling through the City Gates from the rain-flayed hills, feet wrapped in muddy rags, asking directions from the first citizen they meet, "Sir, can you tell me the way to Metzger Street?" There they will sleep in the corner of their cousin's tiny rented shack, rise at dawn to wait with the restless crowds on Brandplatz and Barfüsserallee, beg for work at tuppence a day.

A slow, muddy flood of humanity swills around Rettich, searching for coin. And from Bishop von Stahlem's butcher's fingers, a bright rill of papal silver flows.

Pope Innocent has fled from the chaos of Rome to Lyon. From Lyon he has declared Emperor Friedrich's son Konrad dethroned, and Heinrich Raspe of Thuringia the new King of the Germans. Holy Gold flows to German Lands from the Florentine banks, buying support for this newly declared monarch, the *Pfaffenkönig*, the Pope's choice of King. And Bishop von Stahlem holds out his cassock's apron and gathers the Pope's golden *augustales* like a Rhineland milkmaid gathers plums.

Von Stahlem gilds his liegemen's nests, ensilvers his coterie of Lords, Canons and Clerics. His enfeoffed nobles ride proud through the city gates from their country estates, their stallions' hooves shed purple Vogesen mud on the Hagenburg cobbles. They canter to the Cathedral to hang their standards from the Triforium arches that Rettich once carved.

The von Zaberns, von Kronthals, von Rappoltsteins, old Alsatian Gentry, watch on darkly. Supporters of Friedrich and the Staufen dynasty since the times of Barbarossa, they cleave to Konrad, son of the Emperor. And so there are now two Kings of Germany, King and Anti-King, Staufen and Raspe, Konrad and Heinrich. There are two Overlords; Pope and Emperor. There are two masters in Hagenburg, two hearts in the breast of the Rhineland, beating in fractured, bellicose time.

But Rettich wants no argument with anyone. When the talk turns to politics, to Pope and Emperor, he withdraws to the corner, whittles with his knife as if he were back in the fields of Lenzenbach, watching his Lambs.

Rettich's closest friend and companion is Wine, golden Rhenish Wine. And his Friend and Companion has painted Rettich's nose and cheeks a broken crimson, age has scratched lines around his eyes. His hands are calloused, rasp to the touch like pumice stone. His gait is stooped from a thousand shouldered loads. But his hair is still yellow and unruly as harvest straw, and in evening sunlight, it shines.

Two weeks before the Assumption, and this summer eve finds him at the Ehle Wharf Tavern, waiting for his brother

Emmerich. He is on his second pitcher, and it feels as if the sun has been setting forever, bejewelling the Ehle's waters with dancing coins.

Rettich has his own wine glass, stout and greenish, a gift from the glassmakers on the Nanzig road. He pours out another glass of Rhenish gold, holds it up to the sinking orb of the sun, lets the rays filter through, play upon his drunken face. Fractured and swimming in the glass, a figure, striding towards him. His little brother, late on the hour.

Rettich lowers the glass. "Your health, brother. Here." Emmerich wipes his mouth with his sleeve, drinks a long draft. "Thank you, brother." He sinks down to the bench and they look out over the gently flowing Ehle, the tethered, bobbing river barges. "How's trade, Emml? How are Schäffer and Associates?"

"Wonderful. Trade's good. Strong. If only the Bishop didn't take half of it in taxes."

"Lower your voice, Emml, you never know who's listening."

A lustre in Emmerich's eyes, sarcasm, amusement. He holds up his hands. "So, let them come and examine our books of account and see if it is not true! I'm still allowed to speak the truth, am I not?"

"Probably not."

"And your work, big brother? Building a Wall between the Church and the People she's meant to save?"

"Yes. But it's a pretty wall. And your taxes pay my pretty wages. So thank you. I'll pay for the wine."

"Looks like you've had a pitcher already."

"I have. Whilst waiting for you."

"A Rhine boat is late, I was waiting for it. It's still not come in."

The brothers look at each other. Emmerich's eyes narrow. "So. Why did you ask to see me? What's this about, brother?"

Rettich sighs. "Emmerich. It's time you got married. You should have been wed years ago."

"Oh, My Lord. Did Our Sister put you up to this?"

Rettich looks up to Heaven, raises his hands, palms upward in despair. *Of course our sister put me up to this. Who else?*

Emmerich shrugs. "No reputable woman will marry me because I work with the Jews. And what's the point of marrying a *dis*reputable woman? Why not—beg your pardon—just fuck her and pay her sixpence? Like I normally do?"

Rettich can't help smiling. "What if Our Sister, in Her Greatness and Grete-ness, were able to find you a Bride?"

"What. Has she?"

"No, not to my knowledge. But she's offered it."

"Yes, let her try. It would be useful to be married, after all."

"Useful?"

"Marriage hides a multitude of sins, doesn't it, Brother?"

"Emmerich?"

The brothers look at each other, intently. It's Rettich who looks away first.

"How's Ällin these days, Rettlein?"

"She's pregnant."

Emmerich nods, drinks from the glass. Silence stretches out a while. When he speaks, he speaks softly. "Is it yours?"

Rettich looks at his hands, shakes his head, almost imperceptibly. The words are hardly audible; "We've come to an understanding."

"I follow you."

Rettich's hands twitch, wrench up and cover his ears. Emmerich takes one of his hands, pulls it away. "So what? In our village, we all knew everyone's secrets. Boys sleeping together, adultery, village fair fucks. Didn't we? And what happened?"

"We laughed at them."

"That's right."

"But I've been dismissed from teaching. No-one looks me in the eye."

"Well, they say it's a sin."

"It *is* a sin."

"So is Usury. So is working for the Jews. We're filthy sinners, Rettich, us both."

"Master Emmerich?" A plangent voice halts their words. Emmerich wheels round. The voice seems to come from a dark silhouette, haloed by the copper light reflected from the waters below. "Master?"

Emmerich stands. "Is that you, Markl?"

The silhouette rises from the waters of the Ehle, disembarking from a coracle. He holds out his hands and helps another, older man from the boat. They come up the wharf steps to the side of the tavern, and the setting sun's amber light.

Emmerich goes pale as he sees the older man. "Ulrich?" A bandaged head, black with blood. Ulrich nods, his eyes are pained as he grasps Emmerich's hands.

Emmerich swallows with fear. "What happened? Come, sit. Rettich, pour wine."

Ulrich drinks, holds his bruised back as he eases himself onto the bench. He breathes in. "Master Emmerich. The Albe River Bandits are back."

"What? From the dead?"

Ulrich laughs a bitter laugh. "Yes. They came on us like ghosts. From the forest banks. The Watzenau forest. Suddenly they were all around us in coracles, pulled the boat ashore."

"And what did they take?"

"Every penny, every bale, every grain. We had four passengers, and they took them too. Two women, two men."

"Took them?"

"The women were young. Attractive. The men, I don't know what for."

"How many were there of them?"

"Twenty? Thirty? And they didn't just take our boat today, Master. They took two more."

"O Lord. Three boats in a day?"

Ulrich nods. And drinks again.

"Old man, what did they do to you?"

Ulrich looks up. His eyes reflect the last light of the sky. "There was a man. Tall, powerful. Scar down his cheek. He had full, proper armour, chainmail, like a Knight. I thought he was the leader, but no. He asked me, 'Are you the Captain of the boat?' and I said, 'Yes,' and he said, 'Come with me, our Leader wants to give you a message.' And so they took me ashore, and into the woods. We walked some time, through the thickets, with the branches tearing at us. I thought they were taking me there to kill me, like an animal. But then we came to a clearing with a fire, a hut, some men, women making food . . . and that's where the Leader was."

"Who is he?"

Ulrich looks down. "He wore a helmet that had a leather front, covering his face. Only holes for his eyes. I couldn't see him. He turns to me, and he has a strong, deep voice. He says, 'Tell them at Hagenburg, tell them at Speyer, tell them at Worms. I'll be collecting from you. I'll be collecting the Toll that's mine.' And I look up at him and ask, 'What is your name, Sire?' and he takes a stick and beats me like a dog, beats my back, and then my head. And I'm screaming and the blood is running all over my face and eyes, and he says, 'You bastard. Tell them I don't have a Name. Tell them that he who sees my face will die.'"

ANNO
1246

THE STERNKAMMER
(BARON VOLMAR VON KRONTHAL II. ANNO 1246)

L *et's make an inventory of your assets* says my fiduciary
counsel Emmerich Schäffer. He's dangerous, this
Schäffer. He knows too much. Where all our money is,
all our property. Knows my wife the Baroness, my Mistress
Elise, my bastards with her, all my affairs. But the Baroness and
I give him chests full of silver to play with, speculate, invest, and
instead of running off with them into the woods, he writes them
all down in those ledgers of his, and, at the end of each year,
gives us More Money back than we lent him at the beginning.

He's some kind of Magician or something. Where would I
be without him?

*Item one. Ancestral von Kronthal lands, Kron river valley.
From Mohrmünster east to Kirchheim, from the Hägen hills to
where the Kron meets the Ehle.*

*Assets in the von Kronthal ancestral lands: seven vineyards,
five grain-fielded estates: wheat, spelt and rye. Four farmsteads.
Two mills on the Kron. Two quarries: providing Hagenburg cathedral with stone. Seven and ninety serf families, working the land.*

*Item two: Forest, hunting lands: von Kronthal ancestral land.
Aagenau forest, East of the Karrenbach, West of the Rhine.
Thirty-nine serf families: swineherds and foresters.*

*Assets: Saw mill, produces timber for Hagenburg cathedral,
and Hagenburg town builder Fritzl Bayer.*

*Swine meat; four dozen carcasses a year. Sold at Christmas
market, Hagenburg. Has right to be put up for sale before all
other swine meat at market, except the Bishop's.*

Item three: Fishing and shipwreck booty rights, West Bank of the Rhine, the length of Aagenau forest. Thirteen serf families: fishermen, ferryman, tollmaster.

Assets: Aagenau ferry toll for crossing Rhine. Aagenau Rhine toll charged on all passing ships not registered in Hagenburg or Basel.

Item Four: Grazing rights, high pastures, west of Chapel Pass, south of Bishop's Lenzenbach border, north of Zabern-Nanzig highway: ancestral land of the Baroness, née von Moder. Twenty-three serf families, shepherds, cowherds.

Assets: Raw wool tithes, dependent on yield. Two score cattle carcasses, ten score sheep carcasses tribute annual. Sold at Zabern market, where it is the first meat to be sold.

Item Five: City property of the Baroness, née von Moder. Zabern: the streets that line the Zabern river, both sides: thirty seven hearths, paying annual rent.

Item Six: Hagenburg: City property of the von Kronthals; between Rhein and Mayenz gates, North from Brandplatz, West from Barfüsserplatz. Three hundred and seventeen hearths; annual rents.

Item Seven: Winzingtal, Aargau/Black Forest borders, ancestral property of the Baroness, née von Moder. Mixed forest and grazing land, hunting rights, woodcutting rights. Fifty-nine serf families.

Schäffer pauses, his quill poised above the blank parchment. These bloody clerks, they think that with their pens they can do anything. Defeat enemies, "consolidate assets," save the world.

"Bring me some more wine, Schäffer, I'm just drinking dregs here."

"Yes, My Lord."

We're in his offices in the Ehlestrasse, a former store and warehouse. Very fine. Glass-paned windows look out on the Zollturm and the dock; the wharf, the city wall and the river gate. Outside the doorway, the Hagenburg crowds weave and swarm. Lord knows where all these damn people come from. What business do they all have here?

"My Lord." A female voice in my ear. The ruddy-faced Serving Girl, curtseying, proffering me a glimpse of her milk-maid's tits and a fresh draught of wine. "Thank you, girl." I take the goblet and stretch out my legs, warm in leather hose and riding cote. I'm in from Kronthal Castle, on my way to Schwanenstein and Sweet, Mad Elise.

Schäffer is back at his books, waving the Girl away. He frowns. "This is the situation, my Lord. We couldn't make you any money this year. Our returns are down. *Everybody's* returns are down. And it's only because of our skill at investment that you didn't *lose* any money this year. Almost everybody else did."

"Why?"

"The River Bandits, my Lord. That . . . and the tense situation. Wars in Hessen, Lombardy. Pope against Emperor. It makes everyone . . . nervous. And they keep their money in their wallets."

Schäffer's long finger circles in the air and then points at his ledger. "My advice, my Lord, would be to sell your wife's lands in the Aargau borders."

"Sell my land? Have you gone mad?"

"It is an isolated parcel a long way from the rest of your property. It will be difficult to defend if it comes to a war. And it is always useful to have easily transportable assets in troubled times. Coin, my Lord. And war could easily spread. From Lombardy, from Hessen, could it not?"

† † †

War is coming. Let it come. We in the Sternkammer are ready for it.

The Pope is hiding in his miserable fortress in Lyon, and

334 · BEN HOPKINS

from his wicked hands, a river of gold is flowing to buy his allies and armies, to put this upstart Heinrich Raspe on the German throne. The Bishops of Mayenz, Cologne, Hagenburg have kissed the Papal ring, cashiered the Gold, fed it through their fatty fingers to their cronies and vassals, and declared for Raspe.

And We are increasingly alone. Those families of Alsace whose hand has been furthered and strengthened by the Staufen dynasty, we have wealth, but not the bottomless purse of Rome. We meet at the Tavern of the sign of the Star, *zum Sterne*, and call our secret society the *Sternkammer*. We talk about how we can help each other, pool resources, stand up against the Pope, the Bishop and his vassals. How we can hold on to what is ours. But God damn it all, we know what is Victory, but not how to win it, we have the Blood, but not the Cunning. And this Emmerich Schäffer, this little scribe, has more Cunning in his little quill-tip than I have in my whole body. When you cut me, I bleed. When you cut little Schäffer, his wounds run ink and molten gold.

"So, what have you in the Sternkammer done so far? To prepare?" he asks.

"The three main roads into Hagenburg, they all run through our lands, Schäffer. So our men watch the roads, keep an eye on things."

"An eye on things?"

"To make sure the Bishop's vassal knights aren't gathering in the City. If they gathered in force anywhere near Hagenburg, we'd know. That's what we're most concerned about, the Bishop's knights taking the City and defending it from within. So, we watch the roads, Schäffer, and we have three score swordsmen here within the Walls."

My Counsel raises his scrawny eyebrow. "I wouldn't presume to advise My Lord on matters Military."

"Don't even try, Schäffer. You're a Lenzenbach sheep boy.

Your hood may be trimmed with sable, but I know where you're from."

A slight smile from my Counsel. It curls at the edges of his lips. A bit insolently. He asks: "Tell me this. The Bishop has the Pope's money to spend on gaining support for Raspe. Whose support has he bought? I mean, who has actually *changed sides*?"

"Von Sangenheim for one! And the families up by Mohrmünster, the minor families on the Lothringen marches. Turncoats."

"They needed the money?"

I shrug. Where's this leading? "Their estates are small, hilly. They could always do with a hand-out. I heard von Sangenheim's barn had burned down. Now he's building a new one."

"So. This is about Money."

I knock back the wine. "With you, Schäffer, it's always about Money."

He has no shame, this Schäffer. No deference for the Old Ways. He dips his quill in ink, scribbles some figures down in one of his books, and says, as if it were nothing; "Well, Bishop von Stahlem has the march on you, then. He's bought new friends and allies. His money is buying von Sangenheim a new barn. If it comes to a war, he has all these new allies, plus all his age-old supporters; the clergy, the old noble families whose sons are in the Cathedral Chapter, drawing Church Gold. So, who do you have on *your* side?"

Schäffer stands, and looks out the window at the passing crowds. "There is a merchant called Manfred Gerber."

"I've heard the name."

"Three years ago, he led a raid on the bandits by the Albe River."

"A sorry bunch of ruffians."

"Maybe. But they'd killed, raped and stolen from our townsfolk, from pilgrims, travellers. For instance, they stole a cobbler's consignment of leather. He went bankrupt and his children were reduced to begging. A 'small' thing, maybe, My Lord. But People remember these stories."

"Yes. And?"

"Gerber and his associates are building a Merchants' Church on Brandplatz. Last month they needed help carrying the new stone, from the quarry barge here at the Wharf, all the way to the Square. He called out for help, using the Town Criers." Schäffer goes to fetch the wine pitcher from the sideboard. He turns to look at me. "Four hundred people came on a Saturday morning, at dawn, to help carry his stone. Unpaid."

His grey eyes stare at me, unblinking. "My Lord, Manfred Gerber could walk out of these offices here, hold up his arms and call out, and with a click of the fingers, he'd have a dozen hands to help him."

He walks over, across the polished wooden floor. Pours me a generous stoup of wine. "How many could you manage, My Lord?"

"I'm not stupid, Schäffer."

"No, My Lord."

"You want me to go after the Bandits."

"I want you to sell your lands in the Aargau. And, yes, use some of the money to raise a troop to defeat the bandits. For the Bishop is doing nothing about them. Defeat them, hang their mysterious leader in the Cathedral Square, and the City will be yours."

I slam my gloved fist down on the table. "Schäffer! Do you think I am some kind of *Ratcatcher*? I meet my peers in the Field of Honour. I don't scuttle around marshes chasing vermin."

He gives me one of his looks. Those blank, slate-grey eyes. A stare like a cat's. Unnerving. "I thought you might say something like that, my Lord."

He creeps back to his desk, takes up his quill once more. "What a pity."

†††

Evening, in the Great Hall of Schwanenstein. Elise waits on the Countess. I drink, stuff myself with devilled roast pigeon, smoked eel and purée of swede. Schwanenstein Castle is like a Pilgrim's Inn on the road to Cologne, full to the rafters. Musicians, minstrels, jongleurs, poets . . . And the Countess sends round to all the villages from Illingen to the Black Forest, offering work and silver to the prettiest girls . . .

What a pigsty. What a whorehouse. What a change from my cold, devout Castle Kronthal. My brother-in-law, Rutger von Moder, keeps on honeying me to make love to his sister and produce an heir for our combined estates. But it's like clambering onto a toad in winter. I try and explain this to him as delicately as possible. "We're doing our best," I tell him, and he claps my shoulder, man to man, to hide his disappointment.

Tonight, I'm not the only Sternkammer member here. Reichard von Zabern and Lanzelin von Rappoltstein are carousing, trying their luck with the Countess' Handmaidens.

The Count sweeps into the hallway with his hunting braves. He joins me at the High Table, nods towards Elise, who is sleeping on her feet, waiting behind the Countess in the shadows, longing for her bed and her babes. "Not tired of her yet?"

"No, Sebald."

"When you get tired of her, give me a sign. We've all been dying to give her a poke." He's baiting me like one of his hunting quarries. His eyes are bloodshot, wild.

In our bedchamber behind the kitchens, Elise is too tired to make love, but not too tired to argue. "Take Tybolt away? He's not yet two summers old! I'd rather die!"

"He needs a knightly education. He won't get one here. Here he'll just learn to whore and cheat."

"Then take us from here! I beg you! Take us to the City, My Lord. Find me a house in the City. Let me live there. I can weave and sell cloth for a living, and bring up Tybolt and Ysolt myself."

"I like you where you are. Where I can keep an eye on you. Where you're under my protection. And in the City there are laws, statutes, Elise. She who has a home must needs register. And who do we write as the father of your children? Who is your husband? Where were you married?"

"I've told you! Ask Emmerich. There are ways round this. He'll know."

"What's wrong with Schwanenstein?"

"I am a slave! This place is a whorehouse!"

"God damn you, what do you lack? The finest food and clothing? Warmth, space? The children are growing up in one of the finest castles of Alsace! It's what every child in the City *dreams of*!"

"Then why take Tybolt away from here? If this is the Earthly Paradise?"

"He's my Son! I'll do with him as I please! He'll be leaving on his third summer, and that is that!"

She throws herself on the pallet, scoops the children to her side. Sobs, wails, screams, the whole bloody repertoire.

† † †

He's got me Thinking, that Schäffer has, and I don't like it. Thinking makes my head hurt, and it gets in the way of Life. But what taste has Life now? All the salt and spice has been taken from it, grain by grain.

He's right, that straw-haired bastard. The City is there for the taking. The merchants, the tradesmen, they all hate the Bishop now. Even the Bishop's own ministers; the City Families who run the tolls, the mint, the courts of law, the Zorns, the Müllenheims; even they have begun to despise von Stahlem and his court of cronies and pocketing parasites. The

Bishop stands alone, separated from his People, protected only by the clerics and the old Cathedral Chapter families, rotting on their ancient vines.

Lanzelin and Reichard are still snoring. It's shortly after dawn and they're not happy to be woken. Neither are the two village girls they're entwined with, all on one mattress in the lower guestroom of Schwanenstein Keep.

"Come on boys, we're going hunting."

The girls groan, the boys grumble. But when we get the castle ferry across the Rhine and head for the Watzenau Forest, the boys start asking questions. After all, Watzenau is not a forest where one can chase the russet hart on galloping stallions, it's a mess of bloody thickets and marshes, a place for dogged peasants to hunt down boars with sticks and spears, to snare rabbits and quiver at the hoot of an owl. It's a forest such as haunts children's stories, all thorns, kobolds and shadows.

Lanzelin yawns. "Watzenau? What the hell are we going to do there?"

"We're hunting the Bandits, boys."

That gives them pause.

I've never been to Watzenheim before. A desolate Rhine-bank village of stinking huts and pig slurry, crouching on the edge of the hostile forest. The only visible inhabitant, a twisted codger threading twine, stares at us as if we were the unholy Turk.

We follow the one narrow, pitted road into the forest. There's an ancient Imperial milestone nearly covered with briars, and then, after that, the branches close in. Our horses have to trot through in single file.

"Volmar, Brother," says Lanzelin. "They say the Bandits are two score swordsmen now. What good are we three against them?"

"One Knight is worth ten men, Lanzl."

"That doesn't reassure me. Did you argue with Elisl? Is that why we're out here?"

I let the branch I'm pushing aside spring back and fly towards Lanzelin's face. He ducks.

"Lanzl. Everyone else needs one hundred armed men and a Priest to say Communion before they can even go to hunt down a mouse. But we are Old Knights of Alsace, Lanzelin, and we are not afraid of a few footpads."

I don't need eyes in the back of my head to know that Lanzelin is sharing a look with Reichard. Well, let them think it, let them think I am mad. Maybe I am.

I am the Baron of Kronthal, my family goes back seventeen generations. True, the von Kronthal estate is not what it used to be, but my cold, dull marriage to the heiress of the von Moders has fixed that. I have more gold than I could ever spend in a lifetime, I can buy any woman I want, any wine, any indulgence, any pleasure. And instead I am here, in a dark forest, thinking of my Reputation.

This is the disease of Politics. And Schäffer has given me a fatal dose.

ANNO
1247

THE MASTER
(ANNO 1247. MANFRED GERBER VII)

The Baron von Kronthal doesn't look bad for someone who has spent four months traipsing around Watzenau Forest: his hair long and clean, a freshly shaven chin. He doesn't stand as they enter, doesn't offer his hand, merely nods at their deferent bows. Slouches in Emmerich's cushioned chair as if it's a throne.

"Master Merchants, all, thank you for coming," he says, once they have taken their place. Perched on benches, standing, leaning against the office walls of Schäffer and Associates in Ehle Street, the Merchants of Hagenburg, summoned by the Baron's command.

"I'll be honest, I don't care much for this place. Hagenburg. It's a stinking mess, and every day it gets worse. Someone should burn the whole place down and start again from scratch. Still, it is, for better or worse, my home. And as the son of one of the oldest families in Alsace I feel I have to protect our City. Our Bishop is more concerned with lining his friends' pockets with silver and punishing porters who've had too much wine . . . "

"Well said!" ventures Manfred, alongside a general muttering of approval.

" . . . so it falls to me and my liegemen and fellow noblemen to take action against these Bandits."

Baron Volmar von Kronthal stands from his chair, his feather-capped head nearly touches the office ceiling. He takes a goblet of wine from Emmerich Schäffer's outstretched hand.

"I and my brave Knights have reconnoitred the area on both banks of the Rhine, from Illingen and Schwanenstein to the Albe mouth and beyond, and from Rheinau to Watzenau forest, North towards Speyer. We have found many traces of the Bandit troop, we have engaged with them once, but as the odds were some forty to five, we withdrew. We have captured and questioned some seven men and boys we found making their way to and from the robber pack."

The Merchants look amongst themselves, wary, eager.

"We have ascertained the following. There is a core group around the Bandit Leader. None of the men we captured had seen or met this man, whom they refer to simply as *the Master*. He keeps distant, makes the plans and dispenses both justice and booty throughout the band. His orders are carried out by a lieutenant, named Staubmantel, a man who bears the scars of war, and who, it is said, fought in the Crusades, an experienced fighter.

"At the centre, there is the Master, surrounded by his lieutenants and confidantes. Then there is the main attack troop, which is some dozen armoured fighters. Then, joining them, from all around, mercenaries, footpads, chancers, thieves. Anyone who wishes to try their luck for a small share of booty.

"The bandits have no base, no camp. They have some favoured places deep in the Watzenau forest, and sometimes venture to the marshes across-river from the Albe. They are always on the move. In the winter, they disband. In the summer, they reach some sixty strong. They have enslaved women who act as camp whores and cooks. They have boys who act as messengers.

"I and my men have identified their preferred resting places. We have plans of attack. To be sure of victory, we will need some ninety fighting men. Horses. Supplies. As soon as the winter is over, as soon as the snows have melted and the thaw waters lowered, we will be ready.

"A war chest will be placed in the Pfennigplatz Counting House, under armoured guard. I myself, Volmar von Kronthal, will place a hundred marks in the chest. For a short campaign, we need double that. For a longer campaign, we will see. But, Master Merchants, I hope to deliver a quick and glorious victory over these bloodsuckers. These parasites who are sucking the blood from Old Father Rhine."

Applause. The Baron drinks from his goblet, whilst the Merchants of Hagenburg raise their hands in acclamation. Manfred's eyes search out Schäffer's.

Good work, my cunning friend.

† † †

The sullen boy, normally so fractious and quarrelsome, bursts into helpless sobs on the crowded Cologne quay. "Don't leave me here, Father. Don't leave me here."

Can one credit it? Only that morning he had been grumbling that he couldn't wait for Manfred to leave, stumbling round the Oferstolzens' warehouse like a drunken dancing bear. And now he clings to Manfred like a suckling child.

The boy has inherited his mother's dark hair, and now his father twines his hand in the locks that fall from the velvet cap. He tilts the tear-stained face towards his.

"Listen, Boy," he says, "it's not that bad. Herr Oferstolzen will take care of you."

"I don't like him."

"Watch your tongue. Respect your elders."

"I don't want to stay here."

"Boy. This Christmas just gone, you passed thirteen years. And with thirteen, your apprentice time begins."

"Can't I be apprenticed in Hagenburg?"

"You're safer here. And the girls are prettier." And yet a pain creeps through Manfred's heart. He remembers his apprentice years and his own wretched tears when his father abandoned him on the Frankfurt quay.

But who can gainsay it? This is the Way of the World.

"Use your time well, Boy. Learn the trade."

"I want to stay with you and Mother."

"We've taught you all we can. You'll be free of us here. You can get up to all kinds of mischief. With the girls."

The shadow of a smirk twitches across his son's young face. The fluff of a coming beard, now pearled with tears. Manfred's hand, more tender now, washes the tears away. "I'll be back before you know it, Boy. I'll have business to do here in the summer. I'll bring you some Lenzenbach cheese and a new summer cote. What colour do you want?"

"Blue."

"Like Mother's?"

The child nods, looks down, hiding further tears.

"Farewell, Boy. God be with you." Manfred pats his son's cheeks, walks to the barge, gives the signal to depart.

The ship heaves into the wide waters. The wind is with them today, a bright, steady breeze sweeping upriver. Tears fight at the gates of Manfred's eyes, but he does not let them pass. He turns, showing his son a graven face of manly endurance, and waves.

His son stands alone at the end of the jetty. His body is stooped, rejected. A knife twists in Manfred's heart, a terrible, keening pain.

† † †

Upriver from Cologne, against the flow of Old Father Rhine. A creeping pace, pulled by straining drays. The old boat captain tells river tales of underwater caves full of treasure guarded by River Nymphs and jealous Kobolds, golden-haired sirens singing sailors to their doom, whirlpools that form under the full moon, gateways to the other world.

But Manfred's heard them all before. He sits on the bowsprit, wrapped in the captain's skins shiny with linseed oil. On the Eifel and Taunus hills, winter is easing into Spring, the snows are melting. In the Rhine villages, in Bacharach and Bingen, the streets are bright with Carnival.

The Pirate Season will soon begin.

At Speyer, a surprise. The boat that Manfred boards is a pilgrim barge, carrying the Basel faithful back from the shrine of the Three Kings in Cologne. And at the aft end, sitting in inconspicuous silence, Meir Rosheimer and another Jew.

"I didn't know that you had converted."

Meir frowns, but recognises the joke with a shrug. "Just we thought this pilgrim boat the safest, and they take Jewish money too."

"Well, we are travel companions." Manfred sits down beside them. Meir's troubled, pale companion shifts away on the bench, flinches as if Manfred had the Ague. Meir gestures with his hand; "My brother, Yitzhak, my colleague, Manfred Gerber."

Manfred looks at Meir's brother, curious to see the man that Emmerich has told tales about. A scholar taken with a raging fit on the steps of the synagogue, crying out that the Gentiles were coming to take the Jewish women. It took five men to restrain him and he was sent to a Rabbi in Speyer to be healed. Meir spreads his hands, turns them palms upwards towards Heaven. "My brother has been unwell, but he is now much recovered, thanks to God."

"Thanks to God," says Manfred and smiles at Yitzhak, who fidgets like a child with the hem of his cote. He mutters something that sounds like words of thanks, but one can hardly hear him over the sound of the boatmen's cries. They are pulling away into the current of the river, punts and oars rising and falling . . .

"May I thank you personally," says Meir over the sounds of

the rushing waters, "for allowing Schäffer and Associates to keep its place in the River Trade Union."

Manfred chuckles, pulls his earlobe. "But it's a *Christian company*, Herr Rosheimer!"

"So I've heard, so I've heard," says Rosheimer, and laughs. "And it's nice of you to say so."

"Your Christian mastiff Herr Schäffer made it quite clear to me. That if I cut you out, you'd close down your Rhine trade and concentrate on the Danube and the Rhône. He pointed out I'd lose one third of my custom overnight."

"He's very persuasive, is Herr Schäffer. He certainly always gets his way with *me*. I often wonder who is running our affairs, he or I."

"I think he himself has probably forgotten, Herr Rosheimer."

"I think you're right, Herr Gerber. I think he has."

The boat eases out of the strong counter-current and the gurgling, hissing waters fade into drifting silence. "Be my guests at the Inn at Leymersheim tonight."

Meir's hands rise in defensive thanks. "Thank you Herr Gerber, but we have our own food, and will sleep on the boat."

Manfred turns away and grins to himself. You could offer the Jews a seventeen course meal and wine made from gold leaf and they'd still turn you down. It's in their religion, they can't eat or drink anything made by Christian hands. Once Schäffer tried to explain it all to him, you can't eat bread at Easter, you can't eat pigs or crayfish at all, and one bowl is for cheese and another for meat. It sounded like insanity.

But wherever they go, the Jews take care of their own. When Manfred travels to Mayenz or Speyer, he must find an Inn, pay for his food and his lodging, show generous hands and invite others to his table. Each trade trip costs a fortune. But the Jew, he embarks from his boat and walks to the Judengasse. And there he is given free bed and board, boys to delouse him, a place of honour in the synagogue, a bundle of letters and promissory notes to take with him to his next port of embarkation. He moves from one Judengasse to the next, always well-fed and watered.

† † †

The pilgrims join in prayer. Their priest leads them, singing softly. In the stern, the two Jews huddle over their book. Yitzhak Rosheimer's eyes are closed in fervour, opening only rarely to glance at the page; he knows, it seems, the whole text by heart.

Manfred sits towards the bow, tense and quiet, like a figurehead. He and the Captain scan the trees for signs of attack. They have passed through the worst of it, through the Watzenau forest, where every cry of a crow or rasp of a magpie sends fingers of ice scuttling down your back.

"We'll be in Rheinau soon, God willing," whispers the Captain. "Not far now."

"God willing," whispers Manfred, kisses his Saint Christopher medallion. The sun is low in the sky, burnishing the canopy leaves. Ahead, another boat. Stranded by the shore. Its prow is against the rocks, its body twisted, its starboard gunwale dipping just below the surface of the waters. On the shore, a woman and a baby squat and wail. Two men pace up and down nervously, their eyes scanning the further horizon, hoping for aid. On the boat itself, nine more men and women clutch to the prow, try to push at the rocks, hoping to free the boat from grasp of the mud and stone.

One of the men on the shore turns and sees the pilgrims' boat. He leaps for relief. "Here! Here!" he cries. "Help us, please! The pirates!"

The Captain nods to the helmsman to pull the tiller, alter the course towards the shipwrecked boat. "We can't take them all on, there's too many of them."

Manfred stands, trying to see better. "Maybe we can tow their boat away from the rocks."

"Is their hull not damaged?"

"It's hard to tell."

They pull alongside the stranded boat. On the shore, the woman with the baby wails, "Help us, help us. They took my husband!" A shiver of wind sweeps through the leaves.

Manfred looks at the stranded passengers. Something is wrong. Their faces are not grateful, frightened, hopeful. Their faces are blank. Cold.

The woman on the bank abruptly stops her wailing. She picks up her baby and walks into the forest. A sudden, gelid silence falls. The men on the stranded boat now all have swords, axes. Stepping out from the forest's gloom, a dozen archers, arrows ready on taut, straining strings.

"My name is Staubmantel," says a voice. "All of you. Get off the boat."

† † †

They're not much older than his son, the two of them. Bitter, brutal faces. Rough fingers rub at the weave of his cote, test the velvet of his cap. "A rich one here, a Rich One."

"Bring him to me." Staubmantel speaks.

Darkness is coming. A small clearing in the forest, a bow-shot from the shipwreck shore. A bonfire. A soup pot. Grimy-faced women making food. The bandits, three dozen of them or more; men, women, children. Some with plate- and chainmail like Knights. Some with shields, all of them armed.

A temporary encampment; kick over the fire, pour water on the ashes and it's gone. A movable base.

Staubmantel stands above Manfred, one head taller, maybe more. A scar judders across his forehead and cheek; souvenir of the slash of a sword. "A Rich One, is he?" His chainmailed hand slashes out, lashing across Manfred's cheek. "Don't look at me, you Dog."

Manfred faces the ground as the bandit's hand gropes over his body, clutching at his clothes, the velvet, the supple Anglian wool, the silk scarf. "Merchant are you, Dog?"

"Yes." A whisper.

"Hiding amongst the Pilgrims?"

"Yes."

"Welcome to Fortune's Wheel, Dog. See it spin."

The boys start sawing at his belt with their knives, cutting at the purse straps. Manfred pushes at them. "Stop! I'll just give it to you!"

The boy hits him in the eye with the pommel of his dagger. "We don't take orders from you." Manfred's hands clutch at his throbbing head. The purse falls.

Staubmantel counts. "A handful of pennies and heller. Is that all this Dog is worth?"

"I KNOW THAT BASTARD!" A voice from the fire. Standing now, putting aside his soup. Carious teeth, gapped. One eye long gone, covered by a scarred and twitching lid. Finger trembling as it points at Manfred. "I know him."

Manfred swallows. "I don't know you."

"Because I got away. If I hadn't, you'd have stuck me like a pig." He spits from his rotting mouth. "Staubmantel. This one. He led the raid on the Albe camp."

Frost fingers scuttle around Manfred's heart. And clutch. He gasps. "It wasn't me."

"Manfred Gerber. It must be Manfred Gerber." Staubmantel laughs. "Manfred Dog Gerber. WE GOT HIM!"

"I'm not Gerber!" Manfred struggles against the kicks and blows now raining on him. Wild, his eyes look for the Jews. As if they could help him. As if they would.

† † †

Through the darkling forest, traces of dusk still cling to the gaps between the trees. Stumbling through half-seen paths, brambles, briars. Kicked from behind by his two warder-boys. Hands bound behind his back. Thinking to himself like a prayer, *You'll be all right, you'll be all right. They'll want a ransom. A big ransom, but you'll be all right. You're worth two hundred marks. More. Grete will find it. She'll sell some boats. Borrow from Schäffer. Pawn the house. You'll be all right, you'll be all right.*

A camp in the woods. A makeshift hunting shelter; a mighty beech at the centre, and from its first branches, a roof of wicker and wattle, spreading wide. Under the cover, a pit dug for a fire, a roasting haunch of meat. A trestle table, laden with food and wine. Two of the Basel women, brought here, stripped naked, kneeling, trembling, awaiting their fate.

"We have Gerber! We have Gerber!" The boys shout out. "Master!"

A tall man, broad shouldered, by the fire. Fine cloak of light blue wool, hood of silk. He turns, his steel breastplate, polished, reflects the flames.

Manfred knows the face. He knows it. "This is Gerber?" A deep voice, rich. A refined accent, Old Alsatian, like a nobleman.

He approaches. The boys kick at the back of Manfred's knees so that he falls to the leafy ground, kneeling before the Master. The Unnamed.

The Master looks down at him. The face. Hooked nose, dark eyes. Manfred knows the face. He's seen it in the past. Not in a forest, amongst bandits, in firelight. But in broad day, through incense smoke.

In the Cathedral.

"Gerber? Do you know me?"

"No, sire."

"I think you do."

The Count von Schwanenstein.

The Count nods. "And so you do." He crouches down to look in Manfred's eyes. Manfred's heart pounds. Sickness crawls in his stomach. "A shame. We could have made a pretty ransom with you. But no one may know my name."

Manfred's throat is dry. He stutters, can find no spit.

"Sorry? Do you want to say something?"

"I can help you," he croaks.

"I don't think you can, Gerber." He stands, sweeps his hand, commanding. "Fetch the rope!"

"I can help you! The Jews, the two Jews . . . "

"What Jews is he babbling about?"

The two boys turn from the horse's saddle where they are unravelling the rope. "Two Jews on board the pilgrim boat, master. They don't look like much."

"One of them is Meir Rosheimer. He's worth a fortune. Five hundred marks. Let me go, I'll give you a hundred. One hundred and fifty."

The Count of Schwanenstein sighs. "We're not in a marketplace, Gerber. Here I decide the price of things."

The boys have the rope now. They throw it over a branch. Set a bench there beneath it.

The rope swings. The fire burns. The two pilgrim women sob, turn away. One of them has beautiful breasts. All Manfred wants is to be with that woman, one last time.

The boys bring him to his feet. In Manfred's mind: his son's broken figure on the Cologne quay, Grete's smile, the touch of his father's hand. His mother. He can hardly see her, she died when he was so young.

His knees are trembling so much, they hardly need to kick the bench away. He would have fallen anyway, of his own accord.

† Manfred Gerber (1212–1247)

SHIPWRECK
(ANNO 5007. YUDL BEN YITZHAK IV)

"C ome here, Boy," says Emmerich, his face bright with pride. "Let me kiss you."

Yudl comes, lets the Strawhead Goy take him in his arms and plant a kiss on his grateful brow. "You're learning fast. That's a fine price you got us there . . . A fine price. I'm proud of you."

Yudl's New World; the bureau in the Ehlestrasse, the teeming city dock, the Counting House where foreign coins are weighed and changed. For his apprenticeship Emmerich gives him a purse of silver every week to go and buy wares to sell on the "stopping barges," the ships that dock at every river pier and jetty, selling trinkets, pots, tools and small bales of cloth.

As he walks home through the Hagenburg streets, Yudl shines. He thinks of the web of trade stretching out from his purse's silver, the pewter candlesticks bought here in the Wachsgassl workshop carried by the tireless pedlar over hill and valley to the high parishes above the Rhine. He imagines the pedlar's rasping sing-song as he approaches the village, the toll of his bell, the dogs barking and snapping at his feet, the peasants' worn pennies ruefully given. And then he sees the end of the journey, the final result: the candlestick standing above a smoke-black hearth in the foothills of the Alps. The triumph of trade.

Hands behind his back, Schäffer and Associates' new Apprentice passes through the markets, the hawkers and beggars. The Abomination holds no terror for him anymore; as he walks past he stares it down, forbidding its dominion over him; just a pile of stones and vain idols, an excrescence of the sinful earth.

In the Judengasse he heads for the beth midrash, takes his place in the second row of lecterns, addresses himself to the Word of the Lord. Now that his Father has gone to Speyer, he is free. He studies no more and no less than is expected of any Good Jew. The Rabbi may grumble, but Uncle Meir is on Yudl's side. Yes, they need scholars and scribes, but they also need traders and merchants. When the beth midrash guttering springs a leak, who is it that pays for repairs?

It is a bright, golden late winter, mild and hopeful. Every few days storms gather above the Vogesen and scour the earth with rain, but the darkness never tarries, the clouds scatter in high, soaring winds and the sun returns, teasing forth the buds in the courtyard trees. Outside the haberdasher shop, his Mother sits in sunlight, awaiting custom, and sometimes, when work is slow, Yudl, Meir and Emmerich join her on the low, smoke-blackened stools that once sat round the family hearth. There they talk of the network of trade that Schäffer and Associates are building along the rivers of Rhine, Danube and Rhône. With her profits from the shop, Mother buys shares in the cargoes, and smiles when the letters arrive from Speyer and Ulm, showing her gains. Her heart seems light and easy, laughing happily at their jokes.

And Yudl watches her carefully. And never once does she step out of the bounds of propriety. Always keeping her distance from the Gentile guest, never taking something directly from his hands in case their skin might touch, and if laughing, always covering her mouth and looking to the ground, in case she might tempt him with Frivolity.

Since his Father is gone, the House in the Judengasse sighs with relief, laughter rings out from the kitchen where the women now gather to gossip and sew. The Secret Red Book has gone too, and with it the compulsion to uncover what is hidden; the pale, troglodyte truths beneath the stones.

It will be a Golden Spring.

✡ ✡ ✡

. . . the Nations are torn by division, the Emperor wars with the Hierarch of Babylon, the Gentiles draw lots, take sides, fight amongst themselves. At the Gates of the East, the Mongol horde waits to sweep through the collapsing kingdoms. A letter has come to us from a Jew of Bessarabia under the Mongol domin- ion. He says that the Ten Lost Tribes of Israel wait in the rear of the Mongol armies, beyond the river Sambatyon. Their shining vanguard has been seen on the horizon. It cannot be long now until the Days of Tribulation when—

The voices called him from the street. "Yudl! Yudl! Come quickly!"

The previous summer, once again reading the Book of Secrets. His Father's ravings, his vengeful dreams based on faded letters, copies of copies of copies from unknown sources in distant lands. "Yudl, come quickly! Your father! The beth midrash!"

Yudl puts the book back in its place, locks the library door, hides the key, runs outside. Minchin and other boys waiting for him in the doorway, huddling from the midsummer rain. "What is it?" "Your father! He's gone mad! Mad! He attacked Aberle!"

Running the fifty steps to the beth midrash, racing inside to find his Father, pale and distraught, his eyes rolling in a ghostly, mask-like face. His limbs and body possessed by some uncontrolled power, a marionette plucked this way and that by unseen strings, held down by the Gabbai, two boys holding his feet. Nearby, dabbing his bleeding nose with a rag, Aberle, trembling.

"Father, what happened!" "Yudl, Yudl . . . " his Father's hand reaches out, clutches at Yudl's face. "My son! My son!"

Yudl flinches, as if his Father's hands were claws. He turns to the chorus of shocked and pale faces. "What happened?"— "He attacked Aberle! Jumped on him!"—"Aberle took Yitzhak's place at his lectern!"—"So what, do you kill a man for using your lectern?"—"No, but . . . " Aberle stamps his foot. "I just put my book down on it for a short while, I didn't mean . . . "—"You provoked him on purpose! You want his place at the Rabbi's right hand!"—"And don't I deserve it? I'm a scholar, not a lunatic like him!"

Yudl looks round wildly as the babble of accusations and counter-accusations rises. He finds the Rabbi seated in the corner, holding his head in his hands. "Take him home, Yudl. He needs rest."

As the summer faded and the High Holidays came, Yudl's Father retreated into silence. He hardly left his library, only going to the beth midrash when the Law required it of him. When Yudl went up the stairs to visit, he found him hunched over a book, unmoving, seemingly not even reading, just staring at the Letters as if they were some great, mute mystery.

On the night of Yom Kippur, they lay prostrated on the floor of the beth midrash, wrapped in their shrouds. As the Cantor rose to recite the penitential *chatanu* prayer, his Father cried out, his eyes wide in his face, foam on his lips, "They are coming! They are coming!" And he raced out into the street.

Yudl followed, half-tripping over his kittel, into the damp dirt of the Judengasse. Darkness. From a few shutters, the dim, guttering light of tallow candles, kept burning by the women in vigil, waiting for the men to return from schul. His father stumbled to the alleyway that runs past their house. "The Goyyim are coming! The Goyyim!"

There are the stories, handed down from generation to generation. That the Goyyim wait for Yom Kippur night, when all the Jewish men are in their synagogues, prostrated in repentance. Then they creep into the Jewish quarter and enter the Jewish homes, and take the women in their beds and fornicate with them.

The Judengasse shutters opened, the women, pale in candlelight, stared outside, frightened at the noise. But there were no Goyyim sneaking through the dark streets. Only Yitzhak Rosheimer, frothing at the mouth, and his shamed son Yudl, trying to grab hold of his flailing, desperate arms . . .

✡ ✡ ✡

Yudl dreams that his Father is dead. Drowned in the mikve, struck down by leprosy, killed by robbers. He dreams that he will never return from his convalescence in Speyer. He dreams that (God forbid!) his widowed Mother marries the Strawhead Goy.

Opening his eyes from half-sleep, Yudl tells himself that these are sinful dreams. He knows that the dreaming mind is adrift on a trackless, unknown sea, but that the dreamer is the Helmsman, setting the course. Rubbing his eyes, he sees the first light of dawn seeping through the shutters. He waves his hands, dismissing his dreams, and recites: *I give thanks before You, Living and Eternal King, that You have returned my soul with compassion.*

Early winter afternoon in the Ehlestrasse bureau. Yudl and Emmerich are reckoning their takings, the coins and promissory notes from the year's last convoys. They are alone in the office, the assistants have left early for the Martinmas feast; the first barrels of the year are being breached, crowds are gathering outside the Cathedral for the Festival of the New Wine.

Yudl doesn't look up from the Counting Table. His heart is beating fast. He must say it now or forever leave it unsaid.

"There are people who say that you are my father."

Emmerich holds still. Lays down his quill. Silence. Ink drops from the nib, blotting the page, spreading, a black rose.

His voice shakes. "I would be proud to be, Yudl."

Yudl looks up from the coins and figures. But Emmerich is looking away, staring at the blank wall as if the sad story of the past were written there. "Your Mother and I, when we were young. Your age. We liked each other. She was the most beautiful thing I'd ever seen . . . " He pauses, collects himself. "And she, the Lord only knows why, liked me. She would watch me as I went about my business in the Quarter. Your Father was always in the synagogue, studying. But your uncle noticed. And sent me to Mayenz to be apprenticed, moved me out of the way, out of trouble. Then you were born, with fair hair. And although I was far away, the Gossipers started their work."

Emmerich now turns to face him. His grey eyes are surprisingly still, steady.

That evening, Yudl is at home, alone, sitting in his father's library. The room smells of soot and sadness. Yudl runs his hand over the desk, piling up a ridge of dust. He sits, pulls a random book from the shelf, opens it. Maimonides' *Guide for the Perplexed*, a Hebrew translation from the original Arabic. His Father's favourite.

He starts to read, thinking of his Father's beautiful voice, reciting the Torah. Fervent, musical and true.

On the page, the letters suddenly swim and meld. A haze of words, dim, as if seen through mists. Yudl's hands dab at his eyes as his tears fall on the page and a sob rises up from deep within him, from that forgotten place full of bitter, hateful love.

✡ ✡ ✡

In the beth midrash, an early spring night, the lamps burning. Yudl and the elders of the community face each other on the rough benches. The Rabbi reads the letter aloud.

*

. . . Meir is less convinced of this than me, but he accepts its terrible logic. The Rabbi will know that Maimonides, he of blessed memory, has said that it is a mitzvah to pay a ransom for a captive. But he will also know the shameful case of Levi bar Darga, who paid an excessive ransom of 13,000 dinars for his daughter. And he will know that the Mishnah says that one must not ransom captives for such high sums, for to do so is to encourage the venal to target Jews for ransom in future.

*They killed Manfred Gerber, whose wealth is similar to my brother Meir's. They did not ransom him, but executed him. And they are holding **us** ransom for five hundred marks, a terrible sum that will bankrupt our family and cause hardship to our Hagenburg community which relies so much on the Rosheimer wealth for its well-being.*

*We therefore plead to you. Do **not** pay our ransom. Should you pay it, other Jews and other communities will be targeted and endangered.*

Do not give our captors this encouragement to ransom other Jews.

Be steadfast. Reject the offer. And God Willing, we will find some other way of escape from here. Meir tells me the Baron von Kronthal has started his campaign by now. Maybe he can rescue us.

For they who took us captive required of us a song. But how shall we sing the Lord's song in a strange land?

Yitzhak ben Yisrael

The Rabbi raises his head from the letter. "Woe to those who have talked ill of Yitzhak ben Yisrael," he says. "Who amongst you could have written such a letter?" He places the letter in Yudl's hands, and looks up at the quavering light of the lanterns. "And what shall we do? Shall we heed his wise advice? As he himself indicates, the Talmud can be invoked on both sides of the argument." Rabbi Menahem turns to Yudl. "Bring that One in to us now, Yudl. Let him speak."

Yudl rises from his bench and goes to the doorway, where Emmerich Schäffer is pacing up and down in the dusk. Inside, Emmerich sits on a stool just outside the circle as Yudl reads him the letter in a tremulous voice.

After Yudl has finished, the Rabbi clears his throat. "Tell us, Herr Schäffer. Can we pay such a sum?"

Emmerich shakes his head. "No." He looks at the ground. "Yes. If we call in many of our assets, we can. But it will ruin us." Now he looks up to face the Rabbi. "We should bargain with them."

"Bargain?"

"If anything, it will buy us time."

"We will not *bargain*, Herr Schäffer. It will not be said that the Jews of Hagenburg haggled like fishwives over the price of two souls."

✡ ✡ ✡

Yudl pulls at the rope, dragging his father's coffin across the cemetery ground. It was his dying wish to be buried in penitence, to be dragged forty cubits to his grave.

Waiting by the open pit, the coffin of Yitzhak's elder brother Meir. All the Jews of Hagenburg stand amongst the gravestones. The women wail, their hands form claws, pluck at their cheeks. Yudl's Mother is on her knees, screaming at the Heavens. At discreet distance, the Gentile mourners; Emmerich and his brother, their sister Grete, she herself in a black widow's veil. The workers of Schäffer and Associates, Uncle Meir's business colleagues.

Yudl stumbles to his knees. Rises up again, pulls at the rope. Aberle is there, offering his help, but Yudl has sworn he will do this on his own. He pulls onwards.

His Father and Uncle's bodies, cut down from trees by the shore of the Rhine. A note from the pirate Staubmantel saying: *come collect your dead, you skinflint Jews.*

The two coffins are lowered into the pit. The wailing becomes shrill, keening over the sound of the nearby monastery bells. Yudl kneels by the grave, raises his head, releases a piercing cry. Above him, the linden tree. A raven launching into the leaden sky.

Dear Yudl, this will be my last letter to you. My time is short and I must be brief.

God's ways are mysterious. He has given me but one son, a jewel and a treasure whose value I never truly realised until now. One thing is clear, Yudl, you have a gift. Whether for trade or for Torah, only time and destiny will tell.

Whatever you do, do not squander your blessings as I have, in foolishness and in speculation of what might have been. What has been, has been, and cannot be undone. The past is closed. Only the future is open.

Take care of and provide for your mother. And remember me kindly, and not in bitterness, I beg you.

I love you. Your Father.

Yudl takes the spade from the mound of earth. It is he who will throw in the first clods, and clothe his father's casket in darkness.

UNVANQUISHED
(ANNO 1247. BARON VOLMAR VON KRONTHAL III)

T he fingers of his sword hand are almost completely crushed. And still he screams, "The Count of Schwanenstein! Count Schwanenstein!"

"Release the screws, this is getting nowhere." I sink back onto the bench, lean up against the farmhouse wall. Close my eyes, feel the sunshine as the bandit's screams subside.

Some bandit. Younger son of a poor Lothringen noble, sent to the Crusades for ten years and then disinherited and forgotten. He comes back in rags with his flea-ridden squire. Homeless, lordless, he wanders the roads of the German lands, tells tavern tales of dusky dancing girls and the golden walls of Ashkelon, hires out his sword for a shilling a day to whoever will take him. Ends up in a Black Forest gang of thieves and highwaymen. Hearing of the fame of the Watzenau Bandits, he comes to Alsace and joins the pirate band.

He's only good for the gallows now.

All goes quiet as my men wait for my command. We're in some godforsaken hamlet between Watzenau and Bergzabern. Foresters and swineherds fled inside when we rode in, three score horsemen and two dozen footsoldiers. We threw down our five shackled men. In a farmyard we lit a fire, heated our irons, prepared the screws. Shameful work.

And now this. This nonsense.

Peasant piggy eyes peek from the farm's locked shutters as I lash out at the splayed, twisted bandit. Kick him like a dog. "Count Sebald is my relative, you bastard." He whimpers like a cur. "Kill me, kill me please. A clean death . . . My sword hand's gone . . . "

I stand. "Take this filth back to Hagenburg, and give them to the Judge. I'll ride ahead."

Jerusalem's getting old in the tooth, but he's still a fine steed. The days are long. I'll be there by sundown.

† † †

Schäffer raises an eyebrow. Insolent. "The Count von Schwanenstein?"

"That's what the bastard said."

Schäffer looks down at the floor a few moments. Takes in a deep, long breath. "Well . . . that's interesting."

"What, you devil?"

The Girl brings water and wine, some fruit tarts.

Jerusalem nearly drank the Ehle dry as we pulled into Hagenburg. Now it's my turn. I down the pitcher of water in one. As Emmerich waits for the Girl to withdraw, he looks at me. One of his long, quiet stares. Like a sheep. A cow. Chewing the cud.

The Girl curtsies, closes the door behind her.

Silence. Outside, the sun is setting, the dock is quiet.

I look at Schäffer. "What? Speak."

He raps his desk with his knuckles, stands. "I've been wondering about it for years. The Lady Adelheid's habits, my Lord. Just one banquet must cost ten, eleven marks. And sometimes three, four banquets a week? And the troubadours, the jongleurs, the jewels, the fabrics. The shoes with golden laces. The handmaidens. The tournaments. A mild estimate, My Lord. Sixty marks a week in the summer season."

"The Count's estates cover the whole plain of Illingen. It's fertile land."

"Yes, but I doubt his lands bring him even seven hundred

annual. Herr Rosheimer and I assumed that he has been sell-ing assets . . . just as he sold some land and tithes to you."

"He did . . . "

"But we have heard of no further sales. So we assume he must be borrowing gold from somewhere. A substantial sum, every year. My Lord, we wanted to lend to him! But we could never get ourselves introduced!"

"You know I tried, Schäffer. He was never interested."

"So from whom did he borrow, if not from us? From the Bishop? An old Staufen like Schwanenstein? I think not. From a Florentine bank? Then who was the Factor who did the deal? It's been a mystery to me, My Lord, for years."

"Maybe he . . . " His words worm their way into my ear, making me pause.

" *'Maybe he,'* My Lord?"

"Damn you, Schäffer."

"*Maybe he has another source of income*, you were about to say, My Lord?"

I nod.

"Well, My Lord. It would seem that he does."

† † †

Elise hasn't spoken to me since I had our little boy Tybolt taken away. She screamed like a tigress, raved like a heretic, tore at my face with her nails, leaving scratch-marks on my cheeks that smarted for days. But thank the Lord I had the Boy sent off—he's now safe and sound in the Lorraine, far away from the debacle of Schwanenstein.

It is noon on a bright summer's day but Schwanenstein cas-tle gate is closed. From the crenellations above the drawbridge, the Castellan asks me to turn in my sword.

"Say that again."

"Your sword, Baron. It is the custom."

"Not with me. *Not here.* I am Family."

"Nevertheless I must ask you to deliver your sword. It is the custom upon entering a Free Man's dwelling, My Lord."

"I KNOW THE CUSTOMS OF THE LAND!"

"Then you will have no objection."

Sebald is waiting for me in the Great Hall. The flagstones crawl with his pack of hounds, his throne-like chair perches before the cold, blackened fireplace. He grins. "Cousin, welcome. Wine?"

"Can it be true? You are the bloody Bandit King?"

He says nothing. I look at him. He is pale, his skin is stretched tight on his skull. Always a strange one, Sebald. Like there's two of him. One man in the morning, another in the afternoon. And today it's his Shadow Half, staring me down.

"So you don't deny it?"

He says nothing. Again.

"I've been chasing round the damned marshes like a bloodhound. I killed some of your men. Gave others to the bloody Bishop's sheriff to hang."

"Serving your New Masters?"

"New Masters?"

"The Jews and the Traders. Aren't they your New Masters?"

"It's called 'Politics,' Cousin."

"It is?"

"They're on our side. The Imperial side. If it comes to a war, we'll need them." In the wide, flagstoned hall, my words echo back at me, empty, wretched. "Together we can keep the Bishop in his place."

"Is that what they told you? They play a tune and you dance? Are the Jews and Merchants the new Lords of Alsace?"

"Listen. I swore in front of half the City I would defeat the Bandit King! And then he turns out to be my Cousin's husband. You should have told me. We could have worked something out."

"I have nothing to work out with you, Cousin. You who bought my parcel of land from me like a moneylender on Jew Lane . . . "

"You needed the money!"

"You who tried to peddle me his filthy *'fiduciary counsel'* to help me with my finances, like some kind of back-alley procuress."

"Sebald . . . "

"I am a Knight. And you are a Tradesman's Errand Boy."

Silence. My hands clench at my sides. In the shadows, his liegemen sit on benches. Seven swordsmen. "So you can afford to be bold when I am unarmed?" I step forward. Sebald's liegemen stand. Their scabbards scrape on the flagstones. "You? A Knight? Raping pilgrims, ransoming drapers, robbing women?"

He shrugs. "The Booty of War. And I have spilled no Noble Blood." The Count of Schwanenstein waves his hand, searches for a sweetmeat and tosses it to his hounds. A mêlée of growling, writhing fur. "We *are* at War, Cousin. The real war isn't the Staufen against the Pope. It is We against Them. Them with their Guilds and their fat Purses, buying up noble land. Upstarts. Mark my words, if we don't cut off their heads, they will eat us alive."

"You are babbling and I will take my leave. I will see Elise and take her with me."

Sebald's hollow eyes hold mine. "Elise is not available."

Silence.

"Where is she?"

"In the dungeon. You may not see her."

My fist clenches. The Count's voice echoes, resounds. "Of one thing be certain. As and when I like, I will hang Elise and her little baby slut from the Castle Gate. It seems you got your bastard boy out just in time. Where is he?"

"As if I'd tell you."

He's mad. I see it now. He opens his arms. "We're here. Come and take us, Errand Boy. This castle has never been conquered. Unvanquished. Try your luck."

He sighs. "Now go away."

I stand firm. I may be surrounded by seven armed men, but I do not take orders like a valet. "ADELHEID!" I scream, and propel myself towards the keep's stairway. "COUSIN!" The seven swordsmen reach for their hilts, but at Count Sebald's gesture, they withhold.

She is in her chamber, in a pitiful state. Two of her handmaidens lie beside her on the bed, drunk. The room stinks of schnapps.

"Adelheid, get up. You must help me. Help me see Elise."

"Volmar, are you here?" Her eyes are glassy, ringed with red. "Have you come to rescue me?"

"Rescue you? What from?"

The Countess drags herself up from the bed, pulls her fur stole closer around her shoulders. It is midsummer, and yet she shivers. "From *him*," she whispers, pointing downstairs. "He says no more *divertissements*. Not even a dancing party."

"Adelheid, there are other things to worry about. There will be a battle here, Schwanenstein will be attacked."

She laughs. "Don't you know? It is *Unvanquished*. Wenzel of Nürnberg wrote an Ode to this castle . . . *many men have scaled her proud stone, only to retreat in sickness and dismay.* Of course the castle is a metaphor for . . . *ME!*"

"A magnificent tribute to your beauty, My Lady . . ." mutters one of the drunken handmaidens.

"It is a high honour to have so many odes composed to one, I suppose I have had many dozen . . . " Adelheid continues, chattering like a skylark in the heavens, oblivious to the world below. "An accolade rarely consigned . . . "

"I want to see Elise!" I manage to interject.

"Oh do not speak of that vile girl!" declaims Adelheid and

turns away from me. "Sebald found her stealing my jewels! Her hand wrist-deep in silver! And she tried to escape! He has had her imprisoned. Why he has not had her flogged I do not know!"

"Adelheid, it is not true. Adelheid . . . !"

"Either bring me cheerful news, cousin, or leave! I am in mourning!"

"In Mourning?"

"For the Death of Joy!"

Outside Adelheid's chamber, the seven swordsmen await me, weapons drawn. I launch myself at them with my fists, and they leap upon me with pommels and knees. We wrestle like fools all the way down the Keep's stairwell.

Count Schwanenstein's liegemen throw me out through the Gate, toss my sword after me across the cobbles. Like I'm some kind of drunken lackey being thrown from an Inn.

† † †

Arrows like hailstones break upon my carapace. We push on towards the dry moat, the raised drawbridge, the plunging gap, throw our torches, the bales of dried straw. The men cower under the Tortoise Shell; a roof of timber, wicker and hide, now spiked like a porcupine from the torrent of arrows. Young von Zabern's Squire is hit in the ankle. Someone else in the thigh.

The torches are good. Two bales have caught, start to smoulder on the ledge by the drawbridge. If they don't pour dousers, the whole thing might go up.

"Back! Regroup!" I shout out over the drumming of the blows on the tortoise roof. Three or four wounded is too high a cost for this feint, this test of the Schwanenstein defence.

Under the Tortoise, we stagger back through the squall of arrows. The storm recedes as we pull further out of range, the sound of the blows replaced by the screams of derision from the crenellations. Schwanenstein's packs of wolves are howling. "Run away, run away you scum . . . "

We look up at the castle, rising on its shoulder of rock above the Rhine, unvanquished. Already the water butts are being winched on the Gatehouse Tower, lifted above the parapet, ready to pour.

Below, in the moat, on the ledge beneath the gateway, the straw is raging red and orange, retching smoke. If it could burn a short while longer, then the drawbridge would catch.

But here comes the rain. The water butts tilt over the gatehouse wall; a cascade of water. My crossbowmen fire a volley at the water-winchers. Their quarrels clatter against the fortress stones. Miss.

A billow of grey, wet smoke, and it's over.

† † †

Late summer. Early Autumn. All Saints'. Every day we harry them. Approach the walls in our tower, under our tortoise shell, under the shelter of shields. Shoot crossbows, arrows, throw burning bales, and, when the wind is right, burn pitch and let black smoke billow into their crenellations. Shout insults at them. Tell them the news about their wives. How Frau Metzgin, wife of Staubmantel's right hand man, now sucks pizzle in the Rheintor Bath House, one penny a suck.

Out of the range of their arrows, we put on shows. We light fires, grill freshly-slaughtered venison, drink luxurious horns of Rhenish wine, dance and sing. Joust, just to show we have the room to ride our horses. Hunt on the Schwanenstein hunting lands, and parade the rich spoils; hares, does, boars, a fine chestnut hart. Emmerich's men wave sacks of coin, offering a fine price to He Who Will Open the Gate. We seduce them with riches. We mock them with Freedom.

But they do not give.

Every day their archers are in position, ready to fire as soon as any of us stray within range. Every day their men are ready with water, with fire, to repel our advances. Every night their guardsmen patrol the walls.

And twice they have even caught us complacent, dozing in our tents, supping on soup. The drawbridge dropped down, and a swift strike of a dozen cavalry, riding amongst us, swords slashing. Seven dead. And then back inside the gate before we could mount a counter-attack.

Shameful. We will not be caught like that again.

And yet the days draw on, and no crack is seen, no breaking down. Schwanenstein stands, proud and hawk-like on its outcrop of unvanquished stone.

Ex Tenebris
(ANNO 1247. EUGENIUS VON ZABERN VII)

B eing blind is not without its advantages. Primary amongst the long list of unexpected blessings, the substantial diminution of Society that I am expected to endure. Most of my fellow Canons seem happy to leave me alone in my quarters, sitting quietly with my disfigured face obscured by shadows that for me no longer have any significance. Sunlight I can *feel* on my skin, its warmth. But, for instance, candlelight means nothing to me. Here is a binary opposition that no longer has meaning: Light. Darkness. Both are reduced to an undifferentiated Meaninglessness. A Zero.

And in this beautiful Nought, I now live.

† † †

Hieronymus does visit me daily, but only to check that my needs are met, that my food and wine have been brought to me, my chamber pots emptied. And, upon my request, he reads to me. From the Holy Scriptures, but also often from the new writings that are emerging from the academies, from Albertus Magnus and Roger Bacon. They have a sensibility that is pleasing to me, a wish to find concord between our God and the World in which he has seen fit to place us; namely a world that is made of Numbers and Facts and Laws which seem to be immutable. Maybe it is true that one day Our Lord will decree that the sun will rise in the West, but I doubt He will bother to do so. He will not disrupt the divine order of the world just to prove Brother Bacon wrong.

I would be untruthful were I to say that my Blinding was a blessing pure and simple. In fact it took me more than two long years to reach this state of Acceptance in which I repose today. The first weeks were plagued by physical discomfort, stabbing pains running from my eyes down my neck and along my arms, and by mental tortures far more difficult to bear. These, generally speaking, took the form of "*if only I . . .*" and concerned me rearranging the sequence of events in such a way that I never was blinded and that all my Enemies were cruelly and viciously punished instead.

It took a long time to eschew these foolish thoughts and to dispose of them into the same trough into which I now throw all manner of former absurdities. Had it really been I, Eugenius von Zabern, who had seen "auguries" and superstitiously believed in signs? How could I, a man of intelligence, have believed that the Lord Our God so organised his world that a crow would fly thrice in circles around the calvary of St. Arbogast and that the sun would cast a crown of gold around my head in Arles Cathedral, just to inform me that I would one day be Bishop? Does not God have more significant concerns than to pluck the strings of the world to make auguries and signs for his humble servants?

I am ashamed that I ever even gave passing credence to such idiocy. But no longer. The darkness of the Zero in which I live is Total. It casts no shadows and half-lights, no uncertainty, no Roman *chiaroscuro*.

It, like Truth itself, is Absolute.

† † †

And so I have retired from the clamour and agitation of the City to the quiet of the hills, to Avenheim Monastery, where the restless souls of noble families are sometimes interned. Indeed, the Brother who helped install me in my austere cell muttered that this room had once belonged to Achim von Esinbach, adding, in a whisper, *'the Suicide.'* In a certain way I am grateful for this coincidence, as I feel a sense of guilt about that young man's death, for maybe, partway, my machinations contributed to his demise. And so his spirit is here in this room to remind me of my former Vanity, and of all the foolish Schemes that were its issue and offspring.

In the damp, lingering cold of the end of the Year, Hieronymus comes to me in my cell and informs me that I do, for once, have a Visitor.

"Well then, send him in."

"My Lord, she is *Female*."

This is intriguing. My Curiosity wishes immediately to be assuaged, yet I also wish to extend this state of anticipation for a little while longer. So I do not ask who it is, and instead request Hieronymus to guide me from the monks' living quarters, where no women are admitted, to the Refectory, empty at this hour, where this unexpected meeting will take place.

Here Hieronymus helps me onto a stone bench, and I hear the woman's voice. "Thank you for agreeing to meet with me, My Lord."

It is Grete Gerber.

"Frau Gerber." She doesn't know that I have recognised her by voice alone. There is no need to tell her, it would only increase her already substantial vanity.

"Tell me what it is that I can do for you."

† † †

Naturally, I am aware of the scandal of Schwanenstein. Our Bishop took the view that the Count of Schwanenstein, as a Canon of the Cathedral and the scion of one of the Chapter's oldest families, should be left unmolested and offered up for trial by his fellow Canons, followed by contrite confession to His Grace himself, and repentance for his crimes: maybe a pilgrimage to the shrine of Saint Odile, or a month in a monastery on a lenten diet.

This is indeed how we Canons of the Cathedral have, in general, dealt with the misdemeanours of our fellows in the past, and it has always been judged sufficient. But on this occasion, in view of the Count's numerous crimes of robbery, rape and murder, this "closing of the ranks" of the upper echelons of Hagenburg society has been met with ill-tempered dismay by the citizens of the city. Even the Bishop's ministerial underlings, the judges, officers and officials of the City Families, increasingly alienated from their high-handed overlord, have demonstrated a sense of outrage.

And so Bishop von Stahlem, cowed and fearful of popular uprising, has exercised a form of benign indifference, and allowed the siege of Castle Schwanenstein to continue. His neutrality in the matter is doubtless a sensible policy. In any case, it was much of a muchness to me: after my Blinding, I had withdrawn from the Political World without the slightest pang of regret. But here, now, is Mistress Gerber, calling me back to the Whispering Chamber and the infernal labyrinth of intrigue. "If you could just talk to the Bishop, My Lord. I am sure, as the former Treasurer, your word must carry weight in matters financial."

"You wish to 'borrow' half the Cathedral work force and take them to Schwanenstein? To build catapults?"

"Just for a couple of months."

"I cannot see if you are blushing when you say such things."

"Maybe a bit, My Lord. My brother tells me they are not so busy in winter."

"True. As I recall, they spend the winter 'working' in the tavern whilst still drawing a salary on the Bishop's shilling."

"We will take them from the taverns and put them to work, My Lord."

"You are doing this for the good of their souls, I see. And you want stone from the building site? From the quarries?"

"The rubble, My Lord. The unusable debris."

"And what will the Bishop receive in return for his debris? For leasing you his Cathedral workforce to aid with the siege of Schwanenstein?"

"The Good Will of the City. I think he could do with it."

"And cheap at the price! How about, assuming the siege is successful, the Schwanenstein estates?"

"This price is too high. But everything is negotiable, is it not?"

I have been happy to reside in darkness and allow the whispers to whisper unheard, to allow the cataracts of the world to rage in an unseen, unheeded distance, and concentrate on God, on Numbers, and on the new Thoughts that make their deep, considered way to me from the academies of Paris.

But now I feel myself drawn back to the world of Action. For some reason, maybe it is the memory of her attractive figure, the intemperate glow in her eyes, her shameless yet captivating disdain for the Noble Estate . . . but I *like* Grete Gerber. She makes me think of another world, entirely unknown to me, where the majority of people must live. A world now forever beyond my reach, where, after a day's work, one would lie in a woman's arms, and, falling asleep, forget the laws, concepts and numbers that rule all human life, and simply Dream and Be.

ANNO
1248

VANQUISHED

(ANNO 1248. RETTICH SCHÄFFER IX • YUDL BEN
YITZHAK V • BARON VOLMAR VON KRONTHAL IV •
GRETE GERBER III • EINOLF II •
EMMERICH SCHÄFFER I • COUNTESS ADELHEID VON
SCHWANENSTEIN I)

Emmerich Schäffer

Dear Judah,
Once you receive this letter, I will be gone.
  Please believe me. Everything I did was intended for the
Best. I owe my good fortune to your Uncle, and that is some-
thing I will never forget. If, in my actions, I did anything
wrong, I hope you will be able to forgive me. But I trust that,
once you read this letter, you will understand that I intended
only the good of Commerce in general, and that of our
Company in particular.
  In order to explain my actions, I must go back in time to
before the siege of Schwanenstein. You will remember, from
the many conversations between myself and your Uncle, the
mention of one of our informants: a maidservant at the
Castle named Elise Gottlieb. What you—and most people in
Hagenburg—will not have known, is that this Elise has
been, for some years, the concubine of the Baron of
Kronthal . . .

Yudl Rosheimer

Despite the weeks of dark cloud and rain, Spring is coming.
There are green buds on the courtyard linden tree, and the cats
are screaming with their own, peculiar, aching form of Love.
Yudl has found a Bride, a thirteen-year-old girl from the

Kalonymus family of Speyer, the greatest rabbinical family on the Rhine: an honour for Hagenburg and the hushed and wondering talk of the beth midrash.

Yudl delays the wedding until the summer, citing the foul weather, the inauspicious constellations of the stars, but in truth waiting for Schwanenstein to fall, and for a solution to be found for his Mother.

His Mother, thirty-one summers old and still bright as the ruby in the Torah Crown. The tombstone has not yet been set on her husband's grave, and already the tongues have begun to hiss. Aberle's sister says that at Purim, when all were drunk and dancing, she saw Zipporah talking with the Strawhead Goy in Shokhet Alley, and she touched his arm, and laughed without covering her mouth. And Saul the cobbler said he saw her coming home after dark from the Christian part of town, smiling to herself like a girl. Rumours, whispers: the very whisperings that loosened and unravelled his Father's seething mind.

She must go far away. Far away from the Strawhead Goy. Far away from *the slanderers, who whet their tongues like swords.*

✡ ✡ ✡

The river is high, the current swift. The Rhine flatlands glide past the boat, fans of mud, flooded fields. Herons launch into the wide sapphire sky. Yudl dreams of his ancestors, misted in ancient time, warriors and generals, settlers of god-given lands. He sees Joshua returning from Egypt, laying waste to Jericho, blowing the *shofar* until the walls were breached by the Will of God.

He steps from the boat alongside his companions in trade; Emmerich Schäffer, Grete Gerber, Wikerus, Gaufried, the merchants who have funded the Schwanenstein campaign . . . He sees a field of mud, bedraggled tents, ropes stretched from tree to tree along the banks of the Rhine where steaming vestments dry in the newly emergent sun. He sees a host of soldiers, horses, teeming around piles of stones. And he sees four strange contraptions, tall-legged wooden animals like his Bestiary's Giraffe, a long birch-tree neck twisting to the sky. From the end of the pole a leather sling hangs down, heavy with a charge of stone.

Baron von Kronthal sits high on his stallion, still and unmoving amongst the weaving currents of horses and men. At his orders, a clarion blows and silence falls.

Yudl closes his eyes, sways from side to side, and mutters the Words of the Holy Torah. *Vengeance is mine, and recompense. See now that I, even I, am He. And there is no God with me. I kill and I make alive. I have wounded, and I heal. And there is none who can be delivered from my hand.*

Baron Volmar von Kronthal

"Let it fly! Number One! Let it fly!"

This had better bloody work. Number One. The trigger is hammered free. The stone counterweight plunges to the ground, the timbers shudder, the long arm lurches into the air, wrenches its leather sling . . .

Goddamn! The sling catches in the mud, only judders up. The stone arcs, drops to the ground. Our soldiers scatter, running from its path.

Bloody engineers. If none of these damn things work . . . ?

"Number two!" I shout. "Let fly, let fly!"

Number Two. It's our heaviest stone.

The counterweight plunges, the long arm wrenches, flies, the stone soars. The men cheer. It's a sight to see.

But the stone's too bloody heavy. It ploughs through the mud at the foot of the castle walls.

Getting better, but not good enough. I turn, catch Master

Rettich's eye, send him a look. He nods, shrugs, smiles. Him and the Count of Schonach, drunkards both, standing together, the Engineer sent by the Cathedral and the Veteran of the Siege of Damietta, adviser on engines of War.

"Number three! Let fly!"

Three. Our lightest stone! It overshoots! Flying over the walls like a swallow at dusk, plunging into the distance, into God Knows Where!

The men shout, wail, beat drums. We make stones fly like birds, we will vanquish stubborn Schwanenstein! "This is the one, boys! Number Four! Let fly!"

Four. A perfect hit, square and true. Thanks be to God! A sound of cracking, a plume of dust rises from Schwanenstein wall.

Rettich Schäffer

Rettich remembers the night of his Initiation, kneeling in the flawless darkness, praying for light.

The Minotaur is Weight. Weight that pulls at the Cathedral's tendons, drags her down towards the groaning earth, Weight that the Mason must capture and defeat.

Now this Weight is once more in Rettich's calloused hands, the drop of a hundredweight, the fling of a wooden arm, the throw of a quarry block. The Minotaur, in the service of War.

The Count of Schonach claps Rettich on the shoulders, laughing full-throated. "One square strike, Master Rettich, one square strike! We re-locate Trebuchets One and Two! And then we calibrate! And divvy up the stones!"

The quarry stones must be sorted. Not for their veining, their colour and shade, not for the gradual shifting hues of an arcade wall, not for Grace and not for God. But sorted for weight and size. The lighter stones for the further catapult, the heaviest for the trebuchet built close on a mound of earth and brick, shielded by wicker walls.

"Come, men! Listen!" shouts Rettich, and his workers and apprentices swarm, the Good Men of the Cathedral. Masons, stone-cutters, carpenters. Now Men of War.

Emmerich Schäffer

. . . *we had been using the trebuchets for a week and the north wall of the Castle was beginning to fracture, when an event occurred that greatly unsettled the Baron von Kronthal's confidence.*

At dusk, on the battlements, Elise Gottlieb and her daughter Ysolt appeared. Both were naked. And both had nooses tied around their necks.

The next day the Baron summoned me and charged me with the task of negotiating a peace with the Count of Schwanenstein. Reluctantly, I agreed.

In the dark of night, I was sent with a lantern to the South wall. I called up, "Parley! I am sent by the Baron to the Count!" and, after a wait of some length, I was admitted by rope ladder into the Castle. I proceeded to my meeting with the Count, who received me in a private chamber. I had brought to him some plum aquavit from Ihringen, which he quaffed as if it were water, quickly becoming drunk. I outlined the Baron's proposal; the Count would surrender and forfeit all the Schwanenstein and Illingen estates, his men would be arrested and tried and therefore either hanged or expelled from Alsace, Elise Gottlieb and her daughter were to be returned safe to the Baron's hands, and in exchange the Count would be granted safe passage to his remaining estate in the Vogesen with a three knight and one dozen servant retinue.

Then I explained; should he not agree to these terms, all his estates would be forfeit, his castle would be destroyed and all found within it, except women and children, killed.

"I accept," said the Count, to my surprise. And, as maybe you

understand, Yudl, to my acute displeasure. Had we spent a for-
tune in silver and months of work just to have the Count jaunt
off to his Vogesen hunting lodge, unharmed? What guarantee
that, from there, he would not recommence his banditry? And
what weak and half-hearted warning would this be for those
who in future might try and profit from piracy?

I asked, as I had been charged by the Baron, to take Elise
with me as a token of the Count's good faith and intention.
Schwanenstein said, his speech slurred with schnapps, "Take her,
but only if you bring us a new slut in exchange. The men need
something to poke of an evening." When I asked for further elu-
cidation, he explained that since the beginning of the siege Elise
had been used by the entire castle garrison as a whore.

I asked to see the woman and was led to a dungeon room
where the Schwanenstein soldiers were queuing to take their
turns to fornicate with her. I saw her only briefly, but my glimpse
of the woman was enough to tell me that she was in a degener-
ate and forsaken state. Was this still the woman the Baron once
loved?

Yudl. As I walked back through the castle grounds, I quickly
considered all the factors. I had many courses of action open.

And in the end I chose the one I thought best for the City of
Hagenburg. For Schäffer & Associates. For you. And for me.

Baron Volmar von Kronthal

I ask Schäffer, "Where is Elise? Did he not accept the proposal?"

Schäffer shakes his head, avoids my eyes. He looks pale.
"My Lord. Try and forget Elise."

"What, boy? Did he accept?"

"He did."

"So where is Elise?"

"Try and forget her, my Lord."

"Why, Schäffer?"

Schäffer says nothing.

"WHY?"

After a long silence Schäffer speaks like a child who must confess a sin. Coyly looking up at me, fearing a blow. "Sir, she is shared around all the men of the castle. As a Whore."

My hand balls, twitches, lashes from side to side, searching for something to strike. Schäffer flinches. "He says if you want her, you must buy her back from him. Trade her with a replacement Whore."

A blanched, bitter silence. Schäffer clears his throat. "I know some girls from the Harbour Brothel, my Lord, shall I *do the deal*?"

He can hardly finish the sentence. I am already striking him with the back of my hand. Blood gushes from his nose. He grabs his face, squealing like a sow.

"Get OUT OF HERE, you bastard!" He runs from the Tollhouse. I shout after him. "NO TREATY! WE TEAR THIS BLOODY PLACE DOWN STONE BY STONE!"

Grete Gerber

The War Chest in the Counting House gapes open, its store of coin exhausted. The Merchants of the Rhine, grateful for safe passage between Hagenburg and Speyer, throw in their pennies and sous, the Jews, seeing the Campaign as vengeance on the Jewish dead, send what they can, and the Baron von Kronthal and his Sternkammer knights throw in their noble Gold. But it is never enough.

My girls are working tirelessly. The looms clatter, the shuttles weave, the pennies tinkle into my money chest. My little Manfredle is back from Cologne, and wants to fight at Schwanenstein to avenge his father's name. But what fighting? The soldiers lie in hammocks, sharpen their swords, and wait.

When there are stones to throw, the trebuchets winch, pitch and hurl . . . and one more piece of wall comes down . . . to cheers that have grown fainter as the siege wears on.

And then the soldiers return to their hammocks. And wait for the coins to gather in the chest . . . one by one . . . penny by penny . . . until we can pay for the next barge of stone.

† † †

There's a knock at the door, and I'm not expecting anyone. The servants are out at market, so I open, and there's a woman standing there. Wrinkled and over-ripe like an October apple. And beside her, a boy. "Mistress Gerber?"

"Yes."

"My name is Rosamunda Bartsch."

I know the name. It's the widow Manfred threw over for me way back when. And then I look at the boy and nearly die of fright right there in my doorway.

It's Manfred. As when I first met him, seventeen summers ago.

Well, it's not too hard to imagine that I tipped my barrel. Started screaming right there and then, *who the devil do you think you are* and *come here with your bastard one more time and I'll have your tits ripped out* and other such niceties, and started shooing her back into the road as if she were a wasp.

I couldn't help noticing that the boy was laughing, giggling away like a monkey. Like father, like son.

Anyway, I chase her out into the road just as the latrine man is pushing past with his handcart, and God forbid but doesn't she just career and knock right into it. And, *floosh!*, down comes his vat full of shit and the lid breaks off and there's liquid sewage pouring over the road.

Oh Lord! The stench of it! It shuts me right up as I cover my mouth and nose with my hands, and try not to retch. And she too and the Boy, the three of us stumbling around like drunken donkeys, trying to flee the stench. And the latrine man righting the vat, sealing back the lid and shouting *if you've water, madam, bring it me and I'll have this cleaned up for tuppence.*

God damn me if I don't now catch Rosamunda's eyes and we both start laughing. I've never seen a jackal but I laughed like one, tears coming from my eyes. We must have looked like loons, the three of us laughing there and the latrine man staring at us all perplexed. And then the wind changed and the smell came back at me.

The Stench.

Countess Adelheid von Schwanenstein

One by one, it's all being taken away from me. My jewels, my silver, my raiments. Sold like tarnished candlesticks over the castle wall in exchange for hunks of meat and tuns of wine. *To keep the men happy*, he says. I'm afraid of him now. He has that flaw in his eye, like a crack in a mirror, fracturing everything it sees.

Even respect and deference have been taken from me. My handmaidens and I were reading the poems composed in my honour, and when we came to Wenzel's lines about this castle and about me; *many men have scaled her proud stone, only to retreat in sickness and dismay*, they began to titter and giggle. At my insistence that they should explain, they said something unspeakable. *It means that all who fuck you get the clap.* I had them dismissed and sent to the kitchens.

I hardly leave my chambers any more. The castle yard is full of prowling hounds; they haven't run the fields in nine long months. They screech and howl, tear at each other, and no one corrects them any more. The Men are just as bad, gambling, fighting, drinking, sleeping on the stairs below my chamber. Belching in my presence.

From my window I can see them urinating in the corners of the yard.

And I can see the besieging army, cowering in their cowardly tents beyond the reach of our bowmen. Riding up and down on their prancers. Charging their infernal machines with stones.

I can't bear to look when the catapults let fly. Once I stood at an embrasure and watched as the black mass lifted from the field like a crow and then raced through the shrinking air. As it swooped nearer I flinched and fell shrieking to the floor as the impact shuddered in the stones below.

And it has been going on for weeks. This thud thud thud thud thud . . . The North wall soon will fall. Surely, it must soon fall?

† † †

I could hardly raise myself today. One day has become like the other. The castle used to ring with Joy, and now it is an earthly prison.

From my shutters I can see the Enemy. They are racing around in the field below. They have gathered what seem to be barrels and kegs around the trebuchets. There is activity, excitement; a crowd of ordinary people has gathered, as if to watch a Mystery Play. Cornets and trumpets blow as if in Victory.

They charge the catapults. I cannot look, I hide myself in my blankets and stoles.

But the *thud* doesn't come. Not a thud. Just a clatter. A breaking of wood.

I lift my face from the bed.

And then comes the *stench*.

Grete Gerber

Stools from night buckets, from hostel latrines. Urine

rotting for weeks in tavern piss-barrels, shit scooped in piles from Kronenburg cesspits. Gongfermors' poo and fullers' pee, knackers' guts and butchers' offal, tanners' dogshit, swine-herds' slurry, meat left to rot until the maggots breed. That was all My Great Idea.

And it didn't take long once those trebuchets started firing barrels of *that* at them. They say two rotting sheep's heads and a barrel of shit went straight down the castle well, and then there was nothing for them to drink or cook with anymore. And the stink. The stink was unbearable.

So the white flag starts flying, and then there's the Baron and Emmerich going to the walls and shouting up at the Count's castellan to agree the terms of the surrender. And we give no quarter now, none at all. Death for all the men inside. Women and children go free with anything they can carry.

At midday, the crowds start to gather. The drum starts to beat. A shawm starts to blow.

And the castle gate opens.

The drawbridge comes down.

Baron Volmar von Kronthal

I stand at the bottom of the Castle Ramp. My sword is planted on the ground, six archers kneel at my side, their bow-strings taut, waiting for Treachery. I, the Victor, stand and wait. I can see the crowd behind the castle gate; kitchenmaids, cooks, washerwomen, castle boys and girls.

Silence falls. The drum beats. Boom. Boom.

Boom.

And the cortege starts to move out of the gate; the women and children first, as arranged. But the first four women are carrying a coffin, a small one made from barrel slats and patch-work wood. And I already know what's inside. Before they kneel in front of me, I know it.

Elise. And Ysolt. My two little girls.

Grete Gerber

And then after the coffin come the rest of the women and children: stable boys, serving girls, handmaidens, kitchen drudges, all wide-eyed and starving, carrying their little bundles of possessions, wrapped in rags. And the drum beats and the pipes blow.

All the women and the children . . . except the Countess herself. The crowd of onlookers churns, curdles. Cries rise up. "Where's that bitch? Where's that whore?" We wanted to see her scuttling out of the stinking gate with her maids and kitchen scrubbers.

But she doesn't come.

Instead, it's the men, gathering under the gateway. They come out one by one.

The first men have no weapons, they're just servants, stablemen. They walk out onto the steep road, take the first corner, and only then can they see what's waiting for them: the Executioner and his Boys with scarlet hoods over their heads.

The men run. Our soldiers stand on either side of the castle road, prodding them with their spear shafts, kicking their behinds, screaming, laughing, jeering.

A copse of trees lines the banks of the Rhine. And hanging from the branches, a forest of nooses.

Baron Volmar von Kronthal

Her lips are dragged back over her jutting teeth. Her staring pupils fill the whole of her eyes. I hear nearby voices. *She hanged the child. Then herself. God rest their souls.*

I hold little Ysolt in my arms, sink down beside the coffin and fumble with my fingers to close Elise's staring eyes.

Blackness rises from Schwanenstein's conquered stones. The procession continues, the walk of the condemned. I see nothing, I am empty. I am a Victor of shadows.

Yudl Rosheimer

Yudl turns away, he has seen enough, he has seen his fill of blood red vengeance. The forest of nooses sways, a ripe orchard of carrion fruit, full to bursting on every branch.

They are using the trebuchets now, charging the catapults with living bodies. And dashing them against the castle walls.

And then a cry goes up and Yudl must look again. *They're coming! They're coming!* Who is coming? He peers, short-sighted, through the tumultuous crowd.

Baron Volmar von Kronthal

My hands twitch, reach for my sword.

And then they come. The Countess, ragged-haired and bruised-faced, bent double, carrying the Count von Schwanenstein on her back like a mule. She stumbles over the Castle threshold, panting.

"Carry me to the Rhine you useless nag!" shouts Count Sebald, whips her side with the flat of his sword.

Around me, my Men scream with hatred, cheated of their Prize. *The women may go free, with all they can carry.* The terms of the Treaty. I look around for Emmerich, my Clerk, for confirmation. But he has gone.

The Countess struggles down the hill, near-crushed by her burden. I run alongside, and bark at them over the chorus of jeers. "WHAT DID YOU DO TO MY ELISE YOU ANI-MAL?"

"Nothing. Why didn't you take her when you wanted?"

"WHAT?"

"I told your lackey Schäffer he could take her, but he didn't want to." He bites the Countess' neck. "Don't drop me you bitch! DON'T DROP ME! Take me to the Rhine!"

I told your lackey Schäffer he could take her. But he didn't want to.

"Where is Schäffer?" I turn around, reeling. A parade of leering, screaming faces, twisted in hatred. "WHERE IS SCHÄFFER?"

Einolf

"DO YOU REMEMBER ME, MY LORD?"

"Get out my way!"

"NO."

She stops, the Countess, on staggering feet. The boy of eighteen summers stands before her, an Apprentice, all dressed in green. His feet are planted wide, his left hand held out, showing his flattened palm. *None shall pass.*

He points to his neck where a pendant hangs. A waxen heart.

"Do you remember, My Lady?"

"Boy, out of our way."

"NO!" The boy's hand suddenly whips out and grabs her throat. In an instant, the baying crowd is still.

The Count and Countess flail, wide-eyed, but the crowd is a hushed, closing circle, tightening, blocking all escape. The boy's hand slackens, loosens, retreats.

The Count, mounted on his tottering steed, holds out his sword. "Who are you, Boy?"

"My name is Einolf, My Lord."

"Einolf?"

"It is to you I owe my Cathedral Orphan life."

The crowd pushes closer. Schwanenstein spits. "I don't remember."

"My Lord. First you *made* me an Orphan. And then paid Blood Money on my life."

"I made you a . . . ?"

"You raped my mother. You killed my mother. And then bought for me a New Life."

The Countess' knees buckle, break. The Count falls with her, rolls in the dust at the Apprentice's feet.

"Your covenant taught me a trade, My Lord. Do you know what it is?"

The Count of Schwanenstein kneels, scowls, spits. "You think I care?"

Now Einolf raises his arms. In his hands, cheesecutter's wire. "Well, can you guess, My Lord?"

The crowd roars. "A cheesemaker! A cheesemaker!"

And Einolf lunges. The wire circles, sings. The sharp wire cuts at the Count's white outstretched neck.

And he pulls, the boy. Pulls so that his veins strain, and his face squeezes red. His eyes bulge. And the cheesewire wrenches. Left. Right. Left. Right. Deeper. Deeper. And the Countess screams. And the Count's sap spurts red.

And still he cuts, the Cheesemaker's Apprentice. Through vein and muscle, through grizzle and cord. And then with his stamping foot he snaps the spine.

And holds up the head of Schwanenstein.

Yudl Rosheimer

He can see his Bride's legs trembling beneath her clothes, her hands clutch at each other, twitch. Her face is veiled, her body concealed by a long, fur cloak. It won't be long now until he can see her, behold the face of his Wife.

A prayer shawl is cast over the heads of Bride and Groom as Rabbi Menahem holds aloft the wine and recites the Seven Blessings. Without thinking, Yudl's lips mutter the familiar words, he looks around the dozens of guests; Jews, Gentiles, rich, poor, a motley collage of colour, of smiling faces. His Mother's eyes, shining with tears. He has found her a husband in the Kingdom of Bohemia, far from here. "You just cast me away, Yudl? Now that I have brought you to adulthood, you have finished with me?"—"God forbid, Mother, how can you say such a thing?"—"I just did say such a thing."—"I thought you would be happy!"—"Happy to be separated from my Son?"—"Happy to be reunited with your family in Prague!"— "I should be happy?"—"You always wept and prayed you would see them again! Well now you will, so be happy!"—"Be happy? I want to die."

But now, as the Rabbi gives the Bride the wine, his Mother's eyes shine.

Yudl searches the guests for the Strawhead Goy. Rumours of a feud with the Baron, a misunderstanding, a sourness spoiling the sweet victory of Schwanenstein. Why has he not come?

Aberle is at Yudl's side, with a goblet wrapped in a cloth. He places it beneath his feet. Yudl sings. His voice is fine, like crystal. Like his Father's.

If I forget thee Jerusalem
may my right hand forget her cunning
If I do not remember thee,
let my tongue cleave to the roof of my mouth,
if I prefer not Jerusalem above my chief joy

Yudl raises his foot, smashes it down onto the glass. The bride removes her veil; a girl of thirteen summers, a trembling, beautiful child.

✡ ✡ ✡

Yudl is drunk. The bonfire's flames leap high, fountains of

sparks reach to the darkening sky. The guests are dancing. Spinning. All Hagenburg is celebrating the Conquering of Schwanenstein, the freedom of the Rhine.

Through the mêlée and roundelay, a Boy coming towards him, holding something in his little hands.

A letter, addressed to him, in Emmerich's handwriting. "He said not to read it today, sir. Tomorrow he said would be better. He sends greetings to you, sir, and love, he said. To you on your day of Joy."

Emmerich Schäffer

. . . Yudl, as you will soon surely hear, Baron von Kronthal has sworn to kill me. For lying to him. For not saving Elise and Ysolt Gottlieb when I was able.

And so I am gone. Do not try and find me, for I will leave the Empire altogether. I do not know yet where I will go.

Yudl, your mother and I were together one time in the year of our Lord 1231. Our Love was forbidden, and I was sent away—a separation that near destroyed my Heart.

It can benefit no one for this to become known beyond the three of us, it can only lead to difficulties for your mother. This is why it has been kept silent so long, and why it is only now, when I am leaving, that I say this, that I may be your father.

Do not think harshly on us, Yudl, we were young, younger than you are now, and drawn to each other by Love, which knows no laws or boundaries.

I am leaving as soon as I complete this letter. I will need funds for my journey and to start my new business, wherever that will be. From the Baron's coffers I have taken 200 marks. This is theft, pure and simple, from the man who has threatened to kill me. It is wrong, and a sin, but so be it.

From the coffers of our enterprise, I have also taken 100 marks. I am aware that this is a great sum, but I pray that you will not begrudge me this capital, which I believe I have earned. My "theft" will leave you with little coin, I know, but you will know how to realise some assets to continue trading. You have learned well.

I am sorry I could not be at your wedding, Yudl. I hope it will be an auspicious match.

Goodbye, Yudl. I thank God for these last five years, in which I have been able to be close to you.

Emmerich Schäffer

ANNO
1254

A Pilgrimage
(anno 1254. Rettich Schäffer X)

S ometimes a ship comes in with a cargo of Rhenish wine, and then a barrel is placed at the centre of the German House and boys are sent running through the narrow streets, calling out in their guttural Greek voices, "Rhine Wine, reinwein! Rinevine!" . . . and, as if it were the Sirens' call, all the Germans of the city come crawling out of their lairs and hiding places and pile their pennies on top of the barrel. And when there is enough coin, the barrel is breached and stoppered, and the shop stays open until the last drop is drunk and the dawn rises over the Asian hills across the water.

It is a Sunday, and Rettich is at Mass in the small German chapel when the door flies open and the boy runs in. "Rinevine! Rinevine!" he shouts, just as the Priest is presenting the Host in its ivory box, and the dozen kneeling worshippers unravel with laughter. Father Ekbert shoos the boy out of the door. "I'll start again, shall I?"

The service over, the Priest says a few half-hearted words about not drinking on the Lord's Day, but then, without too much reluctance, is persuaded to cross the lane and drink just one glass for the Love of Christ. The Honourable Merchant Emmerich Schäffer is already there, leaning back in a rocking chair, his soft leather boots propped up on top of the barrel, his silver pennies glinting on the rusty iron rim.

Rettich sits down beside him, gives him a Sunday kiss. "Peace be with you, brother."

"And with you too." Emmerich leans closer as the chapel

congregation files up to place their coins on the barrel top. "Rumour's out that there's some folk in from the Rhine. Came in on the same boat as the wine. I've sent my Boy to scout them out."

Emmerich stands, flicks through the pile of coins, silver and bronze. "Come on, we need one more shilling nine pence! Dig deep, you skinflints! I'm thirsty!"

† † †

Two years, before, in Hagenburg, a pane of glass the size of Rettich's palm, wrapped in cloth. The glass is blue as sapphire, blue as the Ocean that breathes in Rettich's mind.

"Come outside, we must hold it to the light." The young Factor steps outside the Lodge with Rettich, stands patiently as the Master Stone-cutter holds the glass to the sun, and then to the darker part of the sky. "Beautiful, not even a single flaw. Nary a bubble. And what a colour! This was given to you, you say?"

"In Venice, Master."

"Venice? I know no-one in Venice."

"And maybe there's no one as knows you in Venice, sir. The man that gave it to me is a Factor like me. He travels the Adriatic and Ionian seas."

"This means nothing to me."

"He sails to and from Venice in commission for Greek merchants. He was looking for a factor who trades the Rhine. He found me, and bade me deliver this package to you in Hagenburg. It's all I know, Master."

"So who has sent this to me?"

"There was a piece of paper, Master."

Rettich looks up, surprised. The young Factor is holding out a scrap of parchment. "It fell from the package when you took out the glass, sir."

Rettich takes the paper. Only a few words, a cursive hand.

via dei fondachi, Konstantinopolis

† † †

Dombaumeister Werlinus von Nordhausen holds the glass in his whiskery fingers, turns it against the light that falls from the lodge window. A lump rises in Rettich's throat; the memory of Master Achim, twenty years ago in the very same place, holding up the weak, lemony yellow glass, frowning with sweet dissatisfaction, searching for Sunlight.

"Beautiful, beautiful . . . " mutters the Dombaumeister. "From Constantinople, you say?"

Rettich nods. He knows what will be coming next.

"Do we have a price?"

"No, Master, no price was quoted. Merely an address. The Road of Storehouses, Constantinople."

"A shame. It would be good to know its price. Forgive me for saying it, but we could do good business with this glass. A Royal Blue like this. When I hold it to the light I see a Virgin surrounded by dark blue sky and stars. I see a John the Baptist by a deep blue river, I see a Knight reposing in glory on a bed of bluest silk and velvet. And you, Master Rettich?"

"I see the Ocean, Dombaumeister."

"But you have never seen the Ocean, Master Schäffer. I saw it once, in Normandy. It was grey."

† † †

The Rhine Harbour tavern, *zum thrunkenen Cahne*, a late autumn afternoon. Grete has given him an introduction to a Haulier who transports goods from the Rhine through the Black Forest, then down the Danube towards the Orient. A squat Bavarian, stinking of beer and mules.

Rettich looks round the harbour tavern, the calloused

hands of boatmen gripping worn tankards, the even more cal-loused and worn-out whores, the perilous allure of travel. He tries not to sound too green. "They tell me Constantinopolis is at the end of the Danube river?"

"And further still, Master, further still."

"And so, it is far?"

The Haulier laughs, moves closer to Rettich. "Well, where's the furthest you've been from here?"

"The Lothringen borders."

The Bavarian laughs. "And that's *far*? A pigeon can fly there and back in a day."

"Well, so how far is far?"

"You cross the Rhine. And then through the Black Forest to the Danube, that's one week of hard travel. And that's just the beginning, Master. Follow the river. It's another week to Ratisbon, a fine city. And then on through Bavaria. At least you're moving with the current, and if you can get a good ves-sel, you can make fair distance in a day. But even then it will take a week to cross Bavaria. In one month you will reach the end of the German Lands, but even then your journey has only just begun. After the Germans come the Bohemians, the Magyars, the Slavs. Towards Constantinopolis there are forests so great that in ancient times whole Roman armies were lost in them and died of hunger. Beyond the forests there is a Great Plain that stretches to the Edge of the World . . . "

Rettich's heart is racing. He closes his eyes and sees visions; pulsing, flickering, like the light through a swaying canopy of leaves. Landscapes are awoken by the Haulier's words, whole worlds are brought into being from where they lay sleeping in his imagination. Rippling hills, cliffs and gorges of limestone glide past his drifting river barque, temples with strange, twisted spires rise in hazy, unknown distance.

The Haulier's voice lowers, softens. "And at the end of the river there is a wide, black sea, whose ends cannot be seen.

And across that sea is Constantinople, a city of a thousand chapels, the capital of the Latins and the Greeks."

† † †

The last errant Germans have been found in the hive of Constantinople streets, and the pile of coins is large enough for the Factor's price. Rhinelanders, Saxons, Franks and Swabians line up with their glasses, leather cups, pewter mugs. Rettich is given the hammer and spigot; hands that once fashioned the Hagenburg Cathedral's stone, hands now for hire in the thousand chapels and churches of Constantinople, breach the oak-wood cask, let flow the wine.

Rettich leans back beside his brother, holds the glass to the light, a weak lemony radiance, borrowed sunlight. Emmerich snorts. "Are you just going to look at it all day?" Rettich swirls the wine, runs the liquid over his tongue. Honey, apples, the yellow flowers that gild the April hills. "Remember, brother? Lenzenbach in spring?" Emmle nods, drinks deep, whistles a lonesome shepherd's song.

Rettich closes his eyes, purses his lips, whistles along. The refrain recalls a cool breeze in the Lenzenbach hills, the mauve and aquamarine of the Western sky, the cold, rising stars. It is two years since he left his homeland, two years since he has seen fresh, rich Rhineland green. On his journey he has seen the parched, bone-coloured hills of the Holy Lands, sheltered in the meagre, blue-black shade of cypress trees, sought parched atonement on the baking slopes of Golgotha.

"Rhinelanders! I was told there were Rhinelanders here?" A booming voice from the Middle Rhine. A tall, shiny-headed merchant stands sweating in the German House doorway, waving his cap like a fan against the afternoon heat.

"We're here!" calls Emmerich, proffering the stool where his feet were resting. "And where are you from?"

"Worms."

With a flourish, Emmerich wipes the seat with his sleeve. "Worms! And when did you leave?"

"This March."

"A newcomer! And so, what news?"

The stranger sits as Emmerich pours him out a draught of wine. His eyes squint, assessing. "Your accents sound more Alsace, Upper Rhine. Colmar?"

"Lenzenbach. Hagenburg."

"Hagenburg?!" His eyes shine bright. "And what was the last news you heard?"

The two brothers look at each other. "Last season. A boat came in from Venice in the autumn squalls. September. A factor from Cologne, he passed through Hagenburg in June."

"Then you'll not know!"

"*What'll* we not know?"

† † †

"Father? Papa?"

His daughter's voice recalls him to the Real World. Once again he has been travelling in his mind, gliding down a deep blue river, the colour of the Glass. "Yes? Mechthild?"

"Will you hold him a minute?"

A full moon face, rouge-cheeked, dribbling, his tongue feeling the sore coming of his first tooth. His grandson, Reichart, known as Rettl, like him. Rettich holds him up to the pale winter sky. "Fly, Rettl, fly!" Above them, high in the flawless air, a "V" of four score pilgrims, journeying to the promising South. Rettich smiles to himself. Does he now even envy the Geese?

He stands with his grandson, holds him gently over his shoulder, pats his back . . . pat pat, pat pat. Looks to his family gathered round a winter bonfire in the backyard of Grete's house on the Müllergass, roasting chestnuts, drinking hot spiced wine. Himself now a Grandfather. Grete's Manfredle to marry in spring. The Cycle of Life.

Grete is at his side, pulling her sable stole closer against the evening cold. "So, you've decided to go? Tell me why again?"

"To repent my sins where Our Lord was Crucified."

"And the real reason?"

"To source blue glass for the Cathedral."

"And the real reason?"

"I want to see him."

"Why be so sure it's him?"

"Who else would send me a sample of glass from Constantinopolis?"

"I'm sure he's dead. Why else would he send us nothing in four years? Not even a letter?"

"He never liked his family much."

"Except you."

"I left him alone, that's why."

"So leave him alone now."

"Grete, I'm going. And I want you to make sure that Ällin and the children are all right in case I don't come back. I'm leaving money and a bequest . . . "

"Rettich, you understand less about money than a hermit."

"You forget that I once bought your Freedom with a complex financial transaction."

"You borrowed twenty-seven marks at ten *per centum*, how complex is that?"

"So help me."

"I will. We'll go to the notary and you will sign a paper that confers your estate to me until your return. I'll manage everything, don't you worry. Little sister will manage everything."

The bonfire's sparks spiral into the gloaming, the hired minstrels play, his grown-up children dance. Carved pumpkins glow in the gathering darkness, hollowed and filled with candlelight. Around the autumnal city, the new wine is being breached, pigs are being slaughtered, drunken revellers stumble into Saint Martin's crisp, frosty night.

What holds him here?

† † †

Rettich's last day in Hagenburg, Maundy Thursday. The snows have thawed, the rivers have returned to their banks, discharging their melting waters into unseen oceans. Outside the Lodge, the Easter crowds flood the Cathedral Square, forming knots around the stages of the penitents and players. Inside the Lodge, indolent holiday dust gathers on the tables, awaiting Christ's Resurrection before Work resumes once more.

On a scrap of parchment Rettich writes;

> *blu glas for the outer panes*
> *of master Achims rose*
> *via dei fondachi konstantinopolis*

He takes the soft cloth that he has used for twenty years to wipe and polish his tools. With the cloth he wraps the note and the glass, binds them with twine.

What did Master Achim call it? The *escritoire*, for which there is no German word, the small drawing desk where he used to work and dream. No longer used, it leans in a dark corner, one leg crooked, a stand for glasses and bowls, a prop for tools.

Rettich still has the Key.

Inside, dust and disorder, months of disuse. Spiders have lived, constructed cathedrals of silk, reigned over their worlds, and died. Gently Rettich lays the cloth-wrapped glass beside his copies of Achim's drawings: the statues of the Western Façade, the Great Portal. And, drawn from murky memory, uncertain and incomplete, his copy of his Master's vision of the Universe, the great Western Rose, a window where all the Colours of the World unite and fuse, where Creation's manifold forms meld in purest white, fired by the Love of God, the Sun's life-giving Light.

He shuts the lid, closing the Rose in darkness. He locks the lock. Hangs the key on a nail on the wall.

And leaves.

† † †

The Merchant of Worms spreads his hands. "You'll not have heard. Hagenburg is in turmoil."

Emmerich leans forward. "Go on."

"The Bishop and his City are nearly at war with each other."

"It's been that way since Bishop Heinrich was enthroned."

"But now it has got worse. A War is coming, it's what they all say."

The two brothers sit, leaned forward, on the edge of their stools.

"One day this last Winter, a boy was just playing in the street and one of the Bishop's Vassal Knights charged past as if it were a tilting ground. The horse's hooves struck the boy in the head, in his chest, his leg. And he's left dead.

"The boy's Mother, screaming, walks through the streets, carrying her son's twisted corpse in her arms. From the Mayenz Gate, through Barfüsser Platz . . . and a crowd forms behind her, wailing, shouting. She makes her way to the Bishop's Palace, and kneels on the steps, demanding Justice."

The Merchant leans forward, lowers his voice. "And she is just beaten away by the Bishop's police."

Silence. Outside, the city is sunken in evening heat. A dark violet dusk sinks down from the Anatolian hills. The Merchant of Worms drinks, clears his throat. "The people are enraged.

The crowd that followed the woman goes now to the Cathedral Square. And, walking home through the Square is a young noble from one of the Bishop's families. A priest. The crowd set upon him. They club him to death, throw his corpse on the Cathedral steps."

Rettich flicks his eyes to his brother, pale in the evening gloom, now sitting forward, transfixed.

"The mob gathers, swells, arms itself with clubs, staves, knives. Workers, tradesmen, merchants, even some Zorns and Müllenheims."

"What?" whispers Emmerich. "The Ministerials too?"

"Yes. Believe this. Even some of the City Officials have changed sides, turned against the Bishop. So the Bishop's men retreat to the Palace, to the Towers in the City Walls, to the armouries and gatehouses. The Bishop's Knights and Cathedral Canons hide, fearing for their lives. The mob runs to the tavern *zum Sterne*, where Baron Kronthal drinks. They call on him from the street, begging him to lead them in uprising, in overthrow."

Emmerich cannot wait. "And the Baron? What did he say?"

The Merchant of Worms stands, throws his hands in the air, laughs. "He wasn't there! He was hunting in his country estates!"

Emmerich slams his fist down, toppling his glass. "*I knew it!* That useless fool!"

"By the time he came to the City, the Mother of the dead child had been given seven marks blood money, the most hated Knights had fled to their country estates, the Militia were back, patrolling the town. The crowd had dispersed, gone back to their daily work."

Emmerich shakes his head, looks at Rettich, his eyes flashing. "I should have been there!"

The Merchant sits again, pulls his bowl of food towards him, finishing his tale. "But mark my words, Men of Hagenburg! This will not end well. Hagenburg is a City waiting to rise."

†††

Emmerich taps the boatman on the shoulder, speaks in his approximate Latin, "Carry on, the shore along," and then in Greek, "*Piyene gialo gialo . . .*"

They lean back in the boat. A cooling breeze sighs in from the Marmara Sea. Rettich remembers Werlinus von Nordhausen and their argument about the Blue Glass. "When I hold it to the light I see a Virgin surrounded by dark blue sky and stars, I see a Knight reposing in glory on a bed of bluest silk and velvet. And you, Master Rettich?"

"I see the Ocean, Dombaumeister."

"But you have never seen the ocean, Master Schäffer. I have seen it. In Normandy. It was grey."

"I've seen it in my mind, and it is Blue."

And it is such a blue, on a day like this. A blue such as only dreamers can conceive, the Blue in the mind of God when He first created Blue.

The Cathedral of Our Lady of Hagenburg? She seems a ghost, a thankfully forgotten shade. What was once Master Achim's Holy Vision had become, under Werlinus, a Whore offered to the highest bidder. The Bishop's Knights competing to commission glass windows with their coats of arms, statuary of saints that bear their own likenesses, Holy Virgins with the faces of their wives.

It is bitter medicine to think of the past. To think of the hopeful young Shepherd stepping from the river barge, holding his brother's hand, and striding for the first time into the Hagenburg crowds. To know now, with the melancholy consolation of older age, that Hope and Innocence can never last.

And all that Hagenburg struggle and tumult between Bishop and City, for Rettich, it all seems as distant as his youthful dreams. Here, the Sun's honest light dispels all gloom. And Emmerich, God bless him, has bought some land by the side of the waters at the foot of the Pera hill, a grove of hazelnut trees overlooking the straits. Rettich will build them a cabin there, a little house of beech and pine. But for now they have hung hammocks from the fruit-laden branches where they can swing and slumber in the dappled shade.

Today they have brought some bread, honey and wine, some cheese and olives. The boatman will wait for them. They can sit, drink and eat, sleep in the hammocks through the afternoon heat.

"Emmle," says Rettich, "I'm thinking. I don't want to, but maybe I should return home."

"Whatever for?"

"I feel old. I feel pains in my chest in the mornings."

"Then rest, brother. You've earned it."

"Should a man not die at home? With his family all around?"

"A man can die anywhere. It's all the same. The only important thing is how he lives."

Rettich dips his bread in honey, takes a gulp of wine. He lies back in his hammock, and sways. The hazelnut's boughs are blown by angels' breaths, by a restful breeze.

On the waters the silver sunlight dazzles, the fishermen's coracles bob and dance. Darkness will come, but will come slowly, she will creep from the sea to the shore, a welcome guest.

† Rettich Schäffer
(1210, Lenzenbach, Alsace–1256 Constantinople)

END OF BOOK TWO

BOOK THREE
THE PEN
(1260–1273)

PROLOGUE

ANNO
1349

O Hagenburg
(anno 1349. Quirin von Lenzenbach I)

O n the morning of Saint Valentine's Day, the Year of
Our Lord 1349, an armed crowd, led by the Butchers'
and Tanners' Guilds, broke into the Jewish Quarter
of Our City of Hagenburg. With them they had brought the
tools of their trades; meat cleavers and sinew knives, bone mal-
lets and hide-scrapers. The assault was brutal and fierce.

Some Jews tried to protect their families with kitchen
knives and wood-axes, some of the Jewish women slit the
throats of their own offspring rather than let them be taken by
the mob. Those Israelites who were not killed in the struggle
or sacrificed by their own hand were dragged in chains to the
Burning Ground. For the purpose of this assault was not the
Salvation of the Jews' souls from the errors of their faith, but
their Pillage and Destruction.

As soon as a Jewish home was emptied of its inhabitants, a
plundering began. All property was taken: pins, knives and
linen, bowls, plates and candlesticks. From the homes and
trading shops of the Moneylenders and Pawnbrokers much
coin was despoiled and pledged items returned with triumph
to their former owners. Elsewhere floors were broken open,
plots of land and courtyards dug up with mattocks in a fevered
search for buried treasure. So certain were the mob of the
secret, hidden wealth of all Jews that even the homes of the
poor and indigent were torn apart.

In the Jewish Cemetery gravestones were broken with mal-
lets and scattered, and a pyre built, and a trench for burning.

One month before, Basel had burned her Jews locked into a wooden house on an island in the middle of the Rhine, Mayenz would soon burn hers on its execution ground with a fire so hot and high that the Cathedral's very lead gutters melted and ran. Here in Hagenburg, the Jews, nigh on a thousand souls, were burned on the desecrated graves of their own ancestors. Spared were only those young women who, upon being disrobed and their headdresses unravelled, were discovered to be of great physical beauty. These Jewesses were forcefully baptised and then forcefully defiled.

I and my colleagues in the Council, threatened by the butchers' mob when we called for the slaughter to cease, could only later return to the burning ground in stealth and darkness. An uncanny sight, the embers of the conflagration still glowing, and amongst the red pulsing jewels of the cinders, an ashblackened ossuary of human bones.

Be it on our heads, and the stain on our hands. For weeks we had striven to prevent this massacre, but in vain. This was a mutiny, a revolt of the working people, led by their representatives in the Guilds. The Butchers and Tanners, to a man indebted to Jewish moneylenders who had lent them hard silver in times of flood and famine, who had sold them hundreds of head of cattle on the never-never when times were harsh, were the leaders of this insurgency. And the rest followed in the hope of easy gains, and the settling of petty debts.

But now the Sun has darkened, the Lord has turned his eyes from us in anger, and Disorder and Calamity are unleashed upon the world. In Hagenburg, the Jews have paid the price for the great misfortune that is now upon us. It was they who were blamed, tried, judged and burned at the stake.

Some months before the burning, given up to torture, a Jew of Geneva had confessed that he had plotted with the Jews of Toledo to bring the Pestilence and the Great Calamity that now rages through the world. This forced confession had been enough for the Guildmasters of the Rhineland to draw the conclusion that if they murder their Jews, they will be spared the scourge of Plague.

Yet now, only months after the immolation of the Jews, the Plague is here in Hagenburg.

I have seen the first corpses, laid on a cart, unshrouded and unshriven, for No One, neither priest nor relative, would come near them for fear of contagion. They were piled against each other, faces contorted in terrible rictus of horror, their skin black-blotched, open sores clotted with scabrous blood.

The Executioner's men, at a high price, and mummed in leather and wearing blacksmiths' gloves, loaded these first carts and took the bodies beyond the walls to the Pit that has been dug, at my instructions, for this purpose. I have specified that the grave should be able to contain one thousand bodies. And I wonder now if that will be enough.

At the instruction of His Grace the Bishop, I have drafted a Proclamation, to be read in the Public Gathering Places and in the Cathedral, that the ill-gotten gains of the sack of the Jews should not be kept by their Purloiners. The thieves are instructed to leave their thievings on the Altar of the Frauenwerk, for the fabric of the Cathedral of Our Lady of Hagenburg, in the Hope of Her intercession in the punishment of their blackened souls.

It remains for me, Quirin von Lenzenbach, to consider my own legacy. For if the Pest takes me, as well it might, should I not also fear for the future of my soul? I would not die a Hypocrite, preaching in the corners of the street, and knowing in my own heart a similar sin. For it is said that my own family's wealth was once stolen from the Jews of Hagenburg, it is said that my esteemed grandfather Emmerich's position and prominence, the noble title *von Lenzenbach* itself, was bought with stolen Jewish gold, with the treasures of the so-called "Rosheimer Fortune."

This is a sin that I myself have not committed. But can one repent of a Sin, and yet keep the profit and benefit thereof? And does not the taint of transgression seep through the generations?

If I must act to salve the sins of my fathers, I must need act soon. The Calamity is upon us. The Apocalypse, the End of Time.

The Cathedral bell slowly tolls, the streets are empty. Those who have not already fled the city cower in their homes.

O, Hagenburg, woe upon thee.

BOOK THREE
THE PEN
(1260–1273)

*

VIII: MONEYLENDERS' LANE
(ANNO 5022. YUDL BEN YITZHAK ROSHEIMER VIII)
*

IX: CHRIST IS RISEN
(ANNO 1262. EUGENIUS VON ZABERN VIII)
*

X: THE CHRONICLE OF WALTHER VON KOLZECK: PART II
(ANNO 1262. WALTHER VON KOLZECK II)
*

XI: VULTURES
(ANNO 1262. BARON VOLMAR VON KRONTHAL VII)
*

XII: THE CHRONICLE OF WALTHER VON KOLZECK: PART III
(ANNO 1262. WALTHER VON KOLZECK III)
*

XIII: BRUSHWOOD
(ANNO 1263. BARON VOLMAR VON KRONTHAL VIII)
*

XIV: ORVIETO
(ANNO 1263. EUGENIUS VON ZABERN IX)
*

XV: PRINZBACH
(ANNO 1263. BARON VOLMAR VON KRONTHAL IX)
*

XVI: THE STRAWHEAD GOY
(ANNO 1264. EMMERICH SCHÄFFER II)

*

INTERLUDE II–ANNO 1318

THE ROSE
(ANNO 1318. ALBRECHT KAIBACH II)

*

XVII: BLOOD
(ANNO 1269. TYBOLT I)

*

XVIII: THE WOODEN DOLL
(ANNO 1269. GRETE GERBER V)

*

XIX: INK
(ANNO 1270. EMMERICH SCHÄFFER III)

*

XX: KALISZ
(ANNO 5030. YUDL BEN YITZHAK ROSHEIMER IX)

*

XXI: THE SILVERED SOW
(ANNO 1271. GRETE GERBER VI)

*

XXII: VON LENZENBACH
(ANNO 1273. EMMERICH VON LENZENBACH NÉ
SCHÄFFER IV)

*

XXIII: INFINITY
(ANNO 1273. EUGENIUS VON ZABERN X)

ANNO
1260

SNOWDROPS
(ANNO 5020. YUDL BEN YITZHAK ROSHEIMER VI)

Herr Rosheimer? Herr Rosheimer?"
The wintry gloom of the Hagenburg Counting House. Lamps burn over the Counting Table, hanging on long chains from the dark, stone ceiling. Müllenheim the Monetarius, his pale, blinking face golden in lamplight, leans towards Yudl. "Others are waiting. If you would be so kind . . . "—"Yes, Herr Münzmeister, I will . . . I was . . . distracted."—"So I see. Would you like me to help you?"

Yudl runs his fingers over his cheeks and eyes, returning his absent mind to the business in hand. He has made a pile of coins on his right; the coins of which he is uncertain. "These coins, Herr Münzmeister?"

The Master of the Mint pulls up a stool and sits by Yudl's side. "These *Händelheller* coins are good. We are taking them at twenty for nineteen." "Twenty for nineteen! This is a good trade you're making, Herr Münzmeister."

Müllenheim shrugs, pulls a face that says *take it or leave it.* "We need coin, Herr Rosheimer. And we need coin *out there,* circulating from hand to hand, from buyer to seller, from trader to trader. We don't need it hoarded in chests and under the bedstead. And we certainly don't need coins like these . . . " and he rakes from Yudl's pile a small handful of old Hagenburg pennies, stamped on one side with a faded crown. "These we take and melt down, and issue to the bearer new pennies valent, equivalent to the weight in silver that comes from the melt." And he makes a sour face. "If there's any bloody silver in them at all. These are some fifty years old, when times were hard."

Yudl raises an eyebrow, pulls his cap from his hair, and scratches his head. "I could lose a couple hundred shillings in this '*Recoinage*' of yours."—"Everyone will gain in the long term, Herr Rosheimer." The Master starts to pick out the faded, tarnished pennies and put them in a pot. "The new coin we are striking with the Prinzbach silver will inspire confidence. What you merchants need is uniformity in currency. Uniformity and clarity."

Yudl replaces his cap. "And for that we sacrifice some five *per centum* of our fortune?"—"A fortune based on fifty-year-old copper coin is not a fortune, that is our contention. We all need a coin we can trust."—"Nevertheless, it's a sly trick of the Bishop's."

A mocking exhalation of air. The Master of the Mint smiles. "Of course, the Recoinage bears the Bishop's seal. But don't, Herr Rosheimer, confuse all this with the Bishop himself. For years that sick old fool has done nothing but eat pigeon pie, hand out trinkets to his sycophants and beatings to anyone who farts near a Priest."

The Monetarius stands. "It's *we* who run this City on the day-to-day, don't forget it." The "*we*" echoes in the Counting House strongroom, reverberating darkly. "We who run the Mint, we who tally the accounts, who collect the Tolls, write the statutes, administer the courts. It's *we* who keep the whole city on its feet. And we formulate a plan to give strength to the Hagenburg currency, and what thanks do we get from you?"

Yudl's hands rise up in protest. "I was only grumbling, Master Müllenheim. Don't I have a right to grumble if you give me nineteen new Hagenburg pennies on my twenty old *Händelheller*?"

Master Müllenheim grunts, sweeps the pennies from the city of Hall am Kocher onto a pewter plate. "With your permission,

Herr Rosheimer, Wikerus the Younger is waiting outside to make the tally of *his* coin. So, let us make an inventory of your coinage banked here. And place all the good coin back in your beautiful strongbox."

The fine strongbox that Yudl has inherited from Uncle Meir, the silent vessel of the Rosheimer Fortune: varnished wood bound in bronze buckles, painted with the coat of arms of the town of Rosheim and with words written beautifully in the Holy Script: *The refining pot is for silver and the furnace is for Gold, but the Lord tests the Heart.*

"And these ones?" Yudl asks, taking a pouch from his pocket.

The Master of the Mint bends over Yudl's shoulder, and plucks out a golden coin, holds it to the light. On one side, a fleur-de-lis, and on the other, St. John the Baptist enhaloed, holding a staff bearing the Lamb of God. A golden Florin, the glorious standard of surgent Florence.

"A beautiful coin, a beautiful coin," he murmurs. "Have no fear, young man. These coins you may keep. A full Mark you will get for this, anywhere in the Christian World."

✡ ✡ ✡

It was last year in the beth midrash, late on the afternoon of Shabbat. As the last prayers were said and the men prepared to head home for the *havdalah*, the unknown Stranger rose from his bench in the corner.

He was tall, his ginger beard was long, and in his eyes was a fomentation. "Jews of Hagenburg!" he called, and his voice was soft, but even so the room fell quiet. "You have been wondering who I am, and why I am here. Many of you have asked me, but I have given no answer. Now is my time to speak."

When he had arrived in Hagenburg, his boots had been caked in purple-brown mud from the winter roads, his heavy wool cloak bespeckled with grime. But now his boots were polished to a shine, his clothes pristine. His voice rang out in the darkening temple. "I have been sent to you by his grace Duke Boleslav of Kalisz! A righteous gentile such as the lands of Ashkenaz have never before seen! I have travelled here from his bounteous lands, a fertile plain fed by the gentle Prosna river. In his Dukedom the rivers teem with pike, the ponds with carp, and the cattle grow fat on the emerald grass. In the forests, silver birch, raspberries and blackberries, mushrooms and fowl. In the city of Kalisz itself, cleanliness and order such as you may only dream of in the stink and crowd of Hagenburg."

In front of the ark, the everlasting light flickers, and there is silence in the beth midrash. Yudl's eyes search out Rabbi Menahem, but he is leaned against his lectern, eyes closed, facing the floor, listening, rapt.

The Stranger smiles. "Jews of Hagenburg, I do not pretend to paint to you a picture of Earthly Paradise. True, the winters are cold. True, in autumn, the winds blow and in the spring, the rain falls, like anywhere else in this tearful vale of Ashkenaz! But, in Kalisz, by order of the Duke, the Jews are free!"

Yudl looks up, studying the Stranger's glowing countenance. He knows a salesman when he sees one, knows the preamble that precedes the harder sale.

"The Jews of Kalisz are free to own property in town or country, free to practice any trade. The Duke concedes the Jews these rights in a written proclamation, of which I have a copy here." And from his cloak he pulls a roll of parchment, which he slowly unfolds.

Yudl steps forwards, bows slightly to the Stranger, and takes the pergament. "The Duke writes in Hebrew?" The Stranger's eyes shine, gently mocking. "No. The Duke writes in Latin. This is my rendering of the proclamation in the language of Ashkenaz."

The letters swim in Yudl's eyes, a German written in the Holy Script, a strange and profane concatenation of sylla- bles . . . *in the name of . . . His Highness . . . Duke Boleslav . . .*

Yudl looks up from the extraordinary document. "And what are you to the Duke of Kalisz, Stranger?"

The Stranger turns on his heels, and his cloak circles his polished boots. A showman. He smiles, showing his gap- toothed mouth. "I am a 'locator.' Charged by the Duke, at his shilling, to travel the river road of the Rhine, and find settlers for the bright new land. I hide nothing from you! True, I receive an emolument for every settling family that stays more than three years. But like you, dear Sir, I am driven in my cho- sen trade not only by the love of silver."—"And what is this other thing that we are driven by, Stranger?"—"By the Love of our Fellow Man."

His clean, soft, supple hand reaches out, and with a gentle flourish, takes the scroll back from Yudl. He holds it outwards to the congregation, turning slowly, presenting it like a Torah Scroll, containing eternal promise.

"I am driven by my wish that the Jews of Ashkenaz may find a true and lasting home until we are called back to Israel." And he sings from the Book of Isaiah, and his voice is high and clear and fine. "*And he shall set up an ensign for the nations, and shall assemble the outcasts of Israel, and gather together the dispersed of Judah from the four corners of the earth.*"

And there are tears of rapture in the Stranger's eyes as the Jews of Hagenburg whisper, "Amen."

✡ ✡ ✡

And how did the legionaries of Emperor Titus lift their ban- ners over the Temple Grounds? How did they raze the Temple's walls, loot its treasures, burn its chambers? How did they slaughter the people of Jerusalem like animals, how did they massacre the thousands, and remain unpunished? Remain the Lords of this World?

Is this not the successor of the Roman Empire in which we now live, is not our King called the Holy King of the Romans, is not the Church that lords above us the Church of Rome? And is this not the Age of Iron foretold in the Book of Daniel? "And the fourth kingdom shall be strong as iron: as iron shall it break and crush all things"?

Yudl stands on the edge of the Quay, staring at the Ehle's drifting waters, his corrugated reflection ripples on the silver surface. Splash! An empty barrel rolls from a docking barge and into the swell. The porter boys shouting, the Quaymaster fishing for it with a hooked pole, but in vain. It floats out into the centre current, heading for the Rhine. *I'll take that off your wages, you dolt. It wasn't my fault, sir, they didn't bind it right. Don't answer back. God willing it will get stuck at the Butchers' Bridge downstream. Well, go and look . . .*

Words, scraps, recriminations, fluttering into Yudl's distracted thoughts. *I have to stop doing this. Drifting off, like an old man.* He rubs his eyes, takes off his cap, scratches his scalp. *Itchy all day.* Around him the teeming life of the Market Quay, the overstuffed heart of Hagenburg.

And yet by the river, the air is sweet. The damp winter wind coming from the distant Vogesen hills, still blanketed in snow. Yudl feels in the lining of his coat, pulls out a scrap of cloth that his wife that morning had sprinkled with rose water. He holds it to his nose. *Ready.*

And he heads into the chaotic streets. Entering the labyrinth that surrounds the Cathedral Square, the stink begins. The stench of pissbowls and chamberpots, dung and refuse, scattered in piles, a soft, wet mass of filth underfoot. The smell of ripening and rotting human waste, clutching the throat.

Yudl walks in the centre of the lanes, head down, clutching

the scented cloth to his nose. *In the streets of Kalisz, cleanliness and order such as you can only dream of in Hagenburg.* The Stranger's words, so enticing now. And in Yudl's mind he is flying, like Habakkuk . . . the Angel of the Lord carrying him into the skies, holding him by the hair, borne by clean, mountain winds. The tangle and filth of Hagenburg far below, the tottering rooves of matted straw, a flight of crows passing over the City's rising walls . . . and then he is soaring over the Rhine and the drifting barges, across the wooded hills of the Schwarzwald, East towards the rising sun, East towards the City of Prague where his Mother now lives, and onwards towards the bounteous, emerald plain of Kalisz . . .

"Watch where you're going!" In the Schmiedgassl, a serving girl bumps into his shoulder as she passes. And Yudl walks on, through the Inferno. Hammers pounding on horseshoes, beating out nails, links in chains. Red fiery sparks cascading from the blacksmiths' workshops onto the road, hissing as they fall into the slush. Glimpses into the smithies, dark, smoke-blackened rooms, the smoulder of furnace and incandescent charcoal, ochre light on the smiths' intent faces as their hammers sculpt the glowing iron.

Yudl walks on. Isaiah again. *And it shall come to pass, that instead of fragrance there shall be a stench . . .* It seems every measure of ground is claimed and occupied, everywhere full. The walls of the houses crowd around the scuttling citizens, trapping in the evil smell. Here, away from the water and the wharf, the Vogesen's freshening wind will never reach. Here the air is stagnant, sulphurous with the furnace fumes, brackish with human filth.

In front of Yudl, the narrowness widens, the darkness lightens. His mind returns to the present day, to the tumult and miasma of Ashkenaz. The Cathedral Square opens, and there is once again light and air.

But even here there is no respite from the wearying parade,

the tattered pageant of Hagenburg. Performers, hawkers, beggars, preachers. A peasant girl with a basket of the first snowdrops and aconites, smiling. "Flowers, sir, for your lapel?" Yudl lets fall the rosewatered cloth, declines. "No thank you, madam."—"Just a penny, sir. For your wife? A token?"—"No thank you, madam."

Regret. Maybe his wife would have liked a posy, a harbinger of Spring. "Excuse me, madam. A tuppence posy, why not?" "Yes, sir, a tuppence posy." Her dirt-nailed fingers select a clutch of flowers. Placing the basket on the muddy, cobbled ground, she ties a ribbon around the stems.

Yudl reaches into his cloak, discreetly he looks around. *Is anyone watching?* The gold for the journey is deep inside his shirt, strapped to his chest. He can feel it hard against his skin. *Still there.* His fingers tickle themselves into the pouch in the gabardine's hem where his daily pennies are kept; old Hagenburg coin.

Yudl thinks of the Flower Girl, kneeling in the grey dawn to pluck the flowers from the foothill woods, and trudging the brown-slushed roads to the City Gates. One of the thousands who flock to the city markets, whose livelihood is to scavenge the scraps that fall from the High Table of Hagenburg. Even in Yudl's short lifetime, how has the City grown, how it has popped its buttons, sprung its overstuffed laces, swollen against its straining walls. And struggling to keep up with its gluttonous appetite, the city's council and officials, registering, taxing, legislating, minting new coin to try and hold the flood of trade as it bursts its banks . . .

And the Bishop? An absent, incompetent Overlord, terrified of the tumult that flows through the streets, huddling with his clerics and knights, leaving all in the hands of his Ministers. The Ministerial families Müllenheim, Zorn, Doroltzheimer, holding back the flood with their quills and statutes, the New Lawgivers of Hagenburg, their fiefdoms the Courts, the Councils, the Committees, the Mint.

"Tuppence, sir?" Her hands proffering the clutch of flowers, white bells nodding, chiming. "Yes, of course." His fingers tease out two old Hagenburg pennies. "Here you are, madam."

Clutching his posy, he walks on, skirting the Cathedral, the giant Temple of Hagenburg, its western end still muffled in scaffold. Slowly, achingly slowly, being remade; taller, cleaner, brighter, adorned with graceful, idolatrous statues and grimacing fiends. *Gargoyles they call them. Gargoyles ... gar ... goyle, gargle, they gargle the rain.*

Rain? Today, low, bruised clouds, rolling, reforming, a gathering wind. The promise of a later storm.

Around the Cathedral's skirts, an Arcade of stalls and shops, selling icons, figures of their Saints, selling the Bishop's wine, meat and crops. Episcopal produce, sold in the Cathedral's shadow, exempt from the taxes that all other vendors must pay. *The Council wants to tax the Bishop's goods. The Bishop refuses. The Council insists. The Bishop threatens the Councillors with excommunication. The Council retreats, grumbling, plots revenge ...*

To fill the financial gap, they raise the taxes on the Jews.

We pay taxes to the Bishop of Rome.

We pay taxes to the Emperor of Rome. The same Rome that destroyed our Temple.

Grete Gerber, passing by, hands clutching her fine skirts, lifting them above the matted filth of the cobbles. *Avoid. Turn. Lord, may she not see me.*

"Judah!" she calls. Her commanding voice. It could silence a gaggle of hissing geese.

Smile. "Mistress Gerber! How are you, madam?"

"Passing well," she says with air and affectation. Beside her, the young bastard "Mayenz Manfred" and the widow Rosamunda Bartsch, her constant companions and familiars. "And you, have you thought any more about my offer?"

"I wasn't aware it was an offer."—"My *appeal*."—"I must be honest, my position is unchanged."—"What can I do to change it?" She smiles coquettishly, hand on hip, a shade of the spirited girl she once must have been.

Grete's head swivels, searching the crowds. Is anyone watching? Listening? Hagenburg, now, is full of Spies. "Help us, Judah, and we can help you. A profit share. The spoils of war."

Yudl shakes his head, leans closer to her, speaks quietly, nearly a whisper. "They tell me the Bishop is sick again. I prefer the policy: *wait and see*. Maybe a fair wind will come, Frau Gerber."—"I see only hail and rain."—"Good things come to those who hope. I must go, I have business in the Judengasse. Good day, Mistress Gerber."—"And to you," she frowns, pleating up her skirts once more.

And Yudl moves off, pressing the posy of flowers to his nose. And enters the Brüdergass, and the labyrinth once more.

Will she ever cease? Milking me for money, silver for her Cause?

Yudl turns, looking over his shoulder. *Is anyone following me? Did anyone see us talking?* The upper stories of the houses lean inwards, stretching out to entrap every inch of space, shadowing the lanes and hiding the streets from God's judging eyes, from Sun and Moon. But where God cannot see, Others are watching.

The City is taut, troubled. The two opposing sides study each other for signs of weakness or gathering strength. If Baron Volmar rides in from his Kronthal estate, as soon as he has passed through the Vogesen Gate, whispered word will be racing to the antechamber of the Bishop's Palace. And if the Bishop's Vassals descend from their distant townships to pay tribute to their overlord, then, speeding ahead of them on the Pilgrims' Road, the Baron's outriders, bearing the list of numbers and names.

In the streets, watchers, informers, spies. Spies for the

Bishop, spies for the ministerial families: for the Zorns, Müllenheims and Doroltzheims, spies for the Sternkammer nobles: for von Kronthal and von Rappoltstein, spies for the merchants, spies for the beggars, spies for the Jews. A penny here, a farthing there, crossed over their grimy palms, and the traffic of the day is for sale; who met with whom, who passed, who visited what tavern, and even *the Baron's valet bought two pounds of eels at the Fischmarkt* could be a penny's worth in the whispered currency of the times.

And Grete Gerber, wealthy widow, is raising money on the quiet. In league with Baron Volmar and the City Families, with the Münzmeister's Müllenheims and the Zorns and Doroltzheimers, she is matching merchant coin with noble and ministerial Gold. *She wants her fingers on the "Rosheimer Fortune," wants me to invest in Weapons, to arm the citizens. To buy a boatload of swords and spears from Magdeburg, crawling upriver from Cologne.*

Even if the war between Pope and Staufen has drifted South over the Alps to Naples and Sicily, even if Peace and Trade now once again sail the broad river road of the Rhine, Hagenburg remains drawn-daggered and teeth bared, the Bishop against his own Citizens. *A coming storm. Invest, invest in gold. Florentine Florins. Not the Hagenburg penny, shilling and mark.*

Soon home. In safety, in the Judengasse. He looks again through the passing crowds. *No one. Good. God willing, no one saw.* His cloak, a simple woollen gabardine, black-dyed. His stockings white linen, his coat black worsted. No colour or flourish, nothing to call attention to him, no signal of his wealth. He passes amongst the living crowds, a modest ghost.

✿ ✿ ✿

The Rabbi is expecting him, already waiting in the small

back room of the beth midrash. A storeroom for damaged books and parchments, a pile of bowls and spoons for communal meals, a broom leaning against a basin. A polstered chair, where the Rabbi sometimes sleeps. "Yudl, come in."

Yudl enters, closes the door behind him, bends to kiss the back of the Rabbi's hand.

Yudl sits on the proffered stool. "How are you, Yudl?"—"How should I be?" The Rabbi smiles. "Like a man with many blessings. Worried."—"That's exactly how I am, Rabbi."—"Then tell me how is your family. Your wife?"—"Very well."—"Your son, your daughter?"—"You see more of my son than I do. How is he doing?"—"A good student."

Yudl passes his hands across his face. "I have brought the money." He reaches into his clothing to loosen the strap that fastens the purse to his chest. As he fumbles, Rabbi Menahem studies him, saying nothing. Yudl feels his gaze, probing. And knows that he sees inside him, at least part of the way inside.

The swollen purse is now in Yudl's hand, heavy with coin. "My word!" Menahem exhales. "You have brought half the Mint of Hagenburg."

Yudl nods. "I think we should pay our taxes early this year."—"Who in the world pays their taxes *early*?"—"We do. When we are worried that if we wait, the price will rise again. And that these coins will no longer be pennies valent."—Rabbi Menahem raises his hands. "Spare me further explanation."—"I will."—"I have no interest nor understanding in these matters."—"I know."—"Then I defer the matter to you."

Yudl eases the purse open, and pulls out two smaller pouches from within. "This is my donation to our poor."—"Bless you." The Rabbi's hand reaches out, his eyes turn away and face the wall. Yudl places the pouch in the Rabbi's hand. Without looking, Menahem places it inside the charity box on the shelf by his chair. His lips mutter a blessing. His eyes close. Then re-open, fix on Yudl.

Yudl places the second pouch in the Rabbi's hand. "And this is for the journey to Kalisz. My cousins will come tomorrow, stay Shabbat, and leave the following morning. May the road money come from your hand, not mine."

Rabbi Menahem nods sadly. His gaze mistens, dreaming of the journey. "I pray you are right about this, Yudl."—"Is it better to know something, or not know something?"—"It is better to know something."—"Then it is right for them to go. Then we will know if the Duchy of Kalisz is as he says."—"It is a long way."—"Our ancestors came further, from Israel to the Rhine."—"They did. I often wonder why on earth, why?"

The two men look at each other, smiling. "And now, Yudl, tell me what you are worrying about."—"The Temple of Jerusalem." The Rabbi's eyes are still smiling. "Is *that* what you are worried about?"—"Emperor Titus destroyed our Temple and then made the Jews pay to build a new temple, to Jupiter, in Rome, did he not?"—"I believe so."—"And, so to say, we pay the great-great grandchild of that tax to the present-day Holy Roman Emperor?"—"Yudl . . . "—"And we just do this? The Jews of Israel resisted Rome."—"And look what happened. Jerusalem was destroyed."

Yudl fidgets nervously on his stool. He is looking at the floor, but can feel Rabbi Menahem's concerned gaze examining him. "Yudl, your father was plagued by the same kind of thoughts."—"I know. Aren't we condemned to follow our Fathers?"

The Rabbi sighs. Yudl looks up and meets his gaze. The Rabbi looks away. "With you I don't know."

Rabbi Menahem spreads his hands. "Look at the Torah. *Two nations are in thy womb.* Jakob and Esau. The wombs of our Matriarchs gave birth to both *our* Ancestors and those of the other nations. Let us be at peace with our neighbours, and at peace with ourselves. You are Who You Are, Judah. And thanks to you and your acumen, our beth midrash has a new roof and new books, our taxes are paid on time and in full, the poor eat meat on the Sabbath. We thank you."

Silence stretches out between them. Through the closed door, the murmuration of the men reciting in the beth midrash, a gentle choir of singsong voices, falling and rising with the cadence of the Holy Word. Yudl takes off his cap, scratches his unruly scalp. "I am no longer so interested in my work. It feels . . . hollow. Like a show. Like the Easter Players who perform in front of the Cathedral."—"I have never seen them."—"Playacting. They play roles, pretend to be lovers, pretend to be angels."—"God forbid."—"And I, if I make a good sale, set up a winning deal. I play pleasure, make seem that I have joy in victory. But inside I no longer feel anything but weariness."

✡ ✡ ✡

The Cathedral's bell tolls, but there is still an hour before sunset. It tolls again, sustaining . . . fading from bronze to beaten silver, at the edge of hearing.

The bell tolls again. A flock of starlings, startled by the bell, somersault, screeching, through the leaden sky.

Yudl, standing in the Judengasse, only a few paces from Home, wipes his hands over his tired eyes. The traffic in the lane has stopped, faces turn to the sky, towards the Cathedral's distant dome, as if expecting to read in the heavens the meaning of the bell.

The bell tolls again.

"Close up your shops," says Yudl quietly to the shopkeepers who have gathered around him. "Tell our folk to stay at home. No open displays of . . . laughter. Joy."

Behind him, as he leaves, the Jews slip silently into their shuttered homes. Beyond the Judengasse the gathering, murmuring crowds begin, summoned by the bell. Yudl doesn't have to go far. At the corner of the Schriwerstublgass, Johannes, the parchment and ink merchant, stands with his black-stained hands folded over his apron. "Herr Rosheimer, heard the news?"—"Not yet."—"The Bishop has passed over."

For some moments they stand together, watching the tawny tide of humanity making its way towards the Cathedral Square. Yudl shrugs, wearily. "I wonder what will happen now."

✡ ✡ ✡

By the time he has returned to the Jewish Quarter, all is shrouded in twilight and silence. The Judengasse is empty, not a soul stirs. Behind the shuttered windows, no sign of life, as if the houses themselves were shrouded in mourning.

Yudl stands, his hand leaning against his house's front door, hesitating. All day, he had looked forward to this moment, his homecoming, when his children cry out with joy.

Maybe today I will teach my son of lampblack, he thinks. *The making of ink.* He turns, and leans his back against the cool oak of the front door. His fingers reach into the fold of his cloak, and pull out the posy of snowdrops and aconites.

Hurrying along the empty lane towards him, out of breath and wheezing, Yudl's stocky Christian assistant Elbertus. As he approaches, he waves. His face bears an expression of earnest importance. "You have heard?"—"I have heard. You're a bit late, Elbertus."—"The Square was so crowded, I could hardly move."—"And what is the atmosphere?"—"Tense, Herr Rosheimer. But the Town Watch are there in force."—"Then go back, and keep an eye open for us. On days like these it only takes a few people to start blaming the Jews . . . "

Elbertus nods gravely, taking the responsibility onto his broad butcher's shoulders. "Good evening, Herr Rosheimer."— "Good evening."

Elbertus' bulky form retreats through the dusk and gloom, disappearing into darkness at the distant corner of the Schriwerstublgass. Stormy winds blow, sending the Judengasse's shop signs swaying. Yudl turns to face his doorway, and knocks thrice, twice; the signal of his return. In his right hand, the posy of snowdrops for his wife, an offering for the temple of their prosperous, peaceful home.

POLYPHONY
(ANNO 1260. EUGENIUS VON ZABERN VIII)

Once I had Eyes and could see. Once I was a respected member of the Chapter of the Cathedral, and could count on my allies and colleagues. I lived in Avenheim Monastery, and dwelt in silence and meditation.

And now, one by one, all of this has changed.

I have Scars where my eyes should be. I am the only Canon of the Chapter who stood against the election of Bishop Walther von Kolzeck, and I am shunned. I have left Avenheim, and live in the City, in the clamour and chaos near the Vogesen Gate.

I am surprised to find myself quite content.

† † †

In the mornings I rise, and after my prayers and ablutions, feel my way to the chair by the window. I unfasten the shutters and sit by the opening, letting the sounds of the street drift up to my listening ears. At this hour the Vogesen Gate has recently been opened, and pouring down Vogesen Street a legion of country folk making their way to the markets of the City. Some have handcarts that trundle clattering over the cobblestones, some are laden with baskets tied to their backs and groan and puff their way up the incline towards the Cathedral Square. Some call out their wares as they walk, hoping for a sale on the road to lighten their burden. And amongst the chorus of voices, I have begun to recognise individual characters in this numerous *dramatis personae*, the heroes and heroines of this lively Shadow Play that unfolds itself beneath my window.

After the clamorous influx of peasants, the music of the street ebbs somewhat, finding its diurnal pattern. The same hawkers pass at practised intervals, calling their wares in singsong cadences, the same beggars perch in the same shady corners, repeating their worn phrases *ad infinitum*, "for the Love of God, a penny, Sir," "Charity, madam, for these hungry mouths." A Leper passes twice before the midday bell, his clapper rattling to warn of his passing. The shopkeepers, when there is no custom, gather at the sides of the street, gossiping like fishwives.

There was a time when I would have found this repetitious parade of sounds a torture, but now I find in it something compelling: the roundelay and song of this city, unstinting centre of my existence since my birth some sixty summers ago.

And indeed, I was born here in this very house; the City Residence of the von Zaberns; two fine storeys of Kronthaler sandstone, a square of buildings surrounding a courtyard, a stable and a small vegetable garden. Here I spent my childhood playing beneath the linden tree, studying in the library, eating in the dining hall of the western wing, sleeping and dreaming in this very room.

Now I have returned, in darkness. And am surprised to find the darkness so full, so full of music and voices, the polyphony of Life.

† † †

One week after the burial of Bishop Heinrich von Stahlem, Hieronymus stands at the door to my old Monastery cell, and announces the arrival of Canon Walther von Kolzeck, leading candidate to be the new Bishop of Hagenburg.

"Let him in."

The sound of footsteps, jingling; spurs. The soft crepitations of chain mail links folding together as he, ignoring all Etiquette, sits uninvited on the stool opposite my chair. His scabbard scraping on the floor. Armed, armoured. A warrior.

I wish I could see his expression as I raise my scarred face in his direction. "My Lord von Kolzeck, let's not stand on ceremony. Please sit."

After a pause that I can only describe as "mildly embarrassed," he says, "Forgive me, My Lord, I am already sitting."

It takes me substantial effort not to smile.

He clears his throat. "I know that you don't like me."

"I do not know you, My Lord. When last I saw you, you were a young tyke, running round your father's heels."

"You did not accept the gift I sent you."

"I am blind. I have no use for silver plates."

"Nevertheless I wish to canvass your support in my election."

"Then tell me why I should give you my support."

"My Lord, even the Canons of the other . . . more Staufisch families have pledged their hand to me. Even they realise that our time is misaligned. That there must be a rebalancing."

"And I too recognise this to be the case. You are wrong to be concerned whether I like you or not. For instance, I rather liked Bishop Heinrich von Stahlem. But his inept rule of this Diocese has been a disaster."

"There we agree."

"And what do you see as the cure?"

"Well, it's obvious. The powers once invested in the Bishop must be wrested back from the Council and the Ministerial Authorities and returned to the Bishop's Court. The control of benefices, tithes, taxes must be put back under episcopal authority. The Bishop must appoint, as he did of old, all members of the Council and Ministerial positions."

"I see. A return to the Good Old Days."

The young Walther von Kolzeck swallows his irritation. I can hear him shifting on the hard, uncomfortable stool I keep in my cell for my more vexatious guests. "You must agree that the worldly power of Hagenburg should be reorganised?"

"Indeed," I concede, leaning forward. "But I see some things differently, My Lord. Why do you have so much support? Let me tell you why."

"I am listening."

"Pope Innocent was so obsessed with breaking the power of the Staufen in Alsace that he showered this Diocese with gold. And Bishop von Stahlem used that gold to buy anti-Staufen allies, enrichening and furthering the smaller families and the country lords of the Marches. But, now that Pope Innocent is dead and the Staufen war has moved to Southern Italy, that flow of gold has stopped."

Von Kolzeck sits still now, his breathing deep and slow. He is listening.

"And so these new young Lords. Your most vocal supporters. They are looking for a new source of income. And now we have You. Walther von Kolzeck, with your family the owners of Prinzbach, the biggest silver mine in the whole Rhineland. And you say you will break the power of the city ministers, reorganise the wealth and benefices of the Diocese. In short, you will break up the present order and make out of what is left a nice, new, big trough. And they want their noses in it."

The stool scrapes against the flagstones as the young lord abruptly stands. "Maybe it is because you are blind, My Lord. But you don't see what's happening beneath your own nose."

"And what is that?"

"The City of Hagenburg growing into a cesspit. A Sodom, a Gomorrah. It is lawless, filthy, out of control. The Councillors, left by von Stahlem to their own devices, pass their own laws, raise their own taxes, build their own houses on the Bishop's land! The People have grown Godless, they despise the clergy and nobility. They spit at Priests and Nobles on the open street!"

I raise my right hand in the darkness, a rhetorical gesture, requesting careful audience. "Yes, the City has grown beyond all imagining, and is out of control. But if you think that this great, crowded city can now be administered by a small episcopal court as in the times of my Master Bishop Berthold, you are greatly mistaken."

My hands reach out towards him. "Time for reorganisation of the disarray left by His Grace von Stahlem, yes. But this must be *slow*, *gentle*, diplomatic work carried out in tandem with the ministerial powers." My hands clasp together. "And one thing is certain, My Lord von Kolzeck, of this kind of gentle, detailed, careful work you are not capable. You will not have my support."

† † †

With these words, spoken in the bleak, lenten, late Winter, I sealed my ostracisation from the rest of the Chapter. One by one even the older, more circumspect Canons pledged their hands to von Kolzeck and—lest we forget—to the flourishing fortunes of his Prinzbach silver mines. After his hasty election, some of them visited me in my cell in private to mutter disingenuous excuses for their behaviour, admitting that "it was maybe a risk" to have elected such a young and untested firebrand, but that "the times call for strong leadership," and other such simple-minded homilies. Sycophantic, greedy, and alarmed by the almost palpable hatred directed at the clergy from the mutinous streets, they pulled their cowls over their heads and hoped that strong medicine would cure the rot at the heart of Hagenburg.

Now it is three months since I left Avenheim Monastery. Von Kolzeck, God bless his youthful, gormless heart, has—so far—been able to achieve nothing. In his impetuous, self-regarding arrogance, he forgot the basic stepping stones he needed to tread before he could achieve his wished-for Glory.

Firstly, the rather important detail: he is not an ordained priest. And so he cannot be enthroned as Bishop until he has taken orders. And a Bishop may only be ordained by an *Arch*bishop.

This little obstacle he had dismissed as easy to surmount whilst canvassing support, waving a letter from the Archbishop of Mayenz, a friend of his father's, in which the Archbishop declared himself ready to ordain von Kolzeck at his convenience. But—and my poor little heart breaks to recount it—as soon as von Kolzeck was elected, the Archbishop was summoned to Viterbo to conference with the Pope, and so is now somewhere in Italy until further notice. And so von Kolzeck must wait until the conclave has finished and the German Archbishops ride north from Italy . . . or he must himself run off over the Alps to find them, and pray to God he somehow doesn't miss them on the way.

These little details. So easy to overlook, when one's eyes are fixed on a glorious horizon.

And, I am perversely happy to say, Worse has just come.

It appears that Von Kolzeck's young comrade in arms, the Count von Lichtenberg, has got himself into some serious trouble. It seems that the Count had heard—wrongly, as it turns out—that Hagenburg's ancient adversary, the Bishop of Metz, was also away in Viterbo at the Papal Conference. He decided to use this opportunity to display his Alsatian mettle and invade the Lorraine, annexing some of Metz' territory for the glory of Hagenburg and, naturally, for the House of Lichtenberg itself.

And now von Kolzeck has a little War on his hands.

The news has just arrived from the borderlands that the Bishop of Metz has counterattacked, and the polyphony outside my window is aquiver with rumour and noise. And I sit here and listen, with the morning sun on my face, and have to smile at the folly that appoints warriors to do the work of wise men.

THE CHRONICLE OF WALTHER VON KOLZECK: PART I
(ANNO 1260. WALTHER VON KOLZECK I)

In the history of the noble families of the Alsace, no Rise is more precipitous, and no Fall so calamitous, as that of Walther von Kolzeck, the 62nd Bishop of Hagenburg. Some noble families rise to greatness through a series of advantageous marriages, some through warlike deeds and the forceful annexation of lands, and some through simple good fortune. It was the fate of the von Kolzeck family to belong to the latter category.

The ascendency of the von Kolzeck family began with the discovery of silver ore in the sands of the Prinzbach river. Before this discovery, Werner von Kolzeck, Walther's father, had been a minor landowner notable only for his unyielding loyalty to the Bishops of Hagenburg. Whenever a war party was raised by the Bishop, whenever the Bishop's vassals and allies needed to show a display of force, Werner von Kolzeck was always first to volunteer. This he did with a zeal that only thinly disguised his true ardour; the wish for favour and advancement.

No sooner than silver had been discovered on his lands, Lord Kolzeck sent, at some substantial cost, for mining experts from the Harz Mountains to come and prospect the Prinzbach valley. His investment proved a canny one, and the Harz metallurgists discovered clear evidence of silver deposits in the Prinzbach hills.

Lord Kolzeck was not laggardly in his exploitation of this good fortune. Borrowing from the wealthy Hagenburg Jew

Meir Rosheimer against the future profits of the mine, he hired miners and began to prospect and excavate, finding ever more evidence of rich mineral wealth. His joy was complete when, in recognition of his unbending loyalty and in expectation of von Kolzeck's coming prosperity, Bishop Berthold von Diez, shortly before his demise, offered a Canonry to the von Kolzeck family. This place on the Chapter of the great Cathedral of Hagenburg, along with its golden benefices, Lord Kolzeck bequeathed on his younger son, Walther, then a promising and precocious boy of seven summers.

By the time that Walther, at the age of thirteen, was sent to the von Lichtenberg family in Buchsweiler to continue his knightly education, an abundant seam of silver had indeed been struck and the hamlet of Prinzbach had transformed into a fortified town on the edge of the Black Forest. With this discovery of a deep and wide seam of silver, the House of Kolzeck had become, in prospect, one of the richest in the Upper Rhineland, their wealth matched only by the von Habsburgs and the combined estates of the von Kronthals and von Moders.

The young Walther was never left incognizant of the growing importance of his House and of the Great Roles he and his brother were expected to play in the power games of the Alsace. His Father was not coy in expressing his unbridled hopes for his sons, his ambitions not even shying at the prospect that Walther might one day become Bishop, and his elder brother Herrmann Holy Roman Emperor!

In Castle Lichtenberg at Buchsweiler, near Zabern, Walther's knightly and spiritual education continued. In matters military, he was instructed by the elderly Count of Lichtenberg himself, in matters ecclesiastical, by an austere Dominican, Johannes von Emsen.

Father Emsen was a man of strong, and sometimes controversial, opinion. He contended, for example, that the

Dominicans' first intervention in the spiritual life of the Rhineland, the Inquisition of anno 1232, had not been prosecuted vigorously enough. He believed that heretical, insurrectionary ideas remained within the corpus of the Upper Rhine, and that secret heresiarchs were active in the shadows, fomenting the people towards unrest. He saw around him, in the conditions of the present day, a sinful unravelling of the time-honoured organisation of society; peasants leaving their fields for the iniquitous life of the cities, children disobeying their parents in the questions of marriage and choice of livelihood, open, shameless disregard for the authority of Elders and Priests, and a tendency in intellectual circles to divagate from the sanctioned precepts of the Church Fathers.

Under the stern tutelage of Johannes von Emsen, Walther learned to look upon the world as essentially Fallen, a cracked and sinful vessel, broken since Eve's original sin, and only redeemable by the valiant heroism of true Warriors of the Church. Walther swore fervently to his fearsome teacher that he would strive to right the wrongs of the world.

Thus Walther grew into manhood under the influence of two, at least partially, contradictory visions. His Father, who wished for him nothing more than he should become Bishop of Hagenburg. And Johannes von Emsen, who, in his sermons and homilies, likened Hagenburg to Nineveh, Sodom, and Gomorrah. And so it became Walther's destiny to be elected to Lord over a city that he had learned to regard as a pit of evil. He was to become Suzerain over a nest of vipers.

† † †

Walther von Kolzeck was elected to the Bishop's Throne in anno 1260, at the age of twenty-three. His election had been won on two prime bases; his Father's apportioning of substantial gifts to the Canons of the Great Chapter, and

Walther's promise to cow and contain the upstart power of the ministerial families. These latter had exploited the chaos of the previous Bishop's, Heinrich von Stahlem's, reign, to their own benefit. Under von Stahlem, the city of Hagenburg had grown substantially in population and in the wealth of its trade, at such a rate that the episcopal administration had struggled to contain it. The Ministers, correctly sensing that their Lord von Stahlem had no taste for municipal matters and the day-to-day running of the affairs of the city, had taken up the administrative burden onto their own shoulders. In doing so, they had also not forgotten to feather their own nests, endowing themselves and their family members with various posts and functions amply remunerated from the public purse.

The *ministeriales*, and their more lowly colleagues the Merchants, whose tax coin kept the ministerial class in clover, had grown rich together, and they, despite their vulgar birth, clothed themselves and disported themselves in the manner of the nobility. They rode on palfreys and coursers, wore coloured silks, bore arms as if they were Knights, formed their own drinking societies which met in the closed rooms of the more genteel taverns, and showed open disregard for the authority of the Church, the Bishop's Law Courts and the hierarchy of noble birth. If Hagenburg had become a sink of vice and a sprawling labyrinth of iniquity, then—it was so contended in the Chapter House of the Cathedral—it was the Ministerials to blame.

According to the old statutes of the City, it lay within the Bishop's right to appoint his own ministers, judges and town council—a right which had been eroded in the chaos of the times. It was this right that Walther had sworn to uphold. It was his fervently avowed intention to disinvest the current ministers of their powers and, from *tabula rasa*, to start afresh.

† † †

However, shortly after his election to the *cathedra*, Walther von Kolzeck was to experience two major reversals of fortune, one ecclesiastical in nature, one military. Both calamities were, viewed dispassionately, out of his direct sphere of control, but the sensation of misadventure engendered by these twin catastrophes would come to blight all his successive attempts at redress: from the beginning of his Episcopal Reign, Walther von Kolzeck was seen as a man of ill fortune.

Firstly and briefly to deal with the ecclesiastical misadventure. Pope Alexander IV, increasingly alarmed at the incursions of the Mongols into the Eastern borders of Christian Europe and concerned by the Orthodox Nicean Greeks' encircling of Latin Constantinople, had convocated an emergency meeting of the leaders of the Church, to which all German Archbishops were summoned. The absence of any Archbishop in the surrounding lands had unfortunate consequence for Walther von Kolzeck, in that there was no Archbishop on hand to ordain him as Bishop. And so, for many long months at the beginning of his reign, he remained a mere "Bishop elect," lacking in religious power and authority.

And his power as the temporal leader of the Upper Rhine was sorely tested by his first attempt at a military excursion. This was necessitated by the impetuous actions of the Count von Lichtenberg the younger (the elder Count, Walther's military tutor, having recently died). Emboldened by his childhood friend's ascension of the Hagenburg episcopal throne, the young Count had invaded territory adjacent to the Lichtenberg estate; territory belonging to the Bishop of Metz. Metz had vigorously counter-attacked and reconquered his domain, and, finding little resistance, had continued to annexe a large parcel of the Lichtenberg lands in retribution.

Bishop elect Walther von Kolzeck was compelled to defend

the territorial integrity of his Diocese, and immediately sent word that all loyal lords and liegemen were to gather in the Cathedral Square of Hagenburg on the following morning to ride out to war against Metz and the men of Lorraine.

Unfortunately for Walther von Kolzeck and his mission, over the preceding years, the bitter sentiment felt by a large section of the Hagenburg population towards the hegemony of the Bishop had developed into a form of organised resistance. The people of the city had learned to arm themselves, to form their own militia, such as the army that had defeated the wicked Count of Schwanenstein, himself a Canon of the Great Chapter of the Cathedral. And support had gathered around the charismatic figurehead of Baron Volmar von Kronthal, the leader of the city's Schwanenstein campaign.

History does not record the names of the authors of the conspiracy that now defeated Walther von Kolzeck in his wish to ride to the Count of Lichtenberg's aid, but suspicion must surely fall upon the scions of the leading ministerial families, such as Niklaus Zorn and Michael Müllenheim, municipal potentates who had made clear their opposition to the new, young Bishop. Maybe Baron von Kronthal was also personally involved in the shameful events of that day, but no record of his participation has been bequeathed to posterity.

What is a matter of record is as follows. As the Bishop elect and his loyal liegemen gathered in the Cathedral Square with the intention of marching out by the striking of the Terce bell, groups of unruly, rebellious townsfolk, in the main drawn from the lower strata of society, formed in the sidestreets and narrow lanes that surround the square. From these boltholes and rat-warrens they periodically emerged to shout foul abuse and to hurl stones and refuse at the gathered Knights of Alsace.

Disorder broke out in the episcopal ranks as individual knights, feeling their Honour impugned by the vulgar mob, chased the ill-doers into the city labyrinth, intending to punish those guilty of defamation and insult. In this they failed, the narrow lanes and uneven cobbles proving an impossible field of combat for knightly warfare, and because the unruly rabble never stood ground to fight, but rather fled deeper into the warren of streets, enticing the knights—or so the warriors feared—into possible ambush.

It was well after midday that the Bishop elect managed to regain control of his assembled knights, and march them to the Mayenz Gate. All the way along the Mayenzer Allee, the shameful deprecations of the mob continued, but at the Gate itself, even greater dishonour awaited.

The Gate was locked. In outrage and disbelief, Walther von Kolzeck summoned the Gatekeeper, who knelt trembling before him, and wept when he confessed that "men" (he could not identify the culprits) had come, beaten him, locked the gates and stolen away with the keys. News now reached the desperate Bishop elect that all four gates of the city had been locked in the same disgraceful manner. He was trapped within his own city walls.

Maybe at this juncture, the young Lord might have decided to build battering rams and break down the gates from within, but this would have taken much time, and would have necessitated the co-operation of the City's craftsmen. And at this crucial moment when sensible deliberation and quiet counsel may have yet won the day, Walther von Kolzeck and his men became surrounded by a jeering, screeching mob of "citizens," whose cacophony alarmed the mounted company's horses.

His options limited, and the situation becoming increasingly perilous, Walther von Kolzeck, doubtless with ashamed and heavy heart, ordered the disbandment of his company, and returned, under the armed guard of some of his most loyal men, to the safety of the Bishop's Palace.

† † †

Here he found little respite from his woes. His father, Werner von Kolzeck, enraged at the damage caused to their House's reputation by this aborted excursion and cowed retreat, forgetting that his son was now, by virtue of his election, his Lord and superior, berated Walther in front of his liegemen with such bile that he had to be removed forcibly from the audience chamber. After this distemperate storm had cleared, visibly agitated, Walther sat down with his advisers to write letters to their allies in the countryside, begging them to march to Hagenburg and to their aid. Couriers were found and disguised as peasants and tradesmen so as to be able to smuggle the missives outside the city walls.

An evening mass was celebrated in the Palace Chapel, at which Johannes von Emsen officiated, and where fervent prayers were offered to the Lord in the hope of His swift and just intercession in these parlous worldly affairs. In his sermon Johannes von Emsen made clear his contention that the jeering mob of "citizens" had doubtless been organised, and even paid to play this insurrectionary role, by shadowy masters, namely by the Ministers, the Jews and the Merchant Guilds.

† † †

It was only some days later that the City Gates were opened for the Bishop elect, and then in circumstances that none of his circle could have predicted. Their spies and messengers had brought in a series of reports and missives which, when taken together, had painted a picture of some confusion. Only two matters seemed certain; one most pleasing, the other, most troubling.

Pleasing was the imminent arrival in the Hagenburg plain of a troop of knights and soldiers loyal to the Bishop, led by the Abbot of Murbach. Troubling was the news, made uncertain by rumour and counter-rumour, that Baron Volmar von Kronthal had, without the Bishop elect's request or permission, liberated the contested Lichtenberg lands, and made peace with Metz. A settlement had apparently been made to return the Alsace-Lorraine border to its time-honoured place.

On the fifth day, an ensign in the livery of the von Kronthal-Moders arrived at the Bishop's Palace, and conveyed a courteous summons to come to the tilting grounds outside the Vogesen Gate to a parley with "the victor of the Metz-Lichtenberg dispute," the Baron von Kronthal.

The invitation was accepted, and von Kolzeck and his men rode, doubtless with some apprehension, through the now calm streets of the city to the now open Vogesen Gate.

A short and decisive public dialogue then ensued. Von Kronthal remained on his horse in front of the ranks of his assembled knights, squires and liegemen. On the hillock of the Bishop's Haldenheim Castle in the middle distance, the Abbot of Murbach and his troops waited, ready to engage in battle if the person of the Bishop elect was threatened. Ranged on the city walls and around the Vogesen Gate, a large crowd of Hagenburg citizens had gathered.

Von Kronthal spoke first. Indicating the army of the Abbot of Murbach on Haldenheim hill, he called out, "Is this a battle that you wish to call?"

Von Kolzeck answered in the negative. It is recorded that he said, "I will not call it! Soon, Baron, it will time for the Vintage. And if we fight, the war will be long, and if our grapes are not picked and trod, then calamity will befall Rich Alsace!"

This answer was pleasing to the assembled citizens, and trumpets sounded in his support.

After noting that this answer was gratifying both to him and to Hagenburg, the Baron von Kronthal, now joined by one of the scheming leaders of the ministerial families, Councillor

Niklaus Zorn, posed a further question to the Bishop elect. "And now, will you listen to your City? Will you rein in your hotheaded nobles whose intemperance has brought upon us this war with Metz?"

And by his side, Councillor Zorn demanded to know further: "Will you listen to your Ministers, who require of you a New Order and a Statute Book that reflects the City as it now is in this modern, burgeoning time?"

Walther von Kolzeck's reply is recorded as follows:

"Baron, Councillor. I am not yet enthroned. I am not yet this country's Lord. I will retire to my estates. I will consult with Rome. I will consult with my elders. I will hear advice. I will listen to all parties and with God's Will I will adjudicate well and return to this city and humbly seek to rule under the Eyes of God, just to all men."

And with these words the colloquy ended and Walther von Kolzeck, attended by his troop of loyal men, rode off to Castle Haldenheim, whence they then departed, under cover of darkness on the evening of the same day, to the safety of the fortified walls of Prinzbach on the far bank of the river Rhine.

† † †

Despite Werner von Kolzeck's fury that his son had once again retreated in a display of weakness, it was clear to any dispassionate observer that Walther von Kolzeck had nevertheless been canny in showing himself in sympathy to the trade of the City and its all-important Vintage, and in buying himself some time to regroup, take stock and make plans. Most vital of all for the Bishop elect was to effect his ordination, and in full pomp and display of strength, ascend the Bishop's throne. This would, due to the absence of the German Archbishops, take some time.

Walther von Kolzeck had therefore displayed some acuity

and had saved himself from immediate disaster. Nevertheless, he had also seen, at first hand, the vulgar contempt in which he was held by his own citizens, and he, in the system of beliefs he had inherited from Johannes von Emsen, was inclined to see in this a sinful imbalance that must be called to Reckoning. No milder concepts such as compromise or diplomacy made gentle incursion into the rage of his judgement. Ensconced amongst his sycophantic retinue in the comfort of his Prinzbach castle, he made plans and strategies that were bold, fierce, and coloured with wounded pride.

Indeed, the cause of his further misfortunes could no longer be ascribed, as with the misadventures of his delayed ordination and the foolishness of the younger Lichtenberg, to ill-starred fate. The blame for the precipitous downfall that followed can only be laid at Walther von Kolzeck's own feet.

The twin Vices of Pride and Ambition are like two shining black stallions riding together on the same span. Their uneven tempers cause them to pull apart, sending the Chariot they are so impetuously racing hurtling into the depths.

ANNO
1261

BELL, BOOK AND CANDLE
(ANNO 1261. BARON VOLMAR VON KRONTHAL V)

He'd sent his monks ahead of him to lay the groundwork.

Three of them, two magpie Dominicans and a shit-brown Franciscan, marching through the slush on a damp winter's day up to the forlorn gates of Castle Kronthal. "We pray for audience with the Baron," they called up through the grille-work.

So I gave them audience, and why not? I've got nothing better to do at home these days. I can't even argue with the Baroness. As soon as she passed child-bearing age her brother had her packed off to Castle Moder, claiming, with a patently fake smile, that he "missed his little sister" and wanted to spend more time with her. The inference was fairly clear: he's worried that I'll poison the poisonous, cold bitch, then remarry and father an actual heir. And then that'll be the last the von Moders see of the lands she came with as dowry.

The last years before her womb ran dry, she would come to my bedchamber and beseech me, whilst fingering her medallion of the Holy Virgin, to give her a tupping. Every time she did so, I could almost see her brother Rutger von Moder prodding her scrawny behind with a stick, whispering from behind the arras, *"Make us a bloody heir, you useless sack!"*

The pity of it. But now that sickening boudoir comedy is over, and Castle Kronthal is left to me, my dogs and my servants. And—as today—the occasional visiting petitioner, requesting audience.

One of the Dominicans, a Roman, only spoke in Latin. I suppose that was meant to impress me. The other two were from the East of the Black Forest and yodelled Schwäbisch German like goatherds. They sat by my great fire, their damp habits gently steaming, the slush slowly melting from their stinking boots, and told me that their Master, Walther von Kolzeck, wanted Reconciliation. He wanted to restore balance to Hagenburg, establish the reign of Virtue, *et cetera*. It was true, they said, that the newly ordained von Kolzeck was gathering his loyal liegemen to march with him to Hagenburg for his enthronement, but I shouldn't be alarmed, *et cetera*. And they gave me a piece of parchment, heavy with the Bishop's seal, in the name of God, ensuring my safety and foreswearing any wish for the use of arms.

I gave them some warm wine and venison stew. Let it never be said that I am inhospitable to guests. Then I sent them off to sleep in the village priest's house in the valley. My hospitality has its limits.

† † †

It's not that they lied to me. No. Merely they had, the cunning bastards, used flutes for trumpets. The way they talked, it seemed that Bishop Walter would gather up a few score braves, trot into the City, meekly pick up mitre and crozier, quietly coronate himself and then retire to the Bishop's Palace for a few cups of wine before beginning the gentle work of Peace.

And here he is, marching in through the Vogesen Gate, at the head of a procession whose damned End our men on the walls can't even see, and the drummers of Schlettstadt are pounding, the trumpeters of Colmar are blaring, the banners of a hundred families are waving, and I and my brethren wait on our steeds by the gate and count the horsemen riding in.

We count and count until we lose count. It's nearly a Thousand.

The Cathedral Square looks like a tilting ground so full it is of horses and squires and fluttering pennants. And inside the Cathedral itself . . . when it's time to recite the Lord's Prayer it sounds like a blacksmith's at the gates of Hell; one thousand knights in plate- and chain-mail clatter to the flagstones on bended knee.

I and my braves from the *Sternkammer*, we have our place near the front. Our banners hang just behind the standards of the Grand Nobles, the old families who've had sons in the Chapter for generations.

But now they've put up this bloody Rood Screen, an apron of stone hiding the Choir, even from close to the front of the Nave you can't see a bloody thing of the service, just hear the echoing words. The Nave is still only two-thirds built, and the vassal knights are crammed in every corner, perched on blocks of half-hewn stone, leaned against scaffolds. The Town People can hardly catch a peek, so full is the place of Armour. Boys and girls squeeze through steel greaves, trying to glimpse the new Bishop. Mistress Gerber and the other Guildmasters are all pushed into the back arcades.

It's clear: he's not going to break his Sworn Promise. The newly enthroned Bishop is not going to perjure himself before God and have me, Reichard, Lanzelin and the other *Sternkammer* Knights massacred here in the Cathedral. His Dogs are well leashed, well prepared. No one will raise their hands against me and mine.

But we're the day's prize buffoons. And revenge must be sweet for Walther. This is honeyed recompense for his Humiliation at my hands before the city gates last summer.

The choir sings a *laudamus*. It means von Fucksack must have been consecrated on the Bishop's Throne. And now he comes, the young mitred fool, ascending the stairs of the Rood

Screen, carrying his crozier as if it were a sword. And the assembled clanking saucepot knights rise to their feet and cheer.

Walther drinks in the adulation as if it were the new year's wine and then calls for silence. His speech is short and clear enough. There is an imbalance in Hagenburg, a sinful Disorder. There is not enough Respect for the power of the Church. The ministerial officials appointed by Bishop Berthold and his predecessor some forty, fifty years ago have turned their Offices into their own Fiefdoms, appoint their own successors from their own clans, pass their own laws, raise their own taxes, live from the tithes, sweat and labour of the Poor. *Et cetera.*

But from now on the Bishop will be Lord once more. And his name is Walther von Kolzeck, arrogant fool of twenty-four summers.

Sacristans arrive, wreathed in white and purple robes, bearing wooden crosses and the Cathedral's silver crucifix. Banks of candles are lit by the sexton and his boys. The Choir chants a lugubrious Psalm. Kolzeck lifts his arms aloft. "Those who will not obey the will of the One True Church cannot benefit from her Mercy. Sinners, dissenters, return to the Church and you will find her merciful. In opposing her you risk your Eternal Soul. Return, repent and be forgiven. Or be obstinate in your defiance and face the torments of Hell alone."

"Today is the Feast Day of the Purification of the Virgin. Let it be heard and recorded that I give you, the City Council and City Officials, until Pentecost to come to me in the spirit of peace to negotiate, in good faith, a new book of statutes for the City of Hagenburg. A new book of statutes that will restore to the Bishop the powers that you have expropriated for yourselves. A new book of statutes that will repeal the Flour Tax that weighs so heavily on the poor, a new book of statutes that will enforce the powers of the Episcopal Court, whose judgements you now disdain to obey. Until Pentecost I give you, Officials of this great city."

"But. You who have, in your pride and arrogance, actively defied Hagenburg and fomented unrest against the holy sovereignty of the Bishop, you have been seen. You who have conspired with Metz, who have raised arms against the Bishop's seat to force concessions, who have locked the City Gates against the Bishop's soldiers, your names have been noted down in the holy ledgers. Come forth, kneel and show your fealty to your Bishop, or face the ban of the church and be cut off from Salvation.

"Baron Volmar von Kronthal, Knight Reichard von Zabern, Baron Lanzelin von Rappoltstein, Councillor Niklaus Zorn, Councillor Michael Müllenheim, unless you now come forward and pledge your loyalty, I place you henceforth under the ban of the Church!"

We look at each other like schoolboys, smirking like fools. Can this be true? Can this be true?

Above us, the funeral bell begins to knell, heralding the death of our eternal souls. Oh Jesus and Mary, can this be true?

At the pulpit, at the High Lectern, the Bishop intones again, "I place you under the ban of the Church," and his hands reach for the heavy, gem-encrusted Holy Bible, and close it firmly shut, as a drummer begins to drum. Boom boom boom, echoing throughout the stones. The Book of Life is closed to us. Oh Jesus and Mary, can this be true?

The chaplains wave their long white sleeves above the banks of candles, and, as if in one breath, they all go out. The Rood Screen hulks in the darkness and we are cut off from the Light of the World. Oh Lord in Heaven, can this be true?

The Bishop descends the stairs, carrying the Crucifix. The bell knells long and slow, the drum beats its funereal boom . . . Bishop Kolzeck chants once again, "Baron Volmar von Kronthal, Knight Reichard von Zabern, Baron Lanzelin von Rappoltstein, Councillor Niklaus Zorn, Councillor Michael Müllenheim, I place you under the ban of the Church!" And the crucifix plunges onto the cold stone floor, clanging like the mighty strike of a blacksmith's hammer.

PENTECOST
(ANNO 1261. GRETE GERBER IV)

I've been told they came up here from Italy. It's like a chain: every new place they come to they find new members, and some old members drop off and go back home, their penance done. But every one of them must at least stay thirty-three and a half days: one day for every year of Christ's short life.

For nearly two weeks now they've been camped outside the Basel Gate, about a hundred of them, and twice a day, at Terce and None, they scourge themselves. It's quite a sight, and I should think everyone in Hagenburg and the surrounding villages has come to see them, at least once. They strip to the waist, and then with knotted ropes and hooked chains, flay their own backs and shoulders bloody. And they cry, like a murder of crows, *Repent ye, for the Kingdom of God is at hand!*

Every second day they leave their camp and process through the Hagenburg streets, scourging themselves as they go, singing their dirge-like songs, screaming, weeping real tears and shedding real blood, and, gathered in the Cathedral Square, they perform strange spectacles of sin and repentance. A man and a woman act out the adulterous Lust that brought them into Sin, an old man mimes how he murdered his neighbour so as to steal his land, a boy of fifteen, shoulders flayed to shreds, flits through the crowd, showing how he cut purses and picked pockets before he embraced the Cross.

And then, throwing themselves into the dust, covering

themselves in dirt, they chant and scream: *Do not fight, brothers and sisters! Love each other! Do not divide! Unite! Repent! The last days are coming! Let there be Peace!*

Even though their Show makes the hairs stand up on the back of your neck, their call for Peace hasn't worked here. Not at all. Pentecost has just come and gone, and the Bishop's threats have worked for nothing. No reconciliation, no processions of humble, repentant City Councillors crawling on their knees to the Bishop's Palace to renegotiate a new Book of Statutes. Oh no.

On Pentecost the Bishop took to the pulpit and, quaking with anger, cried that no less a personage than the late Emperor Friedrich himself had confirmed the right of the Bishop to choose his own City Council; a right long since forgotten in the greed of the times, where everyone in office merely takes what he can and enriches himself. The City of Hagenburg, he cried, was now a trough of silver where fat swine come to swill, and the farrow of the poor feed on scraps and starve.

I was there myself, with the other Guild Masters. What is there to say? It's not that he's wrong: the Ministerial Families have stuffed their fat behinds into the seats of office, them and their clan crowding the council and all public positions where a shilling is to be skimmed, it's true.

But what of the Canons and the Noble Families who own the land and whose sons fill the Cathedral Chapter, squatting over their tithes and benefices, over their golden prebends, their rents and tolls, sucking up all the fat of the land?

The Bishop forgets to mention them, doesn't he?

The only difference is . . . the City Families, the Mint Master and the Tollmaster and the Tax Collector and the Burgrave, all the City Councillors and Officials, they actually *talk* with the likes of us, Guild Masters and Artisans, Merchants and Factors.

But the Bishop and the Canons and the Nobles? They treat us like dirt.

So we Guild Masters know whose Side we're on. And it's not the Bishop's. And for all his talk of the little farrow, the starving piglets of the City's Poor, and for all his talk of cutting taxes to suckle them up to his big fat udders, the Poor know this too:

Better a City Family Pig than a Noble Snake.

And in the Cathedral, at his pulpit, despite the Canons who crowd the choir applauding at his back, he can feel it, the Bishop. He can feel his shouted words falling into a big, black well, falling and falling . . . into cold silence.

And so, screeching with pique like a spurned little girl, he— can one believe it?—excommunicated the entire City. With some chanted Latin, with the Bible, the bell and the candle, with a pergament he waved at us, bearing the Seal of the Pope Himself, he cut us all off from Salvation . . . and condemned all of our souls, all thirty, forty thousand of us, to unshriven Hell.

And then he turned on his heel, marched out of the door, mounted his horse from the southern steps, and galloped off with his liegemen through the Vogesen Gate.

Well, that got rid of him for a while, I suppose.

† † †

But what this means, whatever those Scourgers may plead for, rolling in the dust and begging for Reconciliation . . . is War. We all know it. Both sides are sharpening their swords, polishing their armour, and signing up men, swearing allegiances, buying allies, hiring mercenaries. Getting ready for the fight to come.

I'll play my part, I'll do what I can. I'll do everything in my power to force this bastard Bishop to his knees.

† † †

But it's like trying to turn Lead into Gold. He's not giving way. "Yudl! Remember Schwanenstein! That was a big risk too. Baron Volmar is ready again. His allies and friends are ready. An army of more than a thousand men. They're taken care of. They'll pay their own way. And the arms we needed have been bought; I've seen to that. Just we need more coin, a lot of it, NOW. To turn Rudolf von Habsburg over to our side."

"And why's he worth so much?"

"He's a great military leader, ambitious, strong. He's fought and married his way into a *lot* of land, haven't you heard?"

"I've heard."

"He has several hundred experienced fighting men. And he's argued with the Bishop and he's ripe for turning over to our side. With him, victory is assured."

"Victory is never assured, Mistress Grete. And the Baron von Kronthal? Why can't the Baron lay down his own coin?"

My hand thumps the table top. "He hasn't any left."

"He's worth thousands."

"You're right, but it's all in land. Owned in common with his wife. They're not speaking."

"How sad."

"And he can't sell now, the price would be low and it would take too much time, and—"

"Where's Emmerich when the Baron needs him? I remember him advising the Baron to have plenty of coin in times of war."

"Yes, where *is* Emmerich Schäffer, the Director of your Company, Yudl?"

Yudl sits there at his huge desk where Emmle used to sit. His eyes squint, his body twitches, uncomfortable with the pressure I'm bringing to bear. He must be but twenty-nine summers, just a bit older than my Manfredle, and the richest

Commoner in Hagenburg, the owner of the "Rosheimer Fortune." He slides his black cap over his tousled fair hair, smiles a thin smile. "He prefers to be a silent partner of late."

"Do you know where he is?"

Yudl doesn't answer, his face unmoving, blank, revealing nothing.

I fix his grey, black-ringed, cat-like eyes. "And if we heard he was dead?"

He looks pale, unsettled. "Have you?"

"No. But what if?"

Yudl tries to hide his nervousness, smiles and shrugs. Then he starts laughing, and gets up to pour us some water.

The name on all his company's legal records, on his Books of Account, is "Emmerich Schäffer," the Christian face of the enterprise, now a half-forgotten ghost.

Yudl hands me a cup of water. I sniff at it. "Which well is this from?"

"From the Judengasse. I had it drawn this morning."

"Is the Judengasse well clean?"

"It is the only one we Jews haven't poisoned."

"Ha ha." I drink. It seems sweet enough.

Yudl sits down again, touches the tips of his fingers together like Emmerich used to do: these annoying gestures transmit themselves from person to person like a pestilence. "Mistress Gerber," he says. "Gladly would I invest, once more, in a military campaign against a bandit or pirate . . . "

"The Bishop IS a Pirate!"

He looks at me steadily, calmly. "But not against a Bishop, Grete. If the word comes out that the Jews are funding a war against a Bishop, then, I swear to you, my People are finished. From the Alps to the Baltic you will be throwing us in the rivers to 'baptise' us, and burning and hanging us. Don't ask me again. I will never fund your campaign."

† † †

One day, four years ago now, I was in the shop front of our house in the Müllergass, arguing with a Draper from Cologne who claimed we had copied and stolen his patterns on our last range of fabrics (I would say we were "inspired by" his work, but that's beside the point) when a sunburned man in a broad-brimmed hat called through the open shutters, "Is this the residence of Mistress Grete Gerber?"

"It is," I said, grateful for the interruption.

The tall, mysterious man stepped in from the street and looked at me with a grave, pious expression, and said, "Forgive me, madam, I am the bearer of bad news. Your brother passed away last year. In Constantinople."

In shock, I am unable to ask the question, "Which brother?" The man, seeing my consternation, nodded gently and said, "I am told his suffering was short. He wanted you to have these, which I have from the hands of a Greek trader in Venice. I have brought them with me on my travels."

A bundle, loosely tied in string. He unravels it to reveal . . . a stonemason's chisel, a wedding ring, a small carving in oak of an angel, holding a heart . . .

Tears crowd my eyes. Suddenly I am keening, sobbing, gasping for air as I sink to the stool beside me. At first my grief is all too real, but then, sensing the discomfort of the Draper of Cologne standing beside me, I play it for all it's worth.

It has the desired effect: the Draper of Cologne, realising his moment for complaint and compensation has passed, dons his hat, bows, and retreats into the street.

† † †

I slam the door of Schäffer and Associates. Outside, Rosamunda and Mayenz Manfred are waiting. They can see from my face that it didn't go well. But my mind is made up. It is time now for Emmerich to join his better brother. It is time for Emmerich to die.

"Let's go and see the Lawyer. Right away."

We set off towards the Cathedral Square and the Schriwerstublgass. Rosamunda and Mayenz Manfred look at me. "You've gone pale, Gretele," says Rosamunda. "Have you seen a ghost?"

Lord knows I have done bad things in my Life. I have lied, I have cheated. And the Pavilion? That was theft. And throwing Elise out to the meagre mercy of the Streets? That was cruel.

But this? What I am now considering? If it has the stamp of Statute upon it, does that take away its Evil? Does the Judge's Seal deflect the damnation of my Eternal Soul? When I stand before God, can I invoke the Hagenburg Book of Law?

It's as if Rosamunda knows what I'm thinking; her hand reaches out and holds my shoulder. Trying to give me courage.

Thank the Lord for these two companions. Rosamunda's bastard Manfred, the rascal, has more of his Father in him than my boy. And old Rosamunda turned out to be good company, once I got to know her. She told me everything, how my Manfred paid her to move to Mayenz once she got pregnant, how he organised her a paper marriage to keep the Church off her back and sent her eight shillings monthly to keep her quiet.

It was she who gave Manfred's name to the Inquisitors, back in Year of Our Lord 1232. I was shocked when she confessed it, but then it's true that Manfred had just knocked her up and thrown her over for a little country maid called Grete. I understand: I would be ready to commit a sin if he'd done the same to me.

But then she tells me, Manfred, one of the times he was staying with her in Mayenz, on one of his "business journeys" down the Rhine, got drunk and told her that he himself had given Names. When they were pushing him hard, threatening to burn him and his father, he'd given up the names of all his rivals in the boat trade. Wolfram, Michael of Müllhausen, Kärten, even old Günther.

Günther confessed and was humiliated and shaved. Peters and Kärten were burned. Wolfram fled Hagenburg for two years. And Manfred, God preserve his black soul, doubled the size of his business.

Is a Sin a Sin when it leads to Good? That's what I'm asking myself, as the three of us walk together to the Lawyer's office. What Manfred did, that was just for his profit, and that's a Sin, pure and simple, what he did. A Sin.

But what if a Sin leads to the Good of Everyone?

To do Good, don't you sometimes have to do Evil first?

† † †

It's the Thursday after Pentecost and since the Bishop stormed out of the town gates four days ago, there hasn't been a cloud in sight. The Lawyers' bureaux are hot as ovens, and as I sit down on the clients' bench, a flush comes over me like I've never had before. Sweat drenches me, my eyes flutter, it's all I can do not to keel over and drop to the floor like a drunken carter.

"Grete, you're red as a peony!" screeches Rosamunda, and calls out for a cup of beer. Mayenz Manfred pulls open the shutters. A draught of hot foul air sucks inwards, slamming the doors of the building shut like prison gates.

When the door to Magistrate Vergersheim's office is opened, I am leaning out of the window, Rosamunda is fanning me with a flat wooden dustpan like a madwoman, my under-shirt and petticoat are drenched through and I'm still pink as pickled beetroot. And who should be walking out of the Magistrate's office, but Count Rutger von Moder and his sister the Baroness von Kronthal! And me with my face looking like shredded red cabbage! For shame.

I do my best to curtsey and put my wimple to rights, but the Great Nobilities sail past me as if I were a pins-and-buttons lady. I wonder what business the likes of them have in a law office, but I suppose everyone needs to waste their money on lawyers these days.

"So, Mistress Gerber, you've decided to go through with it?" asks Vergersheim, from his doorway.

"Your assistants should have warned me you had Nobility in there. I would have powdered my face."

He laughs, ushers me in and waves his hand over a roll of parchment lying on his desk. "It's all ready, madam. It just needs your signature, and then the seal of the Judge, a formality."

"Are you sure?"

"The Law is clear, madam. Seven years is all that's needed, seven years. And no word has been heard, no sight seen, of your brother Emmerich since the Year of Our Lord twelve hundred and forty-eight. A good, round Devil's Dozen of years. So, Mistress Gerber, if you will excuse the expression, your brother Emmerich is *legally* dead. His estate falls to his next male kin, which is Rettich. And Rettich, upon leaving on his pilgrimage, signed control of his estate to You." And here he holds up the yellowed pergament that I, in the spirit of sisterly care, had, all those years ago, persuaded Rettich to sign.

The Magistrate looks at me. Probably he sees what a state I am in, and smiles kindly. "Sign, madam. And tomorrow the City Bailiffs will distrain those goods and chattels that belong, legally, to you."

"Can you . . . arrange to . . . distrain them. On Monday?"

Vergersheim looks at me, awaiting an explanation.

I can feel a large pearl of sweat gathering on my eyebrow. I wipe it away, brusquely, waving away evil thoughts. "Just to let him . . . have one more quiet . . . happy, what do they call it, Sabbath? With his family? Before . . . "

Vergersheim laughs. "You have become quite sentimental."

"I do this with a heavy heart."

"Then go and repent. Go and visit the Scourgers outside the gates. It's all the fashion."

He laughs again, and unrolls the parchment, facing towards me, for me to sign.

"Quill and ink are here on the table, madam."

I rise, slowly. But even so, my head is dizzy. To steady myself as I reach for the quill, I turn to practicalities. "How much will I owe you, Magistrate?"

I dip the quill in the rich, black ink.

Magistrate Vergersheim's long-nailed finger taps on the parchment, where a Cross marks the place I am meant to sign. "Oh, nothing, madam. In this case, the commission we take from the estate will be quite sufficient."

NINEVEH
(ANNO 5021. YUDL BEN YITZHAK ROSHEIMER VII)

A ll the clerics are leaving the City."—"What? All of them?"

Yudl stands, his face frozen in an expression of surprise, before the locked door of Schäffer and Associates. Elbertus, his young and hefty assistant, ruefully shakes his head at the state of the world. "All of them. I've just come down from the city walls. Go and look if you like, Herr Rosheimer. They're all leaving; priests, monks, nuns. They're locking the churches and monastery gates and leaving. At the Bishop's orders."

Yudl takes the heavy key from its chain around his neck. Unlocks the door. "Tell me what this means, Elbertus."

They walk up the stairs together to Yudl's bureau on the upper floor. Elbertus opens the shutters, letting the light in through the windows of fine glass. "The excommunication of the city was no idle threat. Now there will be no one to take confession of the dying, no one to bless a marriage, no one to baptise a child. Pardon the expression, but he's sending the whole city to Hell."

Yudl sits in his chair, leans back. "Elbertus, between them all, the clerics and their institutions spend a lot of money here. If they're really all leaving, and leaving for a long time, then that's half of Hagenburg's daily trade just . . . pff!" and with his fingers he mimes the snuffing out of a candle.

Yudl looks at Elbertus and sees that the young man's eyes are now closed in reflection. "Herr Rosheimer, it seems you were wise to sell most of your assets and buy up in Florentine gold."

✡ ✡ ✡

The more Pious, like his Father of blessed memory, called such things "Goyyim matters" and showed disinterest, turned away, retreated behind the closed door of the beth midrash. But Yudl can't resist. It's not every day you can see all the clerics leaving the city.

On the Vogesengass, he is one of hundreds who have come to see the strange procession. They pass in silence, a covey of Franciscan monks, their belongings piled on handcarts pushed by lay brethren, their stern faces shadowed in their hanging hoods.

A few wags shout out catcalls; "Good Riddance!", "And don't come back!" "Who needs you anyway?", but most watch in tight-lipped unease as the guardians of their salvation proceed out of the city gates, heading for monasteries and abbeys in the Rhine Plain and the Vogesen Hills.

Yudl leaves the mournful parade and retreats to the shade of the linden tree by the Sankt Petrus well. He takes from his purse the letter from Kalisz, a letter that always brings a smile to his face.

Judah Rosheimer, onorabl kuzzin, jenerus patron in this our voyage.

We got lost.

We kuddent find Prag like you told us, kuzzin. Evil tungs gave us fals cownsil and we got lost. Forgiv us it is so long before we wrote but we was in Saxony. A green land of many trees and fat cowz and abundans. A misterius mountain roze from the plen, and we followed that and then cross the Saxon plen a city of Brezlow and then on after that we agen found the way. As other Jews were kommin on the way.

But we are now here in a villij of Kalisz and all is well. Here we are now two hundred Jews and mor are kommin every day.

The eart is rich the river is full of fisch like the man he said and the Duke is jenerus. We havent seen him yet.

The pezants are fat eat sossij and have pigs and cows. We buy the old cows and make our leather. Trade is good. We are building a beth midrash to the glorie of G-d. The other Jews speak funny German and eat strange foods. The pezants speak Slavnik. We need a proppa Rabbi becus this one he is not good.

Komm Yudl and all will be well and we will be yoonited in G-d. It is not the land of milk and hunny but it is good. Better than Rosheim we rekkun.

In memry of our frends and famly, may the Lord bless this epissl and its voyage to your hands, onarabl kuzzin Judah,

Danl, your kuzzin, now in Kalisz

A small crowd has gathered outside the locked gates of the Franciscan Friary. The Scourgers, that group of penitents who flagellate themselves into ecstasy in the fields beyond the Basel Gate, walk in circles in the shade of the two plane trees that shadow the monastery walls.

"Hagenburg, woe upon thee!" shouts their leader, with froth-flecked lips. "Be like unto Nineveh! Clothe yourselves in sackcloth and ashes, kneel in penitence, and escape the Wrath of the Lord!"

✡ ✡ ✡

Yudl walks across the Pfennigplatz, stumbling. Even here, in the centre of Hagenburg's mercantile wealth, the lopsided cobbles and broken flagstones need urgent repair. Looking down on him, the fine Town House of the Müllenheims, with its three storeys of purplish Kronthal stone. The *Zur Münze* Inn, marked with a sign depicting three golden coins, where the patricians of the City Mint drink and conspire.

The Guards at the Counting House doorway hold up their

halberds, blocking Yudl's way. One of them opens the door and calls inside, "Rosheimer's here!"

Yudl frowns, squints in the sun. *What's this?*

Münzmeister Müllenheim appears in the shadow of the doorway. He won't look Yudl in the eye.

Something's wrong.

"What do you want, Herr Rosheimer?"—"I want to my strongbox. I need some coin."

Müllenheim winces. "Then you've not heard."

"Heard what? Let me inside!"

Müllenheim shrugs, and nods to the halberdsmen, who withdraw their weapons.

Inside, the lamp hangs low above the Counting Table, and upon the table lies Yudl's strongbox, lacquered, brass-buckled, and painted with the arms of Rosheim and the words of Proverbs. Surrounding the strongbox, leaning over the table, the two other Mint Masters; Wikerus the Younger and Johann Zorn. And two armed men. Bailiffs.

The men are all poring over a long vellum scroll. Their eyes glint in the lamplight, like demons examining a freshly-damned soul.

A lump rises in Yudl's throat.

"My strongbox? What is this?"

Müllenheim sighs. "Herr Rosheimer. It is being distrained."

"*Distrained?*"

"Here, look." And he reaches out to hand Yudl the scroll.

By the Power vested in me by His Grace the Bishop of Hagenburg, I, Judge Arnim Doroltzheimer, do declare:

† The citizen of Hagenburg, Emmerich Schäffer, born Year of Our Lord 1215 in Lenzenbach, last known residence Haus Zum Schwarzen Stein, Langer Weg, last seen in Hagenburg in the Year of Our Lord 1248, is, for reason of his prolonged

absence from the city and in the want of any Signs of Life,
herewith declared, for the purposes of his estate, legally
deceased.

† According to the documents duly received, registered and
below listed, the inheritor of his estate is recognised as his sis-
ter, Grete Gerber née Schäffer, born Year of Our Lord 1216 in
Lenzenbach, resident in Hagenburg, Haus Gerber, Müllergass.

† Therefore the assets, property, chattels and coin of the
concern "Schäffer and Associates," owned and directed by the
abovementioned late Emmerich Schäffer, hereby and forthwith
are transferred to the ownership of his inheritor, Grete Gerber.

† In accordance with the wishes of the inheritor, Grete
Gerber, the concern "Schäffer and Associates" is to be liquidated
forthwith and all assets both within the office premises and
stored within the Counting House rendered to her with imme-
diate effect.

The document continues, but Yudl can read no more. The
armed men are standing, walking towards him with measured
step.

"He keeps his keys around his neck, on a chain," says
Müllenheimer, softly.

Yudl cannot move, he is paralysed, as the Bailiffs of the Court
of Hagenburg pull his keys over his head.

He looks, stammering, at Müllenheim, at Wikerus, at Zorn.
"You must stop this! Aren't you my friends? My colleagues? My
brothers in trade?"

The Masters of the Mint cannot meet his eye. They look
down at the table, at their folded hands.

"But what can we do, Herr Rosheimer?" says Müllenheim.
"It is the Law."

QUILL, INK AND PARCHMENT
(ANNO 1261. BARON VOLMAR VON KRONTHAL VI)

This is too easy. Von Kolzeck hasn't even left a proper standing garrison, just some cooks and servants, ostlers and valets, half a dozen men at arms. When they see we have a battering ram and mean to use it, they open up the castle gates.

We give them a short time to pack their belongings together. Soon they scuttle out under the raised portcullis, sacks stuffed with poultry and game plundered from the kitchen larder.

They scurry down the hill towards the distant city walls. It's late afternoon; they'll be in Hagenburg by sundown.

But Haldenheim Castle is now ours.

We ride in and loot what's left; plenty of episcopal silver, fine wine, spices, a good pound of black pepper, a jewel-studded Bible worth some hundred marks. I take the Bible. My men call to me to open it at random and see what my Fate will be. The thing weighs some twenty pounds so I wrestle it down onto the cobbles, strike it open and point my finger.

Nunc igitur, ego Nabuchodonosor laudo, et magnifico, et glorifico regem cæli, quia omnia opera ejus vera, et viæ ejus judicia, et gradientes in superbia potest humiliare.

Something about What's-His-Name praising the King of Heaven, God humbling the proud. Well, make of that what you will. It doesn't mean much to me. "Who was Nabbuchoddonozza?" I ask.

"King of Babylon!" says Reichard von Zabern. He had a proper education.

"What did he do?"

"He lived a thousand years."

"Well, that's promising. What else?"

"I'll ask Great Uncle Eugenius."

"Don't bother."

Finished with looting and fortune-telling, we drag the battering ram through the gates and use it to knock some big holes in the crenellations and stone defences. And then our carts of firewood trundle up to the gate.

It's dark by the time we've finished unloading the wood and stacking it around the inner buildings. It's a shame, really. Quite a pretty castle, and the country stronghold of the Bishops of Hagenburg for generations. But it stands above the winding waters of the Ehle, the Mayenz-Hagenburg pilgrims' road and the Hagenburg plain. It guards the City and the surrounding fields and vineyards. And so it has to burn.

We gather at a vineyard farmstead below the castle knoll as my men set the fires. The nervous owner brings us stoups of his last-year's wine. He's worried that his vines will catch fire, can't stop hiccupping, making "aaiiii" noises and pleading, "Please be careful, My Lord, please be careful!"

As the castle goes up in flames, I can't blame him. It's a terrifying sight; a fire that reaches high into the sky, lighting the vineyards around us a flickering, infernal orange.

It's a bloody fine spectacle.

† † †

Since that draper woman Grete Gerber got her hands on the Jews' fortune, the game has changed. We packed her fine new hefty strongbox covered with Jewish writing onto the back of a mule and marched it under heavy guard over to the Albrechtstal where Rudolf von Habsburg was holed up.

We settled on five hundred marks to bring Habsburg over

to our side. Not that I was involved in the negotiations; we left it to Mistress Gerber, Councillor Zorn and von Habsburg's clerk to strike out the deal. Count Rudolf and I spent the time riding round the Albrechtstal, hunting and frightening the local milkmaids.

The Gerber woman struck a hard deal for her hard coin; a fair share of the spoils if the war ends in our favour. That's the new Way of the World. We'll do all the fighting, and she with her Jewish gold will make off with a friar's slice of the takings.

Signing up with von Habsburg was a wise move, but it didn't have the desired effect, at least not to begin with. Bishop von Kolzeck panicked when he heard the news, disbanded his men home to their estates, and went himself into hiding, presumably to look for new allies.

We considered forming an army and riding after some of his closest supporters, such as the von Lichtenbergs and the von Tecks, and engaging with them one by one . . . but this would only wear us down and leave us open to surprise attack as we roved up and down the roads of Alsace and the Aargau. The truth is, until both sides have a proper army in the field and in the same part of the country, this war is not going to start, let alone come to an end. And when's that going to happen?

When you read the poems and the books of Chivalry, it's as if we Knights all meet in the field of honour by some kind of gentlemanly prearrangement, and the most virtuous and handsome side wins. But the reality is all just Politics. Meetings, sworn vows and deals, buying alliances, forging partnerships, pledging spoils and advancement. And both sides are doing it, and both sides are hedging and hawing, tinkering with the details of their coalition, dragging it out, postponing that time when, and come it must, we all face each other in the Field and hack at each other with sword and spear.

Look at von Habsburg, the sly fox. As soon as he changed sides he started going round the towns, meeting local dignitaries, striking deals, looking to expand his territories and make out of our victory a spur for the fortunes of the House of Habsburg. Anyone who stands in his way, like the town of Müllhausen, whose Mayor called him a "traitor," he goes and beats them until they change their mind. He's besieging Müllhausen now, whilst I'm stuck here, doing the donkey work, chasing the Bishop's liegemen out of their properties near Hagenburg and burning down the Bishop's castle. Making a safe area around the City where we can engage the Enemy when the time is right.

Von Habsburg has a bevy of clerks in his entourage: advisers, counsellors, scribblers. Not me. Since that snake Emmerich Schäffer tricked and robbed me, I've been doing my own dirty work. But in these modern times, if you want to do anything, you need quill, ink and parchment. That much I learned from that bastard Schäffer.

I have to do it. There's a lot at stake in this coming war. When I defeated von Schwanenstein I ended up with most of the plain of Illingen as victor's spoils. And if I defeat von Kolzeck, even greater booty is in my sights. The Prinzbach silver mines.

And so the next day, after inspecting the charred ruins of Haldenheim, I ride into town for a consultation in the Court Offices with the pen-pusher Magistrate Vergersheim. They say he's the best lawyer in Hagenburg.

Since the Excommunication, the City is tense and fractious like a drunken dockside tavern just before a fight breaks out. As I ride my way to the Schriwerstublgass a crowd gathers behind my Ashkelon's haunches, cheering me on my way. "Go and beat that Bishop of ours and drag him back here in chains, My Lord!" "Beat that bastard Bishop like a dog and bring him to heel!" And one bitter man calls out from a tavern doorway; "You Noble Lords! Go and fight it out now before we all die of hunger!"

It wasn't so long ago that I thought I could spend my life carousing and living off the fat of my estates. But now I'm on my way to see some ink-stained lawyer, and the world and his wife are looking to Me to lift the Bishop's curse.

† † †

In Vergersheim's bureau, I shift in my seat and try and tell him what's bothering me, keeping me awake at night. But he looks at me like I'm not making any sense. I'm not surprised. None of this gibberish comes naturally to me. "What I want to know is . . . What did Schäffer call them? My *assets*. Who owns them. I mean. If I die. Who . . . ?"

Vergersheim smiles. Thin-lipped, pale. Like his skin has never seen the sunlight. "You mean, My Lord, you have concerns about your succession?"

"Yes."

"You and the Baroness have no offspring, am I right?"

"You are right. But I have a nephew. A decent von Kronthal Knight."

"The Baroness has a Brother. Count Rutger von Moder."

"She does."

"And his nobility trumps that of your nephew."

"Don't tell me that bastard von Moder will inherit everything?"

"Nearly half of your estate came to you in marriage. The von Moders have a claim to all if your marriage is issueless."

Not that this is News to me. But when this Troglodyte says it, it feels somehow more irritating, more real. Before, when I just had the ancestral and dowry lands, it was all much of a muchness to me. But now that I also have most of the old Schwanenstein estate, plus Prinzbach and other spoils of war in my sights, it feels too much to let slip away . . .

When I mention Prinzbach, the Magistrate is overcome

with delight like a muzzled truffle pig sniffing its prize. "Oh, the Prinzbach mines! Well, wouldn't that be quite something, My Lord!" But then he fidgets. "Excuse the *impertinens* . . . but is your wife the Baroness still . . . *menstruans*?"

I have no idea what he is talking about.

He squirms. "Is she still womanly . . . fertile?"

Oh, I see. "No. And I haven't touched her in years."

"Then we can expect . . . well . . . no future issue . . . from the marriage?"

"No we bloody can't. Ever since she dried up, they've salted her away in Castle Moder like some barrel of pork."

"Protecting their investment, I see."

"Yes, and I can't blame them. When she lived with me, she was always ailing. It's a sin I know, but I did hope she would kilter over and croak. But in Castle Moder I hear she is in the bloom of health. They've been fattening her up like a veal calf."

Vergersheim curls and contorts like some damned cat trying to lick its backside. He squeaks. "My Lord, may we speak frankly and openly, *inter nos*?"

"Yes, just speak plain German with me."

"Yes, My Lord. Have you any bastards?"

Well, I asked for it. I control the urge to strike him across the face.

"Children conceived outside of your marriage to the Baroness?"

"I know what bastards are. Three I know about."

"Male?"

"Just one. Tybolt."

"Age? Status?"

"He is some seventeen summers now, I suppose. I haven't seen him for a few years. But he's a fine lad. Has had a decent education, in the household of a knight of Lorraine."

"Well, this is promising. Would you ever consider him worthy as your heir?"

It's my turn to go pale. "His mother is . . . was . . . a bloody handmaiden! A chambermaid!"

"And yet he is your only direct male heir. Would you consider it?"

"How can you . . . ? Can you . . . legally . . . make him . . . ?"

"Not I, Baron. That does not lie within my meagre powers." Vergersheim offers his thin-lipped smile, blinking like a lizard in sudden sunlight. "The Pope has such authority, and no one else."

"The Pope . . . ?"

"There are precedents, My Lord. It can be done. It is . . . *very* expensive and sometimes difficult to petition the Pope to annul a noble marriage and legitimise another . . . illicit relation. But it has been done before."

"How?"

"We would write a petition. We would need the support of a higher cleric. An Abbot, a Bishop. Then it is a matter of paying the clerks in the Papal Court . . . "

"Counsellor Vergersheim. If there is one thing that is *certain* to provoke the von Moders, then to disinherit them in this way would be it, no?"

"Yes, it is a challenge indeed! They would maybe need to be . . . well remunerated."

"And the mother? Of the boy?"

"Of course you would need to marry her. Is that a problem?"

"*Marry?* She's dead!"

"On paper, Baron. Just on paper."

On paper. Baroness Elise von Kronthal, the late chambermaid daughter of a heretic weaver, my lawful wife. But just on paper.

Kunigund von Moder, a whore who illegitimately shared my name and Castle Kronthal bed for twenty years. But just on paper.

And fine, young Tybolt, son of noble, lawful blood. By a few strokes of the pen and ink, a von Kronthal for ever. Heir to my fortune.

Vergersheim is smiling at me, and I don't like it. I have the feeling that even his smile is expensive. "My Lord, can I offer my services to you? I would be delighted. I already have some experience with dealing with nobility," he trumpets, whilst hypocritically affecting modesty, averting his humble eyes, fidgeting with his ink-stained hands. "I do have other noble families on my . . . client list."

"Not the bloody von Moders, I hope?"

His face winces and jerks like a grouse caught in a wire. "Oh I couldn't possibly say! Confidentiality, my Lord . . . is of vital . . . importance in my profession!"

I look at him for a while. I'm not one of his type, a wood-louse who spends his life crawling about under stones, but I think I know what all this twisting and twitching must mean. "Well, Vergersheim. You can't work for both of us, can you?"

"No . . . I . . . ," he stutters. Looks up from his hands. "You are right, My Lord. I work on a ten *per centum* commission basis, plus fees. And if you should so wish it, as of now, as God is my witness, I shall work only for you."

† † †

As I walk away from his fetid offices, I try and remember if I always detested clerks and secretaries, officials and recorders. Certainly Schäffer made me change my mind for a while. He dazzled me with all his wizardry, and I couldn't see the snake beneath the cloth of gold.

Annul my marriage and give all to young Tybolt? Can I do this?

I have to consider it.

One thing's for certain. The Staufen are all but finished in the German Lands. When this is all over there'll be one new leading family in the Alsace and the Upper Rhine.

Von Kolzeck's. Or von Habsburg's. Or mine.

INTERLUDE

ANNO
1318

VISITATIONS
(ANNO 1318. ALBRECHT KAIBACH I)

When i was young like you, my children,
i would believe anything
if you told me one can build a ladder to the moon
climb up, sit on the edge of its silver disc and look down on
the earth
i would believe you
if you told me that the cat had given birth to mice
i would run to her litter to see the miracle for myself

in short
i was a little fool

and so there was i
an apprentice in the masons' lodge at the cathedral
and the other apprentices made fun of me
they told me "the dombaumeister needs to see you"
and so i would go to his bureau and interrupt his work
and he would shout at me "what the hell are you doing
here?"

and so i was always getting into trouble
and i was always being punished

but one punishment changed my life

i was fifteen summers old

the year was written: the year of our lord twelve hundred
and sixty four
and in Hagenburg
a new Mason's Lodge was being built at the corner of
Cathedral Square
and the old one, which was then little more than a big
wooden shack
was being taken down to build a fine patrician house in its
place
for the whole of the Cathedral Square was being rebuilt

and my punishment was
to stay behind after work and after the curfew bell
and sort and clear the storage rooms
even if took all night

and so i worked
piling up old broken stools for use as firewood
old blunt broken tools to be melted down and made afresh
old parchments with faded sketches and calculations to be
rescraped as palimpsests
and i was hungry and tired and sad and wanted my supper
and my bed

but then i came to an old escritoire
a drawing desk
with broken legs
and a document chest under the writing surface
locked with a key

i searched here i searched there
but no key was to be found anywhere
and so i took a hatchet
raised it above my head

and brought it down
and broke the chest open with one great blow

and, children, what did i find?

old parchments and little packages, wrapped in cloth and
twine
a treasure
a veritable treasure!

i brought close the lantern
and untied one of the parchments
and there i found
that which would change my life

a drawing
—not such a perfect drawing, mind, in the way it was
drawn—
but an imperfect drawing of perfection itself!
the western portals and façade of the cathedral
as yet unbuilt in those days
and such beauty!
and a drawing of the Western Rose
unfinished and only half coloured
but in design, exquisite

and i opened one of the two packages wrapped in cloth
and found
nestled in with scribbled notes,
as big as the palm of my hand,
a piece of yellow glass
amber like sunlight
and a piece of blue glass
azure, deep and rich

like the blue of a summer sky on a harvest evening

and i held them up to the light of the lantern
and i looked down at the drawings
of tiers of statues
of prophets, monsters and saints
and i was filled with joy

† † †

children, at first i did not know what this treasure was, what
it could be . . .
all i knew was that it was some great and magical mystery

i searched in the escritoire, in every corner, pulling out dust
and fragments and cobwebs and dead flies
until i found one last note, mildewed and crumbling
written poorly in an uncertain hand,
which said
these be copies by an unfair hande of the greater master's
originals, now lost

and then i knew
i knew what i had found

copies
made by some apprentice or artisan
himself no draftsman, to be sure
of the work of dombaumeister von esinbach
the first ill-fated Master of the New Cathedral
who had mixed with heretics
lost his mind
and taken his own life

an unholy terror filled me

outside the Cathedral bell sounded the dead of night
the hour when ghosts walk the earth
and i alone
a boy
in the dark, abandoned lodge
with these unholy vestiges of a troubled past

praying the lord's prayer to ward off evil
i wrapped the parchments and the glass in my satchel
and
finishing my work
crept home
through the dark and empty streets

now children, you know i have a fair drawing hand
some say the fairest they have ever seen
well
even as a youngster
my greatest joy was to take quill and ink and parchment
and draw from life
a leaf, an apple, a sleeping cat

and so
when i could
i would buy parchment
and
using the copies i had found
i began to draw

for what were left to me in that old escritoire
were but fragments
a statue here, a portal there, a cornice,

as this unknown artisan had remembered them in his mind
from the wondrous design of Master Achim

this artisan would scribble beside his imperfect sketches
notes like:
these be the old proffets i think in the second teer of statu
abov the portal
and here he would draw wild old staring men
their eyes upraised to heaven, receiving visions from On High
their hands outstretched, from which flame would burst
and i would scratch my head at this wild-eyed man with the
flaming hand
and wonder
is this ezekiel? daniel? jeremiah?
this is no prophet i can recognise from holy scripture

and slowly
over the years of my companionship
i adapted what i saw
i took the spirit of the drawings
and made it mine
rendered it in my hand
and in a way that spoke to my faith in the Lord Above

out of chaos, incomplete confusion,
out of passion and inspiration and intoxication
i made order
i made a harmonious whole

† † †

The Priest has been and gone, the air is thick with incense.
Candles made from the molten wax of the Cathedral's holy
Paschal Candle burn around his bed.

He has made his Peace with God.

Sins of Anger, Arrogance and Pride he has confessed, youthful Lust, Envy of those set before him. Gluttony and Greed have tempted him, but have never consumed his soul, of Sloth there is no mention—there is not one day that God has given him in which he has not worked, studied or prayed. And no mortal sins weigh upon him; he has been faithful to his wife and to his God, has not killed, has not stolen, has not borne false witness, has honoured father and mother.

He has left a quarter of his estate to the Hospital of Saint Johannes, a quarter to the Cathedral's altar of the Frauenwerk, and a half to his two sons. His finest horse he leaves as a mortuary bequest to the Bishop. Two cows to the Convent in Finckweiler, to the Glory of blessed Saint Elizabeth of Thüringen.

In the chapel of St. John the Baptist, masses in his name are to be sung for a year of Sundays.

He is ready for Death.

His words come slower now, fainter. His grandchildren and great grandchildren gather round the bed, leaning closer.

† † †

wrapped in cloth with the yellow glass
was a note in the artisan's unpractised hand
yello glass—follow the vogesen to the lothringen border,
after border the winzbach river,
follow upstreem into the dark wood where the charcole burn-
ers burne,
ask for glassmaster harrimann

a clue, an instruction
but written some forty years ago
by esinbach's apprentice?

*

surely glassmaster harrimann will have passed away
and with him
the secrets of the yellow glass?

children, once i turned Master Stone-cutter
and my time was more my own
i set off for the lothringen border

it was autumn
and the days were drawing colder
night was falling as i walked my horse up the twisting
winzbach vale
higher and deeper into the woods
the light was fading
and i was beginning to fear that i must make my bed in leaf
and loam
when
up ahead in the dim gloaming
the red glow of fire

"god give you good evening!" i called out
and heard nothing but the cawing of crows gathering in the
tree tops

and i walked on
until i saw
a clearing
and a huge mound of smoking turf
under which a glowing fire was burning

upstreem to where the charcole burners burne!
just like the note had said

i called out again
until, from a small hut, unseen in the gloom of the nearby forest
a man emerged and gave me good evening

"i am looking for harrimann the glass maker" i said
and the man said "i am he"

i looked closely, but this man could not be more than thirty summers old!
"are you sure?" i asked
"i know who i am," quoth he, "but who are you, sir?"

"i come from the Cathedral of Hagenburg" i said
and held out the yellow glass
and children!
the man broke out into joyful laughter and clasped my shoulders in his big rough hands

he said "i am Harrimann like my father and grandfathers before me!
And my father Harrimann told me about the gentlemen from the Cathedral
and the yellow glass
and told me the secret of its making

we have been waiting for you, Sir, for some forty years!"

i smiled and said
"until the Western Rose of the Cathedral is ready to receive your yellow glass,
you will be waiting forty years more!
we have not yet even finished the Nave . . . "

and so, with tears of joy and laughter in our eyes
we sat down in his hut,
and ate a hearty meal of rabbit and mushroom stew

and that is how
children
the sun-yellow glass for the Rose was found

† † †

Achim von Esinbach, Renard Durand, Werlinus von Nordhausen, Konrad Illmann, Albrecht Kaibach, a chain of hands. In place of crown and crozier, they bear set-square and chisel, their brows are not anointed with Holy Oil but with mortar and dust.

In turn they accept the task accorded them, to build the Temple, a place where harmony and order hold temporary reign over the unruly earth.

Albrecht Kaibach's hands are like maps of the world, veined and furrowed, roughened by stone. He folds them over his heart and waits for Death or, if the Lord should grant it, one more day on earth.

The children have now gone, the room is silent. From outside, like the whispering of attending angels, the sound of the ever-falling rain.

ANNO
1262

Moneylenders' Lane
(anno 5022. Yudl ben Yitzhak Rosheimer VIII)

He used to be a tailor. He used to sell silks by the yard, sew tunics, embellish with ribbon and gold piping the garments of noble ladies. His fine shop in the Schneidergass proffered arrays of colour and the scent of cloves, the bolts of silk and samples of ribbon cascaded from the shelves like a peacock's tail unfurled.

And then Hagenburg's Guild of Tailors was formed. And only members of the Guild might work as Tailors, and Jews might not be members of the Guild.

And now Mannekint, an old man, sits huddled in tattered fur and sackcloth in the gloom of Moneylenders' Lane.

"This is no life for you, Yudl," he says, blowing into his old, frozen hands.

Yudl looks up at the slender corridor of pale blue sky between the gables. The sun is slowly edging round, gilding the cornices in sparkling gold.

"I'm too old," says Mannekint, "to find new ways, but you are still young. Why did you send your mother away? Go and join her in Prague. Or go to Kalisz and join your cousins. Here there is nothing for you anymore."

Yudl's eyes are ringed with rheum, his face roughened by a winter spent on the Moneylenders' bench. "Why say that, Mannekint? This war is good for our business."—"And when the war is finally over? How many will be able to repay their loans?"—"That is the challenge. The trick, it seems to me," says Yudl, "is to set the interest just right. Not so low as to let them pay off the loan too quickly, and not so high as to ruin them entirely. Just to keep them . . . *just so*. In constant repayment. That is the skill of the matter." And his bitter grey eyes survey the sodden ground.

Mannekint shakes his head. "Your uncle is turning in his grave."

"Let him turn. I lost his fortune."

Yudl closes his eyes. *Naked came I out of my mother's womb and naked shall I return thither. The Lord gave and the Lord hath taken away. Blessed be the name of the Lord.* The Book of Job, his Father's favourite of the holy scriptures. Yudl has inherited his faded, ink-blotched, annotated copy. At night, in his crowded, noisy home, he tries to follow the red thread of his Father's thought, tries to follow his Father's footsteps through the maze of ink.

And his days he spends in Moneylenders' Lane. A dark, pitiful alley running between the busy Judengasse and the multitudes of Rheintorstrasse. Leaning two-storey wooden houses teem with the poor families of Jewish tinkers and hawkers, pawnshops present their melancholy displays; pots, pans, wedding rings and trinkets, dowry linen and thumb-blackened Books of Hours. And up crooked, narrow stairs, the cramped counters of the Moneylenders, where quill and ink wait ready to record the next hungry loan, the next part-payment scraped from the pittance of wages and the ever-empty housewife's purse.

As the morning wears on, the Sun glistens round the edges of the rooves, and Light creeps onto the edge of the Moneylenders' bench. Yudl, in pride of place, blinks in the weak, wintry radiance. His vitality has been drained, leeched by Care. His Home is now a weary place, crowded by two families; his and a cattle trader's, moved here from Schlettstadt, paying hard, much needed silver for the rent. His Wife, daughter of the great Kalonymus family of Mayenz, takes in washing for pennies, sews parchment scrolls in exchange for bread from the communal oven. *The beauty of Israel is slain upon the high places: how are the mighty fallen.*

"Yudl, your debtors are here." Mannekint's voice wakes him from his sunwarmed daze.

Yudl rubs his eyes, dazzled by the sun, and sees, crowned by winter's midday, Widow Krämer and her two sons, escorted by two City Bailiffs.

Widow Krämer kneels at Yudl's feet, on the broken, filthy cobbles. Her trembling hands clutch together, raise imploringly. Her exhausted eyes are red with tears. "Please, Sir, please. Mercy. I have nothing left to give you. Please, please, write off the debt. As soon as I have found work, I will pay you. I beg you, Sir, have mercy."

Yudl looks at his hands. "No, madam. I cannot. That is not how it works. Do you know why?"—"Why, Sir, why?"—"For if I write off your debt, then the word will go out that one can be in debt to Rosheimer and escape the forfeit. And then who would pay me the money they owe me? Why should they? And if no one pays me, I have no capital. And if I have no capital, I can make no more loans. And you, madam. Has my loan not kept you from the streets these last months, has it not fed your children these last weeks?"—"It has. You have saved us, Sir. Now I beg you, have mercy, have patience . . . "—"I have had patience, madam. But today the extension of the extension of the extension has played out, and I can do nothing more."

The Widow groans, a deep, animal cry of despair. Mocking, joyful sunlight brightens the tears in her eyes. "Sir, there must be something . . . "

Yudl shakes his head. She will be taken now to the Debtors' Prison in the dungeon of the Rheintor Tower. Three months, on bread and water, in the crowded dark.

She stands, her despair curdling into bile. "And my sons? Will you have them thrown to the streets?"—"The Church has

charities."—"All the monasteries and churches are closed!"—
"In Hagenburg, madam. There are other places beyond the
City Walls."—"How should they go there? They are too young
to travel alone!"

Yudl stands, turns his face towards the wall. "You should
have thought of that, madam."

She screams. A wail that harrows the eardrums. Her sons
clutch at her tattered coat as the Bailiffs close in and grab her
struggling arms. "You Devil! YOU DEVIL!" she screams at
Yudl.

A small crowd has gathered, as it always does when such
scenes are played out. Some laugh, cruel and shameless laughter. Some cast down their eyes. One man screams, "BLOOD-
SUCKING JEWS!"

And she's gone, dragged by the dogged Bailiffs, her children wailing behind her like beaten spaniels.

The crowd disperses. The spectacle ends.

The sun creeps over the beth midrash roof, and is gone.

In the darkened alley, old Mannekint shakes his silver head,
strokes his silver beard. "Look at us. Is this what we are now?"

Yudl covers his face in his hands.

He walks round the corner into the bright parade of the
Judengasse. Hawkers cry, shopkeepers perch on stools in the
brief, pale sunshine.

At the door of the beth midrash, Yudl cries: "How goodly
are thy tents O Jacob and thy tabernacles O Israel!"

Pale faces look up at him in the studious gloom, startled by
the sudden voice.

Yudl heads to his lectern at the Rabbi's right hand. Waiting
for him, propped open by two stones, a worn and faded parchment scroll. The Book of Job.

CHRIST IS RISEN
(ANNO 1262. EUGENIUS VON ZABERN VIII)

I t is not the worst Mass I have attended. When I was the Bishop's Treasurer, on my peregrinations through the more woeful districts of the Diocese, I was at times forced to attend services where the Priest hardly knew Latin and where the congregation did not know whether to kneel or stand. Once even, in a village church reeking of mould and goat tallow candles, just as the Priest held aloft the pyx, bellowing out his *hoc est corpus meum*, a sheep wandered up to the altar and richly defecated on the consecrated ground.

This High Mass, held in Hagenburg's Merchants' Church of St. Niklaus, in defiance of Bishop Walther's ban, and at which I myself officiated, was not nearly so deficient. But my singing voice is hoarse and tuneless, my officiants, Hieronymus and two beggar friars—the only other clerics that could be found in the excommunicated City—had never officiated before, the altar is unconsecrated, the Church roof not yet completed, letting in sporadic rain, and the bells and chalices were borrowed from the Town Criers and the Tavern *zur Sonne*.

Nevertheless, the nearly-completed Church was thick with incense and the perfume of the town's multitude of merchants and traders, who crammed into every available cranny in their Easter finery. And they, and here one must credit them, despite the rain, my rasping crow's voice and the improvised holy vessels, stayed in devout and respectful silence as we stumbled through the Easter Vigil liturgy.

Now the Mass is over, they tweet and chatter like the swarms of swallows that wheel at dusk above the Cathedral Square. I cannot see them, but in my mind's eye I think of a menagerie of peacocks and cockatoos, a rainbow of ostentatious silk.

And they have cause to be buoyant, a right to chirp triumphantly to St. Niklaus' half-built canopy. The war is starting to go their way.

Since the end of last year's Vintage, small armed bands on both sides of the conflict have ranged the Alsace and the Black Forest. At times they have skirmished, at times they have besieged the villages and smaller towns, but in the great main, they have merely plundered and vandalised the property of the opposing side. Vineyards, grainstores, estates have been burned up in conflagration, ransacked and despoiled.

To begin with, if truth be told, this was theft and opportunistic brigandage, and nothing more. The granaries of Hagenburg's merchants in the Rhine Harbour were brimming with the Diocese's stolen grain, the city markets inundated with pigs and cattle rustled from the Bishop's pastures; episcopal meat normally sold by statute at a premium now slaughtered in the Market Square by city butchers and sold cut-price to the cheering crowd.

On the other side, the Bishop's men have razed Baron Volmar's estates by Illingen, burned the city vintners' vines, and von Kolzeck's men, dressed duplicitously in Habsburg colours, have retaken Colmar which last year pledged itself to Rudolf von Habsburg's shield.

But slowly, Habsburg and Kronthal have rallied control over their exuberant, ill-disciplined men, over their bands of brigands and mercenaries, and have consolidated and strategised. Field by field, village by village, vineyard by vineyard, they have cleared the land around our City of the Bishop's vassals, emptied abbeys and monasteries of loyal clerics, forced the bailiffs of the Bishop's estates to change sides and pledge themselves to the City's cause.

And now, for leagues around the City, not one pennant or standard is raised in the Kolzeck colours. And the inference and challenge is clear.

If Bishop von Kolzeck wishes to be Lord of this City, he must come and take it. He must come, and come soon, in force, to the Hagenburg plain.

† † †

The Paschal candle has been lit. And from it, one by one, the congregation come with their own lamps and tapers to take flame from the Holy Light. *Christ is risen*, and the Merchants' Church is festive and bright.

"A thousand flickering flames, my Lord. A pretty sight!" whispers an awed Hieronymus in my inclined ear. "And an auspicious, Holy one, God willing," he adds, from fear. Hieronymus, however he tries, cannot shake his mortal dread that he has transgressed against the Holy See, served Mass in an excommunicated City, broken his obedience to his Bishop, and thereby, to Rome.

It is a fear with which I myself can mainly dispense. My soul's loyalty is to God, and not to any worldly Lord. And does the Creator of this magnificent Universe cavil over tavern chalices and unconsecrated altars? And does the Lord of the World uphold the edicts of the vain fool Walther von Kolzeck when he, in schoolboy pique, casts his own citizens into darkness excommunicate?

I, for one, cannot credit it.

"My Lord," Hieronymus whispers in my ear. "The worshippers. They want your blessing."

"What, all of them?"

"Yes, My Lord, I think so."

"Well I don't think so, Hieronymus. Let us leave."

Hieronymus' arm reaches out to help me to stand. Immediately a chorus of protest rings out in the nave. "Lord Canon! Don't leave! Bless us! Bless us!"

"Bless me!" calls out a loud, ringing, woman's voice.

Grete Gerber.

"Let me be the first to receive your blessing, My Lord!"

My hand, feeling its way in front of me in the darkness as we try to descend the steps from the altar, is obstructed by something soft, warm, encased in cloth. A woman's head.

The woman's hand grasps mine, and plants a kiss upon my ringed fingers. Then takes once again my hand and places it back upon her inclined forehead. "Bless me, My Lord. Bless all of us," says Grete Gerber. "It is nearly a year that we have been in the ban of the Church."

Then her voice lowers an octave and she whispers. "Thank you, My Lord Eugenius. The City will not forget this, so long as you live."

As his army crossed the Rhine at Taubensand and marched north-west towards Hagenburg, von Kolzeck was certain of victory. The position of Bishop of Hagenburg still claimed unswerving loyalty amongst the majority of the Lords of Alsace and the Upper Rhine, and his army was both more numerous and more experienced in warfare than that of his opponents. The Bishop's army comprised a greater number of horsemen, a greater number of heavy-armoured knights and a greater number of professional soldiers and mercenaries. The City army, in contrast, was made up of von Kronthal and von Habsburg's core troops—admittedly experienced and effective warriors—plus some rather diffident and opportunistic mercenaries, and, making up nearly half the host, mere citizens of Hagenburg called to the fray by the bells of the city, poorly armed with a medley of weapons more suitable for farming, tanning and animal husbandry than for warfare.

The morning of the battle was bright and sunny. Von Habsburg and von Kronthal had taken position on the gentle slope that rises beside the village of Wolfsbergen, a hamlet of some twenty houses a short ride from the city walls.

Bishop von Kolzeck, seeing that the opposing side seemed unwilling to leave its position, and judging that the very modest hillock on which they were ranged offered no real advantage to the enemy, gave a brief, spurring speech, and ordered the attack.

His knights and cavalry charged. It was a fearsome sight at which many of the Hagenburgers baulked and fled. Sensing victory, the Bishop's liegemen, comprising the flower of chivalry and knighthood of the Alsace, charged on towards the crest of the small hillock on which the main unit of von Habsburg and von Kronthal's troops was gathered. Here, fierce fighting was engaged, with the Bishop's army gaining the upper hand.

What happened next is frightful to relate. Von Habsburg, knowing the comparative weakness of his army against the Bishop's, had hit upon a lowly and unchivalrous strategy to weigh the odds in his favour. He had instructed the citizens of the city, as soon as fighting had been engaged and the charge of the enemy had slowed to a walk, to enter the fray, and with their knives, scythes, pitchforks and clubs, to maim and kill the enemy's horses.

This they then did, with terrible, bloody efficacy. Butchers, tanners, merchants and porters slithered between the hocks and hooves of the fighting knights' chargers, and plunged their blades into the horses' chests, used their woodaxes to cut at the horses' fetlocks, slicing and sawing and hacking, until the field of Wolfsbergen was awash with equine blood.

Naturally, as soon as the Bishop's Knights' steeds were cut away from under them, they plunged, in their heavy armour, into the mess of blood and mud underfoot. Here, trampled by their own dying, flailing horses, several died. But the greater number were grabbed by the common hands of the citizens, and dragged to the edge of the battlefield, where they were cudgelled and pummelled into submission.

† † †

Bishop Walther von Kolzeck, who had remained in the rearguard to survey the battle, and who had planned to charge with his smaller troop at a crucial moment to turn the tide of victory, remained, for a short while, paralysed with shock and terror. He and his companions witnessed their company's stirring charge on the enemy troops, and then watched on with incomprehension as their great Knights, one by one, were cut down from their steeds, and fell into the bloody hands of the lowly fortune hunters. Von Habsburg and von Kronthal's hardened warriors then moved into the fray to complete the slaughter of the Bishop's now bewildered troops.

It swiftly became clear that the battle had been lost. Von Kolzeck, upon hearing of the death of his beloved elder brother in the fray, lost what remained of his composure and confidence. His mind clouded with grief and confusion, his spirit broken by the sudden collapse of all his glorious plans, the Bishop became incapable of leadership.

Seeing their overlord overcome with incapacitating melancholy, his closest associates determined to sound the retreat. The Bishop and his retinue then turned and fled the shameful scene.

VULTURES
(ANNO 1262. BARON VOLMAR VON KRONTHAL VII)

After all that nonsense, it was over in a matter of moments. That fool Walther von Kolzeck sent his Knights a-charging before his footsoldiers were in proper formation. And the Knights charged well enough, a great phalanx of bright armour and glinting swords. Their pageboys must have been hard at work all night with oil and cloth to polish all that gleaming steel into a shine.

My back's been hurting a while now, so I held off from the vanguard fray. But after the first wave of our Knights went out, I came hard behind. That young Count of Lichtenberg was making eyes at me, so I went right at him. We managed a few feints and parries, then I hit down hard on his left shoulder, a veritable blow.

But then the trumpet sounded and all chaos broke loose. Out came Habsburg's common city dogs. I'll credit them with blood and balls, no doubt about that, the way they rushed in amongst a great-hundred or more destriers and coursers, not to mention armoured Knights lashing out with sword and mace.

Count Lichtenberg's horse reared and screamed, panicking wild. The young bastard nearly fell down there and then, but he caught his arm tight in the reins and brought the destrier to heel. They lurched back towards the Bishop's camp, and I would have followed them to finish the fight, but already the battlefield was just a mess of blood and flailing horses.

What a vile sight. It was like a knacker's yard, a slaughter-house on Martinmas Eve. Fine stallions thrashing in the mud, their eyes rolling, froth spitting from their jaws, their fetlocks cut to the bone by a butcher's cleaver or woodsman's axe. And the city's tradesmen and porters, covered in blood from head to toe, dragged the armoured Lords through the horses' gore like carters hauling turnip sacks.

Where in Hell were the Bishop's infantrymen? I swerved Ashkelon round and back up the mound to look. They had started to advance. But late, far too late. And seeing Lichtenberg and others fleeing the field, and hearing the keening whinnies of the butchered horses and the curses of the unseated, blood-soaked Lords, they faltered, and then broke and ran.

And it was all over. Like that. The work of months, in a few feints and parries.

† † †

Sometimes Victory is not quite as you'd imagined it. And our Victory could not have been more complete, more resounding. But it was an unsightly one that left a sour, metallic taste, like sucking on a tarnished coin.

As soon as the Bishop's ragged, scattered forces sounded the bugle for retreat, the Hagenburg hounds were let loose on the Killing Ground. Out came beggars, pimps, hawkers and whores and swept the field like starving vultures, pulling armour, weapons, amulets and medallions off the fallen corpses, cutting off chainmail in clinking bundles. I even saw one young carpenter's boy—he could not have been more than thirteen summers—who, unable to pull off a nobleman's signet ring, merely reached in his pack, took out a saw, and started carving away at the wrist, cutting off the man's whole hand.

Turning away I saw, beyond the piles of twitching, groaning horses and noble dead, ranged along a hawthorn hedgerow, hundreds of hostage pages and Lords. Some of the greatest Knights of Alsace were there, stripped to their braies and shirts, their faces bruised and lopsided from the pummelling of cudgels, their wrists and ankles tied in rope and cord.

And it's here that the Great Haggling began. The Common Men of Hagenburg, who had—let us freely admit it—risked their lowly lives to bring down the Lords and their horses, now demanded a reckoning in hard silver.

"My Lord," called out a group of porkbutchers to me, "how much will you pay us for this Baron von Finstingen?"

The Baron von Finstingen was, thankfully, already beaten unconscious as this conversation took place, lying bound in the mud, stripped of his priceless armour and wrapped in a horse blanket. Otherwise, can you imagine it, haggling over his ransom price as if he were a coil of sausage?

I looked the covey of butchers straight in the eyes. "I will name you no price, sirs. The Clerk of the Count von Habsburg will be with you presently. It is he who will take charge of the prisoners."

"We won't take less than a square mark, My Lord. Any less and we'll keep our prisoner and make the deal with his people ourselves."

I shake my head. This must be nipped in the bud, straight away. "There you are mistaken, men. Where will you house the Lord von Finstingen whilst you wait for his ransom price? In your smokehouse alongside your sides of bacon? And how will you deal with the House of Finstingen? Will the Baroness von Finstingen haggle with you porkbutchers as if she's buying a pound of chops?"

"We can haggle as good as any Lady."

"Men. Know your Place. These Lords will be taken into our custody and housed in the Chapter House of the Cathedral, as befits their station. Not in your pork shop."

They stand. And there is mutiny in their avaricious eyes. "But it's us who captured him."

"And you will be well compensated. We thank you for your valorous actions on this day. God give you a good evening."

I wanted to take the Baron von Finstingen myself right there and then. Bundle him on my back and take him to my tent. Clothe him in my spare robes. Treat him with honour. For to see him lying there in the mud, bruised and beaten by sausage-butchers, I could feel no sense of Victory, only of Shame.

And if the defeated Lords are not now treated with respect and distinction, the battle will not end here. It will echo through the years to come, and no honour will redound to my name, but only infamy.

And so I walk through the field of blood. And look upon the prisoners lying in the mud against the hawthorn hedge. And I look into the faces of the Hagenburg victors. Their faces, stained with gore, bear expressions of insolent triumph. For they know what they have done. They have brought about a Levelling. It was they who drew the Mighty down from their proud chargers and levelled them in the mud of Wolfsbergen.

But these Levellers, they'll all be bought off with money. And that's how it will end here. With purses of coin pressed into their bloodstained hands.

The Chronicle of Walther Von Kolzeck: Part III
(Anno 1262. Walther von Kolzeck III)

The convincing victory of the City of Hagenburg at the Battle of Wolfsbergen induced a brief period of euphoria, celebration and confidence amongst Hagenburg's citizens, yet proved to be but a Chimera, an illusory triumph. Firstly it must be noted that the Bishop and his dependents (his court, the clergy, the tradesmen and professions that served these dependencies) formed such a large part of the Hagenburg economy that their continued absence debilitated the city's trade, causing increase in want and hardship. Secondly, although the Bishop had been militarily defeated and rudely apprised of the City's martial might, there existed no instrument or mechanism by which the City might remove von Kolzeck from his throne and seat of power. This could only be achieved by his Death, by the intercession of the Pope himself, or, in some rare and controversial circumstances, by the Holy Roman Emperor. All three of these options seemed vexingly remote: Bishop von Kolzeck, at the age of twenty-four, was still a young man and in the bloom of health, the Pope could not be expected to support the City in its vendetta against one of His own anointed primates, and the Emperor at the time, Richard of Cornwall, an Englishman, was seen as distant and uncomprehending of the political workings of his own Empire, and surely unwilling to embroil himself in a local controversy.

Sporadic fighting continued throughout the summer of 1262. The City's troops, now much reduced into a small band of experienced fighters, used the threat of force to persuade recalcitrant villages and townships to renounce their loyalty to von Kolzeck. When not engaged in this process of policing and enforcement, von Kronthal's men plagued and harried the Black Forest valleys and the east bank of the Rhine around Prinzbach, the von Kolzecks' stronghold. Here they often seized the all-valuable consignments of silver issued in armed convoys from the Prinzbach silver mines, thereby forcing a temporary closure of the mine, a severe blow to the von Kolzecks' finances.

For their part, the knights and troops who remained loyal to the Bishop sallied intermittently forth in increasingly desperate and unsuccessful attempts to reverse the tide of misfortune that had swept upon them. A bold, surprise attack on Hagenburg itself, made in the deluded hope of freeing the ransomed prisoners in the Cathedral Cloister, was a bloody disaster. A bid to retake once-loyal Colmar for the Bishop also ended in ignominious failure. Gradually, von Kolzeck's allies and supporters returned to their estates, his mercenaries left in hope of more profitable employment in other lands, and any prospects of a change in Walther von Kolzeck's lamentable fortunes looked remote indeed.

Nevertheless, conditions in Hagenburg were becoming increasingly desperate. And so it was that the Councillors of Hagenburg, led by Niklaus Zorn, wrote a letter to Bishop von Kolzeck couched in respectful and even emollient terms, requesting his return to his seat of power, and a peaceful and productive negotiation of a new City Statute.

The travails of Walther von Kolzeck could, hypothetically, have ended here if he had accepted the City's offer of peace. But he and his embittered advisors saw the letter not as an offer of compromise but rather as a poisoned chalice, a guileful lure to enter a trap. Even if the idea of "bargaining" with the common ministerial class could be entertained, they believed that von Kolzeck, as a defeated warlord, had no lever-age or power in the negotiations, and that the Councillors and Ministers would be able to force his position. In consequence they believed that the only recourse was to form a new army with the aid and support of the Pope, and to defeat the City on the second attempt, on the battlefield.

Had they known and considered the parlous state of the Hagenburg economy and the hardship endured by the mer-chants and traders of the City, they would have realised they had a strong position in any possible negotiations, but of things such as trade and the exigencies of daily life in Hagenburg they had no experience, knowledge or understanding.

† † †

A Dominican emissary bearing letters of entreaty was dis-patched to Italy and the Papal Court. Bishop von Kolzeck implored His Holiness for his aid and assistance in the form of finance from the Papal coffers (to be repaid at interest upon Victory) and, of more vital importance, a Papal Bull exhorting the rulers of adjacent lands, the Bishops of Metz, Basel, Konstanz and Mayenz, the Abbots of the greater abbeys and monasteries, the Noblemen of Hessen, Westphalia, Lothringen and Swabia, to come to von Kolzeck's aid and join in Holy War against this ungodly, insurrectionary city of upstarts and rebels.

No answer was forthcoming. To Walther von Kolzeck's mis-fortune, the Pope who had anointed his appointment to the *cathedra*, Pope Alexander IV, had passed away the year before. The new incumbent of the Papal Throne, Urban IV, clearly did not regard this Upper Rhineland dispute, dramatic as it was, as high on his list of priorities. Before being elected Pope, Urban IV had been the Patriarch of Jerusalem, and the recent seizure of Latin Constantinople by the Orthodox Nicean Greeks was his primary concern; records from the time attest to his attempt to raise a crusade to recapture the city on the Bosphorus. At this time he was also negotiating with Manfred, illegitimate son of Staufen Emperor Friedrich II, to lead the crusade in exchange for papal recognition of the Staufen as Kings of Sicily; a highly fraught and controversial political gambit.

In this context, it is eminently comprehensible that Pope Urban IV saw the travails of Bishop von Kolzeck as undeserving of his immediate attention. And there is maybe another factor to consider: Urban IV was a commoner, the son of a cobbler of Troyes. It is possible that his sympathies did not automatically lie with the Alsatian nobility, but with the councillors, traders and merchants of Hagenburg.

Whatever the reason, the von Kolzeck camp waited in vain for succour from the Papal Throne. Summer passed, autumn came, and one by one their remaining allies slipped away. Werner von Kolzeck took to drink. Walther von Kolzeck, who only months before had been a bright, energetic youth, vital and confident, always the centre of attention in any situation, became melancholy and withdrawn. Outside their castle walls, Prinzbach had become a ghost of its former self. Work in the mine had almost completely come to a halt as the depredations of Baron von Kronthal's mercenary bands made it impossible to dispatch the silver out of the Prinzbach valley and to the markets of Hagenburg, Nuremberg and Cologne. Many of the mine workers had left, seeking employment elsewhere. The settlement, once a thriving mining community, declined into lassitude and snowbound silence.

At the beginning of Advent, Walther von Kolzeck fell ill. One of his teeth became rotten and infected and had to be removed. The doctor prescribed *lattwerge*, a tincture of opium drunk dissolved in wine to remove its bitterness. The infection soon healed, the toothache abated, but Bishop von Kolzeck continued to imbibe ever greater doses of the restorative medicine.

Some say he died at his own hand. Some say he died from surfeit of *lattwerge*, taken in intoxicated error. But most say he died, simply, of Grief. Grief that all his dreams had been crushed, Grief that he had risen so rapidly, so high, on the Wheel of Fortune, and then been sent, battered and floundering, into the depths of Ignominy.

The last words he has left to posterity are those he spoke only days before his death. *May my name be blotted out, may my deeds be forgotten, may, when I die, there remain no trace of my passing.*

Even this, his final wish, was unwisely made, and is unlikely to be granted.

† Walther von Kolzeck, Bishop of Hagenburg
(1238–1263)

ANNO
1263

BRUSHWOOD
(ANNO 1263. BARON VOLMAR VON KRONTHAL VIII)

S oft voices, talking in a Lothringian village dialect I can
hardly understand. Laughter and the rustle of leaves,
crackling of twigs. I look up from my bivouac, my eyes
blurred with sleep.

It's not long after dawn, and they look like beetles, insects. On
their backs, strapped with leather ties, huge bundles of brushwood.

They haven't seen me. Haven't seen Ashkelon, who stands
nearby, his breath steaming in the air. We're hidden in the
copse where I took shelter late last night.

They crawl their laborious way upwards towards the
Saargemin road, stooping to pick up sticks and fallen branches as
they go. Reaching the road, they untie their huge burdens, sit
down and rest. Eat bread, talk. A family of them—mother, father,
a daughter, a son.

From my hidden vantage point I watch them as I strike
camp, folding the sheep hides I slept on, giving Ashkelon his
morning sack of oats and green spelt. They sit cross-legged,
passing crusts of bread and a gourd of water between them
without ceremony or invitation.

After a short rest, they take up their huge, brushwood burdens again, and, singing a peasant song, a canon in four voices,
they walk on down the Saargemin road.

† † †

I waited a while before I visited the prisoners in the

Cathedral Cloister. I left time for tempers to calm, for the demon Revenge to loosen its grasp on the hearts of the vanquished. I'd given word to the gaolers to indulge their noble whims, and by the time I came by, they had raised money from the Jews and brought in carpets and goose-down cushions, fine wine and whores. The cloister cells looked more like some Saracen serail than a cold, German gaol.

To sweeten my arrival, I had two tuns of the Bishop's wine rolled in behind me, and that smoothed matters a great deal. Not that we all sat down together, embracing and drinking Brotherhood, but at least none of them tried to murder me.

Habsburg's Clerk had prepared them all: sign a declaration of loyalty to the City, a renunciation of alliance to von Kolzeck and his dwindling band of supporters, pay the ransom and then they're free men. They didn't like it much, but after a while they could see which way the wind was blowing. A Ransom is nothing to sing about, but tighten your belt and collect your rents from your lands, pray for fine harvests and good prices for your meat, wheat and wine, and in two or three years you'll be back in the saddle. It's taking noblemen's land that leads to feuds and endless trouble, and we're not touching their property, just the weight of their purse. It'll make them bitter for a while, maybe, but not hateful for generations.

The only landowners we're looking to disown are the von Kolzecks themselves. I want Prinzbach and the mines. And the way it's going for them, with all their "loyal subjects" running from them like they've contracted leprosy, old, heirless Werner von Kolzeck will have to concede it soon.

Chivalry? That's what the captured Knights were carping about when I visited them in their whorehouse prison. "Where was the Chivalry in cutting down our steeds like common highwaymen? Where was the Honour and Glory in that, My Lord Baron?" And I, shamefaced Victor with laurels of ransomed silver, laughed and said, "Well, whatever it was, it worked, didn't it?"

But they're right. The whole thing, from start to finish, it was all just politicking and deals. Five hundred marks of stolen Jewish silver to buy the arms of the House of Habsburg in the first place! And then, in the end, clerks and secretaries haggling over the ransom contracts like grain traders at the Rhine Gate Harbour.

No Chivalry. Just Marks, Shillings and Pence.

In the end, they didn't have any choice. One by one, the captured noblemen signed the contract and the renunciation, paid the ransom and rode off to their estates to nurse their wounded pride. Every day a wife, sister, brother or nephew of a prisoner would ride up to the Counting House from their country estates, and with resentful looks and bitter tears, empty pouches of silver coin, golden candlesticks, jewelled necklaces and bracelets into our brimming Victory Chest.

When the last prisoner had paid and left, Habsburg's Clerk, Mistress Gerber and I went to the Pfennigplatz to divide the spoils. I couldn't quite believe my eyes when Münzmeister Müllenheim doled out my share—enough to buy Heaven and Hell and have some farthings left over for Purgatory. Von Habsburg and I are now very rich men, and that draper woman Gerber who put up the Rosheimer silver to buy von Habsburg's hand has more than doubled her investment—she's now as wealthy as a Countess, and she a damned shepherd's daughter.

I've not seen von Habsburg himself since the days after the battle. He's been touring the townships and buying up land and allies, skirmishing with the Bishop of Basel about some property dispute in the Aargau. His Ambition seems so restless that I get exhausted just thinking about him. But I know I need to follow his footsteps. The war of arms is over, but the war of quill, ink and parchment has just begun.

† † †

Mists are creeping from the River Saar in the valley below. The sun will burn them all away once he rises over the eastern hills. It's early spring and the forests are a mix of dark ever-green, light new leaf and pinkish blossom, a patchwork of colours. All very pretty if you have the whim for it, and today I've got a light heart and lungs full of cool morning air. It's been an age since I rode out on my own, camped in the open under the stars like some lovesick young fool.

As I come into a village on the banks of the Saar, I catch up with the brushwood family; the four of them like worker ants carrying huge loads on their backs. They're still singing, and, as I pass, the man and boy take their caps from their heads and bow, and the ladies curtsey. And I nod and call out, "God give you good day."

In Hagenburg and around the city, they all know me. Even the hauliers, the carters, the peasants stooping in the fields, sifting the soil for pebbles and stones. They all call out and wave, "Von Kronthal! My Lord! God bless your hands! Strength to your arms!" But here in the Lorraine, I'm just some other nobleman kicking past on his fine horse from one castle to another.

I'm vain like the next man, no need to lie. But being No One for a while, to pass in cap-doffing silence, it's not going to do me any harm. I'm riding alone with neither servant nor liv-ery, even my sword tucked into the saddlebags, sheathed and hidden, trying not to attract attention.

The less they know in Hagenburg about this journey, the better.

† † †

Magistrate Vergersheim, what can I say? I do realise that

the man works hard on my behalf and is therefore in some way deserving of my regard. But as soon as this wincing gibbon starts wheezing and whining like a punctured bagpipe, all I want to do is have him gagged with sackcloth.

"My Lord, I do notice that you still have no Baronial Court. No counsel, no advisers other than my good self," he flutes at me, and spreads his long, whiskery hands. "And if the rumours are true, My Lord, you are in need of diplomatic counsel . . . I have some capable men I could present to you for interview, should you desire it. It seems, despite your popularity with the Common Man, you are not now held in high esteem by your fellow noblemen."

This is the kind of importunate counsel I have to endure. Even that devil Schäffer never had the gall to advise me on how to deal with my own kind.

"I have no need of any more bloody pen-pushers and ink monkeys, Vergersheim. One is enough for the present."

Vergersheim goes pale. "My Lord," he says, his voice deepening with suppressed indignation, "there is no need for you to insult me."

I seem to have prodded a boil. But he's right, there's no need to insult a twisting imp like him; it's like hitting an oak tree at five paces. "Vergersheim, let's keep this strictly business. You work on the bloody petition. And leave my fellow Lords to me."

From white, his face swells to dark red, like a bruise. Like a big red cabbage.

And yet he's not wrong about my fellow noblemen. Directly after the victory over von Kolzeck I was the toast of the *Sternkammer*, and they all lined up to drink Friendship and Brotherhood with me. But as the ransom gold rained into my coffers, and as the rumours spread that I had Prinzbach and half the von Kolzeck estate in my sights, the atmosphere slowly soured. There were dark mutterings in the corners of the Wine

Room, backs were turned when I took my table, and many of my fellow Lords seemed to find it hard to look me in the eye.

On Pentecost Sunday we started drinking as soon as the Cathedral service was over. The cook of *zum Sterne* is from Lenzenbach, and he'd ordered half a dozen young, tender lambs to roast in the oven and serve with herbs and crumbled Lenzenbach cheese. It's divine, and when he cooks it, the *zum Sterne* is always full.

By nightfall the place was like a harbour tavern, all drunkenness and abandon. Out of nowhere, von Ährenfeld sits himself down at my table, and says, "So who's next, My Lord Baron? Which family?"

"What are you talking about?"

"First you end the line of Schwanenstein, and pillage their estate. Now it's the von Kolzecks. Which noble house are you going to destroy next?"

"Yours, unless you watch your words, Reimbold."

"The Horse Butcher of Wolfsbergen. Soon you'll be selling noble blood by the pint."

I launch myself at him, ready to pummel his face into the table, but Lanzelin and Reichard hold me back. I shout at him so much that I even froth at the mouth like a mad dog. Von Ährenfeld goes pale and flees into the night, and it takes everyone a good long time to talk me down from challenging him to mortal combat.

"We're all drunk, Volle my brother," says Lanzelin, clapping my shoulder, "it's the Wine, it's all just the Wine."

But it isn't, and I know it. The next morning, when I awake with a throbbing head and pitch black melancholy, I sit for a long time watching the shuffling Hagenburg crowds from my townhouse window. Since Wolfsbergen I have become one of the richest men in the Alsace. And like all wealthy men, it is my fate to be surrounded by envious enemies and grasping swine.

I need to build up friends and allies from scratch. And I

need to secure my succession. My mind aches just thinking about it.

† † †

Someone must have ridden ahead to tell them I was coming, a lone Lord on a fine horse. Sir Raldingen himself canters out to meet me at the edge of his estate. As he recognises me, his face pales, and he nods sadly, as if reluctantly accepting a troubled Fate.

"I've been dreading this day, My Lord," he says.

"Dreading?"

"Too strong a word, maybe. But we'll miss him. He's part of the family."

We find Tybolt at the castle stables, grooming the plough horses, his breeches spattered with mud from the fields. When he sees me, he can't quite believe his eyes. Drops the grooming brush, wipes his hands on his apron, looks everywhere except at me, embarrassed.

I dismount from Ashkelon and he kneels before me to kiss my hand. "I'm sorry, my Lord, I am dirty. If I knew you were coming . . . "

"Never mind that. Stand up, my boy. Let me look at you."

He stands, and I hold him at arm's length. He's nearly as tall as me, thank the Lord, not a titch like his mother. But he's got her eyes, soft and wounded-looking, and her thin auburn hair. A burr of fluff on his cheeks, the trace of a moustache, nothing much to show for his eighteen summers. Or is it seventeen? I can't quite remember.

He's a strange mixture, this Tybolt. Half man, half girl. Strongly built like me, but something womanish about him, soft and giving. Looks like he's about to start crying. Or dreaming.

A mixture.

But that's, I suppose, what Children are.

"Get your things ready, Boy. You're coming with me."

† † †

More haggling, more Trade. And now with Sir Raldingen. Payments on account, ten marks for Tybolt's palfrey, three marks for his sword, compensation for loss of a hard-working farmhand. This must be what it's like being Rich: you pay through the nose for everything. If you start bargaining, they eye you with a wounded look that seems to say, "What's a few shillings to a Great Lord like you?"

But soon enough we're on our way, back through the fields of the Lothringen plain, up to the forests of the Alsace border.

Me and my Son. My Son Tybolt. My Son.

God damn it, but it does something to me. To turn around in the saddle and see him riding beside me, my flesh and blood. He's changed his clothes, has a dark green velvet riding coat, a feathered cap, long polished boots. A fine-looking boy. My eyes are always searching the road ahead, flicking into the sun-mottled shadows of the forests, looking for danger, for bandits and thieves.

Like I'm his Protector.

And I keep looking back at him, studying, assessing. "Don't grip the reins so tightly, Boy. Makes you look like a girl. Like you're afraid of falling. Let them loosely twine over your thumb. Like this."

He looks at my hands, corrects his grip accordingly. Nods earnestly, almost bowing to me in his saddle. "Yes, My Lord."

At the village on the banks of the Saar, the Brushwood Peasants are outside their little thatched farmstead, chattering away like a bunch of sparrows as they sort through their haul.

I rein in Ashkelon and stop a while to watch. Under the shelter of a wattle roof they are piling their sticks, and the children are making cakes of cow dung and straw to dry in the sun. Summer will soon be upon us, and there they are, already storing up their winter fuel.

"How much for a bundle of wood?" I ask. "We need later to make a fire."

They all look up at me and Tybolt, their chattering stops. Their hands fumble at their filthy smocks, as if ashamed of their dirt.

"Take what you wish, My Lord," says the father, in his Lothringian drawl. "We are honoured."

"Tybolt, take enough for a good fire," I say, and reach for my purse.

Tybolt dismounts, and with the help of the muttering, trembling mother, ties up a bundle of fuel.

"Take this," I say to the father, and lean down to place six pennies in his hand. He falls to his knees, tears bursting from his eyes as if I'd just told him that his time had come to die.

† † †

"You know how to make a fire, don't you?"

"Yes, My Lord."

"Well go on then. Here's tinder and flint."

Tybolt nods, takes the tinderbox in both hands, with a slight bow and genuflection as if receiving the Body of Christ. He's gauche with me, reverent, like a valet or page.

"Tybolt."

"Yes, My Lord?"

"You can call me 'Father.'"

Tybolt's soft eyes flick up at me in the dusk, a strange, bewildered look. I smile ruefully.

"I mean . . . when we're alone."

He nods, with a touch of sadness. And then sets off into the brush, looking for kindling.

We've left the road into a gully where the flames of our fire won't be readily seen. The sun has set and the sky between the trees is spangled by the first stars.

Tybolt gets the fire going and I unpack the bread and sausage. I'm thinking of that peasant family, together night and day, and chattering away like the birds in the hedgerows. A family, working together, living together, singing together.

And me? My life? A chain, a chain of chess-moves. Get my Son from his guardians. Take the Prinzbach silver mines. Raise the money I need to buy an annulment from the Pope. Consolidate my lands and moneys. Secure my legacy, my line of Blood. And no one can know. No one can know about any of this. If my wife's family catch wind of it before it's done, there'll be strife aplenty.

Tybolt looks at me, nervously. Sees me staring into the fire, the bread unbroken, the sausage uncut. "Father?"

The word trembles in the air, dances like a spark from the fire. I swallow, and utter three syllables that sound to me both magical and strange.

"Yes, my Son?"

"What are you thinking about?"

It's a bloody good question. Lord save me, I should stop thinking. I'm getting too philosophical in my old age.

Orvieto
(ANNO 1263. EUGENIUS VON ZABERN IX)

It is not with any pleasure that I find myself, once again, in Italy.

Early autumn storms protracted our journey. Afraid of the open seas, our barque crawled the waves of the Tyrrhenian Coast, lurching, pitching, surging the breaking crests. In my eyeless darkness, suspended on a hammock in the goods hold, weightlessly gliding and plunging into one unseen Abyss after another, I fancied myself Jonah in the belly of the whale.

I don't think I have ever prayed quite so much in my life.

Jonah languished in the whale's innards for three days and three nights. My ordeal lasted three times that long before the barque spat us out at some lonesome Sienese fishing port where the cries of the gulls sounded like souls in perdition and the ground beneath us seemed to pitch and weave as if it were the sea's very echo. Here we ate fried fish and noodles in butter, drank tart Tuscan wine, and then lay two days and nights in shivering fever in the village priest's mouldy vestry.

Jonah continued his journey on land to preach to the fallen, sinful city of Nineveh. I, however, marched on, guided by Hieronymus' shaky, seasick hand, towards Orvieto, where Pope Urban IV has pitched his Papal Court. And for this I thank God with all my heart, that our present Holy Father has had the good sense never to set foot in the contemporary Nineveh, that depraved, vicious bordello, Rome.

†††

Since my election to the Bishop's throne, I have known no rest nor leisure. Gone are the quiet hours where Hieronymus would read to me from the Scriptures or the new treatises of scholars from Paris and Naples, gone are my diverting vigils by the window on Vogesen Street.

Now I reside in the Bishop's Palace, and from Lauds to Compline, receive visitors, hear petitions, dictate and hear dictation of hundreds of letters, sit with ministers, councillors and clerics, give orders to my staff and my underlings, and, in any rare occasion where I find myself alone, discuss with myself the issues that weigh upon me, or turn in Prayer, hoping for divine inspiration, to the Lord.

Most pressing has been the need to heal the wounds of the recent conflict. To achieve this I, the Bishop, must concede powers to the City, but, so as not to appear too weak or over-pliant, must do so in moderation, and in the slow, ripening full-ness of time. Here, I disappoint everyone. My noble colleagues and Canons by deliberately weakening our hand, and the Councillors, Guilds and Merchants, by giving them less than they desire.

Meanwhile I am carrying out an audit of the assets of the Diocese (what a falling off there has been here! I left the finances in a robust state in the Year of our Lord 1243, but in the intervening twenty years, profligacy and disorder have undone all my painstaking work), and am trying to find ways of increasing our income, and spending what we have on Works whose value will be of immediate benefit to the Citizens, to assuage their angry thirst for reform.

Of great importance, both symbolic and financial, to the success of these plans has been the tacit support of the "Champion of Wolfsbergen" and the "Vanquisher of Schwanenstein," the very wealthy Baron Volmar von Kronthal.

I invited him to see me shortly after my election. Not with any substantial feelings of optimism or excitement: I have spent too long in the company of the Knights of the Alsace to expect much more than a deficient understanding of the World As It Is, coupled with preening Arrogance and a rebarbative Vanity.

The Baron von Kronthal fulfilled many of my expectations, but frustrated others. It is true that his intellect is on the level of a middling Cathedral Schoolboy, but he has no pretentions to possess any wisdom, and thus has the charm of a dilatory student who knows he is nevertheless his Teacher's Favourite.

"I wanted to come and see you anyway, Your Grace," he says, casually kissing my ring. "May I sit?"

"Please do," I say, gesturing in the direction of the polstered chair opposite, a throne-like object, reserved for special guests. I used to sit in it myself, in my conferences with Bishop Berthold.

"Why did you want to come and see me, My Lord Baron?"

I can hear him shifting in his chair, coughing. "Wine!" he calls to the servants who are, I gather, hovering in the antechamber.

"No value in mincing words, is there?" he grumbles. "I wanted to ask for your help in the matter . . . " He pauses as his wine is poured, and waits for the servant to withdraw. Then he lowers his voice. " . . . of the annulment of my marriage to the Baroness."

This is a man who besieges impregnable castles, goes to war with his own Bishop overlord; he is neither cautious nor retiring. Nevertheless this is a precipitous opening sally by any measurement.

"An *annulment*?" is all I can manage to exclaim as a rejoinder, needing time to marshal my thoughts. After brief deliberation, I consider that an equally rapacious counter-thrust is the only response. "I hear you will be taking ownership of

Prinzbach as the spoils of victory of Wolfsbergen. I want a share in the incomes of the mines for the Diocese."

"If you can secure the annulment, you can have the share in the mine."

"Twenty *per centum*."

"Done."

God damn my Haste. I could have asked for more.

† † †

On an open, even road I could, in theory, ride a docile steed—a Mule, for instance, at a walk, guided on the halter by a servant. But even then there is the fear that the animal, startled by a sudden noise, or stung by a wasp, might bolt and take me with it, plunging into the uncharted darkness, and bucking me to crack my head on branch or stone.

And so I am condemned to walk, guided by Hieronymus' gentle hands, or ride in the back of carts alongside the sacks of pomegranates gathered from the autumn orchards. And so we make slow progress as we climb the Latium hills.

Yet, as we come within a few leagues of Orvieto, the road thrums with voices, busy with trade. The Pope's soldiers guard the approaches to the papal city, and provisioners and merchants throng the lanes, herding livestock, carting wine and cheese. And for the more genteel class of travellers, palanquins and bearers are offered for hire.

Hieronymus guides me into the palanquin's cushioned interior. It is small and I must bend my long legs to fit inside, but as soon as I am seated, I am heaved aloft and the bearers set off in synchronised stride. I swing gently, in perfumed cushions, and a sweet breeze tickles through the curtains. Like a babe in a cradle, swaddled and rocked, I fall into a blissful sleep. And only awake, some hours later, when we are outside Orvieto's city walls.

† † †

That he wants to disinherit his cold, devout wife and her fractious, devious brother Rutger von Moder, that he wants to set the shield and colours of von Kronthal as a leading force in the Empire, I can well understand. And that I want a rich, powerful ally, whose Strength stands counter to the rapaciously growing fortunes of the House of Habsburg, is self-evident to anyone who understands the politics of the Upper Rhine. Better two warlords in competition, friendly or otherwise, than one all-powerful Monolith.

The Baron von Kronthal's lawyer, the scheming, well-moneyed wretch named Magistrate Vergersheim, attests that the Baron married Tybolt's chambermaid mother in a secret ceremony in Castle Schwanenstein. And that the Baron's marriage with the Countess von Moder was never valid, because it was officiated by the Abbot of Mohrmünster, who was later burned as a heretic.

These lies and half-truths, sealed in an affidavit, and honeyed with a hefty gift of two hundred marks from the Baron's treasury, I bear in secret with me to the Holy Father. In secret, for if the Baroness' family, the proud von Moders, should hear of it, then they will use every weapon in their arsenal to protect their interests. They will need to be sweetened with gifts, calmed with compromise. They will keep the rump of the von Moder lands, but lose all gains contracted with the Baroness' marriage. I shall have to compensate them richly with some positions of grace and favour in the Diocese.

An awkward and challenging affair, and yet it is a matter of tradition, so I hear, for the Pope to grant one boon to a new Bishop. And here is one that will fill his coffers, help fill mine, and will bind the fractious strength of von Kronthal into beholden, thankful loyalty to the Holy See.

I am confident of success.

††††

When last I was at the Papal Court, I was a mere Canon and Treasurer, now I am a Bishop. Nevertheless to be here is a lesson in Humility and Patience.

In Hagenburg, I am Suzerain and Overlord. Here, I am merely one of many Bishops vying for the attention of the Holy Father. And it is slowly becoming clear that to achieve all that I wish will take several weeks.

And yet it is not unpleasant to be here. As a visiting Bishop I am accorded great courtesy, and am invited to banquets, Holy Masses and discussions of doctrine. I am a guest in the city's *palazzi*, I am introduced to great Noblemen, the leading bankers of Florence and Venice, once even to the magnificent scholar Thomas of Aquino, whose writings Hieronymus and I have very much admired.

To begin with, I begged of Hieronmyus descriptions of the palaces and courts in which these many colloquia took place. "A hall flagged in white stone," he would whisper in hushed tones of awe. "Walls of striped black and white marble, with . . . circular columns . . . topped with capitals carved with oak leaves . . . " And so he droned on.

After a while, I decided it best to leave the new world of Orvieto to my imagination. After all, I rarely think in Images any more. It is hard to describe, but the World for me has become a fluid current of aural and abstract sensations. I remember, only distantly, the appearance of things, and rather think in terms of space, distance, and the music of voices and sound.

And Orvieto is full of voices. A constant flood of discussion and negotiation. In the areas where the Papal Court holds sway the common tongue is of course Latin, but in the side streets and the makeshift encampments outside the town walls one can hear conversations, salutations and imprecations in all the languages of Christendom. All the world is here, gathered around the centripetal hub of the great wheel of Fortune.

And so it is with some Curiosity that I hear, retired from the wearying hubbub in the quiet of my bedchamber, the sound of Hieronymus conversing with a stranger in the familiar cadence of the Alsatian dialect.

"Who is there, Hieronymus?"

"A . . . merchant of some kind, Your Grace. He claims to know you."

"From Hagenburg?"

"From Hagenburg."

"Send him in."

I sit up on my divan, and await the mysterious visitor. His footsteps approach, he bends to kiss my ring, and then he says, to my mild astonishment, "Your Grace, I am Emmerich Schäffer. I hope you remember me?"

I do indeed remember him. But I had assumed, like most of Hagenburg society, that he were Dead.

"My Word. This is a surprise. Please sit, Herr Schäffer. And tell me how you come to be here."

"That, Your Grace, would take some time."

"Then tell me, Schäffer. But please, with some concision."

This he then attempts to do, and fails, but I cannot entirely blame him. It seems the poor man has travelled all over this wide earth, finding nothing but increasing misfortune. After his disgraceful abscondment from Hagenburg and many misadventures on the high seas, he had eventually set up a relatively successful business as a middleman in Constantinople, introducing Buyers to Sellers, "like a pimp," as he puts it. But the conquest of Constantinople by the Greeks forced him once more to flee, and since then he has been wandering the Mediterranean and Adriatic coasts in search of new mercantile ventures. And now he has joined forces with a Moorish investor to try and sell a new innovation to the Papal Court.

"And what is this new . . . thing called?"

"It is called 'paper,' Your Grace. Here."

And he places in my hands a . . . sheet, like a sheet of parchment, but lighter, much lighter. Its surface is smooth like silk, but press harder as one traces one's fingers over it and one can sense faint contours, tiny bumps, furrows.

"What colour is it?"

"White," says Emmerich Schäffer.

"Greyish," corrects Hieronymus.

"Does one use it like parchment?"

"Yes. But it is more flexible, more absorbent, and much cheaper to produce. From old rags. Think of all the parchment in daily use in the papal court! With the use of paper, think how much time and money could be saved!"

I have to smile. "Then you are in the wrong place, Herr Schäffer. The Papal Court has many concerns. But saving money and time are, I believe, not high on its list of priorities."

† † †

I am right in my assessment of the workings of the Court: its work is done in opulent languor. After several weeks' wait, we receive gratifying news from the Papal Secretary that the Baron von Kronthal's annulment will be granted. The Pope's official decree in this matter, bearing his seal, will be conferred to me along with my pallium by the Holy Father himself after a Holy Mass, "at the next available opportunity."

And so we wait.

As we wait, we spend increasing amounts of time with Emmerich Schäffer. It is quite clear to me that the man is an amoral opportunist and a scheming scoundrel, but at the same time I cannot deny his brilliance and cunning. And he proves very useful to us as a Spy, mixing as he does amongst the lower echelons of the various entourages, an environment rife with Gossip and Rumour.

"Your Policy of favouring von Kronthal meets with approval," he tells me, sipping Umbrian wine, for which he has an immoderate penchant and which makes him unduly garrulous. "Earlier papal policy furthered the fortunes of the Kyburg-Habsburgs in the region, as a bulwark against the Staufen. Rudolf von Habsburg was quick to make the most of the situation, as you know, but is now seen as too powerful. So they like the idea of a rival family, you were right, Your Grace. They are still worried that Manfred or Konradin von Staufen will make a claim for the Emperor's throne, and are trying to distract them from it by concentrating their efforts on the Kingdom of Sicily, which the Staufen fear losing . . . "

And so he goes on.

I remember Guido Terzani—God damn him to Hell. All his talk of the "Nine Circles," the hierarchy of influence, and his milking of my purse for every step I took, every morsel of information and advice. All I needed was an Emmerich Schäffer, a fox, a weasel, to burrow amongst the gossipmongers that mill around the Court. And his services are for free. Well, nearly. He has already "borrowed" three marks from me.

The dynamic of our relationship changed on our second meeting, in which I casually asked if he had heard the news of his sister Grete's expropriation of the Rosheimer Fortune. He answered in a rather thin voice that he indeed had not heard this news, and then continued with another topic of conversation, as if the matter was of no great concern to him.

Yet Hieronymus told me later that Schäffer had gone pale upon hearing my question, his face showing signs of visible distress. And since then, Emmerich Schäffer has made it clear to me—as clear as constant hint and inference can make it—that he would like nothing better than to return to Hagenburg and serve as my Secretary and Adviser.

But one anxiety stands in the way of his return: he fears the Baron von Kronthal, from whom he stole a large sum of money, and who swore to have him killed.

† † †

My pallium has finally been sent to me in my chambers. It is as yet unconsecrated by the Holy Father, but the Maker of Vestments wishes to try it upon my shoulders, and make any necessary adjustments.

For a piece of clothing that has cost me some thousand marks (the Diocese of Hagenburg's "tithe" upon appointment of a new Bishop), I feel it should be made of golden thread, but it is merely a loose collar of blanched, fine wool. Nevertheless its appearance is harbinger of Good News: the Pope will consecrate the pallium, anoint me as Bishop, and deliver his boon— the annulment of the von Kronthal—von Moder marriage—on this coming Advent Sunday.

Our long stay in Orvieto is coming, finally, to a successful end.

PRINZBACH
(ANNO 1263. BARON VOLMAR VON KRONTHAL IX)

H e looks at me with his soft, mournful eyes. It's not that he reproaches me, but his sadness is unbearable. He mopes as he tends the fire, mopes as he pours the wine, mopes as he eats. When I make a joke, he smiles. But his smile is like drizzling rain, dousing all mirth.

I can't take it any more. "All right, Tybolt, very well, you may ride with me to Prinzbach."

His eyes shine. And when he thinks I'm not looking, he gives a little jump of joy.

Oh, the sweet relief.

We're in the old Bailiff's Cottage I've lodged him in, on the edge of one of the Kronthal estates. The old Bailiff died some months ago, and his widow's glad of young, manly company until her son comes back from apprenticeship. But here in the drab, empty foothills, young Tybolt languishes in tedium, stares out at the falling leaves and the drifting rain, and since he's been here, he's been sulking like a thrice-kicked cur.

At least if he rides with me to Prinzbach, I might have some peace.

And after all, some days past now, a letter came from the Bishop in Orvieto, written with circumspection but no uncertain hope. *Your matter has been settled, I await only the formal papal seal. God willing, I will return by Fourth Advent.*

The missive was delivered by liveried episcopal messenger as I was drinking in the *zum Sterne*. Autumn storms have been raging down from the Vogesen Hills these last long days, and as the herald—against all protocol, but in humane recognition of the evil weather outside—was admitted into our *Sternkammer* room, a draft of autumn air near blew out all the lamps and candles.

"From the Bishop, My Lord," said the messenger loud and clear, bowing and brushing a wet birch leaf off his shoulder, as if he hadn't already attracted enough attention by his entrance. And so all eyes were upon me as I dismissed him with thanks and broke the seal on the parchment roll.

"Just some business I have with the Bishop," I said to the room in general after I had read the brief note, and took a swig of wine, as if it were nothing. But I could feel the eyes of the whole *Sternkammer* upon me, sparkling with suspicion and curiosity.

In good heart and high spirits, I passed by Vergersheim's offices to tell him the good news. I even clapped him on the shoulder as if he were one of my braves. "Once the seals are dry on this and Prinzbach I'll be needing your services again, so get ready. You were right, Vergersheim, my boy. For the new von Kronthal court I'll need a whole legion of penpushers and ink monkeys!"

But Vergersheim merely winced and looked darkly into his folded hands.

"Oh, brighten up, you woodlouse! Come out into the sun and play! Doubtless you and your bevy of clerks will milk me for thousands! So celebrate!"

Even the promise of showers of gold didn't manage to raise a smile. "Maybe you spoke with that shepherd's son Schäffer in this way, My Lord, but I am a Magistrate of the Court of Hagenburg."

He's no joy at all, this Vergersheim. He'll have to brighten up and lose his airs and graces, or I'll find another counsel who's decent company. I calmly remind him, "Know your place, Vergersheim. If I wish to joke with you, I shall. I am one of the first Lords of the Alsace."

"Yes, My Lord," he says. "You are right. Forgive me."

† † †

We set out towards the Rhine and the Taubensand crossing to Prinzbach. Despite the wind and the shuddering waves of autumn rain, Tybolt is happy as a truffle pig to be riding abroad on Baronial business.

The roads are drenched. And empty, thank the Lord. There's no one abroad on days like these, even the peasants are huddled in their hovels, all their windows stuffed with rags and dung, sleeping in fuggy darkness, eyes dead to the world outside.

Prinzbach itself is a sorry sight. Most of the barracks and miners' shanties standing empty, the fortified walls dank with rain. Only the tavern and the chapel and a clutch of houses have smoke curling into the overcast, stormy sky.

I'm here to set up the garrison. Old von Kolzeck, soaked in wine and lost in grief, held out until All Hallows and then could take no more. He and his few remaining, ragged braves slunk back to old Kolzeck Castle two valleys away, tails between their legs and bottles of aquavit in their delirious hands.

I wish them a Merry Advent-Tide. But now the Prinzbach mines belong to me. (And twenty *per centum* to Bishop von Zabern, let's not forget. From his letter, it looks like he's held up his end of the deal.)

In the smoky tavern, we hang our clothes up to dry and sit in our underwear, wrapped in sheepskin blankets, devour the hearty Black Forest ham pottage, and knock back young golden wine of this year's vintage.

Young Tybolt gets tipsy, starts telling some stories from his life in Lothringen. I've seen it before in boys his age: that gauche eagerness, that desperation to Impress. And maybe the stories are funny in some little, backwater estate in the Lorraine. But I sit there with gritted teeth and a painted-on smile, and try and push out some generous laughter.

I notice the Landlord's Daughter is glancing dreamily at Tybolt, so I tell the boy to get us some more wine, and while he's at it, talk to the girl. She's not bad looking for a Black Forest wench, has big blinking calf's eyes, some good meat on her haunches, plenty to get stuck into for a young lad. "Once the garrison arrive tomorrow there'll be two dozen more mouths to feed round here. Ask her about provisions and supplies—we'll need food round the winter. Make yourself useful so I don't have to organise everything myself."

He nods happily, pleased with the responsibility. And I'm released from his lame-limping stories.

Looking over at him later, leaned up on the counter, nattering with the Girl, all smiles and sideward glances, an idea comes to me that'll catch two birds with one seed, keep Tybolt safe and out of open view, and toughen him up, show him the sharp side of the sword.

† † †

When I tell Tybolt that he's staying at Prinzbach, he starts up with his mournful face again. It's early morning, my head is throbbing like all the devils of Hell are dancing in it, and I'm in no mood for Pouting. "You'll do as I bloody say, and no moping about it. That Landlord's girl likes you, Boy. She'll keep you warm at night as the winter draws in."

He smiles shyly, nods, pulls his coat around him. And it's true, the weather has turned. After the storm that raged all night, the dawn came up crisp and bitter. And the hazy blue sky is now deepening to black in the West. It looks like the First Snows are coming.

The Miners—what's left of them—want to show me, their

new Lord, the silver mine. They take us to a muddy hole in the side of the hill, where a half-blind old lady sits, wrapped in sheepskins, and polishes and primes the lamps. Her crooked fingers poke in the ashes of her fire, and she plucks out a glowing coal with her bare hands to light the wicks.

"This way, My Lords," says the Foreman, and leads us deeper into the cave, through grey sludge and piles of stones, to where rough wood struts bulk the low, dug-out ceiling. Tybolt and I have to stoop. "It wasn't made for men such as you," says the Foreman. "We Miners, we're all short and stocky, like Dwarves."

A hole drops down, deep into the ground. Wooden ladders are clenched to the rock, held in place by iron rods. "I'll light the lamps as I go down," he says. "And then you follow, My Lords, one after the other. The ladder might not take the two of you at the same time."

Tybolt goes first, I follow after. From somewhere deep below, the ringing sound of hammer and chisel, blow after blow.

Three ladders down, and there is solid rock beneath my feet, dry, crunching dust. The lamp in the Foreman's hand breathes, glowing amber and gold. "Come," he says. We turn one shadowy corner and then another, catching a glimpse as we go of a lone miner, kneeling on a sheepskin, chiselling glistening ore by the light of his lamp.

We come to a small, dim chamber, carved into the rock. "Have you ever seen total darkness, My Lords?" asks the Foreman, and before we can even answer, the mischievous dwarf blows out his lamp.

For a few, brief moments, the green echo of the lantern-flame glows in my eyes, but then dims into a black so deep, it's like the Essence of Nothing. I wave my hands in front of my face, but there is not even a glimmer, not even a shifting of the shadow to show that they are there.

And we stand there, in the black heart of silver, in the darkness of the earth from which all wealth is hewn, and listen to the sounds of our beating hearts. And in the perfect blackness, I start to think.

Is this what Hell is like? Is this what awaits the Sinner, a cold, intangible, infinite Darkness?

For the first time in my life that I can remember, I become afraid.

My breath starts to come hard and fast.

"Peter!" shouts the Foreman, suddenly, somewhere to my right. "Bring your light to the chamber!"

"Right-o!" comes the distant cry of the lone miner.

"Tybolt?" I ask, suddenly afeared, somehow, that my Boy is gone. That I am here alone.

"Here, My Lord," says Tybolt, and his fingers, feeling their way, find my upper arm.

Then a glow, still faint, as the miner with the lamp approaches, and the darkness is lifted. I can see Tybolt's pale face. He looks at me and asks, beneath his breath, "Father, are you well?"

He has seen my Fear.

I turn away and cough, as if all that is troubling me is a cold. "I am well, my Boy. I'm well."

† † †

The garrison soldiers, under Vogelsang's command, ride up at midday. They got caught in the storm, bivouacked in some Black Forest farmstead, and they look even more like brutal animals than they normally do.

"Dismount, men! Get some hot food inside you!" I shout, and draw Vogelsang aside to meet Tybolt. The Bishop should be home in a matter of weeks. It's time to bring the boy slowly out into the world.

"This is my Son, Vogelsang. Show him how it's done. Discipline. Organisation. How to provision and maintain a garrison. He has plenty to learn, but he'll take over from me one day."

Vogelsang's tired eyes narrow as he takes in Tybolt's frame, his fingers play with the scar on his chin. "I didn't know you had a son, My Lord."

"Well, I do, Captain. And soon the World will learn it."

"How do I address him?"

"As 'my Lord.' He's a von Kronthal. But don't overdo it. He's your pupil now, Vogelsang, and if he steps out of bounds . . . "

"I'll put him in chains on bread and water. But I'll give him a nice cushion for his noble arse, My Lord."

"You've got the frame of it, Captain. I entrust him to you. He's tougher than he looks, that's all I'll say."

Vogelsang nods, bows. Takes Tybolt's upper arms in his hands. "Strong arms, My Lord. Let me have some breakfast, then we'll start."

Tybolt smiles, looks at me. I can see he's anxious, but also proud. I take him in my arms, give him the Kiss of Peace. He looks me in the eyes, steady and calm, as if witnessing my moment of weakness has given him strength. And now that I've acknowledged him to the world, no more pouting, all his moping has gone.

I dislike long farewells. "I'll come back for you by Christmas."

† † †

The first snows have come, turning to slush in the lower plain, but draping the upper hills in ermine white. I need to arrange to have the rest of Tybolt's things brought to him in Prinzbach, then all I can do is wait. Wait and pray for the Bishop's safe return to Hagenburg.

And whilst I wait, I need to gather my friends around me.

I've been neglecting them, my *Sternkammer* braves. It's time for carousing, carousing and joy. An Advent-tide feast in Castle Kronthal. Sled rides through the hills to my hunting lodge, roast goose and hot, spiced wine.

The woods by my Zabern estates are swaddled in white. Pine needles like nails of frost, the silver birches like silver filligree, skeletons of rime. On the path through the forest, I can see traces of horsemen who've passed this way maybe hours before, their hoofbeats re-dusted in windblown snow.

Visitors? Or the ostlers, exercising my steeds?

I spur Ashkelon to a canter—it's too early for ice to have formed on the paths, it must be safe. Obedient to my touch, he welcomes the new pace. He must sense we'll soon be at the manor house. A stable, a nosebag, a bed of warm straw. I can feel him straining, wanting to break into a gallop, but hold him back. In my Youth I would have relented, thrilling to the speed of the race, uncaring of sliding snow and hidden ice. But now . . .

Suddenly he whinnies, stumbles. He wants to buck . . . I catch sight of it for an instant: a *rope*. Snapped taut, across the path, between two pines.

But it's too late. Ashkelon's fetlocks catch. We plunge. Down, hard. To the ground. And my mind goes black. As black as that infinite darkness I'd seen at the heart of the world.

† † †

"Wake up. Wake up, you mongrel."

I'm lain flat on the snow. Somewhere I'm bleeding—I can feel the sticky wetness, smell the sour, sweet blood. My back is in agony, pain sluices up and down through my twisted legs.

I open my eyes. And look into the face of my brother-in-law.

Rutger von Moder squats above me in full armour, his face red from the cold. His breath steams as he growls, spitting out his words. "Where is the Bastard? We were told he rode out with you, you dog."

I say nothing, try and breathe. Try and push myself up, on one elbow.

I look. Behind von Moder, three more armoured men. Von Ährenfeld. Von Moder's son Reinhard. The Count von Lichtenberg.

Now, I am sitting. Blood is dripping on my shoulder and my upper arm from a cut somewhere on my head.

"Never mind," says von Moder. "We'll get the Bastard later."

Nearby, Ashkelon writhes and whinnies, his legs broken.

"Ashkelon . . . " is all I can say. My beautiful one. My friend.

"So, when it's *your* horse, it's not such glorious victory, Brother? Get up, you Horse Butcher. Get up and fight."

My back. Is it broken? I can't seem to stand.

"I can't get up . . . "

Von Moder spits and reaches out his hand. He pulls me upright. I teeter like a drunken carter, draw my sword and plant it in the ground. To hold me steady.

Vergersheim.

It must have been Vergersheim. For a share in the thousands that the von Moders will reap from my Death. Because I insulted him. Because I told him to know his place.

The New Lords of this world. Nib-cutters and ink monkeys.

"Are you ready, von Kronthal? Can you stand and fight like a man?"

I lift my sword from its planting in the ground. Yes, I can stand.

From my back, hot jabbing needles of pain stab my legs and arms. But I can stand and fight.

I can stand.

† Baron Volmar von Kronthal (1212–1263)

ANNO
1264

THE STRAWHEAD GOY
(ANNO 1264. EMMERICH SCHÄFFER II)

Dearest Judah,

At last I have been able to return to Hagenburg. The Baron von Kronthal is dead; it is said he was ambushed by robbers in the Zabern forest. A doubtful story, maybe, but whatever the cause of his demise, it has liberated me from his death sentence, and finally, after some sixteen years, I am able to return home.

It will I hope not surprise you when I say that the first place I went upon arriving in the city was the Judengasse and your house. Please imagine my great sadness and disappointment to discover that you were not there. From what I was told, I have missed you by a matter of months.

They tell me that you are either in Prague or in Kalisch, and so I send this letter to the Jewish elders of Prague, with the request to forward it to wherever you are. I hope and pray that it will find its way to your hands.

Judah, words cannot express my anger. I have learned of the way that my sister has robbed you, deprived you of all you own.

But hear what I say. I am now back in Hagenburg, very much alive, and not dead as the courts ruled me to be in the iniquitous case of this act of robbery. I am in a good position, as the secretary of the righteous new Bishop, Eugenius von Zabern (whom you will doubtless remember).

The matter is legally fraught and far from straightforward, and my sister Grete is wicked and stubborn. Nevertheless *please believe me when I say that I will do everything in my power to restore the company of Schäffer and Associates to its former status.*

This, Judah, I promise you, in recognition of the tender esteem in which I hold you. Not one day has passed in these sixteen years in which I have not thought of you with love and regard. You have been with me in the docks of Constantinopolis, in the bazaars of Aleppo, in the alleyways of Ragusa, by the canals of Venice. Judah, by the ruins of the temple of Jerusalem, I had your name remembered in prayer by a holy man. He said it would bring you good fortune.

I hope it will.

I will write again when I know more. Please inform me of your whereabouts and of your well-being.

I promise to do what I can to restore your fortune.

Emmerich
The Strawhead Goy

SECOND INTERLUDE

ANNO
1318

THE ROSE
(ANNO 1318. ALBRECHT KAIBACH II)

The Pilgrim comes, in his heart a prayer to offer to the Almighty, for the soul of his mother, for the sickness of his ailing child. From his distant village through mud and rain, through the perils of an uncharted journey, he trudges ever onwards on weary feet until he comes to the stir and clamour of the City Gates.

And then into the tumult of Hagenburg.

The Pilgrim, bewildered by the crowds, holds the sight of the Cathedral's dome before him and advances with caution through the multitude. He has heard the tales of the city's dangers, of theft, of fraud, of the siren calls of Temptation, Debauchery and Vice. He sees a cornucopia of goods and provisions, piles of hot meat pies and great coils of sausage, pyramids of fruit, glazed hams and glistening baskets of fish. He sees painted women clad in silks, he sees Lords and Gentlemen, beggars, whores and thieves. Urchins throng to his hands, offering him services, girls, a room at the Inn. Anxious and ashamed, he pushes on through this rich new world, his footsteps summoned by the clear, gentle tolling of the Cathedral Bell.

And then, finally, he stands before his goal, the Cathedral of Our Lady of Hagenburg, and sees, rising above him to a heaven that now seems closer than it ever was before, tier after tier of carved and chiselled stone, thousands of stone men, women, angels, monsters, hundreds of representations of his Lord Jesus Christ, the apostles and prophets, the tender Virgin.

He wants to fall to his knees, but does not dare, he fears the laughter of the city crowds, instead, he crosses himself fervently, again and again, and then, breathing deep, enters the Temple, enters inside, and walks into a high, echoing chamber of vaulted stone and coloured light.

† † †

i have told you the story of the yellow glass, children
but now let me tell you the story of the blue glass
a glass of a blue so fine and deep as the sky itself

when i found it in the old escritoire
it came attached to a note
a simple note
an address in Constantinopolis
far, far away
in the land of the Greeks

now, i could follow the yellow glass to the Winzbach vale in Lothringen
but to go all the way to the Levant?
travel for days and weeks over land and sea?

no, that was beyond my means

but one day
it must have been year of our lord twelve hundred and seventy two
for we had near completed the nave
and had nearly finished dismantling the old cathedral's western towers
i heard in a chance conversation in the new lodge
that one of the Bishop's advisers

had lived in Constantinople

imagine my surprise!
and so i went to see this secretary Emmerich Schäffer
a rich and influential diocese official
and when i showed him the blue glass and the scribbled note
he smiled and said "that is *my* hand! i wrote this!
how did you come upon it?"
and so i explained my story of the old escritoire

imagine my wonder when i learned from Schäffer's mouth
that it was his own brother, a Mason named Rettich
who had been that mysterious amanuensis
who had transcribed the designs of Master Achim all those many years ago!

on hearing that i had taken Rettich's drawings
completed, adapted, reinterpreted them in my own hand
he asked me to show them to him
in the presence of none other than Eugenius von Zabern
the Bishop himself
and so, children, the time had come
to unveil my secret work of many years

now, that great Bishop was blind
and so he himself could not see what i had done
but others were brought to the audience chamber
priests, canons, secretaries
and all admired and acclaimed what there they saw
and filled the Bishop's ears with praise

"are there any signs of heresy?" asked the Bishop, blind and stern and the theologians looked, and could find only sanctity

"your grace," i said, "there were, in Master Achim's designs
some motifs and figures for which i could not account,
and those i have replaced
with familiar figures from scripture
such as here
i have depicted the wise and foolish virgins,
our lord's parable from the gospel,
my hope being
that pilgrims of the fairer sex
may look upon our cathedral and receive moral instruction"

whereupon the Bishop laughed and said
"indeed, that is surely an idea that Achim von Esinbach
would never have had.
that young man's head was always in another world
from the one in which you might live, Master Kaibach.
instruction of such kind was far from his mind
but rather Visions of a New Jerusalem."

the Bishop's face then became sad and he said
"and yet his fate has often weighed upon my soul.
I treated him poorly, that poor young man
and if, somehow, in your work
his life lives on,
then i am glad of it.
now kiss my hand."

and i knelt and kissed the Bishop's ring
"you have my blessing," he said

and that is how i, my children, became

at the tender age of twenty-three
the new dombaumeister of Hagenburg

all my life i have spent around this cathedral
and all my life i have seen
the pilgrims who come from the distant villages
nervous, pale, cowed in awe
in their souls
the terrible fear of damnation
and in their hearts
the thirst for salvation

and what i have done i have done for them
to raise their thoughts to the heaven on high
to lift their spirits from despair and darkness
to offer hope of salvation,
of another life in God
a reunion in another world

and all of this it comes
from that discarded escritoire
thrown amongst rubbish, cobwebs and dust

† † †

The Rose.
If he had a dying wish, it would be to see the original draw-ing, to see, just once, how it was truly meant to be.

A sketch is all he has inherited from Achim von Esinbach and his amanuensis. A radiating corolla of corrugated concen-tric circles, tinted by Rettich here and there with dye and paint, and annotated in his peasant's hand: *as I remember, here blak, here wite . . . here pure blu . . . here sunyello, here leafs of red . . .*

A riddle, a ghost of a vision, beatific and strange.

And in his days as a young Master he puzzled over it, and puzzles still. Is it the Creation here represented? Is at the centre, darkness? Surrounded by pure white Light? *. . . and God divided the Light from the Darkness . . .*

And God made the firmament and divided the waters . . . Is this the Blue? The Blue of heaven and the ocean deep?

And God said let the earth bring forth grass . . . and the fruit tree yielding fruit after its kind? Green . . . and Red?

Is the Rose a vision of the Universe when she was young?

Now the stone framework for the Rose is nearly ready, but other generations will guide its genesis, other masters will complete it. Albrecht Kaibach, Master Builder of the Western Façade, will not see its final form.

The children are now gone. When he struggles to open his eyes, he can see amber in candlelight, the worn faces of his wife and sons, holding vigil.

"Sleep, my love." His wife's voice, whispering in his uncharted darkness. He no longer feels his body, all weight and pain is gone. Unanchored, he drifts like flotsam on the gentle waters of Old Father Rhine.

† Albrecht Kaibach
(1249–1318)

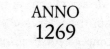

ANNO
1269

BLOOD
(ANNO 1269. TYBOLT I)

The Accused confessed to all the murders,
and gave the following deposition.

I arrived at Castle Moder in the guise of a travelling salesman. I had been apprised earlier that day that a group of salesmen were planning on showing their wares at the castle, and so I joined their group, and arranged that I would be seen last by the Baroness and Count.

I was admitted to their chamber, where I knelt before the Baroness who was seated upon a divan, and opened the cloth that concealed my so-called wares; some worthless trinkets and baubles that we had robbed from pilgrims in the previous weeks. Lying on top of the jewellery, was my sword.

"There is nothing here for me, young man," said the Baroness.

"No, look, My Lady," said I, and showed the sword.

"What will I with a sword?" she asked, and I declared, "This, My Lady, is a very special sword," whereupon I unsheathed it and showed it to her, and said, "This is the sword that my father gave me, my Father, the Baron Volmar von Kronthal."

Whereupon there was a look of confusion in her face, and then terror.

At that very point when I was certain that she had understood who I was and the import of my presence there in her chamber, I brought the sword down upon her with great force. She, the Baroness, was already screaming and flinching away from my attack and so my first stroke only served to slice open the front of her neck. With my second blow, following immediately after, I struck off her head.

The Count was now already running from his lectern in the corner of the room, and screaming, with all his might, "To Arms! To Arms!"

I leapt over the divan and caught up with the Count von Moder just outside his chamber doorway, where he, unarmed, retreated like a rat into a corner.

The corner afforded me no angle from which I could strike at him. I was therefore forced to stab him with the point of my sword. I stabbed him numerous times, I cannot tell you how many times I stabbed him.

Where did you stab him?

I stabbed him in the face, in the eyes, in the throat, in the heart, in the stomach, in the groin, until he sank to the floor and I could be certain that no surgeon could ever sew his guts back together again.

And then I fled. The castle servants had heard the alarum and were running around in confusion. Only two of them were armed and it was not difficult for me to evade them and mount my horse. The Castle gates were open to allow the other merchants to leave the premises and so I simply galloped forth, scattering the terrified and panicking merchants out of my way.

I then joined my troop in the forest. They informed me that they had located the son, Reinhard von Moder, who was nearby in the woods, hunting with friends. I and two of my men rode out to meet them. I was bloodstained from the dispatch of the Count and the Baroness, and as we approached Reinhard's hunting party I cried out, "Murder! Murder! My Lord, come quickly!" I told him his father and aunt had been attacked and that I, a merchant, had tried to prevent the attack. I told him his wounded father wished to see him and that his friends, along with my two men, should chase after the attackers who had fled. In this way I inveigled him to ride with me alone.

On the way, as we galloped towards his castle, I unseated

him with my sword. He fell heavily to the ground. I believe he broke his spine on the stone on which I caused him to fall.

I doubled back on my horse and dismounted. He was still conscious, and screaming in terror and in pain. I told him who I was and bade him confess that he and his father had killed the Baron von Kronthal.

He confessed. I pressed him to reveal who else had been there at my Father's death. He refused to speak further and so I struck off his head.

What is this "troop" you mention? Who are these men that you ride with?

When my Father died, those close to him—and here I will name no names—advised me to go into hiding in the Black Forest. This I then did, living in poverty and privation. Later I was joined by some members of my Father's Prinzbach garrison, who had been divested of their post by the mines' new owners, the von Moders. Together we formed a troop and lived from robbery and extortion.

We crossed from the Black Forest to operate in the forests of the Vogesen. It was our intention to find those so-called "robbers" who had murdered my father, and take our revenge upon them. It was later that we received information from my Father's friends that he had been murdered not by robbers but by the von Moders. It was then that I swore to exact a Son's revenge on this family.

And was it also You who murdered the Canon von Moder?

It was I. I do not know if the Canon had been implicated in my father's murder, but I had sworn to erase the name of von Moder, root and branch, and he was the last living scion of that family. I waylaid him in the pissoir of the *zur Glocke* tavern in

Hagenburg, where he—I had been told—often drank after Evensong. I throttled him with a wire and left his corpse in the latrine.

I left Hagenburg just as the city gates were closing and returned to my troop in the following days. I then disbanded them, as my task had been completed.

Thereafter I searched amongst the farms of the foothills for honest work as an ostler, as I am good with horses. I found work on a farm near Kinschheim. But my conscience troubled me and I could find no peace.

One day I travelled to Avenheim Monastery, where my mother is buried outside the walls, to pay my respects at her grave. Whilst I was there, a monk of the monastery asked me who I was and why I was weeping at the grave of Elise of Schwanenstein. My heart filled with Contrition and I confessed to that Monk all that I had done in the name of Revenge.

The Monk told me that I had committed mortal sins and that I would burn in Hell, and that my only hope of salvation would be to confess and accept punishment for my crimes.

And so I do here before you Gentlemen, in the hope of my Salvation. And if God will not forgive me, then I will go to Hell. And when I am in Hell, I will once again seek out those whom I have killed; Rutger and Reinhard, who murdered my Father, the finest man of Alsace.

And, amongst the fires and torments of Hell, I, Tybolt, will, with the permission of Satan, double and triple the eternal punishment of their blackened souls.

For I was there at their mortal demise, and wrought it with my own hands. And I testify to you Gentlemen of the Court, their suffering was but trifling and brief. Blood has its own terrible Justice, and in my veins my Father's blood still flows, and cries for Vengeance.

Here ends the Accused's deposition.

The Verdict, here duly recorded:
The Accused is found guilty of the murder of four persons of Noble Blood and Standing.

The Sentence: To be broken on the wheel and then hanged by the neck. Whilst hanging, to be disembowelled. Then to be taken from the rope, and Quartered by the Sword. To be buried without the city walls in darkness, and in an unmarked grave.

† Tybolt
(1244–1269)

THE WOODEN DOLL
(ANNO 1269. GRETE GERBER V)

In my dream I'm walking through the woods above Lenzenbach village, and Emmerich is beside me, behind me, flitting through the fir trees like my Shadow. It's winter, and our feet crunch in the snow, and that worries me, because when we were little we were never allowed to go into the woods at wintertime because of the Wolves, and our footprints will give us away, the whole village will know, and Dadda will hear and punish us with the belt.

But Emmerich and I, we're as old as we are now, bent and weary. Beneath his roguish red cap, Emmle's hair is white as the snow, and my dark hair is broken with grey.

"Come with me, I'll show you something," says Emmle, and takes my hand, pulling me deeper into the woods, and I don't want to go with him, but know that I must.

He looks at me and smiles, "There's nothing to be afraid of, Little Sis," and when he says that I get more and more scared. Because he was always mean to me, Emmle, always playing tricks on me, always trying to make me look the fool. And I think, *This is another trick. He is going to hurt me. Run. Run away.* But I don't know which way to run. I don't know the forests like he does. He was always off on his own, playing in the woods. Even on Sundays, when the whole village would be kneeling in Church, meek as mice, having the Fear of God hammered into them by Father Willem's sermon on Hell, then naughty Emmle would slip away, creep through the vestry door . . . and be gone until nightfall.

And no one would know where he had gone.

And now he is leading me There. There into his secret hideyhole deep in the wood. Deep and dark where the kobolds drink children's blood, and the wolves of winter keen and howl.

When I was a child, o!, how Emmle would make fun of me, o!, how he would make me cry. And dear, sweet brother Rettich would come between us and try and make peace. And once, just for me, Rettich carved a beautiful, lovely wooden doll.

And how I loved that doll. Big Sister Amaline taught me how to weave and sew, and whenever there was a scrap of cloth for me to work on, I would make that doll some little clothes, and dye them and adorn them with acorn shells, bright red dried berries and curls of carded wool.

But that Doll, one day it disappeared, and I could find it nowhere, and I cried and cried. And all Emmerich did was to laugh and taunt my childish tears. And Rettich, to console me, said "I will make you another one, just like it," and that only made me howl and wail even more, because I didn't want *another one just like it*, I wanted *my* wooden doll, I wanted My Doll.

And Emmerich leads me through a secret hole in a thicket, and up a steep gully slope. And the bramble thorns tear at us, the blackthorn scratches my cheek, and finally he says, "Here, here you are, Little Sis."

And I look up and I see a shrine. A Shrine like the Grandmothers used to make before Father Willem told them it was Unholy. A woodland shrine, with bright ribbons tied around old horseshoes and polished iron nails, hanging from the boughs of an old oak tree, and in the heart of the trunk, an offering.

And the Offering is My Wooden Doll.

And I rush to take her in my hands and kiss her, and as I

pull her from the tree there is a little rain of coins . . . the penny offerings to the woodland spirits.

And I hold my wooden doll in my hands and weep for joy.

And I wake and the dream is over. And I know that it was Emmle. It was Emmle who stole my wooden doll. It was he who took it from me, and hid it far away in the darkness, in the deepest dark of the deep dark wood, where kobolds drink children's blood and the wolves keen and howl, so that he could laugh forever, laugh at my anguish and my childish tears.

† † †

"What doll?" he asks, when I confront him with my dream.

"So you're saying you didn't steal my doll and hide it?"

"Why would I steal your doll?"

His blank grey eyes stare at me, and his cheeky face breaks into a smile. "Grete, are you going mad in your old age?"

We're sitting by the fire on the family floor of Haus Gerber on Cathedral Square. Outside, through the narrow glass windows, a cold autumn shower is sprinkling the panes and the gargoyles of Our Lady of Hagenburg are spouting rain.

Inside it's warm and snug, and the sounds of the cooks preparing the evening meal and the aroma of rosemary and roasting pork fill the house from cellar to eaves. Manfredle and his family are out visiting friends, Mayenz-Manfred and Rosamunda have gone to the cellars for wine, and it's just the two of us, me and Emmle, the last of the five-strong Schäffer brood. For Mechthild and Amaline passed over last winter, and dear Rettich . . . well, it's been nigh on fifteen years . . .

And five years ago, you would never have expected this to happen—me and Emmerich sitting together, chatting like old enemies reconciled. Ever since we were little we always fought like cats in a sack, and when he turned up on my doorstep five years ago like a Ghoul returned from the grave,

I wasn't surprised that the first thing he did was shout at me and call me a devious bitch. That's the way we always were.

But time salves all, and even tricky Emmle has turned back to Family in the end. It's funny how everything turns out. Emmle spent so much time in Vergersheim's bureau trying to browbeat him into returning Yudl's old lacquered coinbox and the "Rosheimer Fortune," that the two of them, those two pen-pushing schemers, have ended up best of friends. And my brother and I, after fifty years of screaming at each other, now meet on Sunday afternoons in Gerber House on Cathedral Square, and drink fine wine and chat like seamstress gossips.

"Well, if you didn't steal my Doll, who did?"

"It could have been any girl in the village. Besides, you were always losing things."

"Hah! I've never lost a thing in my life."

"Except your virginity to the first ginger fool who felt your arse."

"Sssh! The servants might hear."

And I think of those youthful days with my Manfred, and then go all soft inside. There it is again, the Itch. I look up at the crucifix above the hearth, and whisper a brief prayer; *get behind me, Satan.* But why did God give us the Itch if he never wanted us to scratch it? The Priests will tell you that it's all about making babies, new Christian souls to be baptised and offered up to the Glory of the Lord. But I'm now years beyond my fruitful age, and the Itch is pretty much as strong as it ever was.

"Emmle?" I ask, reaching out to poke the logs in the grate.

"Gretele?"

"What do you do for . . . pleasure? These days?"

I can't bear to look him in the eyes, and keep on poking the embers. He drags out the silence—on purpose, no doubt, and then asks, as if he's too dull-witted to read my gist. "What do you mean, Grete?"

"You know what I'm asking. The Itch. How do you scratch it?"

568 - BEN HOPKINS

I dare to look up, and see his insolent, wicked smile, his blank, staring grey eyes. "Well, I know where to look."

"You mean the red-scarfed girls?"

He shrugs, as if to say, *well, who else?*

"It's just as I thought. It's all right for you men, all ever so easy. Well, brother, I want you to do something for me."

"Yes?"

"You know the streets. I'm sure you can get me my heart's desire. For a price. Something young and vigorous."

He laughs. "Sister, have you no shame?"

"No. Why should I? When you gad about with whores? Why shouldn't I . . . "

"WE BROUGHT THE WINE!"

It's Mayenz-Manfred, calling out from below, mounting the stairs with two big pitchers of Dorlisheimer. Rosamunda, now not so steady on her ageing legs, brings up the rear with a plat-ter of ham. Emmerich wags his finger—*naughty girl!*—and then lets it rest upon his lips—*leave it to me.*

I change the subject as quick as I can. "And Bishop Eugenius? Will he meet with me?"

"About the Citizens' Building Committee?" Emmerich looks over to the new arrivals. "Well, now that they've brought the wine, let me say it. For we can celebrate! Manfred, pour it out."

Mayenz-Manfred, plumper and rounder than his Father ever grew to be, bangs down the pitchers on the dining table. "What's the toast?"

Emmerich folds his long fingers together. "His Grace will meet with Mistress Gerber and Councillor Enzelin. At the Palace, the day before Martinmas, after Lauds."

† † †

If you want to get anything done in this City, if you want to be taken seriously, then don't be a Woman, let alone a Woman

Without A Husband. You need to be a Man. And, well, if you can't be a Man because God didn't make you one, then you have to settle for the next best thing, which is to have a man by your side. I call it a "Beard." And Councillor Enzelin—a wealthy, gentle man of few words and few ideas—is a perfect Beard for many of my present endeavours: he has poise and generates respect, but when it comes down to the shillings and the pence, he lets me do all the talking.

Of course, I have to let him think that he is the senior partner of the two of us and I have to live with him taking the friar's portion of the credit for everything we do, but it's a small price to pay for the results I need. And so I meekly trot behind him, walking in his wake like a Saracen wife behind her Pasha, but when the doors are closed and the meeting begins, I unwrap my tongue. And then he sits quietly by my side, looking important and thoughtful, and helpfully mutters his "quite so"s and "so true"s, until, at the end he laughs and exclaims, "Mistress Gerber is quite a chatterbird! But I have to say, I couldn't have put it better myself!"

And so me and my Beard, sweet, virtuous Councillor Enzelin, go about our business of slowly, gradually, changing the world, piece by little piece. And now we have a veritable Challenge: to try and persuade the Bishop to put the funding of the building of the Cathedral into the Citizens' hands.

† † †

I've always had a strange kind of leaning for Bishop Eugenius—when I look back now I realise that even when I hated him, I was secretly rather sweet on him—but he isn't growing old gracefully. Now he's beginning to go deaf on top of being blind, and whereas before he seemed merely to assume that everyone around him was a fool, now it seems an iron conviction.

Yet his ears are still open to Reason, if you can shout it loud enough. And I've always had a good shrill voice.

"THE PEOPLE OF THIS CITY WANT TO DONATE TO THE CATHEDRAL! THEY WANT TO SEE THE BUILDING COMPLETED AND KNOW THAT IT HAS BEEN CONSTRUCTED WITH THEIR FUNDS! BUT IF WE DONATE TO THE CATHEDRAL ALTAR, THE MONEY GOES INTO THE CHURCH'S POT, AND WE HAVE NO OVERSIGHT OVER THE WAY THAT MONEY IS SPENT! IF THE CATHEDRAL FABRIC FUND WERE *SEPARATE*, AND *OVERSEEN* BY A COMMITTEE OF CITIZENS, AND THE *SPENDING THEREOF* OVERSEEN BY CITIZENS EXPERT IN BUILDING AND CONSTRUCTION, THEN THE DONATIONS WOULD INCREASE MANIFOLD! AND THE BUILDING WORK WOULD BE QUICKER AND MORE EFFICIENT! AND WE WOULD FINALLY HAVE A CATHEDRAL AT THE CENTRE OF OUR CITY AND NOT A BIG, CHAOTIC BUILDING SITE!"

. . . is the gist of what I shout in his silver-haired ear, with Councillor Enzelin nodding by my side, and, at intervals, shouting out, "SO TRUE! QUITE SO!"

After he has heard our presentation, the Bishop sits a while in silence. It seems the longer he has been cut off from the world of the sighted, the more eccentric he has become. As he reflects upon our weighty matter, his head twitches from side to side, and his mouth pops open and shut like a carp in a pond.

After many long moments, he speaks. "Very well, Councillor, Mistress Gerber. There is much common sense in what you say. And we shall essay it."

"OH THANK YOU, YOUR GRACE!"

"Schäffer and Vergersheim will draw up the statute. But it shall be so written that it can be rescinded by the Episcopate should the arrangement prove unsatisfactory, or should there be irregularities in the allocation of funds. In short, the idea seems very fine, but you will forgive me when I say, I do not trust the citizenry as much as you do."

† † †

Hagenburg, I have to admit, is slowly improving, slowly changing from a crowded sewer into a place of order and decency. Our new Bishop, guided in no small part by my canny brother, is open to change and development. His Grace's mind is that of a mathematician: he likes order, planning and sequence and frowns upon mess, confusion and muddled reckoning.

It may not yet be the Earthly Paradise, but all is going in the right direction. A rain of statutes has poured forth from the City Hall, regulating weights and measures and the quality of goods put on sale, banishing the "Stinking Trades" of knackers, blacksmiths and tanners beyond the city walls, banning the emptying of chamberpots onto the streets, begging in the residential areas, the banging of drums after sunset. The streets are sweeter and cleaner, the gangs of urchins, beggars and thieves have been swept away, and Trade, after years of stagnancy during the years of war and tension, is flowering once again.

God be praised.

And yet I feel a Tension, I sense Ill-Feeling beneath the new smiling face of Hagenburg. Take the Cathedral Square, for example. It has been cleared and ordered, the mess of the workmen's Lodges and the building debris moved aside, and where there were once ramshackle arcades and wooden lean-to taverns and shops, we have now erected a fine row of harmonious, patrician townhouses—the residences of the foremost merchants and officials of the City—and it is here that I now live, in Haus Gerber, on the northern side of the Square.

And yet I step out of my doorway and what do I hear?

Preachers standing on boxes, calling Hagenburg a Sodom and Nineveh, calling for a Lightning Bolt to fall and strike the crown from the heads of the Lords of the Sword, the Lords of the Cross and the Lords of the Pen, to punish the Luxury and Sin of the wicked, rich merchants, and to set fire to the houses of the evil, moneygrubbing Jews.

And at the public execution of Tybolt—he who claimed to be the bastard son of Baron Volmar—there were loud lamentations as he was brought to be hanged. He a murderer, who had killed four people in cold blood. "Kill all the Nobles!" was the cry to be heard. "Hang the bloody Lords, not their poor bastards!"

And I have to admit it: I know I've said similar things myself, in the past, when I was young. And now that I am a Lady of Substance, with assets and silks and silver spoons and a house on Cathedral Square, I shrink back at the echo of my younger voice.

In the heat of my blood, I called down Lightning on all those richer than me, all those put above me in the fortune of birth. And it seems that the people of the city got a taste for it at Wolfsbergen—to pull Lords from their horses and cudgel them in the mud. And Manfred, God bless him, if he'd been alive at Wolfsbergen, he would have cheered them on. He always said, *One day we will rise up and kill them all.*

It's all a fairy tale they tell us, he always used to say, *that their power and supremacy comes from God, that only they know the pathway to Heaven. One day all their fairy tales and lullabies will come to an end, and we'll rise from our slumber, and we'll take the Lords of the Cross, the Sword and the Pen, and in our rising, tear them all asunder.*

† † †

I have so much still to do. The Cathedral Building Committee is one thing, but I have the second cloth atelier to build, I have to find a good buyer for the river freight business. I have to set up the Merchants' School where our children can also learn to reckon and manage accounts, not just the Latin and Bible hocus pocus they presently learn from the Priests. And now is the time to get these plans into realisation, now that the Diocese and Municipality are open to Enterprise and Reason.

What bitter absurdity it is therefore, that as soon as the Gates of Possibility are opened, I must succumb to illness.

I have pains in my chest. They come and go. Biting, yanking pains that rob me of my breath. A cold, firm hand that grabs and squeezes my heart. And what Emmerich tells me is no succour at all. Rettich, the year before he died, suffered from similar attacks. And then one strong seizure that lamed him. And then one final seizure that stopped his heart for once and all.

† † †

And so I, threatened with the shadow of an untimely death, must needs think of my Legacy. And it is a hard truth, but one that I must bear, that my son, Manfredle, is a Fool. A happy Fool, a sweet Fool, but a Fool nonetheless. To leave my great fortune into his hands would not be wise, he would drink it, gamble it and give it away in warm, foolish generosity to his friends.

So I need to invest my fortune in Land. In fields and vineyards and farmsteads, in hills and moors full of grazing sheep, in forests full of precious timber, in mountains riddled with mines and quarries, yielding precious stone. Then my fortune will be locked in properties that Manfredle cannot squander, and he can live like a Prince from the tithes and rents.

But How?

The Lords own all the Land, and why should they want to

sell their fount of Gold? Whilst one sometimes hears of a
Commoner buying a farmstead, a small estate, a disused flour
mill that he wishes to fix and put back on its feet again, a plot
of land by a lake where he can fish for carp . . . one never hears
of a Great Landowner whose blood is not noble as the German
Eagle.

It's the eve of first Advent Sunday at Haus Gerber, and after
two tumblers of wine, I feel melancholy and weary. "We've
come some way, Emmle. But there's still such a long way to go.
The Nobles still own the Land, the Ministerials the City. You
and me are like village dogs, biting and yapping at their heels.
We bother them, and every now and again they throw us
scraps of meat . . . but we're still dogs."

Emmerich smiles one of his mocking smiles. "You may be a
yapping bitch, it's true, Little Sis. But you're a yapping bitch as
rich as a Countess."

The fire burns in the grate. The others are all in bed.
Outside the night watchman calls out the Peace; *the third walk
of the watch, and all is well!*

Emmerich clears his throat. "In my experience, everything
is for sale."

"But not Nobility, Emmle. Anything but that. If Nobility
were for sale, I would have bought it a while ago."

"If a cobbler's son can become the Pope, why can't a shepherd's daughter become a Countess of Alsace?" Emmerich
drinks his wine to the dregs and stands. "And if there's any
shepherd's daughter can do it, then I'm sure it will be you,
Little Sis."

I raise my eyebrows, say nothing.

Emmerich shrugs, wraps his hood around his white-golden,
tousled head. "Let me know if you're interested, and I will
look into it further. I'm sure I can procure you a good parcel
of land. Good Night, Sis. I'll let myself out."

And he stoops to kiss my cheek and leaves. I sit there, in a wine-gold haze, as I listen to his footsteps on the stairs, the bang of the door, and the sounds of the housemaids shutting the bolts behind him. And then his boots clacking across the cobbles of the Cathedral Square.

Countess Grete, what a joke. My brother can rustle up some young stable boys to pleasure me in my bed on Sunday afternoons when the Servants are all out on leave, but make me a Landowner with an estate . . . ? There are limits. Even to Emmerich Schäffer's cunning and nous.

I pour out the last drops of wine, and look around my beautiful home. The Crucifix above the hearth, edged in gold. The Venetian glasses, the blue-glazed bowl of apples and cloves, the oakwood table and chairs, upholstered in down and silk, the levantine carpets, the silver, star-shaped chandelier.

My lonely bed awaits me, but I have no strength to move. On winters' nights in Lenzenbach when I was a little girl, the house would be as cold as ice. But under the heavy woollen covers of the children's bed where we five little mice slept together, all would be snug and warm. And I would cuddle my wooden doll to my chest and listen to the wind whistling in the shutters. And all around our dark, silent house, the whispering, desolate woods where kobolds drink children's blood, and the winter wolves keen and howl.

ANNO
1270

INK
(ANNO 1270. EMMERICH SCHÄFFER III)

*To His Honourable Highness, Count Rudolf von Habsburg,
from Emmerich Schäffer, Secretary to the Bishop of Hagenburg.*

M y Honoured Lord,
My Master, His Grace Bishop Eugenius von Zabern,
in reluctant recognition of his ailing health, has
charged me with the solemn task of apportioning the assets of
the von Moder estate into deserving hands. In doing so, His
Grace has conferred upon me full powers of discretion, and
assures me of his desire to withdraw, as much as the exigencies
of his office allow it, from the temporal world of men, the more
to devote himself to prayer, to meditation and to God.

*After the most heinous murders of the four direct family
members of the House of von Moder, murders carried out by
the bloody hand of a certain Tybolt, whom some claim to be
the illegitimate son of the late Baron von Kronthal, there
remain no primary heirs to the substantial von Moder-
Kronthal estate. Claims have been made by distant cousins,
some of whom have even engaged legal counsel and written
petitions to Rome. There being at present no incumbent on
the Papal Throne due to disagreement amongst the
Cardinals, Bishop Eugenius has asked me to act swiftly and
to dispense the estate to the political and financial advantage
of the Diocese of Hagenburg, in which all the von Moder
lands are situated, to avoid a lengthy dispute such as that
which occurred with the lands of the House of Dagsburg some
thirty years ago, a dispute with which I believe You,
Honourable Lord, must be familiar, Yourself being one of the
beneficiaries of the eventual outcome.*

I therefore take it upon myself to offer You, Honourable Count von Habsburg, an abundant share in the Estate. In so doing, we recognise You, My Lord, as Knight and Warlord pre-eminent in our lands, as our greatest worldly leader. I am assured by many who are expert in such matters that when the throne of the Kingdom of the Germans and the Holy Roman Empire should fall vacant, it is You, My Lord, who will take the imperial crown. I hope therefore, by this modest offering, to demonstrate the continued Loyalty and Support of the City and Diocese of Hagenburg, and to bind you further in Friendship to the Hagenburg Episcopal Throne.

A final matter. I wish to present myself as Your Servant and Devotee. My honourable sister, Mistress of the Hagenburg Guild of Drapers, Grete Gerber—whom your Secretary Herr Wehelin will doubtless remember—was She who raised the ample funds that brought Your fortitudinous Hand to the side of the City of Hagenburg, and thereby brought us Victory at Wolfsbergen. I, her older Brother, now will deliver to you the Prize of profitable von Moder lands in the Vogesen and the Rhine Plain. You may thereby plainly see that we, Your Servants, have greatly endowed your treasury with our loyal gifts.

My humble request is merely this: should fate accord to you the deserving prize of the Imperial Crown, to remember me. Our lowly house of Schäffer has been blessed by abundant financial fortune and will soon acquire substantial estates in the region of Lenzenbach, but only You, Honourable Lord, will have the power to crown our good fate in noble Gold.

My Lord, I await from your Secretary in the fullness of time a confirmation of receipt of this letter, with a declaration of your continued loyalty, as friend and military protector of the Bishop of Hagenburg, and a confirmation that you will look favourably upon me, Emmerich Schäffer, as your liege and servant. On receipt of same, I will convey to you, as lies within my power, the title deeds to an abundant portion of the von Moder estate.

> *Yours in devotion, Your Servant*
> *Emmerich Schäffer, Secretary to the Bishop of Hagenburg*

† † †

To His Honourable Highness, Baron Lanzelin von Rappoltstein. From Emmerich Schäffer, Secretary to the Bishop of Hagenburg.

My Lord Baron,

As You know, I am your loyal servant, and have taken it upon myself, ever since you came to me for advice on the matter of your Insolvency, to find solutions to the embarrassment in which you find yourself. To date—and this I admit with a measure of shame—the measures that I have proposed have been but temporary and partial, in the nature of negotiating favourable rates for bridging loans from my contacts in the Judengasse, but now I am very content to say that I have a proposal that may, on the face of things, seem unusual, but which will, should you agree, clear all your present debt in one stroke.

In short, the proposal is thus: I will, in my capacity as the executor of the von Moder estate, bequeath to you some lands in the Vogesen, in recognition of your services to Hagenburg. Please believe me when I tell you that the allocation of land to your House will not be greeted with joy in all quarters, but I have laid the groundwork, indicating your valiant actions in the Battles of Wolfsbergen and Schwanenstein at the side of the late Baron von Kronthal, as sufficient justification for your inclusion in the list of recipients.

I appreciate that what you presently need is not more estates, but coin, and in substantial amount.

To this end, you will receive from my sister, Mistress Grete Gerber, the sum of one thousand marks for the rump of these estates which lie adjacent to Lenzenbach, which you will then sell to the Family of Schäffer. You will then pay me six hundred marks, and keep four hundred yourself, which will cover your debts, and allow you to start afresh in a life of solvency and comfort.

The condition for this gift of four hundred marks is simple: your silence and confidentiality. The sale of the Lenzenbach lands to me will be kept quiet for the time being. I know the Bailiff of Lenzenbach personally, and, as his new landlord, will be able to explain the situation to him in discretion.

Should you not wish to contract this deal, I have no further solution to your situation. Your level of debt is very serious and can only otherwise be met by selling a substantial parcel of your estates. I could find you a buyer, should you wish. But the offer I have just made you will save you the embarrassment of selling your House's assets and will restore your name and honour.

If you find the proposal amenable, please ride to Hagenburg at the nearest opportunity and present yourself to me at your next convenience.

Your humble Servant,

Emmerich Schäffer

† † †

To the Honourable Magistrate Heinrich Vergersheim.
From Emmerich Schäffer, Secretary to the Bishop of Hagenburg.

Dear Heinrich,

The matter of the Lenzenbach estates is now in process. I have established that Baron Lanzelin von Rappoltstein will be willing to sell his newly acquired parcels of land near the village of Lenzenbach for the reasonable price, given the revenues that pertain thereto, of a thousand marks. He wishes to sell quickly, as he has substantial gambling debts, as you know.

As Mistress Gerber, as a woman, may not own landed property by purchase, but only through inheritance or gift of a male relative, the land deeds will be transferred, initially, on Baron Lanzelin's receipt of the balance of one thousand marks, to my name.

I remind you of our conversations on this matter, and the benefits that will redound to You for your assistance in this case. Please recommend the transaction to your client.

Your Friend,

Emmerich Schäffer

† † †

To His Honourable Highness, Count Wolfram von Lichtenberg.
From Emmerich Schäffer, Secretary to the Bishop of Hagenburg.

My Honoured Lord,

It is with gratitude and joy that I write to you, and humbly accept your gracious gift of the revenue of the Rohrbach vineyards. Your House has ever been a great servant to the Diocese, and a courageous defender of its northern Marches, and should you profit from the allocation of the von Moder lands, it is only because of your virtue, and not mine.

I will do, as I promised, all that I can to promulgate the candidacy of your son Konrad as the noble and worthy successor to our present, remarkable Bishop. When that Sad Day comes, as come it must, I will prove your most loyal servant.

Yours in Gratitude and Obedience,

Emmerich Schäffer

† † †

Judah Rosheimer,
Borek Village, The Duchy of Kalisz

Dearest Yudl,

It is done. It took great effort, and perseverance, but it is done. I have now, in my sight and in my grasp, the necessary capital to restore our wonderful company, Schäffer and Associates, to its former glory. It will be exactly as you left it. Hagenburg is presently resurgent, trade is buoyant, and there is much that we can do together.

Therefore I beg of you to return to Hagenburg and take the reins once more. I cannot tell you how much it would gladden my heart to see you once again.

Please come, Yudl. Together we can repair the wrongs done to you, for which I am so truly sorry.

Please write and tell me you will do this. I yearn for word from you.

With affection and hope,

The Strawhead Goy

KALISZ
(ANNO 5030. YUDL BEN YITZHAK ROSHEIMER IX)

He remembers the Abomination, and in his memories, it is monstrous in size, reaching to the very heavens like Babel. Its walls, its stones and statues are hazy in his sight, aqueous, as if he is seeing them through a veil of drifting rain and river mists, as if the Rhine itself has burst its banks and flooded the great city, as if the Cathedral is a ship adrift on surging, vengeful waters.

And he remembers the Strawhead Goy walking beside him through the Square, and putting his fatherly hand on his shoulder and bending down to him (for he was not yet fully grown) and saying, *Look, Yudl, look there.*

And the statue he showed: a woman, blindfolded, her body slumping in melancholy and despair, the curves of her pleated gown sighing, pulled down by black Melancholy, her one hand weakly clutching a broken spear, the other a book that is slipping from her powerless fingers.

That, Yudl, he said, *is the statue of Synagogue. That is our representation of the Faith of the Jews. Blind, broken . . . and with the tablets of the Law falling from her hand.*

✡ ✡ ✡

When he thinks back on Hagenburg he sees nebulous images sunken in gloom, feels a choking sensation, a rising panic, the echo of nightmare. Sometimes he dreams he is back in the city, lost in a labyrinth of narrow, empty streets. He is always small, frightened, a little Boy, and the Gentiles are giants towering above him, their buildings are monoliths, towers gashing wounds in the Heaven. And a mocking voice sings, from Numbers. *And there we saw the giants, the sons of Anak: and we were as grasshoppers in their sight.*

But when he awakes, friendly, bright sunshine is pouring through the shutters. And when he opens them, the sky is vast and untrammelled, stretching out over the wide, flat Kaliszian plain. Here in the village of Borek in the Duchy of Kalisz, all is calm, all is in proportion. The sky and the plain seem to stretch out forever. The wind blows, fresh and clear, scented with grass.

Yudl has been chosen as Rabbi for this small, frontier community. The Jews of three villages, strung out along the River Prosna, south of the town of Kalisz. A small congregation, but growing every spring and summer month as emigrants arrive from the distant German lands.

That morning, a letter has come to him from Emmerich Schäffer, bearing with it the oppressive memories of his Rhineland home. It has lain, unopened, on Yudl's desk whilst he has conducted his pastoral business, receiving villagers, answering their questions, calming their concerns.

And now, finally, he is alone in his study. He takes his knife to break the letter's seal.

✡ ✡ ✡

He finds his mother at home. The Rosheimers have built three logwood houses and a stable surrounding a courtyard where chickens peck amongst the cabbages and beans. One house is for Mother, her younger husband and their two children who have come to join Yudl from Prague.

Mother has finished cooking the soup for the evening meal, and is gathering the embers, forming them into a glowing, amber cone, to smoulder until dusk when it will be time to set the night-time fire.

"Mother, he writes and tells me he has the money."—"Then tell him to send it."—"No, he says he will set up the company again. As it was. Before it was stolen from me."

Zipporah turns from the embers, and sits on the bench by the hearth. Her sunken eyes are deep in shadow, her pale cheeks dull silver in the light that seeps through the half-closed shutters. "Then go. If that is what you want."

"No," says Yudl, sitting on the stool facing her. "I have left that life behind. And yet it is a *lot* of money. If I were to return, disband the company, take the capital? Think of what it could do here. What a synagogue we could build, we could bring teachers and scholars, buy herds of cattle . . . "

Zipporah snorts, a gentle reproach. "And the Kalisz peasants? How long before they form a mob and come and hang us for all this newfound Gold? For now they leave us be, for we are as dirt poor as they."

Yudl nods mournfully, and rubs his eyes with the palms of his hands. It's true, the beth midrash here is little more than a stable with roughly plastered and whitewashed walls. When the winter winds blow, the men pray wrapped in blankets, their breaths steaming in the frozen air.

"Maybe you're right, Mother."—"Only you can decide, Yudl. But in our hearts, we gave up that money a long time ago."

Yudl looks up at his mother. Her face is still beautiful despite the lines of age and care that spread across her cheeks. He searches for her eyes, set deep in her face, two points of reflected light, crescent moons. "Mother, when I think of him, I think of a kind man. A man who loved me, taught me, who took pleasure in my happiness."

Zipporah shrugs. "I do not think of him very much at all."—"And yet you loved him? Once?"

His mother flinches, looks down in shame. Listens carefully, as if to make sure that they are alone. Her husband and sons are out at the beth midrash, or grazing the herd. They are alone.

She whispers. "I loved him. But I was just a little girl." Gently she rocks on the bench, her hands twist and turn. "He loved me . . . very much. He talked of taking me, and us running away to Italy. Where the sun shines, and you can pluck ripe figs from the trees. But then they . . . your uncle . . . made him go away. And when he came again, after some years . . . It was as a stranger. He rarely spoke to me. Not until after you were working for him. And all that time I watched him. And I could see, where his heart used to be, there was a purse. A purse full of coin."

She stands, smoothes her dress, and takes the soup pot in both hands. "Do not go. His Gold will only bring us trouble." She walks with the soup pot, and sets it on the table. "Let us never speak of this again."

✡ ✡ ✡

His son Eli has made gloves, fashioned from supple kid leather, varnished over with a secret substance that helps keep the leather dry, and inside, stuffed with warm sheep's wool. At the market in Kalisz, the first twenty pairs he had made were sold out in a single morning. And now he has an atelier here in Borek, where they are making hundreds more.

Yudl watches Eli from a distance as the young man negotiates with two peasants from a nearby village. It seems they have brought a sack of apples to exchange for gloves, and Eli is explaining that it's not enough. They stand outside the wooden shack that serves as the atelier, gesticulating and talking, until the peasant reaches reluctantly into his pocket and pulls out a silver coin.

A cow lows in the nearby barn, the wind shudders the

poplar trees, their leaves turning golden brown. The last days of summer have crept away towards the South, far, far over the Carpathian hills.

Yudl walks on through the village, the logwood one-storey houses and barns, the mud and cow dung, the piles of winter fuel, the saplings and young trees, not yet bearing fruit. In the near distance, the Christian part of the village, with its lines of poplars, its few stone houses, the tiny Church surrounded by apple orchards and, rising above it all, the huge plane tree that shadows the tavern and the village square.

Yudl smiles to himself, a wry, accepting smile. It seems his son Eli is destined for Trade. Eli's bride Rahel, a garrulous girl from Prague, had learned Bohemian from the local children there, and although the language they speak in Kalisz is much different, the rudiments are the same. Eli and Rahel have therefore been the first truly to master the local tongue, and travel between the towns and villages far and wide to thresh up customers for Jewish goods. And for study and the Torah, Eli has little, if any, time.

But so be it. Life here is a struggle, a challenge more to the body than the mind. Felling trees, cutting timbers, building houses, digging wells, planting crops and saplings. The scholars and their books will come when they are needed. All in the Lord's good time.

Yudl returns to his study built into the gable roof of his house. The ceiling is so low one has to stoop, but his chair is soft; the finest chair of his old Hagenburg home. And his Father's library is there, carried with them all the way from the banks of the Rhine.

Yudl writes:

Dear Herr Schäffer,

I thank you for your letter. I have been touched by your

assiduous efforts in restoring my family's fortunes. But at present I have no desire to return to Hagenburg and resume my previous occupation. I have renounced the merchant's life, and my days are now dedicated to study and to God.

Please return to Schäffer and Associates its lost reputation and restore its former glory. Give generously to the poor and the needy. Remain a steadfast friend to our people in Hagenburg. More I do not ask of you at present. After due reflection and further meditation, I will decide whether I will ever be able to return to the Rhine.

Yours in gratitude,

Judah

He will give the letter to his son's hands, and it will be taken to the next market fair in Kalisz, whence, by the routes of Fortune, it will wander westwards over the coming months, borne by Jews who travel from town to town in search of the rewards of Trade, that web of silver thread that spans the world.

Yudl stands and puts his hand against the gable ceiling, stuffed with straw. Here in his study, he has allowed himself one Luxury, a single pane of glass the width of five hands, and the only glass window outside a church in all the surrounding land.

Here, from this higher vantage point, he may look out across the endless Kalisz plain. He may watch the stormclouds forming and the sweeping veils of rain. On sunny days, he can see the clothes drying on the lines, twisting and leaping in the gusts of wind. He can watch the cows returning from the grazing, the scurrying flocks of geese, the children playing, the men returning from the beth midrash.

He stands like this often, and thinks. For he, in his older age, has returned to the questions of his Youth. He has returned to the Slippery Things, the unanswerable questions. *When did it all begin, and when will it all end? What is beyond the end of the Universe and what is beyond the end of Time? If there is Imperfection in this World, then how may it have emanated from the Perfect Source of all Perfect Things?*

And he thinks of the story. That the Soul knows everything, but before it is born, an Angel gives the babe a fillip on the nose, and then all is forgotten, lest the child be driven mad by infinite knowledge on this finite, imperfect earth.

And all we Know, we Knew once before, and we think we Learn it, but it is not so: we merely Remember a part of that Perfect Knowledge that we carry in our soul.

And we look to the heavens, and sometimes in perplexity, and sometimes in despair, we cry out questions to the Lord. But *God maintains his silence and carries the Universe.* And there is never an answer.

He folds the letter, holds the sealing wax to the candle's flame, and thinks of his Father's words. *Gold comes, and Gold goes, the grass withers and the flower fades, but the Word of the Lord shall stand for ever.*

ANNO
1271

THE SILVERED SOW
(ANNO 1271. GRETE GERBER VI)

I remember, back in Lenzenbach, when I was a girl, there was a sow. And the sow had just farrowed. And then she keeled over and died.

And she lay there in the corner of the yard, and all the village children came to see her lying there, with her farrow, all seven of them, whining and griping and suckling, pushing their tiny pink heads into her teats, squeezing her dry of every last drop of piggy milk.

And when her teats were dry, the men came and dragged her up onto a trestle and slit her throat, and bled her into buckets. And then they rubbed hot ash and embers over her hide, to burn off the bristles. And then they shaved her with knives. And then they sawed her up and jointed her, and they hung her, in pieces, in the smokehouse, to cure and dry.

And the farrow? They were too young to sup on grass and meal. They only wanted milk from their mother's teats, but her udders were now boiling in the offal pot, to make a chewy treat.

They whined and keened and squeaked as we chased them round the yard. And when we caught a little piggy, our fathers strangled them, one by one.

A fire was dug and set, and spits were hung across the pit. The seven spitted little piglets crackled in the flames.

The whole village gathered, drinking and dancing. For when God strikes down a sow and seven piglets, there is no weeping. There is black pudding, there is smoked bacon, there is boiled offal and liver sausage, there is succulent, sweet, suckling piglet meat, pulled steaming from the tiny bones.

†††

Like that poor old sow I lie here on my side, unable to move, and the farrow nestle, sucking me dry.

"It was all for the good," says Vergersheim, that snake. "Of course, when Herr Schäffer reappeared in Hagenburg, alive as you or me, it was clear he had a case to reappropriate the assets of Schäffer and Associates, the so-called 'Rosheimer Fortune' . . . plus interest and damages. So we came to a quiet arrangement between us. Clerk to Clerk. We Men of the Pen have a good understanding."

A Quiet Arrangement.

A Good Understanding.

"We protected and preserved your estate, Madam. But considering that your present fortune is substantially founded on moneys expropriated from your brother Herr Schäffer, it does not seem unreasonable that he now should be, jointly with me, Executor of your Estate.

"Do not fret!" flutes Vergersheim, smiling like a Devil. "Your son and grandchildren will be amply provided for!"

Amply provided for. No doubt they will not starve. But the fat and the bacon and the ham and the sausage will be carved up by Secretary Schäffer and Magistrate Vergersheim, and my own farrow will be weaned from my teats with chitterling and tripe.

Emmerich comes to visit me when I am alone. *I got you, little Gretele*, he whispers in my ear. *I got you.*

†††

Since I was struck down, since my heart seized up and clobbered me lame, since my tongue drooled speechless from my dropsied mouth, I have learned what it is to be a silvered sow. My ateliers, sold. My fabrics, my raw goods, auctioned. My river boats consigned to Schäffer and Associates, a name once again on the Hagenburg Register of Trade. My strongbox of coin, still marked with faded Jewish letters, passed back into my brother's grasping hands.

House Gerber on Cathedral Square . . . and my lands in Lenzenbach—conveyed in Emmerich Schäffer's name.

Manfredle screams, and Manfredle wails, Manfredle weeps and clutches my palsied hand. *Mother, they are robbing me! They are fobbing me off with a house on Langer Weg and a pension of forty marks a year!*

But when it comes to feed me soup and mashed-up beet, when it comes to wash my soiled behind, he leaves the work to the serving girls. As if I never spooned mush into his grasping mouth. As if I never wiped up his shitty arse.

As if I never suckled life into him from these dried-up dugs.

† † †

A Benedictine Monk comes to my chamber, places a lighted candle in my hand. His dark eyes gloat like coins in the amber light, and he talks to me of my coming death as if it were his alone to comprehend.

Imagine if you will, Madam, a vast, cold ocean, and on that ocean, a sailing barge. And you upon that vessel, with the thousands of souls who have died that day, from every nation on this Christian Earth.

And ahead of you on the seas you behold, rising to the very clouds, a mountain.

This, Honourable Madam, is Mount Purgatory. And this is the mountain that you, in penance, must ascend.

And think, if you will, that every one of your sins is a block of stone. And think, if you will, of this mountain, that reaches even to the Heavens. And think, if you will, that you must climb, and bear every burden, every block of stone, until the very summit of that dreaded peak.

First you climb, one day, bearing the stone that marks your very first sin. Then, the second day you must descend the road you have already come, and collect the burden of your second sin, and ascend again. And again and again and again and again, bearing on your back the weight of your sins, up and down, and up and down again . . .

Imagine, Madam, if you will, this penitent climb . . . lasting not for days. Lasting not for years. But for . . . Centuries!

He's good, this Monk. There are even glistening tears in his golden eyes.

But I have here, Madam, some remedy. And he pulls from his cloak a parchment scroll. The seal is stamped with two crossed keys, the Seal of Rome.

This dispensation, sealed by the hands of the Holy Father himself, will shorten your journey . . . by a thousand years.

For fifty marks of silver, I can here inscribe your honoured name . . .

My Brother, My Keeper, My Purse-Bearer, has been listening outside the half-closed door. And now Emmle comes, laughing, and takes the candle from my lifeless hands.

"My Sister thanks you, Brother. But you may keep your Pardon Scroll. And leave immediately, lest I kick your scraggy arse all the way back to Rome."

† † †

To cheer me up, they talk about my funeral. How my coffin will be fashioned in varnished oak and borne by Master Drapers from the Guild I helped found. How Mass will be sung at the Morning Altar, the Altar I helped fund. How my silver pennies from my charity chest will be given out in alms. How they have no less than six monks, four silver candlesticks borne by altar boys, the Cathedral Choir to sing the psalms.

But what's that to me? I will already be gone, and my Soul

already on the shores of Purgatory, my hands, now full of ghostly life, clutching at the penitent stone.

My thanks to Emmle, that evil fox. I have no need of Dispensations, no need of Pardons from the parchment workshops of the Papal Throne. For, on those distant shores, a Ghost, I will have my voice again.

Good Lord, I pray that it is not a Sin, but I know my Penitence will be brief. Those two coins they place upon my sightless eyes, I will put to profitable use. I, Grete Gerber, will arrive upon the Purgatorial Shore, and I will trade and bargain, I will wheedle and cajole until I have porters aplenty to shoulder the stones that are inscribed to my soul.

And palanquin bearers to carry me aloft. And fine food for my workers, hot soup and warm, Lenzenbach bread. And the Angels will chide me and say, "Mistress Gerber, this is NOT the way it is done!" And I will say, *In heaven as it was on earth, I have never listened to anyone.*

I will climb that Mount the way I've climbed up out of this mortal vale. From mud and clogs and piles of dung to silver and gold and mother-of-pearl.

And it won't be long before I'm in Paradise, resting my weary feet in a heavenly stream. And I'll look down from my cloud at the Cathedral of Hagenburg, that *my* committee is now helping to build. And I'll see the monks singing mass in my name. And I'll see my farrow, waiting to throw my casket in the freezing ground.

And I'll ask a passing Cherub for a pitcher of wine. And I'll drink to myself. For I know what I've done, and every deed I've done was Mine.

† Grete Gerber
(1216–1271)

ANNO
1273

Von Lenzenbach
(anno 1273. Emmerich von Lenzenbach
né Schäffer IV)

To His Imperial Majesty, Emperor Rudolf von Habsburg, from Emmerich Schäffer, Secretary to the Bishop of Hagenburg.

Your Imperial Majesty,
Allow me to attach to the missive of my Master, His Grace Eugenius von Zabern, Bishop of Hagenburg, my own brief, humble letter.

It is with great joy that we in Hagenburg have heard of your election to the Throne of the Holy Roman Empire, and with even greater joy have learned of your intention to visit our city. Please be assured of Hagenburg's support and loyalty. I look forward, as spokesman for the Bishop on political matters, to discussions with your representatives as to how we can be of service to You, especially in your ongoing dispute with the Bishop of Basel. It will be Hagenburg's honour and joy to provide you with men and arms for your campaign.

I feel deeply humbled by the Honours you have bestowed upon me, Honours of which your Clerk has informed me in his missive, and the terms of which I hereby agree.

With your Imperial Majesty's permission, I shall take the name of "von Lenzenbach," as I myself was born in that verdant vale, and it is where my estates are located.

I remain your faithful and loyal servant,
Sir Emmerich von Lenzenbach

† † †

To My Lady Baroness von Ahrenheim, from Knight Emmerich von Lenzenbach.

My dear Lady,

It is with jubilation that I have received today your missive regarding my proposal of Marriage. The conjoining of our hands will redound to the benefit of both our Houses, conferring upon me Honour and Pedigree, and upon your House, an end to the financial woes that have beset you. I hereby accept all the terms negotiated on your behalf by your cousin, Canon von Lichtenberg. By way of allaying your final concerns, please accept my assurances that the slanderous lies spread by my enemies that I have offspring from a previous illicit liaison (with a Jewess no less!) have no foundation. Success and advancement breed envy, and envy breeds slander and falsehood.

I am impatient to conclude our happy union, and to greet you in Haus Lenzenbach as my honoured and cherished Wife. Yet please forgive me, My Lady, if I ask of you to delay this happy occasion until the stars shine more favourably upon us.

My Lord and Master, His Grace Eugenius, is now gravely infirm. The doctors inform me that it cannot now be long before the Lord calls him to his side. And so I must unwillingly ask of you Patience until this sad day has passed, and the election of His Grace's successor is established, before our hands may be joined in Matrimony.

I beg for your Understanding, and thank you from my heart for your Forbearance,

Your happy husband-to-be,

       Sir Emmerich von Lenzenbach

† † †

Judah Rosheimer,
Borek Village, The Duchy of Kalisz

Dearest Yudl,

As I have heard nothing further from you since your last missive, I must conclude that you are resolute in your decision not to return to Hagenburg. I therefore must tell you that I will now disband Schäffer and Associates. The substantial burden of my other duties prevents me from giving the company my full attention.

I therefore, for the avoidance of any future doubt, here disclaim any further debt and obligation to you. You shall have no claim on my estate or that of my descendants.

Yours in affection,

The Strawhead Goy

† † †

To Bishop Elect Konrad von Lichtenberg, from Knight Emmerich von Lenzenbach

Your Grace,

My grief and sadness at the passing of my much honoured Master Bishop von Zabern is almost surpassed by my joy at the news of your election. If I could play but a small role in your success, then I am most glad of it.

I accept with deep gratitude and humility my appointment as Councillor of the City of Hagenburg. In my view our most urgent task will be to regulate and contain the growing power of the Guilds and craftsmen in the body politic of our City. They must be listened to, and appeased with small concessions to their importunate demands.

I await your summons. As soon as you need my services, I will hurry to be of assistance.

Yours in obedience,

Sir Emmerich von Lenzenbach

† † †

To Haider Schulte, Master Painter,
from Councillor Sir Emmerich von Lenzenbach

Honoured Master Schulte,

Thank you for accepting this commission at the agreed price. The (empty!) coin strongbox in question will be delivered to you, along with this letter, by my valet.

Your task is as follows: to remove the present embellishments (Star of David, crest of the town of Rosheim, lettering in the Hebrew language etc.) and retouch the lacquerwork accordingly. Then, on all four sides of the strongbox, paint, to the finest of your ability, the crest of the House of Lenzenbach, the stencil for which my valet shall deliver to you herewith.

Payment shall be made on your delivery of the finished article.

Yours, with respectful greetings,

Councillor Sir Emmerich von Lenzenbach

INFINITY
(ANNO 1273. EUGENIUS VON ZABERN X)

The Good Lord knows, I have not been one to embrace life on this earth with joy and enthusiasm. I have rather considered my Existence as a continuous trial, an inexorably burgeoning list of tasks which I leave, now that my life is coming to its End, unsatisfactorily unfinished.

And yet I am afraid of Death, and my body cleaves to Life as a babe to his mother's breast. In vain I offer myself the consolations of Philosophy, that all flesh is as grass and must wither and die, that my existence itself is a miracle that I received without volition and must therefore relinquish with serenity. In vain I meditate on the revelations of Theology, that after Death there will be a Resurrection, another life in the spirit, the hope of Paradise.

All in vain. Even in its depleted, exhausted state, my flesh clings to existence and trembles with Life.

† † †

For some time now, I have relinquished the uses of this world, abdicated from the duties of my office, entrusted power into others' hands. In so doing I have been cautious not to give away too much actual Power, but rather the accoutrements and vestments thereof, dispensing to those hungry for influence those daily tasks and responsibilities carried out in the sovereign's name.

For instance, if you had told me as a young Treasurer that

the building of the Cathedral could be put into the hands of the citizens, I would have laughed at you. With what virulence I hated the New Cathedral and its drain on the Diocese's resources and indeed on my own time and vitality. But what better solution than to remove the burden of its construction from the Church and to place it on the broad, vigorous shoulders of the People?

Our fortunate, present Treasurer, Canon von Hagen, has had only on occasion to cast his eye over the Fabric Committee's accounts—unlike my younger self, he has lost no sleep over the funding and administration of the Cathedral's construction. And, under the management of the citizens' committee, work has proceeded apace, the old Western towers have been fully dismantled, and the foundations dug for the new high, majestic, Western Façade.

I have not forgotten my promise to Bishop Berthold, the promise I made when he himself was on his deathbed, to stay true to his vision of creating the finest Cathedral in the German Lands. And to this end I have appointed as Dombaumeister the young Albrecht Kaibach. Under my predecessor, Heinrich von Stahlem, the work proceeded at a slovenly pace and the unity of design and form of the Bishop's Church had been corroded by individual commissions and bequests. These will now be corrected, and the work will return to the original vision of Achim von Esinbach, whose plans Kaibach has retrieved and adapted to the contemporary style: equally ornate, but less emblematic, more lifelike, more taken from Nature.

Soon work on the new Narthex, Towers and Western Façade will begin. I had hoped to live to lay the Foundation Stone. It seems I have hoped in vain.

One by one, my senses have been taken from me: Sight, Hearing . . . and now Touch. I can barely sense my surroundings, barely move on this my deathbed. All I can feel is pain, a dull ache pressing against my chest, conspiring to rob from me my final breath. And then, at times, at junctures increasingly frequent, an Agony.

But I am glad of the silence, if not of the pain that is its ghostly companion. A Ruler's ears are always filled with envious, slanderous poison, with jibes, slights and complaints. At most I have suffered for my promotion of my secretary, Emmerich Schäffer, to Regent in my infirmity. Noble and priestly tongues ceaselessly hissed in my ears that I had given him too much power, but in all conscience, I cannot fault what he has done for this City.

For instance, it is a small matter, but one I truly appreciate, that there is now, thanks to Emmerich Schäffer, in the town hall of Hagenburg, a stone that weighs exactly a pound, a beaker that holds exactly one pint of water, a stick the exact length of one ell, and it is the task of one official, the Master of Measures, to make all weights and measures used in the city conform to these standards.

The Whisperers warned me that Emmerich Schäffer is a schemer, hungry for power, but is this Statute for the Unification of Municipal Measurements the act of some aspirant despot?

Is it then the act of a virtuous man, a Good Deed offered to the Judgement of God in hope of the remission of Sins?

No, it is not that, either. And if the impetus behind his work is not the thirst for power, nor the theological virtue of Charity, then it must be something else, something unfamiliar to me and to members of my noble breed. What brave Knight would debase himself to calibrate a stick? What virtuous Saint would strive to regulate the dispensation of tavern wine in perfect pints and gills?

And yet Schäffer and his kind set about this work with Industry, and it is by these small innovations, by these tiny yet significant increments, that civic life is ameliorated. And it is because of the work that Schäffer and I have done together that I know that, when I die, I will leave Hagenburg a better place.

† † †

No, I have not loved this Life, this World. For good reason it is known as a Vale of Tears. And yet I have not spent my life in weeping, but rather in vexation that the world is full of Fools.

I know it is unspeakable Vanity, but if all the world were as me, if Hagenburg were full of von Zaberns and Schäffers, then we might, with industry and application, create a shadow of the Earthly Paradise here on the banks of the Rhine. And yet instead we struggle against a tide of Idiots, who through arrogance, greed, folly or lassitude, stand in the way of betterment and the common good.

Why then, if that is so, do I so cling on to the gunwales of this Ship of Fools? Why do I not let myself slip into the oblivious waters?

Because, even if my corrupt body is rotten and wracked with pain, even if all my senses have departed from me, leaving only agony and decay, my Mind is still blessed with Life. And, as in the long nights of my Youth, when I could find no sleep, I lie here . . . and think of Numbers.

For Numbers are the bridge between the World of Perfection and this fallen, foolish vale of tears. They exist both in the purity of abstraction, and in the concrete, solid, sinful world. They exist in the ten fingers of my twitching, clutching hands, in the spidery numeric scrawls in Schäffer's books of accounts, they exist in that vision of perfection in this fallen world, the Cathedral, in its circles, in its triangles, in the parabolae of its curls and curves, a beauteous image of the Godhead as a finite, geometrical and comprehensible idea.

And they exist also in pure conception, in the flights of numerical beauty that my mind conceives.

Can one set a limit on numbers? Can one imagine where the line could be drawn and say . . . after this count, one may reckon no further?

No. They have no beginning and have no end. Numbers stretch out, beyond our human limits, beyond our comprehension, to a boundless Infinity. This physical world, my body, my life, will come to an end, but numbers count onwards for ever, towards the greatest of all reckonings that can never, ever be reached.

† † †

I feel the touch of some caring being who kisses my hand, and pours some drops of water into my dry, gasping mouth. Is this Hieronymus? My old, faithful friend?

I can feel the drops of water, one by one.

One.

Two.

Three.

In the crypt of the Cathedral, a tomb awaits me. My body shall be laid to rest, wrapped in a pure, white alb. My crozier shall be laid in my lifeless hands. Masses will be sung in my name. They will anoint my forehead with Holy Oil, and then, when all the rites of death are done, the Masons will heave and seal the heavy stone lid above my mortal remains.

† Eugenius von Zabern
(1201–1273)

END OF BOOK THREE

† Emmerich von Lenzenbach
né Schäffer
1215–1279

✡ Yudl ben Yitzak Rosheimer
4992, Hagenburg—5046, Kalisz

EPILOGUE:
ECHOES
(1350–1351)

EPILOGUE

I: THE CALAMITY
(ANNO 1350. QUIRIN VON LENZENBACH II)

II: KINDLING
(ANNO 1351. THE UNKNOWN MOTHER)

III: SNOW
(ANNO 1351. ZENZI)

ANNO
1350

THE CALAMITY
(ANNO 1350. QUIRIN VON LENZENBACH II)

I have heard these voices throughout my life, drunken voices raised in taverns, bedraggled wild-eyed men shouting from the trestle tables of market squares, calling down Calamity on the world, prophesying with fervour that One Day the People will rise, the peasant, the footman, the carter and porter, and will knock the Crowns from the heads of Kings.

And look, it has happened, or something very like. And what is the all-hallowed Result?

A thousand dead Jews burned in a pyre. Bands of ruffians who toss down their tools hours before sundown and sit drinking outside the taverns, cursing and throwing stones at priests. Petty merchants folding their hands inside their furs and refusing to trade until the City rescinds all tolls and tithes. Marauders and highwaymen on all the roads. Bandits roaming the vineyards and farms.

And truly, Calamity has fallen upon this world.

† † †

In Hagenburg alone, some ten thousand have died from the Plague. And throughout the Diocese, whole villages have been lost, monasteries and abbeys stand empty, sheep wander through abandoned cloisters, pigeons nest in looted churches, in our once splendid vineyards, the grape twists dying on the stunted vine.

The Bishop still rules, at least in name. But Butchers and

Tanners sit in our City Council, cloaked in sable and silver, taking on the airs of the patricians they once affected to despise. The common people, enriched by Death, who were quick to learn that work is plenty and workers scarce, haggle their way to bloated wages and, when a better offer comes, with an insolent shrug of their shoulders, leave off their work, half complete, half done.

A sister dies and bequeaths to her brother, the brother dies and bequeaths to his wife, the wife dies and bequeaths to their son, the son dies and bequeaths to a cousin, the cousin dies and bequeaths to his sister . . . and the sister Lives. She buries her dead, bows deep in mourning . . . and in her shuttered, empty home, when no envious eyes are looking, in guilty lamplight, opens her money chest and tallies her Coin.

And All Who Live today, now that the Plague has seeming passed away, shoulder up their Grief like a sack of chaff, cast it to the wind, and Rejoice. For they have seen Death creeping by, have heard the rustle of his sable cloak, have seen the rictus contort their Loved Ones' faces, smelt the foul pus that oozes from the blackened boils, clenched their hands to their ears to blot out the screams . . . and yet They Live.

The Taverns are full, Musicians play. Jigs and dances, reels and roundelays. But while you dance, who will sow the seed, who will reap the field? Who will pluck the vine and tramp the grape? Who will provide your next year's wine?

So, Hagenburg, wait. Wait till the barrels are all drunk dry.

† † †

And so I am leaving. This house, Haus Lenzenbach on Cathedral Square, I have put up for sale. I cannot think there will be a buyer soon.

In recognition of my family's wealth, and in hope of my resurrection and the Lord's forgiveness of this City's sins, I bequeathed all my remaining worldly goods to the Cathedral's Fabric Fund. And in doing so, I know I am not alone. Whilst the Plague sickened through the city's streets, whilst Death crept from house to house, then the city's sinners repented of their many sins. Many were those who, as the black pustules cracked and burst, pleaded to Heaven and pledged their ill-gotten gold to God. And many of those who had sucked their silver from the burning furnace of the slaughtered Jews, in mortal fear of Hell, laid their purses on the Frauenwerk Altar to buy some remission for their crimes.

The Fabric Committee, which once I chaired, is now swilling, awash with Gold. And from my window here on Cathedral Square, as I wait for the cart that will take me from Hagenburg, I can see the majestic Cathedral rise to the skies. They have finished the beauteous Rose. They have built the scaffolding for the first soaring Spire.

I am told that one can see it from leagues away. From the Black Forest. From the Vogesen Hills.

And so this Cathedral that I have looked upon, from this window, every day of my mortal life, will continue to grow. And it is built on such diverse Foundation Stones. On the Fear of God. On stolen Jewish Gold. On the hope of Salvation, a Resurrection and a Life to Come.

† † †

My servants call, the cart is ready. Loaded with my last, personal things.

I will journey to Lenzenbach, in the Vogesen Hills. My wife, my three sons and grandchildren await me on our family's estates, now managed by my eldest boy. On the green foothills, herds of cattle, sheep and goats. On the lower plains, wheat and rye.

My ancestors came from a village there. They were shepherds, the Bishop's serfs. They watched their sheep and slept the summers beneath the stars. And thus they lived, full centuries long, until dreams of this city led them astray.

It is time to return.

ANNO
1351

KINDLING
(ANNO 1351. THE UNKNOWN MOTHER)

They came from the Lorraine. From a village blighted by the Plague. They wandered South, along empty, haunted roads. And came one night, as evening fell, to Avenheim Monastery, louring in the dark.

They were Mother and Son. He but five summers old. They had no food but dried, black bread. And so they stumbled to the Monastery, in hope of soup, in hope of a bed.

But the Monastery was empty, abandoned, a shell. And as they stood in the twilight of the courtyard above the wide, darkening, Rhineland plain, a last ray of sunlight broke the cloud, and lit, like a Sign from God, the City of Hagenburg, leagues away, in the valley below.

It shone upon the city's sandstone walls, and burnished the Cathedral's towering dome, and lit the spidery scaffold of the surging Spire. And the Mother turned to the Son and said, "My Son, this is where we must go. Tomorrow, God willing, we will journey there, you and I."

For she knew she was sick. A Fever had clutched her since the day before. And the evening was growing colder, the Witch of Winter rode the wind, and the clouds were seething down from the Vogesen Hills.

And her son was shivering, trembling with the cold. So she knew that they must have shelter, a fire, and—God willing—hot food and a bed. She had little strength left, but she dropped to her knees and prayed to the Lord—*oh my God, grant me fortitude.*

And with her last might, she broke the shutters of the Monastery's servants' cellar, and climbed inside. Her son was weeping, his feet rubbed raw, his tiny body exhausted, his eyes red with tears.

She pulled him inside, wrapped him in sheepskin from her bundled pack and took out their two candles, and her tinderbox. "Stay here, my Love, and I will come for you. Here is a candle, so you need not fear the dark. Stay here, I will find what we need, and I will come for you."

† † †

With fading strength, she searched and searched. Her candle's flame hardly seemed to penetrate the dark. But in a storeroom she searched and found . . . a tub of dried peas, sprouting, dried garlic and a flagon of wine.

Her body was shaking, the fever sapped her spirit, tempting her to yield, to lie down and sleep. In the kitchen, she found an old iron pot. In an alcove, firewood, and in a side room, a pallet, and blankets of wool.

She returned to her son, who had fainted with cold. His candle still burned in his tiny, shivering hand. She begged God for Strength, just one more time, and carried her son in her trembling arms. And laid him on the pallet, wrapped him in blankets, and piled the wood high in the hearth. Set the pot on the trestle, and singing a hymn, filled it with dried peas, garlic and wine.

Her eyelids were drooping, her strength almost gone. And yet she had one last thing to do for her Son. She must light the fire, set the pottage to cook, or else they would both die there in the monastery's dark.

And yet kindling . . . she had none. And here she nearly succumbed to despair. But then she remembered one thing in a chest she had seen. Parchments, curled, yellowed and dry.

She returned with the candle, and opened the chest. It was full of writings, drawings and words.

She offered prayers to the Lord, and brought the chest to the hearth. By the light of the candle, she spread out the parchments, and said, "I know it's a sin to burn Holy Words. But Jesus, forgive me, for through this, my Son will live."

She had but few letters, but her fading eyes could read the name on the parchment: A C H I M v E S I N B A C H it said.

And then she took a kitchen knife, and cut the first parchment in strips. And unfolded the second, and was blinded by tears.

For what lay before her was the fairest thing she had seen. A circle of colours, a Rose painted in white, blue, crimson and green.

She crossed herself again, and bade forgiveness once more. Sliced the parchment in strips, and set them on fire.

† † †

She laid down by her Son, held him tight to her breast. She succumbed to Delirium, and called out to her Lord. *O God, o God, save us, I pray. Save me, save my Son, let us live through this night, let us live till the new day.*

Her son stirred beside her, and his lips formed some words. He said, "Mama, who is God?"

And she said, "He who hath made this great world."

Snow
(anno 1351. Zenzi)

and when we got up the world was white white white with snow everywhere all over the mountains and all over the plain and mama said i am sick my boy we have to go take that pot of soup and wrap yourself in the sheepskin and i'll take the blankets and off we go so we went outside and it was cold cold cold and she looked and said do you see that bell we must go up there and so we went and mama fell down and said get me that stick to help me walk so i got the stick and i took hold of her hand and we went up the steps one by one and it took forever but we got to the top and mama said do you know how to ring the bell and i said no and she said pull the rope pull it with all your weight jump on the rope and grab it with your hands so i pulled and pulled and nothing came out and jump she said jump on the rope and i jumped and the rope came down and dong the bell went dong and rang out and i jumped again and dong the bell rang again and mama said good my boy now you ring the bell and when you are tired you eat your soup now i must lie down and she wrapped up in the blankets and lay down in the snow and i rang the bell and rang it again and the whole world was white and when i was tired i ate my soup and mama was asleep and the whole world was white and i rang the bell and then people were coming over the snow and they crossed the graveyard and walked through the graves and waved up to me and mama slept and the world was white everywhere you looked and the world was white white white and mama had told me god had made it so and the whole world was white, it was like magic

† The Unknown Mother
1323–1351

† Quirin von Lenzenbach
1290, Hagenburg–1355, Lenzenbach

† Zenzi
1346–1412, Hagenburg

THE END

ACKNOWLEDGEMENTS

Cathedral was written between 2010 and 2017. I began the book in Saverne in the Alsace and continued it in Istanbul where I was living at the time. Then I moved to Berlin and wrote there and in my "writing cabin" in the Harz Mountains in Sachsen Anhalt. Whilst writing the book I got married and became a father, wrote seven screenplays and made two films, in Tbilisi and Istanbul.

The book is dedicated to my inspiring and brilliant wife Ceylan, who was a constant source of love, laughter and support throughout the long writing process.

Many other people helped with the book's development. I am especially grateful to my friend and film editor Alan Levy, who read early drafts of all the chapters, and whose sharp and sensitive insights helped guide the writing process. Rob Cheek, John Hardwick and my wife Ceylan also read and made very helpful comments—my thanks to them.

Dr. Stephen Mossman and Dr. Renate Smithuis, medieval historians at Manchester University, read the near-final draft and made important corrections and suggestions. I am deeply indebted to them, and to Dr. Hendrik Mäkeler of Uppsala

University for his knowledge of medieval coins. My thanks also to my old friend Dr. Max Jones for introducing me to his colleagues at Manchester.

My thanks also to Dimitris Lyacos, Eran Kolirin and Nick Marston, to Michael Reynolds and Daniela Petracco of Europa Editions, to the team at Conville & Walsh (Jake, Alexander, Kate and Matilda) . . . and to my son Armin, for helping me to play and laugh after a long day's writing.

And finally my thanks to my literary agent Lucy Luck, whose enthusiasm for the book was very inspiring, and whose incisive editing suggestions helped create the book in its final form.

My very heartfelt thanks to all of the above.

Ben Hopkins
Berlin, 2020

ABOUT THE AUTHOR

Ben Hopkins is a screenwriter, film-maker, and novelist. He has lived in London and Istanbul and now lives in Berlin. His films include features and shorts, fiction and documentary, and have won awards at festivals such as Berlin, Locarno, Antalya, and Toronto Hot Docs.